A MARTIAN Garden

The Story of the First Humans Born on Mars

PAYSON HALL

ISBN: 978-1-66782-980-7
eBook ISBN: 978-1-66782-980-7

ACKNOWLEDGEMENTS

Inspiration – Conversation over coffee with Donna Purdum, 2011

Editor - Ana Cotham

Reviewers & Feedback

Ana Cotham, Dale Emery, Theresa Erickson, Mardell Hall, Phil Lundeen, Joey McAllister, Linda Nedney, Scott Penfield, Claudia Suzanne, Mary Winkley, Jacob Glazer

Art

Jacob Glazer – Thanks for turning my poor sketches into great illustrations

Shout out to Mrs. Saladin, my freshman high school English teacher who impugned my talent and future – When I sell my writing she spins in her grave and it makes me smile.

New Rome

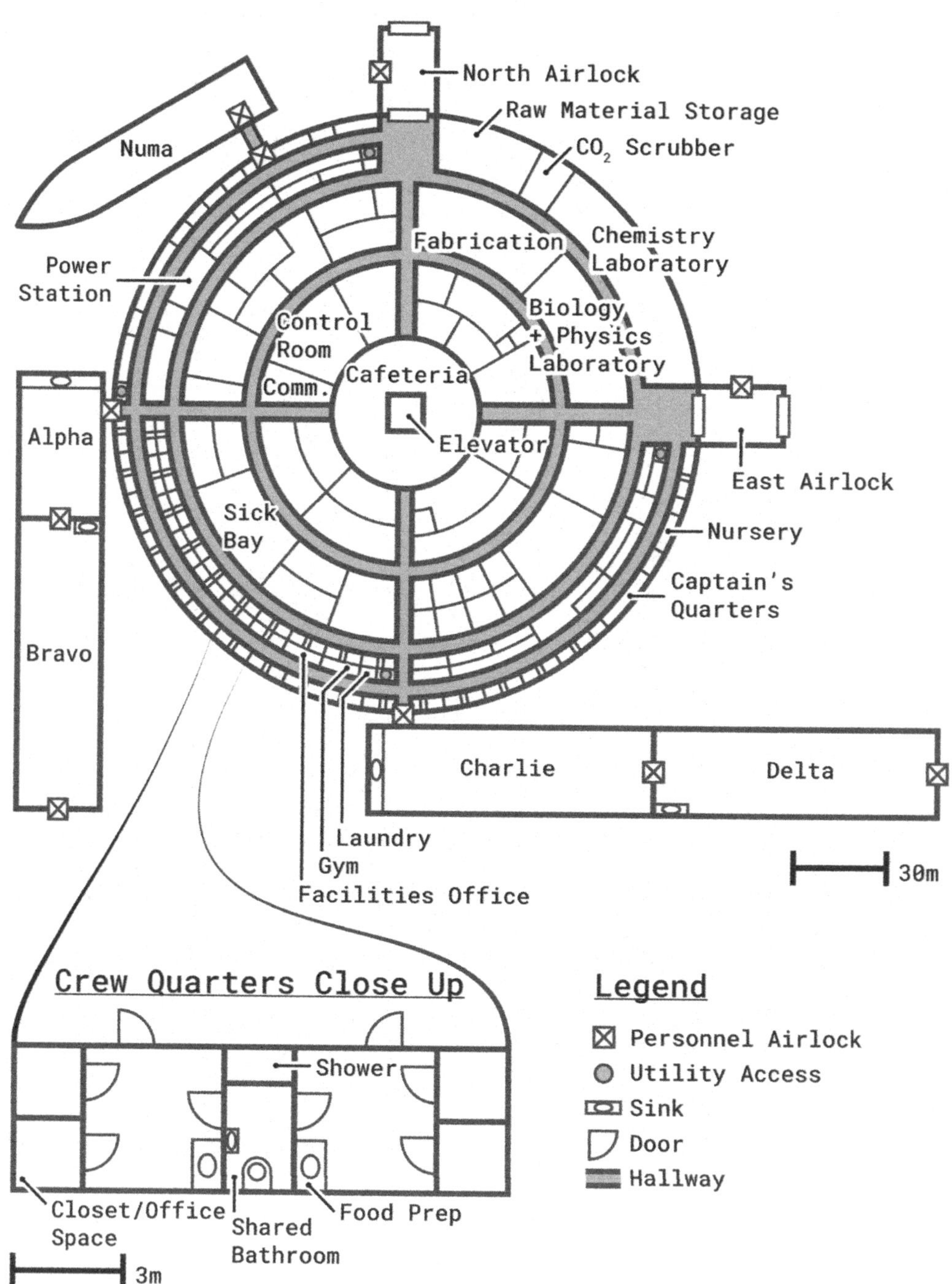

North Airlock
Raw Material Storage
CO_2 Scrubber
Numa
Fabrication
Chemistry Laboratory
Power Station
Biology + Physics Laboratory
Control Room
Comm.
Cafeteria
Elevator
Alpha
East Airlock
Sick Bay
Nursery
Captain's Quarters
Bravo
Charlie
Delta
Laundry
Gym
Facilities Office
30m
Crew Quarters Close Up
Shower
Closet/Office Space
Shared Bathroom
Food Prep
3m
Legend
Personnel Airlock
Utility Access
Sink
Door
Hallway

PART 1: MARTIAN SEEDS

"Don't judge each day by the harvest you reap but by the seeds that you plant."

- Robert Louis Stevenson

CHAPTER 1 – Smoky Rescue Day

Julia was elusive. Her smile mocked as she pulled away from his attempted embrace. He laughed and pursued. She stayed just beyond reach, brown eyes beckoning. Then she was on a skateboard, gliding away from him down the hill. He wondered how the tiny wheels traversed the gravel so smoothly—with that thought, they were on bicycles and the question faded. He pedaled faster, but she remained just ahead of him smiling, never turning her gaze away. She was enchanting. He longed to kiss her full lips, but no matter how fast he pursued, she remained beyond reach. The Pacific Ocean was at the base of the hill—he would catch her there.

Then they were in each other's arms standing by a bonfire on a cool and foggy California night. Their embrace unified them, puzzle pieces fitting together as familiar lovers do. Fulfillment. Contentment. Joy. Bliss … coughing?

Had someone thrown garbage on the fire? The acrid smoke of burning plastic assaulted his sinuses and grated his throat. Somewhere an alarm was sounding. Julia vanished. He looked for her in surprise, but she was gone …

The strobe pulsed blindingly as Porter awoke, coughing and disoriented. The alarm blared and his head ached and swam. The unpleasant smoke from his dream strangely lingered. Smoke was ominous on a space station. He tried to sit up too quickly and felt dull pain in his right knee. As he threw off the blanket, the sight of the pneumatic cast from his groin to below his foot oriented him. He was in sick bay. Memories of the accident flooded back. Images: the slow-motion fall, his leg tangled in the ladder, his knee twisted to an impossible angle by his mass; friends carrying him to sick bay; the concern on Julia's face as he was sedated.

He lay back on the hospital cot. He was groggy and thirsty. He was a notoriously sound sleeper, but this was more. Pain meds, he reasoned. He might have slept despite the noxious air, but the shrill alarm was unrelenting.

A detached voice over the PA system announced, "Fire stations. This is not a drill. Wear exo-suits with helmets." His duty station would be at the North air lock, but he didn't imagine his cast was going into an exo-suit any time soon. He willed the fog from his mind and sat up slowly, tentatively experimenting with his injured leg and examining his tattered trousers and cast. The small white room wobbled as he became vertical. He smelled and tasted the acrid smoke but could barely see it.

He guessed the crutches in the corner were for him—likewise, the cookies and water on the small table by the cot. He drank some water and jammed a cookie—one of Julia's famous oatmeal and raisin—into his shirt pocket. Balancing on his good leg, he hopped carefully toward the crutches. On Earth, his six-foot frame would have weighed about a hundred kilos, about two hundred and twenty pounds. Here on Mars, he weighed ninety pounds. Three years of retraining his brain to the different relationship between gravity and mass here helped him manage a controlled collision into the wall.

He retrieved the crutches and gingerly put weight on his casted leg, discovering that the cast allowed his lower leg and foot to not bear weight. A rigid frame within the pneumatic cast protruded below his foot and transferred the weight around his injured knee to the thigh above. It wasn't comfortable and the cast made his bad leg slightly longer than the good one, but it offered better mobility than he'd hoped for. His knee throbbed mildly with his pulse. He discarded the crutches and hobbled through the door into sick bay proper.

He still couldn't see smoke, but he could still smell it here. As he entered, Dr. Akiko Croix looked up from a flurry of activity and smiled with surprise. "Look who's up and walking! Good to see you, Porter." Gesturing toward the emergency strobe, she added, "Leave us alone for a few hours and see what happens? Ordinarily, I'd tell you to stay off that leg for a few days—special dispensation today. You are officially fit for limited duty ... if you're clear-headed and steady enough for me to put you to work?"

Porter grinned through the pain and nodded. "Knee is sore and a little throbby, but this cast is amazing. Good work, Doc. I have a headache ... but just as likely to be from the alarm and fumes as the painkillers. What's going on?"

Doc was all business as she continued pulling supplies from cupboards and drawers and laid out bandages, drugs, tools, and ointments. "Unclear. There are reports of some problem with the reactor and a fire. Don't know which came first or if they are two flavors of the same problem. Sounds bad. I've been told to expect casualties. The other doc is in route to the North air lock." She pointed to a nearby sink. "Wash up and get ready to be my gopher. And drink some water ... might help with the headache."

As Porter headed to the sink, the doctor touched the communicator panel on the wall. "Central, this is Doc Croix. Porter is assisting me in sick bay and won't be at his fire station. The alarm has officially awakened the last sleeping human on Mars. Can we please silence it now?"

"Roger that, Doc," came the raspy reply.

Taking off his wrist communicator to wash his hands, Porter wondered how Earth audio technology from 2040 could faithfully reproduce 60-year-old disco music with clarity while still making intercom systems sound like cans and string. As he dried his hands, the alarm went silent; the piercing wail echoed in pantomime by the brightly flashing strobe that persisted above the door.

Minutes later, the first bodies began to arrive.

The initial casualties were burn victims, borne on stretchers easily carried by two people in the low Martian gravity. The clothes and skin of the wounded were charred and melted together into an indistinguishable mass. Despite Doc's brief show of checking vitals and trying to resuscitate the victims for the benefit of the concerned stretcher bearers, it was clear to Porter that they were dead on arrival.

The small sick bay began to fill with the casualties, stretchers, and stretcher bearers who had become horrified spectators to the macabre scene unfolding before them. They whispered about the devastation that they had seen in the North part of the station. More casualties arrived. The station had only a few stretchers, and now casualties were arriving slung over the shoulders of comrades.

Porter saw that Doc had her hands full and he motioned toward two of the onlooking crewmembers who seemed unsure of what to do. "Chu, Williams, take these bodies out of here. We need room for the wounded." Given a mission, they acted swiftly.

As they stacked bodies on the stretcher, Chu asked uncomfortably, "Where should we...?"

Pausing for a moment, Porter thought of nearby available space. "Greenhouse Alpha should be out of the way," he said. "Then get the stretcher back to the accident area."

Chu and Williams departed, clearly relieved to have an assignment and a reason to leave the impromptu morgue.

The next two casualties had no apparent injuries, but were dead, nonetheless. Cummings and Bishop, engineers who worked with his wife. Porter guessed smoke inhalation. The air was getting worse with now-visible smoke. Oppressive. Again, he recruited the incoming bearers to dispose of the several bodies brought in moments before, trying to be sensitive and not assign a bearer to dispose of a body that they had brought in. The clutter in the room began to achieve an uneasy equilibrium.

The doctor had a detached look on her face as she checked vital signs and quickly cut clothing from the victims to look for other injuries. Porter recalled she had a military background and guessed her cool efficiency might be a consequence.

Gruesome, cloying smells now hung heavy on the air—a noxious stew of sweat, blood, rubbing alcohol, bacon, and burning garbage.

The eleventh or twelfth casualty to arrive was still alive. Crewmember Garcia who carried her in said she had been found unconscious in the outer ring corridor near the fire at the northeast side of the station. After checking vitals and ensuring an airway, the doctor put an oxygen mask over the victim's face and used a combination of chest compressions and air pressure from the mask to cycle the air in the victim's lungs. Apart from the sound of her activity, it was quiet. The silence lingered. Porter noticed impatiently that the smoke in the air was getting thicker.

Porter reached for his wrist com, discovering in frustration that he hadn't put it back on. It remained by the sink, on the other side of an obstacle course of stretchers and corpses. He punched the intercom on the wall. "Central, this is Porter in sick bay. Check ventilation system. We are getting a lot of smoke pumped in here."

"Roger that, Porter," crackled the reply. "Ventilation system compromised. Suggest Doc move sick bay to the cafeteria where the air is better. Confirm with Doc and we will re-route casualties."

The doctor was still doing chest compressions, stifling her own coughing as she did so. She looked to Porter and nodded assent.

"Central, Doc has confirmed moving sick bay to the cafeteria," Porter said to the wall. "I say again, sick bay moving to cafeteria."

"Roger that," Central crackled in reply.

Porter took a dressing gown from the cabinet and used it to bundle up the supplies that the doctor had placed on the counter for easy access. He handed the bundle to Garcia. "Take this to the cafeteria. Tell anyone you see along the way that sick bay has been moved to there." Crewman Garcia nodded, grabbed the bundle, and moved swiftly out the door.

The PA system announced, "Effective immediately, sick bay has been moved to the cafeteria. Please bring all wounded to the cafeteria. Damage control teams, report status and casualties to central by 1900 hours ... that's five minutes, folks."

A coughing fit erupted from the patient getting chest compressions, and Doc looked relieved. The patient pushed the doctor aside and sat up violently, ripping the oxygen mask from her face while coughing and vomiting and struggling to breathe. Doc tried to comfort and gently restrain her, but her patient rejected the assistance, spitting and croaking in panic, "Daycare ... children!"

The words hung in the air as the patient's coughing continued. The doctor looked at Porter. She seemed unsettled for the first time this afternoon.

"I'll go right away," said Porter. He saw the patient's wild eyes relax slightly at his words. He grabbed some gauze and fixed it to his face with a surgical mask. "You're needed in the cafeteria, Doc," he mumbled through the gauze. "Send reinforcements when you get there." Porter limped toward the door.

As he left, he saw Doc help the patient off the examining table and steady her. Barrymore? Porter thought her name was Barrymore—or Baymore. Marna? Mara? He silently chided himself for being so reclusive. There were only 127 colonists (not counting children) and there was no excuse for him not knowing all their names after six months of team training, nine months in space, and almost three years on planet. He committed to getting out of his greenhouses and socializing more when this was all over. Julia would like that. She was more extroverted than Porter.

He checked himself; he couldn't think of his wife just now. He had to believe she was okay. He needed to focus on the tasks at hand.

The main colony complex was roughly round; three concentric circular passageways divided it into rings and four spoke passages radiated from the central common area at the center of the donut—known as the "cafeteria"—at three, six, nine, and twelve o'clock. The sick bay door was at eight o'clock on the middle ring. The daycare was near four o'clock on the outer ring. Porter exited sick bay and turned left, following the middle ring corridor counterclockwise. The smoke was thicker as he headed east. His feeble improvised gas mask didn't seem to help much, but as the haze got thicker, he didn't dare remove it. At the intersection of the middle ring and six o'clock, he came to an airtight door. These were normally kept open, but in case of emergency they closed to slow decompression or the spread of smoke.

As he fumbled through the door, the lights flickered and died. Emergency backup lights, self-contained LEDs with battery backups, came on. The emergency strobes continued flashing. The smoke was thicker beyond the door. It puzzled Porter that the smoke seemed to have no trouble penetrating doors specifically designed to contain it. He turned south, heading toward the outer ring on the six o'clock spoke. Whatever was happening must be more serious than the dead he had already seen, and they represented 10 percent of the colony's adult population. Where was everyone? He got to the outer ring and went through another airtight door. He glanced at the familiar air lock door at the south terminus of the six o'clock spoke. It led to greenhouse Charlie on the southern side of the station. He turned left, continuing toward the daycare through another airtight door. The smoke was denser here, and his eyes burned. He could hardly see the walls of the corridor. It occurred to him that someone with an exo-suit should be doing this. He had been rash to charge off, but someone had to go, and the doctor was needed elsewhere. He briefly considered turning back to look for someone more capable, but he hadn't seen anyone and there might not be time to seek alternatives.

It was hot in the corridor and sweat and smoke stung his watering eyes. His headache was pounding, aggravated by the smoke. In the haze, he almost tripped over three bundles of rags on the floor. When Porter looked more closely, he realized the blanket-wrapped rolls were children. He bent down awkwardly with his one functioning knee and opened one of the blankets. The infant girl was coughing weakly and gasping for breath. Spreading her blanket on the floor, he stacked the other two bundles next to her on top of her blanket. Gathering the corners, he stood, clutching the bundle to his chest just as a shadow emerged from the smoke. It was an exo-suited crewmember carrying two more bundles.

Laying the blanketed bundles on the deck at Porter's feet, the crewmember flipped open her helmet's visor and said, "Porter! Am I glad to see you! Get these to fresh air, I'll get more!" Without waiting for a reply, she coughed, flipped her visor closed, turned and vanished back down the smoky corridor. Porter thought that might have been Sumi Smith.

Coughing, he awkwardly added the new children to his bundle. It was ungainly to pick up and carry, but low gravity helped. As he stood, it felt as if a hot spike shot through his bad knee. His sweaty thigh had slipped and shifted down into the cast an inch. Now any weight borne by his right leg was pressure on his right foot and transferred to his wrecked knee. He clenched his teeth, focusing on his task. With a grimace, he staggered back the way he had come looking for fresh air, each step agony.

Porter knew he couldn't go far. He called for help, coughing, but heard no response. He had to get the children to breathable air and needed to go back for another load from Sumi. Time was not on his side. It was one hundred meters to the cafeteria, through several airtight doors that would require he put down bundles he might not be able to pick back up. As he shuffled his load and approached the door at the six o'clock spoke, he realized that he was only a few yards from greenhouse Charlie.

The main station complex was circular. Two rectangular greenhouses placed end-to-end extended south from the west side of the station, accessed by the air lock at the end of the nine o'clock spoke. These were greenhouses Alpha and Bravo, the first two greenhouses built. Alpha for aquaculture and Bravo for initial plant husbandry. Two more greenhouses, Charlie and Delta, extended east from the six o'clock spoke. Bravo and Charlie were the "terrariums" where Porter had spent most of his waking hours for the past six hundred days trying to build up atmosphere, soils, and robust plant life to make the colony more self-sufficient. First Bravo, then Charlie, which was just getting productive. Delta construction was nearly complete, but he hadn't begun development there yet.

As he turned toward the air lock door, he realized that others might have sought refuge there as well. He fumbled with the bulky air lock door with his full hands. It was a proper air lock, separating the main station from the outbuildings. Inside was a small square room three meters on each side with an exit door toward "outside" where greenhouse Charlie had been constructed. Inside the air lock was a rack of exo-suits, a first aid station, comm station, and a low central bench. The bench was intended to facilitate suiting up prior to going outside, but Porter had repurposed it as a working area to sprout seedlings and test soil samples. He punched the button on the comm panel. "Central, this is Porter in the greenhouse Charlie air lock. I have children with me who need medical attention. Am trying to assist a crewmember evacuating the daycare center. Need assistance extracting wounded from daycare and tending wounded in greenhouse Charlie. Do you copy?"

Interminable silence.

He considered leaving the children here in the air lock, but though the smoke wasn't as thick here, it had followed him into the small space and breathing was still difficult. His nose was saturated with the smell of burning plastic. There wasn't time to cycle the atmosphere in the small air lock, and he wasn't sure that would be effective anyway given the ventilation problems. He shifted his load and opened the outer air lock door, stepping through it into greenhouse Charlie.

Exiting south out of the air lock, the west wall was just to his right, the south wall was thirty meters ahead of him, and the rest of the greenhouse extended one hundred meters to his left. The greenhouse's receiving area just beyond the air lock seemed worlds away from the heat and smoke he had left behind. It was quiet. There was no pulsing strobe of the silent fire alarm. There was no one here. The dark Martian sky seeped down through the transparent panels of the greenhouse onto soil, plants, gardening tools, and equipment. Cool fresh air embraced his face and lungs, chilling him as sweat evaporated. The lack of smoke made normal respiration seem luxurious. Coughing and gasping for breath, he lowered the blanket-wrapped children and uncovered them. There were five in total. The oldest might have been two years old, the youngest perhaps a few months. Several didn't seem to be breathing. Taking off his improvised breathing mask, he gently compressed the ribcage of each child to clear the airway. Then, covering the child's nose and mouth with his own, he blew in small puffs of air. The first two children promptly responded to his ministrations by coughing weakly and starting to cry. The next two were breathing on their own without him, wheezing and unconscious. The baby didn't respond.

He tried again, but the infant didn't breathe. Porter was rattled. Minutes ago, he had seen Doc triaging the wounded with dispassionate efficiency. Here was an infant perhaps three months old and he didn't know if he could stop trying. He tried again. As he compressed the chest a fourth time, he thought of Sumi delivering more bundles into the hallway just steps away from the air lock. As he blew gently into the mouth and nose, he thought of more children stacked like cordwood, choking in the haze. He told himself that the tears in his eyes were from the smoke. He laid the unresponsive baby gently on the ground, then took its blanket and struggled to his feet. The agony of standing focused his mind. He chided himself that it was okay to cry over lifeless infants, but "real men" didn't cry about physical pain. He smiled grimly at his stupid joke, took a deep breath of fresh air, and shambled painfully back toward the air lock.

As he passed two wheeled utility carts full of dirt he paused, wondering if he could push one with only one good leg. He stood on one foot and dumped the soil from one of the carts, then turned and rolled the cart forward a meter or so. The wheels hesitated on the sand and dirt covering the concrete floor of the receiving area, but it would roll better on the smooth floors of the station. The cart could certainly carry more than he could in his arms. As he wheeled it toward the air lock, he realized it would also be easier to navigate the doors without having to put down and pick up his cargo. He took a few more deep breaths, and then pushed open the heavy outer air lock door.

The air lock was hot and filled with choking smoke. He exited the air lock, propping the door open with a helmet to save time on his return, and headed east on the outer ring, struggling to breathe. He had forgotten his discarded mask. It was difficult to keep his eyes open. He had been gone only a few minutes. Four more bundles were waiting for him, motionless on the floor. He loaded them quickly while calling out, but seeing no one in the haze, he trundled the cart back to the air lock. The cart had been a good idea ... apart from the contortions to initially load the bundles. He used the cart to support some of his weight. His knee screamed at the slightest pressure on his foot, at the slightest shift of weight.

Into the air lock. As he navigated the cart over the threshold, he allowed himself to worry about Julia again. Where was she? Was she safe? His beloved nuclear engineer was surely busy. Doc had said something about trouble with the reactor. It was supposed to be "idiot-proof." Coughing, Porter pushed open the door into the greenhouse and felt anew the joy of breathing. The sounds of children crying were unusual here, but it was sweet music. He moved past the entryway and emptied the contents of the cart gently, but unceremoniously, much as he had the dirt moments before. He lowered himself awkwardly to his side and unwrapped the children. He initiated the mouth-to-mouth ritual for those not breathing on their own. Encouraged by cacophonous evidence of his success moments earlier, Porter smiled and wept as three of the four children responded to his ministrations.

He was exhausted. He wanted to rest. As he struggled to his feet again, he realized that in addition to aggravating his injured knee, he was probably losing the benefit of any residual anesthetic. The agony of every movement made it hard to concentrate. He thought of the hallway. Less than thirty meters. He retrieved and donned the discarded surgical mask, set his jaw, leaned heavily on the cart, and pushed it toward the air lock in short bursts. When he arrived at the door, he hyperventilated slightly, partly to store up oxygen, and partly in response to the pain, then swung the heavy door outward. He pushed the cart into the air lock, then shoved it over the threshold, then right around the outer ring toward the daycare center.

Smoke. Heat. Burning eyes. Strobe. KNEE! Each step was agony.

Another trip.

Another.

Was this the third trip with the cart? The fourth? The previous foray found only one bundle and there had been no sign of Sumi, his rescue partner. He forced himself to make one more trip, just in case. Apart from thick clouds of smoke billowing from farther down the passageway, the corridor was empty. His smoke-strained voice croaked out a call, but there was no reply. While maneuvering the cart to turn it around, he shifted his weight badly and fell, wrenching his knee so severely he might have briefly lost consciousness. He discovered that near the floor, the air was less smoky. He choked in a few abbreviated gasps, composing himself, and contemplated resting for just a moment more ... maybe he would dream of chasing Julia again down the hill to the blue Pacific ... The bonfire. Burning plastic. Sick bay. Children!

Must. Keep. Moving.

It took the last of Porter's resolve to lift his head and fix his gaze through the smoke, back toward the ghostly outline of the corridor junction. He abandoned the cart and crawled toward the air lock, dragging his leg behind him. So much pain. So tired…

He crawled through the airtight doors, then into the air lock. He continued forward in fits and starts and opened the air lock door to enter the greenhouse. Sweet, sweet air. Smoke began wafting past him into the twilit glass building. He rested for a long moment, then turned and pushed the air lock door closed and sealed it, collapsing on the gravel with his back to the door. He struggled for breath for a minute, coughed and then lay still. Just a moment to rest his eyes ... The last thing Porter heard before his consciousness slipped away was the beautiful chaos of children crying.

CHAPTER 2 - SNAFU

Porter didn't think crying awoke him. He was dimly aware of wailing in the background as he slowly regained consciousness, but he was sure he could have slept through it for a few hours more. She must have touched him or made noise, but he didn't remember it. When he opened his eyes, a pudgy toddler of about two with a tangle of golden hair crouched before him, staring at him intently with blue eyes. She wore a dirty blue gingham dress with tiny bare feet peeking from below it. Her face was dusted with dirt and soot. Clean tracks marked the recent passage of tears on her rosy cheeks. She seemed pleased that he was awake.

"Hi there," Porter croaked gently.

The girl smiled in surprise at his animation, standing erect and taking cautious steps backward.

"Who are you?" Porter asked.

She said nothing but watched him closely while keeping her distance.

The small sun was high in the sky, providing a white-reddish light through the dusty greenhouse panels. As Porter sat up, he became more aware of the din of crying children. Looking around, he saw over a dozen children scattered about the reception area. Some played in the dirt. Some wandered among the planting tables and equipment. Others were sitting or lying down and crying. Some appeared to be sleeping. Porter pushed away memories of last night—he feared some of the motionless were not sleeping.

The golden-haired girl continued watching him.

"I'm thirsty," Porter said. "Would you like some water?"

"Wa-duh," repeated the girl shyly.

"What is your name?" Porter asked, thinking he might now have a partner for the conversation, but the girl was otherwise silent.

"Well, let's go find some water and then maybe you can tell me."

Pulling himself up with the air lock door, Porter struggled to his feet. He wished he had kept the crutches. Looking around, he saw a shop broom leaning against the wall. He carefully hopped on his good leg to the broom, tucked the broom head under his arm, and used it as an improvised crutch. The little girl followed a few steps behind, watching him carefully.

Porter took his coffee cup from the workbench and moved to the sink. He rinsed the cup and filled it. He drank half in a quick gulp, and then offered the cup to his new little friend.

The girl backed away uncertainly.

Supporting his weight with one hand on the sink, he bent down and put the cup on the ground. He smiled at the girl and said, "You can have some water when you are ready."

He hopped a step away from the cup and busied himself rinsing and filling a watering can in the deep industrial sink. From the corner of his eye, he saw the girl tentatively approach the cup, then pick it up and drink.

"Where is everyone?" Porter said aloud. "I would imagine they would have gotten to us by now." He looked toward the air lock. The glass of the air lock doors acted like a poor-quality mirror when the sun was this bright in the greenhouse, reflecting back images of the transparent greenhouse walls behind him and the view of the barren Martian landscape beyond.

Inside the air lock, beyond the partial mirror effect of the glass, he could dimly see the fire alarm strobe still blinking silently.

Then he noticed the red-light warning that the air lock was depressurized.

This meant that there had been a failure in the pressure vessel of the main station. The airtight doors should have slowed that kind of failure to give people a chance to respond, but it was a big deal, nonetheless. On the other side of the greenhouse wall, Martian air pressure was less than 1/100th of Earth pressure at sea level. Human life expectancy at that pressure was about one minute, with a merciful loss of consciousness after twenty to thirty seconds before the worst of the symptoms took over. The colony had never had a serious loss of pressure in a thousand days on Mars—a few drills and some dry run tests, but never a real loss of pressure. He told himself that the crew was probably working the problem. He realized that no one might know he brought the children here. The greenhouse would be the last place anyone would look. The children's parents would be frantic!

He reached for the comm band missing from his wrist, cursed, then touched the panel on the wall above the sink. "This is Porter in greenhouse Charlie. I have children from the daycare here with me. What is the status?"

Silence.

A sliver of panic pricked his brain, but he chose to ignore it for now. Comm must be down. He noticed the crying again. He turned and looked at the children around him, then proclaimed to no one in particular, "I'll bet you are all thirsty." He put the strap of the filled watering can over his head and shoulder, leaving it dangling in front of him.

He looked at the golden-haired girl watching him, the now-empty cup dangling from one small hand. "Will you be my helper?" he asked. She didn't reply but paused and then took his hand when he offered it. Together, they moved slowly toward the other children, the girl carrying the cup, and Porter holding her hand with one hand and his broom-crutch in the other.

The next hour was chaotic but productive. The surviving children had been quite thirsty, all thirteen of them. The toddlers managed to drink from the cup, although several were apparently new to the concept and choked and sputtered their first sips. The babies were more challenging. At first, Porter dipped his pinkie in the water and let the young ones suck the water as it ran down his finger, but this was time consuming and didn't go fast enough to satisfy either party. Eventually, Porter realized that a bit of blanket soaked in water was a better delivery system, and he tore strips from one of the blankets to support the four youngest.

Some of the toddlers might have been potty trained before the accident, but the trauma of the fire, the long stretch of unsupervised time while Porter had slept, and the lack of anything resembling a toilet meant that all of the children had soiled themselves. Porter removed the children's diapers and other clothes. He used some of the remaining blanket fragments to give all the children quick sponge baths, trying to soothe the diaper rash that seemed universal after what must have been eighteen hours in soiled underclothes.

He improvised a meal from a half dozen brownies Julia had made a few days ago to tide him over when he worked through lunch. Thinking of Julia and her brownies made him smile—then nudged the sliver of doubt deeper. He told himself that Julia had to be okay. It was just a matter of time. He chose not to contemplate the magnitude of a disaster that would result in silence continuing sixteen hours after the event.

He had no trouble getting the toddlers to eat bits of the brownies, but he quickly learned to provide them in small pieces and soak them in water for the "molar-challenged."

The babies were fussy. Porter was sure they were hungry too. He chewed bits of the brownie and brushed the resulting sludge onto the lips and roof of the mouth of the babes that he suspected had no experience with solid food. They spit out most of what he tried to put in, but they were hungry and motivated, and Porter was patient. Although repeated application probably didn't result in the equivalent of a full meal, most did ingest some calories and more water. He was pleased to see his golden-haired helper mimicking his actions by reinserting some of the rejected food to the babies, and he praised her for assisting him. None of the other children seemed to take much interest in helping.

Once the children were fed, Porter paused to consider his situation, something he had gladly avoided while preoccupied with more pressing childcare needs. He knew that every passing hour without contact from other survivors on the station was ominous. He found it hard to imagine that everyone had—he pictured his wife Julia and almost didn't allow himself to complete the thought—died. Standard fire response protocols would have put many in exo-suits, so even if the decompression was massive and sudden, there should have been survivors. He was disgusted with himself that he had forgotten his wrist com, which would have been an alternative to the hard-wired intercom system and furthermore would have tracked his whereabouts on the station's computer.

He knew the accident was severe. He had seen over a dozen dead in his brief stint in sick bay. The reactor was northwest of the cafeteria. He had run into smoke billowing south from the east corridor near the daycare, suggesting the fire was in the northeast quadrant of the station.

If there were other survivors—he preferred that assumption to alternatives—where would they be? Why would they be so slow restoring pressure to the station? Perhaps they had established a contained area? Maybe they evacuated to hunker down in the hulk of the original *Numa*, the ship that brought them to Mars?

Spaceship *Numa* was the size of a large jet liner and had been constructed in Earth orbit to carry the hundred plus colonists on a one-way trip to Mars. It had been designed to deliver them and land safely and then serve as the foundation for the construction of *New Rome,* the first permanent extraterrestrial human colony. The station had grown out southeast from *Numa* following a well-scripted plan, using local building materials and cannibalizing parts from *Numa* and repurposing them for the colony. Essential supplies and materials had been sent ahead on unmanned missions and were waiting for them at the landing site when they arrived. These supply ships were also cannibalized to help build the station. What had been advertised to the world as a mission of science and exploration was really more of an engineering and construction project in a very harsh environment, or perhaps an elaborate test of the thoroughness of the mission planners—if you forgot to bring something you needed to Mars your options were to synthesize it, improvise, or do without, although requests could be delivered by unmanned vehicle sometime within six to eighteen months, depending where Earth and Mars were in their respective orbits when the need was identified. Most of the initial "science" was learning to fabricate necessary materials from the local resources.

The remains of *Numa* would be a good refuge. It was integrated into the northwest quadrant of the station, but for safety reasons, it used its original ventilation system with limited interface to the rest of the station. After landing, *Numa* initially served as cramped crew quarters during early station construction, but the colonists were quite motivated to carve out less cramped work and living areas for themselves, and the remains of the ship had quickly been repurposed to storage rooms and administrative offices. He imagined Julia, Doc, and other colonists "camping" in the shell of *Numa* with other parts of the station decompressed. What would they have to do to restore pressure integrity for the station at large? Standard exo-suits had enough air for two hours. That meant there was little point looking for survivors in depressurized sections of the station two hours after they lost atmosphere. Searching this part of the station would be low priority, compared to treating the wounded and restoring power and pressure containment. Porter convinced himself that this was sufficient explanation for why he hadn't yet seen other survivors to keep the sliver of doubt from pushing deeper.

He thought about the critical failure of the ventilation system to stop the circulation of smoke and fumes, and realized that his greenhouses, like *Numa*, were not integrated into the primary ventilation system. Ironically, in the case of the greenhouses, this was because of concerns that the greenhouses might decompress and a determination that they were expendable at this early stage of development. The plan was to eventually integrate the greenhouses into the ventilation system to develop atmospheric carbon dioxide/oxygen exchange with the plants and make the artificial atmosphere of the colony more self-sufficient but processing the huge air volume of the greenhouses threatened to overtax the ventilation system. As a consequence, integration had been postponed until the system capacity was increased.

We are alive because there wasn't enough ventilation capacity to integrate the greenhouses thought Porter.

He glanced again at the air lock door. The fire alarm still flashed silently. The red depressurized warning indicator was still glowing. He had failed to close the inner air lock door. He chided himself halfheartedly but was so pleased he had successfully completed and survived the last unproductive trip that he quickly moved past the scolding to longing. He wished that he had access to the emergency supplies in the air lock. He walked to the air lock window and looked inside. It looked pretty much as it always did. He noticed the seedlings he had been sprouting on the bench were desiccated and limp, the water in their leaves having boiled away in the near vacuum. The far door was still propped open by the helmet.

Porter briefly considered opening the air lock door without pressurizing it in an attempt to close the door between the air lock and the station. Even if he could open the door, he was pretty sure the pressure differential would create a wind tunnel that would blow him through the air lock without any hope of stopping. The door between the air lock and the station proper opened toward the station. He knew he would be unable to close it against the pressure of the air in the greenhouse trying to escape. For that matter, he doubted he could pull the air lock door in front of him open against the vacuum. The whole air lock was designed to navigate from a pressurized station to a depressurized "outside" and back. Standing in the pressurized "outside," he had no immediate inspiration about how to use the air lock for the exact opposite of its intended design. He looked through the glass at the first aid kit two meters away from him ... it might as well have been on Earth.

Porter was disappointed, feeling that if he could have sealed and repressurized the air lock, it would have been symbolic progress toward returning the station to normal. He turned and looked out the southern greenhouse wall at the desolate Martian landscape, a near vacuum that was currently -5O C in the midday sun. Perhaps he needed to rethink "normal"?

Porter sat, demoralized, and watched the children settle down as the sun sank in the west and shadows grew long, overtaking the receiving area by the air lock.

There was little to do but try to keep the children healthy and wait for rescue. He had felt so resourceful sharing his brownies with the children earlier. Now he wondered where their next meal would come from. If he assumed he had only the contents of the greenhouse, what were his options? He surveyed his surroundings with new eyes.

The greenhouse was not a very hospitable place for children. It was a large glass rectangle roughly thirty meters wide and one hundred meters long. Greenhouse Charlie was three hundred days old, the third of four greenhouses constructed using a large three-dimensional printer that consumed Martian sand and large amounts of power to create a molten slurry resembling a mixture of concrete and molten glass. The molten goo was then "printed" in place by a computer-controlled nozzle traveling on a huge frame that resembled the inside of a giant Etch-A-Sketch. The foundation was a three-foot-thick slab underfoot that terminated in a three-foot-high wall around the perimeter. Triple-paned, argon-filled glass panels formed the rest of the greenhouse. The clear glass had been synthesized from Martian sand and had a reddish-yellow tinge. The argon was distilled from the local atmosphere and provided excellent insulation. The roof arched thirty meters above the floor. The receiving area near the air lock was Porter's current "office" and work area.

As the colony's primary horticulturalist, Porter's plan was to set up residence in the receiving area of the greenhouse when he got custody. Once production was fully operational, he moved to the receiving area of the next one that needed his attention. Greenhouse Delta, through the air lock at the far end of Charlie, was the newest. It was sealed and pressurized at this point, but still an active construction site.

The receiving area by the air lock to the station consumed the first ten meters of the greenhouse, providing a space for bulk delivery and storage of sand and chemicals, and for assembly of the low grow tables that filled the balance of the greenhouse. By the air lock were Porter's workbenches, seedlings, test kits, and garden implements. There was an arched metal ladder on wheels that conformed to the shape of the walls and roof and could be rolled the length of the greenhouse to facilitate cleaning and repairing the glass. It could also be used for pruning when trees or bamboo grew that tall. Although there was running water in the sink sourced from the station proper, Porter had designed the greenhouses like closed "terrarium" systems. Each greenhouse was designed to reclaim and reuse evaporated water from the air with a condenser. Half of the grow tables in Charlie were filled with soils in various phases of development and conditioning. The rest were filled with various plants selected for their efficiency in creating edible foodstuffs, creating oxygen, and sequestering the carbon from carbon dioxide. At the far end of the building by the air lock to Delta was a small utility area where Porter kept a beehive, a worm farm, and the microbe growing vats needed to create and condition soils to support terrestrial plant life.

The children seemed to have settled in the receiving area, near the mounds of sand and soil where they had been initially deposited last night. If they were going to spend another day here, Porter realized he needed to clean up some of the obvious hazards.

He did a quick mental inventory. None of the plants in Charlie should be dangerous. He should probably ensure that none of the chemicals were easily accessible–the ammonia nitrate and lime that he used so casually to build soils would be poor playthings. He also needed to secure the tools and the remaining cart. He had to find a way to keep children out of the growing area of the greenhouse ... he didn't need a toddler getting into the apiary at the end of the building and stirring up the bees.

"Okay," Porter said to himself, "Maslow's hierarchy of needs on Mars: air, heat, water, and food."

Air. He briefly wondered whether the partially developed Charlie had enough plant life to provide sufficient oxygen and scrub enough carbon dioxide to keep the air continually breathable. The rule of thumb for oxygen production was that thirty cubic meters of healthy plant life provided approximately enough photosynthesis for one adult; he was sure it would be less for a small child. With half of Charlie cultivated at this point—he did a quick estimate—Charlie as currently configured should be able to sustain about fifteen adults. That seemed within a reasonable margin, but Porter realized that the greenhouse atmospheric metrics he normally tracked with detached clerical interest—oxygen and carbon dioxide levels—were suddenly much more important. He no longer had the option of propping open the air lock and manually exchanging air with the station to refine the mix. He walked to the environmental monitor to check the current stats.

Temperature	68° F (20° C)
Pressure	13.14 PSI
Altitude Equivalent	+1000 meters
Relative humidity	63%
Atmospheric Composition	
Argon	72.4082 %
Oxygen	22.1258 %
Nitrogen	05.3979 %
Carbon Dioxide	00.0513 %
Carbon monoxide	**00.0045 %**
Methane	00.0001 %
Hydrogen	00.0001 %
Nitrous oxide	00.0001 %
Ozone	00.0001 %

That was a reasonable mix—slightly more oxygen than Earth or station normal. Nitrogen was precious, so the 78 percent nitrogen common in Earth's atmosphere was supplemented in the colony by argon, an inert gas easily distilled from the Martian atmosphere. He noted the bold font emphasized the elevated carbon monoxide levels and reviewed the history. Levels had peaked last night and had been steadily decreasing. He recalled the smoke that followed him through the air lock. Carbon dioxide levels were good. Carbon dioxide levels needed to be kept below 0.1 percent to avoid some cognitive impairment and below 0.5 percent for human safety. Above 4 percent was life threatening.

Heat. Keeping the greenhouse warm enough for the naked children might be a challenge, particularly at night. The average temperature on Mars was -55° C. Fortunately, the station was near the equator where it was warmer and there was very little atmosphere to conduct heat away from the walls, so their little closed system was exceptionally well insulated. Most of the heat was lost through the floor.

The greenhouses used electrical power to heat the interior of the structure and supplement the diminished sunlight with sun lamps. This was particularly useful when dust storms obscured the sun for extended periods. Some storms could last for months. Each greenhouse relied upon solar panel arrays beyond its walls to generate modest amounts of electricity for those needs, and fuel cells along the wall stored energy captured by day for use at night. In theory, self-sufficient. In reality, the solar power system sometimes required supplementation from the station's grid. Porter had no reason to believe that station power had been restored since its failure the night before. If the remaining colonists thought there were no survivors in the southern part of station, restoring power here would not be a priority. He realized he would have to be conservative about power use to ensure they could keep the area warm enough. With that thought, Porter walked to his workbench and turned off the grow lights nurturing seedling beds he was sprouting. Sunlight would have to do for now. He also turned off the lights illuminating the air lock to Delta. He was the only person likely to go there, and the dark made it less attractive to a wandering toddler if they woke up at night while he was asleep.

The heat loss through the floor was normally reduced in the receiving area because of proximity to the warmed ground underneath the station. If the southern part of the station remained without pressure—and, he presumed, heat—that would change. Porter wished the children had come with clean dry clothes. He walked to where the children lay and saw that the ambulatory had naturally grouped together like puppies in a dirt pile to conserve heat. He noticed that the babies mostly stayed where they had started and were shivering. Using a shovel, he built a dirt berm with a bowl a meter in diameter. He lined the bowl with a tarp and one of the blankets. He moved the infants into the depression and reorganized the blankets, so they were shared and layered among the four. Stirring the young ones led to a fresh round of crying. Porter imagined they were hungry again, but he had nothing to feed them. He hoped the shared body warmth and insulation from the floor would settle them. He bent down awkwardly and touched the cement of the greenhouse floor. It was colder than usual ... fifty degrees, he guessed. The dirt might be sufficient insulation for tonight, but the trick might not work tomorrow.

Water. *New Rome* mined water from beneath the Martian soil, melting the ice and storing the liquid water in holding tanks below the station. There were also sewage treatment tanks and aquaculture in greenhouse Alpha that processed wastewater and purified it for reuse. Porter didn't know how well insulated the pipes were within the station. For that matter, he didn't know how well the holding tank was insulated. He didn't know whether the water capture system had power. He decided it was safest to assume that the tap wouldn't last long. He walked to the sink and refilled the watering can. Testing the stream as it emerged from the tap, he noted the water seemed colder than usual—not a good sign. He looked around for other potential water containers; perhaps some of the chemical containers could be emptied? Apart from the still crying infants, who seemed to agitate rather than console one another, the children seemed settled for the night. Porter thought this might be an opportune time to inventory Delta and to remove the corpses.

He somberly gathered the lifeless bodies of the half-dozen children that hadn't survived the ordeal, and put them into his remaining cart, then limped quietly east out of the receiving area between the long rows of grow tables. The only sounds disturbing the night silence in Charlie were the scratch of the wheels as they rolled over the dirt and sand on the floor and the rhythmic thumping of his broom-crutch. As he got away from the insulating layer of dirt on the receiving area floor, he felt the increasing cold of the cement through the sole of the hospital slipper on his left foot. The dark, quiet rows of tables were both familiar and strange—familiar because he had spent much time here and knew the area so well, and strange as he contemplated that, for now, he had nowhere else to go. Where was everyone? Where was Julia?

Greenhouses Charlie and Delta extended east from the circular station starting at the six o'clock air lock. As he pushed the cart east, he could see more and more of the southeastern side of the station through the glass wall to his north. There was no obvious damage he could see in the dim moonlight. The fire strobes blinked in the windows, but he saw no other lights.

When he arrived at the air lock between Charlie and Delta, he was relieved to confirm that Delta remained pressurized. He had not spent much time in Delta yet. It was still a construction project, not an agriculture project. He had made a few trips out of curiosity and to encourage and thank the construction team, but it wasn't "his" space yet. The greenhouse plans were established on Earth. He was not the nervous building owner worrying about the placement of windows and doors—he was the tenant awaiting permission to occupy. He entered the air lock. It was more Spartan than the main South air lock behind him. There were eight exo-suits and a first aid kit. He made a mental note to grab the first aid kit on his return. Chastised by his experience the night before, he carefully closed the door behind him before opening the door into Delta.

Delta was colder than Charlie. There was no insulating layer of dirt in the receiving area. No grow lights warmed it. Porter turned on the lights. The mostly empty Delta seemed cavernous. His breath misted in front of him. The remnants of construction were scattered about, trash and scraps, a few unused panes of glass, and barrels of raw materials. It smelled of dirt and construction—cement and glue and the faint burned smell created by the 3-D printer. He was pleased to see a medium-sized 3-D printer had been set up to manufacture grow tables, though only a few dozen tables were complete and piled nearby. He was initially surprised to see the movable ladder/scaffold was in place but realized that it was a convenience for the construction teams and was likely one of the first things fabricated and installed. The sink was fixed along the wall that Delta shared with Charlie. That made sense; Charlie had spigots at either end, and in the middle. Delta would mirror that, extending the same plumbing.

He looked again at the raw materials to feed the printer—barrels of sand refined from the first quarry on Mars, about half a kilometer northeast of the station. He wondered how much power it would take to operate the printer. Could he run it just with the solar power system? He looked along the walls and saw that the power cells were in place. He hoped that meant that Delta's solar panels were connected. The lights had come on. He guessed that answered his question.

Martian sand was piled almost a meter high along the length of the north wall. It had been run through a kiln to burn off chemical toxins and ensure that it was sterile, but otherwise it was untreated. Until yesterday, a big part of his mission over the next year would have been to move those tons of sterile rock and sand into grow tables and transform them into soil that could support terrestrial plant life. That task no longer seemed important.

Water. He was distracted. Porter spread a sheet of scrap plastic on the floor and began emptying some of the small plastic barrels of finely ground sand intended for 3-D printer consumption onto it. He guessed the barrels were two gallons each. If he assumed he needed three barrels of water per day … this led him to wonder how long they needed to survive. The sliver of doubt and despair pushed deeper, releasing phantoms of ideas that made him uncomfortable, verging on panic. He looked through the glass wall toward the station. He saw nothing but strobes flashing coldly in the darkness. A week, he decided arbitrarily, because he couldn't entertain a longer period right now. He dumped twenty-one barrels of sand, then rinsed and filled them at the sink. The water was still working, he thought, relieved at the remnant of normalcy. He left the water-filled barrels on the floor by the sink. He was tempted to explore further but felt uneasy being away from the children for so long. His machinations had taken the better part of an hour, and his knee was throbbing.

Porter unloaded the bodies from the cart, wrapped them in plastic and put them on one of the growing tables. Then he impulsively emptied and rinsed two more barrels, placing them in the cart. He headed back to the air lock, turned off the lights in Delta and closed the air lock door behind himself. He put the first aid kit into the cart as he went through.

Food. As Porter reentered Charlie, he turned on the lights near the Delta air lock. The crying had stopped for now. Porter contemplated the crops in the Martian greenhouses. Alpha had been the first greenhouse, devoted to oxygen creation, carbon dioxide sequestration, and wastewater recycling. Alpha was really an aquaculture space. He had helped the chemists and biologists with the setup, but algae weren't his specialty. Food and oil were extracted from the algae, but it was more of a chemical process than an organic one. Alpha was never *his*.

Bravo, the second greenhouse built, was the ag nursery. There, Porter nurtured the cuttings and sprouted the seeds transported from Earth. He still had seed caches in the station, and some here in Charlie—but Bravo was intended to be the most diverse biosphere so that the colony could determine which plants thrived under Martian conditions. Bravo had been subdivided into four microclimates with different temperatures and humidities appropriate for the types of plants being grown.

Charlie, Delta, and future greenhouses were expected to specialize and produce foodstuffs and materials in bulk. Porter had selected and grown the constituent plants of Charlie using a terrarium model, trying to establish an environment that was self-sustaining and always producing. Some of the crops in Charlie, like corn and soybeans, were naturally annuals. Germinating them all at the same time would result in all producing at the same time and all dying at the same time. Although it was most efficient for the plants to follow their natural annual cycle, thriving during summer and being dormant through the winter, Porter staggered the germination and supplemented sunlight with artificial means. This was fortunate for their current circumstance, but also an essential practicality for the colony since a year on Mars lasted 687 Earth days, or 669 Martian days (or "sols"). Now it was Martian mid-spring, April 39, Mars Year 47 – that made it May or June 2042 on Earth. He had early corn slowly ripening in the greenhouse. The stalks hadn't particularly thrived with the sun so distant this time of year, but they were edible and had lots of calories. Without access to the station, he didn't have the means to easily process the ripened soybeans for food, but some of the immature beans could be boiled as a good protein source. Edamame without salt, thought Porter—that would be boring, but nutritious. He wasn't a dietician, but this seemed like a promising start. It might get them through a week, if the children were hungry enough to eat it.

Porter plucked a dozen nearly ripe ears of corn and put them into one of the plastic barrels in the cart. Then he added some green soy seedpods to the other barrel. Satisfied, he turned off the lights and pushed the cart on the cold floor through the darkness toward the Charlie receiving area. It was quiet. No children crying, just the scratching of the wheels and the thump of his broom-crutch echoing in the stillness of the greenhouse on an airless planet two hundred million miles from Earth. Porter had never felt so isolated. The sliver of hopelessness tried to press in further. He willed it away.

He quietly emptied his collection on the counter by the sink, and then filled the barrels with water. Porter realized that he was hungry; apart from the brownie bits he swallowed incidental to pre-chewing them for the infants, he hadn't eaten in twenty-four hours. He stripped the husk back from an ear of corn and ate it raw, following it with the remains of the crumbled cookie he had loaded in his pocket in sick bay an eternity ago. He realized that would be his last cookie for the week. Maybe he would finally drop the extra bulk he had packed on over the last couple of years. It was tough for an Earther to get a good workout in light gravity, but he still ate like a farm boy from habit. Corn and soy mush ... this could be a miracle diet! Perhaps he could start a business selling the mixture by mail to couch potatoes on late night television back home. He smiled at his joke, wishing he had his wrist com to take the "before" picture for his imagined ad.

How was he going to cook? There was no stove in Charlie. Not even a hot plate. The small barrels he brought from Delta were plastic. Even the larger containers holding chemicals for soil treatment were plastic. He could construct a fire pit in the dirt ... or better, on one of the raised growing tables—but how could he heat water to steam or boil? He could roast the corn, but he knew he had to steam or boil the soy. Raw soy wasn't digestible. Perhaps he could heat chunks of concrete and put them into the bucket? This was going to be tedious. He worried that a fire might consume too much of the oxygen ... best keep the fire to a minimum, cooking once per day.

It had been a very long day. The half-moon Phobos on the horizon suggested it was midnight. Porter was tired and his knee hurt. He was thinking about going to sleep, when he realized that he should probably build the fire and cook now, gaining the benefit of some heat and the ability to cook without having to shepherd children. This would also mean that food would be ready when the children awoke ... with dawn, he guessed.

Wearily, he limped back toward the Delta air lock, hoping that some of the plant debris from his pruning a few weeks earlier was dry enough to burn. It was going to be a long night.

CHAPTER 3 – Mush

Porter heated chunks of concrete scavenged from a broken grow table by the fire, then put them into the water to heat it. It seemed forever before the water was hot enough to cook. He interrupted his cooking duties to check the babies when they cried about 2 a.m., the first to wake setting off a chain reaction among the rest. Mercifully, the toddlers ignored the din. The infants had soiled their blankets and were wet. He swapped out the wet blankets and turned the tarp in the dirt nest, then he packed them in again for warmth. He gave each some water through blanket scraps, but he knew they were hungry, and they continued to wail. After nearly an hour, he left them crying and returned to his cooking labors to find the fire near dead. They cried themselves to sleep eventually. When one awoke and started the chorus again an hour later, Porter struggled to ignore the din. It broke his heart. He knew they were hungry. Finishing his cooking task was the only path his exhausted mind could see to soothe them.

By first light, Porter had created about six cups of corn and soy mush. It wasn't awful, but he didn't anticipate culinary awards. No salt. No spices. It was boring. He used the leaves of the cornhusks to hold small portions of the glop for each toddler. He had his coffee cup and the watering can ready. He was serving the four babies "breakfast" as the first of the nine toddlers began to stir. Porter pre-chewed the glop and dabbed it on the infants' lips with his finger. It wasn't a hit. The babies might have swallowed some of the mixture, but they shrieked in protest. He gave them more water, and then left them, discouraged, as he shifted his attention to the toddlers.

Yesterday, the children had been a blur. A novelty. A chore. Things. He hadn't paid much attention to individuals, distracted by the effort of NOT thinking about the situation while trying his best to keep them safe and warm. This morning he was exhausted, but better prepared to interact. He realized their world was upside down too, and they didn't understand what was happening to them.

As they woke, he called to them in a gentle voice, "Are you hungry? Would you like some breakfast?" Perhaps because they were hungry, perhaps because there wasn't much else to do, the toddlers shyly headed in his direction in ones and twos. Some walked, some crawled.

"I made food," Porter said quietly, taking one of the cornhusk plates and spooning some of the mush into his mouth with his fingers. "There is water here too." He took a drink from the cup.

The golden-haired little girl was the first to venture close. Her face was still caked with dirt. Porter handed her the cup and she let her eyes move from him as she drank. "That's a big girl!" he said. "How about some food?" He offered her some of the mush from his husk, but she seemed confused. He put another finger full into his mouth and ate it noisily, with smacking of lips and yummy sounds. That was all the encouragement she needed to try the mush. Porter had to stifle a laugh at the face she made when she tried it. The mush was clearly a disappointment, and she spit it out. "That's all there is for breakfast," he said. She paused, hunger apparently getting the better of her. She experimented again, this time making less of a face, but clearly not thrilled. She swallowed, then sought more.

Porter gave her a fresh leaf full of mush and turned toward a dark-haired girl who had been watching their exchange. Porter only knew the name of one child. The first child born on Mars was a girl named Mary. He remembered because they made a big deal out of it, and Mary was also his mother's name. Mary's father was one of the biochemists, Wayne Shimizu. Porter had worked with Wayne setting up greenhouse Alpha. Because this toddler appeared to be the most mature, perhaps two Earth years old, and likely of Asian descent, he decided she was probably Mary.

"Are you Mary?" he asked. The girl brightened at the mention of her name. "Your daddy is a friend of mine. I'm going to take care of you until your daddy comes back. Would you like some breakfast?" He held out the leaf full of mush, but Mary began to cry.

"Daddy," she whimpered. "I want daddy."

Porter put down the leaf and gently held the distraught girl. "Daddy can't come right now, sweetie. You stay here with Uncle Porter and I'll take care of you till mommy and daddy come back." He held her lightly against his chest. She resisted initially, then surrendered into his arms, sobbing. She took several minutes to cry herself out and then she sniffled, exhausted, and seemed to take some solace in his embrace. He held her a minute more, then refilled the water cup and offered it to her. As he did, he saw that most of the toddlers were now gathered around watching, some silently, most crying quietly. Several were babbling, but he could occasionally catch the words "momma" or "mommy" or "daddy." There were nine toddlers, Earth ages between one and two. Porter felt terrible about being so distracted yesterday but wondered whether he or the children were as ready to interact then as they seemed to be now.

When Mary pulled the cup from her lips, Porter took it from her gently and topped it off with the water can, then turned and offered the cup to a blonde girl with close-cropped hair and blue eyes standing nearby. She took the cup without hesitation and drank. A chubby, light brown-skinned boy with straight dark hair peered meekly from behind her, watching Porter carefully. As the blonde girl drank, Porter leaned back, so that he wasn't visible to the boy, forcing the boy to circle around the blonde girl if he wished to keep Porter in sight. When the boy crept forward, Porter leaned back more. The boy slowly smiled.

"Why don't you share the water with your friend?" Porter asked the blonde girl, pointing. She seemed to understand and turned to offer the cup, interrupting the game of peek-a-boo. The familiarity of their interaction suggested to Porter that these two knew each other. He guessed they were both nearly two. "What is your name?" he asked the girl. She looked at him wordlessly, but not shyly.

"Until we come up with a better name, I'm going to call you Cisco, brave one. I'll call your happy sidekick Pancho, like the cowboy adventurers in those old videos my grandpa shared with me. Is that okay with you, Pancho?" Porter directed the last question to the boy behind her, reinitiating the peek-a-boo game by leaning forward so that Pancho had to circle farther back behind Cisco. Pancho squealed with delight and dropped the cup in his haste.

Porter retrieved the cup and refilled it, shifting his attention to another boy, this one a skinny redhead who had been watching the interactions quietly. Porter offered the cup, and the boy hesitated a long moment, then took it without ceremony and drank. Porter considered continuing the naming game but wanted to give the children time to find their voices. He had just decided to let the game end, when he saw his golden-haired helper begin to share her mush with Mary.

"And what shall we call you, my little helper?" he asked the girl, whose hair was now an impossible tangle. Her blue eyes looked back at him. "How about I call you 'Helper'? Is that a good name?" The girl smiled at the attention but said nothing. "'Helper' it is, until we learn better."

Porter ensured that the toddlers all had water and mush. Like Helper, none seemed thrilled with the fare, and Porter was amused by some of the faces they made—but hunger seemed to win the day and more of the mush ended up in little bellies than on the ground. Cisco even demonstrated that she could speak, coming back to Porter and presenting her husk empty and asking, "Mo?"

Pleased with his progress but exhausted by the long day and night, Porter made one more pass at the infants, ensuring they were clean and dry. He gave them water and tried again to put bits of mush into their mouths. He doubted they ingested more than crumbs. He was concerned about how little they were eating but needed to get some rest himself before the next meal.

He rinsed the soiled blankets in the sink—the water still flowed, but it was colder.

He offered the water cup around to the toddlers again, then drank some water himself and lay down on the dirt mound near the infants and went to sleep as the distant sun rose slowly in the sky on the second day after the accident.

CHAPTER 4 –

First Aid

A few hours later, he awoke to Helper prying his eyes open with her small fingers.

"Pancakes?" she asked hopefully when his eyelids parted.

Porter smiled. "Sorry, sweetie, no pancakes today. Do you want some more mush?"

"No. Pancakes," she insisted patiently, as if he would understand this time.

"I don't have any pancakes, Helper. Let me see what I can find." Porter struggled to his feet and hobbled painfully to the sink to fill the watering can and rinse the cup. The tap still flowed, but the water was icy.

"Helper, would you like some…" Porter said as he turned from the sink. "…Water?" he finished in mild surprise. She had followed and was right behind him.

"Yes peez," she replied cheerfully.

He offered her the cup.

"Would anyone like some water?" he announced loudly. In ones and twos, the toddlers gathered around. He placed the watering can on the ground. When

Helper was finished, he asked her to refill the cup. She seemed uncertain, so he gently took her hand and lowered the cup into the watering can, then offered the cup to the first toddler who had arrived. It was Cisco, the blonde girl. She seemed fearless and took the cup eagerly. Her partner Pancho was right behind her, but the dark-haired boy didn't seem as interested in peek-a-boo just now. After taking a drink, Cisco passed the cup to Pancho, unbidden.

Porter hoped the demonstration would propagate. He realized that he needed to help the children be as self-sufficient as possible and chastised himself for keeping the water out of reach while he slept.

He looked to the air lock. The red light still warned of low pressure beyond the door. The strobe still pulsed silently.

The infants mewled weakly. He filled one of the plastic containers with water and went to the infants, leaving the toddlers to their own devices. Using strips of blanket, he gave the infants water and then cleaned them up as best he could. The foul smell from the blankets suggested they had managed to ingest more of the mush than he realized.

The smallest of the infants was a listless, pale, brown-haired girl. Her cry was feeble, more of a croak. Dried snot crusted her nose. Porter gave her special attention to ensure she got some water and held her close to warm her. Porter decided to call this runt of the litter "Sniffles." He held her until she slept, then wrapped her in a blanket and put her with the other infants.

He glanced to the toddlers and saw that they seemed to have grown weary of the water game but were still milling about. He fetched the cup and moved toward the sink where the last of the mush remained. He filled the cup with cold mush and walked to Helper. "Mush?" he asked, extending the cup.

Pancakes apparently forgotten, Helper put her fingers into the cup and began licking the mush from her hand. The other children began to crowd around, reaching for the cup, but Helper turned away from them and kept eating.

"Helper," Porter admonished, "we only have one cup and we need to share." The girl looked at him for a moment, and then turned away, pretending not to have heard.

"Helper, you need to share with the others." She dipped her fingers one last time and let one of the other toddlers take the cup.

"Thank you, Helper. That was very nice," Porter said encouragingly.

He refilled the cup with the last of the mush a few moments later. When it was emptied again, he rinsed the cup and refilled the watering can, putting both on the ground by the sink where the toddlers could reach them.

His leg was throbbing again, and very painful. He decided his next priority was to see if he could improve his mobility. The initial fit of the cast had been wonderful. The doctor had recommended he stay off the leg for a few days, but he was doing a terrible job of following her advice. Since the cast had slipped, it felt like he reinjured his knee with every step. He doubted the cast was helping at this point, other than to keep him from scratching an intolerable itch. He decided to remove the cast and check his injury. He realized he might still need a splint, so he set out with the cart to gather some bamboo as well as ingredients for the next meal, hoping that he could minimize his walking this afternoon. "A final lap for the good doctor's cast," he thought wryly.

Bamboo had minimal food value. The shoots could be split and boiled to add variety to a menu, but it was not a good source of calories. But bamboo offered many other benefits. Porter cultivated bamboo because it was one of the fastest-growing terrestrial plants, growing several centimeters per day while capturing and storing carbon with great efficiency. It was also evergreen, performing photosynthesis while the annuals withered and died. As a bonus, the rigid bamboo stalks had a variety of uses when properly dried.

As Porter moved down the rows of grow tables, he performed perfunctory maintenance of the plant charges he had neglected the past few days. Normally, cultivating soils and plants was more than a full-time job. Just now he had other priorities, but out of habit, or perhaps motivated by a desire to reclaim his routine, Porter thinned a few seedlings and adjusted watering levels as he went. Charlie didn't have the diversity of Bravo. Porter had planted bamboo, soy, corn, beans, squash, wheat, rice, broccoli, kale, lentils, zucchini, peppers, orange, breadfruit, and pine. Two of the latter three evergreen trees had great potential to supplement their diets in a few years, but otherwise were immediately useful only for sequestering carbon and producing oxygen.

He picked some sweet bell peppers and zucchini, more corn, and more soybeans. Wheat and lentils would not be ready for weeks. Some of the rice looked promising, but he wasn't sure how to hull it with the tools at hand, so he disregarded it for now. He couldn't imagine the children getting excited about broccoli or kale, so he ignored them. He chose several sturdy bamboo stalks about five centimeters in diameter and cut them into three-foot lengths with a hand saw he kept near the bamboo. Bamboo consisted of hollow, woody segments, with a fleshy closure at each of the joints. Porter had seen fancy serving dishes for soup made from bamboo and realized that these could serve as cups or bowls. He fashioned half a dozen "cups" quickly, then loaded his booty into the cart and pushed it toward the receiving area.

The toddlers were playing in the sand and dirt of the receiving area. One brave child had somehow climbed into an empty growing table with a blanket and was napping. Seeing this, it occurred to Porter that the growing tables were raised off the cold floor and would be better-insulated beds than the dirt piles. That was one of the reasons he grew his plants on the tables, to separate them from the cold floor, but he hadn't connected the dots before without an example.

As he pulled the cart to the sink, several toddlers gathered around curiously. He picked up one of the bright red bell peppers, pulled off the stem and split it open with his fingers, pulling it into several chunks and brushing the seeds aside. He took a bite from one of the pieces and made a show of chewing and swallowing, then offered bits to the toddlers. Most of them tried the pepper. Half of them spit it out with a sour face; the other half munched with enthusiasm. He split another and handed out bits to those that seemed interested, and then shifted his attention to the water.

The watering can was about half full. There was no sign of the cup. Porter refilled the can and offered up one of the improvised bamboo cups. He then fetched the first aid kit and a utility knife he kept by the sink and abandoned the toddlers to attend to his leg.

The kit was the size of a large gym bag. The inventory was encouraging. In addition to a paperback book entitled "First Aid on Mars," which seemed helpful, he found an inventory sheet of the bag's contents:

• Amphetamines	• Gauze pads	• Salt tablets
• Antibiotic ointment	• H2O purification tabs	• Sanitary wipes
• Antibiotic pills	• Hydrogen peroxide	• Scalpel set
• Artificial blood	• Hypodermic needle	• Scissors
• Artificial plasma	• Iodine	• Sleeping pills
• Aspirin	• Ipecac	• Soap
• Bandages	• IV glucose	• Stitching kit
• Blankets (foil)	• IV saline	• Surgical clamps
• Chemical heat pack	• Latex gloves	• Surgical tape
• Cyanide tablets	• Laxatives	• Surgical tubing
• Defibrillator	• Matches & lighter	• Thermometer
• Energy bars	• Morphine	• Tongue depressor
• Epinephrine	• Oxygen canister	• Topical anesthetic
• Exo-suit patches	• Petroleum jelly	• Tweezers
• Eye wash	• Rubbing alcohol	• Water

The completeness of the trove pleased him, although the cyanide gave him pause. The book was thick with pictures and a quick glance suggested it was thorough, though he didn't imagine himself "Performing an emergency appendectomy" any time soon. He put an energy bar into his pocket to feed the infants later.

He was preparing to cut off his cast, when he discovered a valve to let the air out without damaging it. He opened the valve to a whoosh of air and felt the pressure of the cast quickly decrease as it deflated. Carefully, he pulled himself along the ground trying to scoot out of the flaccid cast, to no avail. Finally, he used one of the bamboo poles to push the part of the cast under his foot away, and his leg slowly emerged. Beneath the cast, his knee had been bandaged.

Removing the bandages revealed a discouraging sight; a fresh scar indicated where the doctor had operated on his knee. His kneecap, however, was not where it belonged. His original accident, when he tangled his leg in the ladder and fell, had twisted his leg terribly and dislodged his kneecap. He was sure the doctor had set it while he was in sick bay. When he had fallen and twisted his knee again on the last rescue run, he must have dislodged it anew. He grew queasy at the sight, knowing what he had to do, but not relishing the prospect. His leg was swollen and tender. He gently touched the misplaced kneecap and found the flesh around it inflamed and sensitive. He tried to nudge the bone back to where it looked like it would belong. It resisted his efforts. He tried again, noting that the kneecap itself wasn't very tender. He increased the pressure and was surprised by a breathtaking POP as the kneecap returned to its life-long home. He saw stars for a moment, feeling shock not so much at the pain, but the surreal sight of the misplaced bone settling where it belonged. There was a dull ache, but his knee felt significantly better than before. Porter experimented with slightly flexing his leg. His efforts were met with agonizing protests. For now, immobilizing the knee seemed like the best course. He fashioned a crude splint from three bamboo rods and lay back to rest, glad the trauma was over. He fell asleep wondering whether he should use the morphine or simply take aspirin.

CHAPTER 5 –

Making Dirt

When he awoke again, the sun was sinking on the horizon.

He prepared a bed for the babies in one of the growing tables, putting a bit of dirt under them for padding and insulation and to make cleaning easier tomorrow. He cleaned and moved the protesting infants, giving them water, knowing they wanted food. He then tore open the energy bar and chewed it into paste, using his finger to feed them. He seemed to be making progress with all of them but Sniffles, the youngest. She was weaker than ever. Porter tried diluting the paste further with water and getting the child to suckle the resulting film from his finger, but he didn't have much success. She was lethargic and seemed to lack the energy to eat. With a heavy heart, he gave all the infants more water and shifted his attention to the toddlers.

He prepared grow table beds for the toddlers, moving sealed chemical containers to the side of the tables as a stair so that the toddlers could climb in and out at will. He pushed some dirt over the side of the table onto the floor to cushion falls. He fetched the two emergency blankets from the first aid kit and draped them over the table.

Porter worried about the air temperature. It was 18 degrees Celsius or about 65 degrees Fahrenheit and the sun was still above the horizon. He turned on grow lights to warm the greenhouse and supplement the thin sunlight of spring. Then he built a fire with some of the remaining cuttings and made dinner. He cut zucchini into coin-sized bits. It was mostly tasteless but served as filler and some calories and might represent a useful novelty. He reprised the corn and soybean mush from yesterday and fed the toddlers that and the zucchini coins. There were few protests. Hungry children were not fussy eaters. A curly-haired boy refused to eat, but the rest seemed hungry enough. Porter was pleased to see Helper both eating and sharing the zucchini.

Darkness had fallen when mealtime was complete. Porter gave each child a crude sponge bath; then he warmed and dried them by the embers of the fire. He gave particular care to those who still sported significant rashes, dusting their behinds with a water absorbent powder normally used to increase water retention of sandy soils. When bath time was done, he decided to dedicate one of the tables as a toilet. He built a crude ramp and led the children up and onto a table filled with soil. He then announced, "We are going to play the potty game! Everyone try to go potty." As the children looked on, he unzipped the tattered remnants of his trousers and urinated into the dirt, then waited expectantly.

Mary was the first to "score," squatting and peeing in the dirt. Porter made much of her success, proclaiming, "Mary is such a *big girl!*" He pushed dirt over the wet spot that she had made, saying, "This is how we flush in the greenhouse." A few of the other children had similar successes over the next five minutes and Porter praised them and helped them "flush" as well. Eventually, enthusiasm for the game waned, and he began to lead them down the makeshift ramp again. To his horror, several children elected to step off the side of the table and drop to the ground a meter below. As they landed lightly on their feet or fell softly on their behinds, he laughed at how quickly these children were adapting to the physics of Mars. Then chided himself, realizing that Martian physics was all they had ever known.

He showed the toddlers their new beds, hoping the potty game might result in less to clean up in the morning. They surprised him with their willingness to lie down without protest. *Perhaps the cool air has some advantages at night* he thought as he tucked them in with an assortment of blankets.

As he tucked her in, he said, "Good night, Helper."

She closed her eyes tightly and pouted her lips. He thought she was going to cry.

"What's wrong, Helper?" he asked.

"Kisses!" she squealed expectantly, opening her eyes.

"Oh my gosh!" he said with exaggerated surprise. "I forgot the kisses! Here you go, sweetie." He bent and kissed her and gave her a little squeeze. She pressed her lips against his, made a smacking sound that was slightly offbeat, and smiled.

The highlight of Porter's day was walking around the table and giving dramatic kisses to the toddlers in his care. Those that seemed shy got gentle raspberries blown on their bellies instead. The curly-haired boy didn't like the game, so Porter stroked his hair until he calmed down. For the rest, it was the first time he had seen many of them smile.

While the toddlers settled down, Porter rinsed the soiled blankets and clothes and spread them on a makeshift clothesline he constructed between two tables. He hooked up sun lamps to help them dry and help keep the reception area warmer. The water in the sink was very cold and barely running. He refilled the watering can. Noting that his coffee cup was still nowhere in sight, he put a couple of the improvised bamboo cups near the watering can on the floor.

Porter shoveled the obvious human waste and the debris from meals into the cart. He added some Martian sand from a pile in a haphazard attempt to begin some soil formation—normally a much more rigorous process. He decided that this mess could best "age" in greenhouse Delta.

Checking the infants before he left, he found Sniffles crying weakly and shivering while the rest slept. He wrapped the girl in one of the last remaining clean blankets from the rescue and stuffed her into his shirt to keep her warm, and then he set off for Delta with his waste-dirt cart and the empty plastic barrels. As he limped along, he looked through the greenhouse wall at the *New Rome* colony. Between flashes from the strobes inside, the structure retreated into the shadows under a cathedral of stars in the night sky.

CHAPTER 6 – Delta Inventory

As Porter walked toward Delta, he calculated that it had been about forty-eight hours since the accident. He steeled and gave himself permission to think the unthinkable: Julia and the others might be gone. He had feared embracing that possibility would be soul crushing, but he just felt ... empty. Detached. Alone.

He and Julia had been together for ten years and married for eight. They intended to start their family on Mars with the other colonists. When the opportunity to apply for the mission arose, they had discussed it, and quickly agreed to the adventure. They understood the risks, but both thought Mars seemed an exotic and wonderful opportunity to ply their skills someplace that mattered. They were ideally suited to the task. They had different mission critical skills, his in horticulture and hers in nuclear engineering. They were both healthy. They had proven themselves in school and begun to distinguish themselves in their respective careers but had not progressed so far that they were beyond hands-on application of their fields of study. Neither had significant family entanglements on Earth, and, best of all, they were willing to accept a one-way trip to Mars. Porter had understood that there were dangers but had always assumed that he and Julia would face them together. Now he knew that might not be true. He wanted to smell her hair again. He wanted to kiss her neck and taste the salt of her sweat. He wanted to look into her brown eyes again, to be held by her again, to laugh with her again—Sniffles startled and resumed crying, disrupting his gloomy musings.

He arrived at the Delta air lock. Pressure normal. He went through the air lock pushing the cart ahead of him. The air was cool and smelled slightly foul. The bodies? He turned on all the lights in Delta, deciding to move the bodies to the back of the greenhouse and explore the rest of the construction site.

He took the empty barrels he had brought from Charlie out of the cart. He put the plastic-wrapped bodies into the cart and trundled the cart toward the far end of Delta.

As he progressed, he took inventory. There were several dozen grow tables constructed using the 3-D printer he had observed during this last trip. He was pleased to see that the water bladder was installed along the south wall. He noted that the work crews had cleared a path down the center of the greenhouse through the construction debris. The debris consisted of a dozen glass panels of the kind used for the roof, and the remnants of scaffolding. He had heard the construction crews saying that getting the panels properly seated was challenging, but they assured him that once seated the panels were solid. There were several rolls of graphene, an amazingly strong, light, and mostly transparent film of pure carbon atoms; Porter thought these were used to wrap and seal the greenhouses after the glass was in place, but he wasn't sure. He wondered if the rolls suggested these were left over, or if Delta had not yet been wrapped. He passed lengths of rope and spools of electrical cable and a battery-powered, big-wheeled cart for moving construction materials around within the building and across the planet's surface outside. It had probably taken hundreds of trips with this little cart to ferry in all the sand along the north wall awaiting his soil conversion efforts. At the far end of the greenhouse, the air lock was in place, but the sink had not yet been installed. A long hose was attached to the pipes where the sink would have been. Along the south wall he saw a couple of toolboxes on wheels and several trash cans. Porter inspected the far air lock, noting that it appeared intact and stocked. Unlike the mini air lock between Charlie and Delta, this was a full-sized air lock, with a complement of twelve exo-suits and another emergency kit.

He considered his cart's load. There were no grow tables here at the far end of Delta. He didn't want the smells that his load of corpses would produce near the Charlie/Delta air lock. He briefly considered trying to move a table to this extreme end of the greenhouse to bury the bodies but discarded the idea for lack of time and enthusiasm. Sniffles was hungry. His knee was sore. *He* was tired and hungry. He unloaded the bodies from his cart along the north wall about ten meters from the air lock. He arranged them on the ground, covering them with the plastic sheet. It was unceremonious, but he had the living to consider at present.

He dumped dirt from the toilet and other debris into the sand pile ten meters from the corpses. Soil development could wait. He hosed out the cart with the icy water that trickled from the hose and pushed it with one hand back toward the Charlie/Delta air lock, pulling the mewling Sniffles from his shirt and cradling her in the other arm as he went.

As he walked back, he noticed some things he had missed before. There were some rough pads that separated the glass roof panels in the stack for safe transit. He placed a couple of the pads and a coil of rope into his cart. He also found a couple of partially eaten boxed lunches. One had some artificial cheese and a half-eaten sandwich. Another had two cookies and a carton of flavored soymilk. Both had packets of salt and pepper and sugar. Porter realized he had been so busy taking care of the children that he hadn't consumed many calories himself over the past two days. He hesitated, and then wolfed the half-eaten sandwich. The sandwich seemed homemade ... a pseudo-meatloaf sandwich. The lettuce was wilted and the bread a bit dry, but to Porter it was delicious.

Porter felt a twinge of guilt about not sharing the sandwich and decided to give bits of the cookies to the children.

He opened the soymilk and sniffed it cautiously. It smelled okay. He took a sip to wash down the sandwich and began dipping his pinkie in the soymilk and letting Sniffles slurp it off. She was listless, but still had a sucking reflex. He decided the rest of the carton would be for her alone. The older infants seemed to be doing all right with the mush and water, but he was worried about this youngest. He didn't want to add another body to the pile.

It took half an hour to get an ounce or so into the infant, drops at a time. Eventually exhaustion displaced her hunger and she began falling asleep between suckling his fingers. Porter swaddled her in her blanket and stuffed her back into his shirt, then resumed his journey toward the air lock. Before leaving Delta, he filled four empty barrels with water at the sink and put them in the cart. Then, inspired, he attached the hose to the water bladder and left it running. Then he turned off the lights and went through the air lock back to the Charlie reception area. Sniffles slept the entire trip.

He swapped out the wet and dirty blankets from the infants and turned the soil in which they were laying. It smelled pretty ripe, but the filth and wetness were turned under. He could change it again in the morning. He nestled the infants back into their beds, and then tucked the sleeping Sniffles in among them. He covered the pile of them with one of the thick packing pads retrieved from Delta. For the moment, everyone was sleeping except Porter.

CHAPTER 7 –

What Next?

Porter elected to fix breakfast for the children before he slept. He unloaded the water, rope, and remaining pads, putting them on the work bench beside the sink. As he headed toward the grow tables to scavenge ingredients for breakfast, the sad prospect that he was alone revisited him. For two days he had been in survival mode—working with the assumption that he simply needed to keep his charges safe and fed "for a few hours" until the colony reconnected with them. If the rest of the colony were lost, what would he do next? He could imagine surviving a few days, maybe weeks with the children using the resources of the greenhouse, but it might be a year or more before help could arrive from Earth. There were no regularly scheduled flights. *New Rome* was the first and only colony on Mars. Perhaps the most merciful thing would be to gather sufficient cyanide from the emergency kits and mix it into the mush?

How long could he keep these children alive and healthy? He planned crops in consultation with Gerta Schultz, the colony's dietician, but balanced diets weren't his field of study. In the short term, he knew the children needed calories and water; he even knew enough to ensure they had protein. But growing children? Calcium, phosphorus, selenium, magnesium, zinc, vitamins, iron

... okay, Mars had plenty of iron, but the rest? Life on Earth had evolved over a billion years to utilize and need the materials available *on Earth*. Mars was a vastly different situation.

Porter had spent hundreds of days trying to synthesize soil for the greenhouses—adding chemicals and microbes and organic material to inorganic Martian sand to bootstrap vegetation. He had made progress, but he had no illusion that he had recreated Earth soil, with its subtle mix of minerals and microbe-level ecologies that made those minerals available to the higher levels of the food chain. For goodness sake, he was having trouble keeping his worms alive! He had no business considering long-term care of human children.

He turned on the lights near the Charlie/Delta air lock.

One foot in front of the other ...

He decided to check his worms. He had worm farms in two of the grow tables near Delta and used those farms to populate the other grow tables with pioneers. He relied on these farms to replenish the pioneers when he accidentally poisoned them by adding chemical enhancements to the soil too quickly or drown them by over watering. The farms he treated with the utmost care. He also had worm farms and bees in Bravo. The idea was to divide his stocks among the facilities so that catastrophe in one greenhouse would not cause the loss of all.

The worms looked healthy. Several new cocoons suggested the worms continued propagating, unconcerned about their distance from Earth or the occasional misfortunes befalling their kin here on Mars. "Protein source?" Porter wondered aloud. To the worms, he added, "Sorry, guys, forget I said that." He added a fistful of plant debris from a pile near the wall to each of the farms, checked the moisture levels, and then shifted his attention to his bees.

Honeybees, electric fans, and hand-operated paintbrushes were the only pollinators brought from Earth. Bravo and Charlie each had a small colony of bees. To keep the bees fed, Porter selected flowering plants for each greenhouse that had different blooming cycles. Timing the blooms had proven tricky for the first "seasons" because of the double-long Martian year and the increased distance from the sun, and Porter had nearly lost all the bees while he sorted it out. Fortunately, he had brought a broad selection of wildflower seeds to determine which would thrive, and he dedicated several grow tables to germinating and growing these when he realized the problem. Bee populations had stabilized, but it had been a near disastrous ecology lesson. He didn't want to take time to open the hive, but he heard the buzzing of bees regulating the temperature and everything sounded normal. He needed to keep the children away from this area. An inquisitive toddler would get no forgiveness for disturbing the hive.

He checked the condenser. It collected water from the air in the greenhouse that was in turn used to water the plants. The bladders along the wall had a capacity of five thousand gallons and were about half full, as they should be. Worried that the water supply from the station might be disrupted, he attached a hose to Charlie's tank to add more to it and adjusted the atmospheric controls to increase the relative humidity in the greenhouse. He would get as much water as he could from the station while it flowed.

Breakfast. Not feeling creative and knowing that he had an abundance of ripe corn and soybeans, Porter collected the ingredients for his mush, then looked about for something to add variety. Bell peppers had been appreciated, and he picked a few. The zucchini hadn't all ended up on the ground, so he picked a few of those too. Rice and wheat would be interesting when they were ready to harvest, but he would have to find a way to grind them. He also needed more efficient ways to cook. Utensils would be nice. He thought again about the 3-D printer in Delta and the toolboxes he had seen. Perhaps when the sun was shining tomorrow, he could experiment with making some pots and bowls and spoons and a mortar and pestle.

Tonight, it was getting late. He put the vegetables and some debris he could burn into the cart and moved west to the receiving area and the table he used for cooking. Soon the fire was going, and he was heating chunks of concrete to warm water for the soybeans. For days he had been putting one foot in front of the other, just trying to help the children survive. He was weary, but realized he needed to get more organized for the slow-motion emergency he was experiencing. It might last longer than a few more hours. The thought began to overwhelm him, but he pulled back from despair. Small steps - tomorrow he would explore using the 3-D printer to improve his cooking tools.

CHAPTER 8 – Naming

It had been ninety days since the accident. There had been no signs of activity from the station proper, and Porter had accepted that there were no other survivors. Julia was gone.

He had discarded the notion of giving up—for now; quitting wasn't his disposition and, anyway, the energy and enthusiasm of the children was infectious. He couldn't imagine not caring for them, not trying to help them survive. Like his plants, the children needed him. If there was a path to keeping them alive and healthy, that was Porter's mission now.

His knee was still stiff and sore and forced him to limp, but the range of motion had improved a bit. He had discarded the splint weeks ago. Once his leg had healed sufficiently to remove the splint and allow him to wear an exo-suit, he had been tormented by the desire to make a night reconnaissance journey to the main station. He had so many questions about what had happened. He told himself that there might even be survivors, although in truth he could not imagine a plausible scenario to support that fantasy. Ultimately, the safety of the children dissuaded him. The first rule of exiting the station for the harsh external environment of Mars was: NEVER GO ALONE. The smallest mistake or minor malfunction could be fatal without a buddy to assist you. He didn't fear for his own safety but knew that the children would perish quickly if something happened to him. If he had seen any signs of life in the station, he might have justified the risk, but he couldn't bring himself to put the children in jeopardy to chase ghosts or to satisfy his curiosity. This dilemma tormented him.

His current priority was making the greenhouse self-sufficient in practice, not just in theory. At first, he had told himself they needed to survive "for a few days" until they rejoined the other survivors. As the days stretched to a week, he realized he needed to plan seriously for the long term. He relished the opportunity to build and operate a terrarium like the one he had as a child, but the stakes were now much higher and there was no margin for error.

At the same time, Porter was learning about child rearing in a whirlwind on-the-job training session. He and Julia had been looking forward to being parents, but neither of them had younger siblings or much experience. He had babysat neighbor children sometimes when he was a boy, so he wasn't afraid of kids—but that was the extent of his prior experience.

Except for Sniffles, all the "infants" had graduated to toddler status over the past few weeks. They couldn't walk, but all could feed themselves with help, and they were starting to crawl. Porter wasn't sure if this was simply the passage of time, an example of necessity accelerating development, or if low gravity facilitated early mobility.

Most of the time, Porter kept Sniffles slung around his neck with a cloth scrap. The baby girl had lost a lot of weight in the first weeks and Porter had feared he would lose her but she was doing a much better job of eating mush now. He was pleased to see her getting healthy, though she was still frail and small. She didn't have the energy or perhaps the will to crawl yet and seemed to chill easily, but she seemed content to bounce around in the sling, quietly watching as Porter went about his chores.

In addition to Mary, Helper, Cisco, Pancho, and Sniffles, the other children had received "Porter names" and came to respond to them over time. The three newly graduated infants included a girl named "Pigpen" and the twin boys. The dark-skinned twins seemed able to crawl into trouble faster than most of the older children could toddle. Porter had awoken from a nap one afternoon to discover they had crawled up the ramp and were playing in the dirt of the "restroom" grow table. Their delighted smiles when he found them reminded him of the blue twins from the Cat-in-the-Hat books. When he put them on the ground, they immediately headed for the ramp again, compelling him to install a simple gate at the bottom of the ramp to keep crawlers out. In honor of their mischief, Porter named them "Thing1" and "Thing2."

Pigpen was a pale, frenetic little girl with wild brown curly hair who could not seem to stay clean for more than five minutes. She seemed to be bonded with the twins and rarely strayed far from them. To Porter, this was an advantage ... if he found one of the three, the other two were usually somewhere nearby.

The other toddlers got names that were descriptive and easy for Porter to remember. "Ginger" was a red-haired girl with a moon face and green eyes who seemed ever cheerful. "Scar" was an apparently healthy boy with dark brown skin and straight black hair who had what appeared to be a surgical scar on his chest.

"Red" and Cisco were the boldest explorers among the toddlers. Porter had discovered the fair-skinned boy with curly red hair and freckles clambering into the worm pens near the Charlie/Delta air lock one afternoon—the first toddler to make it that far. Porter was mortified and Red seemed to relish attention.

"Scooter" was a light brown-skinned girl with straight black hair who didn't yet walk but scooted herself on her behind from a sitting position, pulling with her legs and helping with her arms. She could scoot almost as fast as the toddlers could walk.

"Curly" was the olive-skinned boy with curly black hair who danced to his own drummer. Porter had initially thought that Curly might have been brain damaged or extremely traumatized by the accident, but had come to accept that Curly was just very particular about the way of things and easily excitable—a definite challenge in the early days. Curly seemed to be less emotionally fragile now that a routine was being established, though he kept to himself and never spoke.

Thirteen surviving children, a baker's dozen. Porter was growing attached to them all, with a special fondness for Helper, Sniffles, Cisco, and the Things (although he couldn't reliably tell the twins apart yet, their energy and inquisitiveness amused him).

To Porter's delight, about half of the children began demonstrating signs of bladder control at night, and many used the designated grow table to poop. This reduced the workload and the noxious odor level in the reception area significantly. At some point Porter realized that the fans designed to facilitate wind pollination of corn and some of the other plants would also serve to disperse the smell of feces and urine. He ran them periodically during the day to serve that dual purpose before he could make his nightly "soil development" run to Delta to dispose of the more noisome organic byproducts created by a pack of children and a grown man.

When Porter found Red climbing into the table holding his precious worms, he got serious about building barriers to keep the children contained and out of harm. He cobbled together a playground of sorts in the receiving area, walling it off from the rest of the greenhouse by turning a dozen tables onto their sides. For now, the barrier was sufficient to keep children contained in an area thirty meters wide and ten meters long. Their sleeping table stuck out from one greenhouse wall. The "potty table" protruded from the other. Porter rolled the movable arching ladder over the play area and tied three knotted ropes to it, spaced a few yards apart, to make swings. He also dumped soil into the center to serve as an insulator from the floor and a pad for falling children.

The wall kept children out of the Charlie receiving area with the sink and air lock area to the west, where he had set up his cooking station. The barbeque he created with the 3-D printer was crude, but more efficient than the open pit fire he had been using. He had put all the chemical containers behind the barrier for safety.

The water from the station had stopped flowing several days after the accident. The condenser in Charlie was doing a fine job of recycling water from the atmosphere and Porter had stored water in Delta's bladder as well as in the empty sand barrels and grow tables.

He sprouted two tables of hardy grasses and wildflowers in Delta to begin serious soil development and to keep the air breathable. He intended to make Delta as self-sufficient as Charlie eventually, but the decomposing bodies and human waste made Delta an unpleasant place to work right now, so developing Delta was a low priority.

Porter stepped up production in Charlie. As in Delta, he planted some hardy grasses that would grow in sterile sand if well-watered. He infused the sand with a chemical compound that bound water into a gel to slow evaporation. He also added trace minerals, some microbes, and adjusted the pH. His plan was to turn some of the plants under every few weeks to help build up the organic material in the sand so that he could expedite the transition to richer soil.

In some of the tables where he had already been carefully developing soils, he returned to work at an urgent pace. He cautiously introduced worms and planted additional beans, corn, soy, and squash. He also nurtured some sprouted tomato seeds by the sink, hoping to introduce them to the soil when he could confirm that the worms were thriving. He didn't have many tomato seeds in Charlie. The bulk of his seed stock was in his office in Bravo, where he had been experimenting with a broader selection of plants and soils.

He was not much of an artist, but he had been able to operate the 3-D printer in Delta to create more grow tables and crude "stone" implements: two big spoons for cooking, the barbeque, a rough kettle and lid for making soup, a skillet, and a large mortar and pestle to grind seeds and beans.

His first use of the 3-D printer had been a near disaster. The printer used a lot of power to melt the sand it consumed as input and deposit it as instructed by the attached operator console. The first evening he had used the printer, he had completely depleted the power reserves. When he returned to Charlie, there was no power there either. No power for the grow lights that kept Charlie warm. Fortunately, it was early summer, the nights weren't as cold, and heat had built up in the greenhouse during the lengthening day. Porter stoked the fire all night and the temperature didn't drop significantly enough to harm the plants or the children. The next day Porter found the power controls for Delta and was pleased to see that Delta could either share power with Charlie or be independent. The instructions in the switch box were quite clear, thanks to an anonymous electrical engineer. He switched Delta to operate independently so that the power draw to run the 3-D printer didn't threaten Charlie's power supply and let both systems bank solar power in their batteries for a few days before daring to use the 3-D printer again.

The quality of Porter's cooking hadn't improved much, but it was being conducted more efficiently. He had developed a routine of tending the plants in his care and harvesting both food and fuel several days in advance. This allowed him to dry the stalks and clippings for fuel more thoroughly with the grow lights and better plan meals. The new barbeque used less fuel and burned hotter, allowing faster cooking. This meant more use of grow lamps for heat, but this modest power consumption did not seem to be stressing the power system, and plant growth meant more carbon removed from Charlie's atmosphere.

The daily menu had evolved from mush to a thick "soup." He made more bamboo cups; now each toddler had his or her own. Soup let him make better use of some of the other vegetables, like kale and broccoli, which he could grind and stir into the broth for diversity. He had used one of the salt packets salvaged from the lunch boxes to make the first batch "special" and ease the transition. The sodium-deprived children ate with enthusiasm that first day, except Curly who shrieked in protest at the change in fare, flapping his arms like a baby bird trying to take flight. Porter tried to encourage and cajole him, but he just became more upset. Finally, Porter cobbled together a small amount of the standby mush and put it on a cornhusk for Curly. Curly quieted and accepted the food. When Curly had finished and held out the husk, indicating he wanted more, Porter said, "All gone," and offered soup. The apparently hungry Curly warily accepted the soup for seconds. They had repeated the ritual for a couple of days, Porter making less mush each time. Finally, Porter made no mush: "All gone." Curly had accepted the soup from then on. Curly moved at his own pace.

As daily life became routine, Porter had more time to think about Julia and the others. He wanted to know what had happened to them, and it tortured him to defer those answers. He had initially convinced himself that "rescue" would come a few days after the accident. As it became clear that there were no rescuers left on Mars, Porter had to accept that "rescue" might be a matter of twelve Earth months or more.

The last manned flight to the colony had landed a few hundred days before the accident and departed a month later. It had ferried a handful of new colonists and supplies from Earth and returned to Earth with a payload of minerals mined and refined at the colony. The trip wasn't cost effective, but it was necessary, and the payload helped to defray the overall expense. It had been the second manned supply ship since the colony's founding.

For the thousandth time, Porter wondered what Earth knew about the accident. There was normally a continuous data feed to Earth, so mission control would likely know more about what happened than he did. How would Earth respond? Could they know there were survivors? Would they see the mission as a rescue, or "recovery"? Rescue would be a priority, but recovery … there was no telling how long before a recovery mission might come. The cost of transit to Mars was astronomical. If the data feed had suggested no survivors, the first trip might be historians long after he and the children were dead. He wondered if communications would work if he got back into the colony.

It was maddening—he was a few hundred meters from food, clothing, medicine, a radio, raw materials, and *answers*. Julia might be trapped there. Others might be stranded there. He had shelter and food here. They might need him. There were the seeds in Bravo. No one was tending those plants. If something happened to the stock in Charlie, Bravo might be their only hope—if he didn't let everything in it die. He looked at Charlie's west wall. The east and west walls were windowless. He stared at the wall as if he could see through by force of will. Beyond the west wall, across one hundred meters of Martian rock and sand, was greenhouse Bravo. In his mind's eye, he saw Bravo protruding slightly south and stretching north out of sight behind the colony where it joined Alpha. He could picture the four climate zones he had fashioned in Bravo: hot and moist, hot with moderate humidity, temperate and moist, temperate and moderate. He recalled with pride the rich diversity of plant life he had been nurturing.

For the thousandth time, Porter convinced himself to make a foray to Bravo that evening when the children went to sleep. He imagined himself suiting up in the dark for a short solo excursion, when he thought, for the thousandth time, about Carter.

Jorges Carter had been the first colonist to die on Mars. When they had begun building the station out from *Luna* everyone helped with construction, eager to get out of their cramped accommodations. They had initially done everything "by the book," as they had been drilled before they left Earth. No one traveled alone. Everyone had a buddy. Everyone was tethered to a buddy or a piece of equipment. The safety protocols slowed down construction, and building was running behind schedule, but for the first six months, everyone had played by the rules without much exception or grumbling. Over time, the rules seemed to get in the way more and more. Colonists carped about the long hours and delays caused by career risk managers making rules from the safety of their desks on Earth while imagining what Mars would be like. More and more, the safety rules seemed silly. Eventually, they began to break down. The tethers were the first things to go. Operating machinery around people tied to one another was a safety hazard itself. The tethers were worn at the belt of the exo-suit. You clipped to your buddy's tether and it reeled in or out as you moved together or apart. A clutch in the mechanism activated if you moved apart faster than a meter per second—the idea being that if someone fell from a cliff or into a crevice, the brake would stop the fall.

Jorges Carter had been off-tether when they observed their first "blowout." They had been excavating the colony foundation near Bravo when they had felt a rumble like a minor earthquake under their feet. A geyser of red sand sprayed up into the sky as a pocket of gas escaped from beneath the Martian surface. It had been beautiful, a huge plume of dust, sand, and rock streaking skyward, launched by gas pressure but, meeting almost no resistance from the negligible Martian atmosphere or weak gravity, it shot up a hundred meters like dull red fireworks. There was no corresponding sound.

The radio channel had been awash with "oohs" and "ahs" when someone had anxiously said, "Carter? Quiet everyone! Carter? Does anyone see Carter? He was standing by where the sand blew up, but now I don't see him."

Forbes, the head of the crew, checked with Central. "Central, this is Forbes. We have an emergency. Missing party member. Please provide location and status of Jorges Carter."

"Forbes, this is Central. According to his transponder he is twenty meters west of your location and approximately fourteen meters below you. Sorry, Forbes, no pulse."

The crew had all stared at the flat expanse of sand, with a slight depression that indicated where the gas had erupted moments before. Mars had swallowed Carter.

Blowouts happened every few days in warmer months. They seemed more common in the summer, perhaps the result of melting water ice or dry ice under the surface breaking a natural vapor seal. The geologists explained that it probably behaved like quicksand on Earth, with the gas taking the place of water welling up from beneath the sand. Their best guess was that the sand beneath your feet would suddenly be insubstantial, and you would essentially free fall for the duration of the gas expulsion, and then be quickly crushed by the settling sand when the gas was finished.

Most of the colonists agreed that being crushed instantly was preferable to being buried alive. But to avoid either fate, people were much more rigorous about tethers after Carter. In his honor, people began referring to them as "Carter Tethers."

The wall was still opaque. For the thousandth time, Porter's excursion daydream faded. He looked away from the wall, aware of the sounds of children playing. It was agony but exploring Bravo would have to wait. He hoped the light and water schedule he had established were robust enough to keep the climates intact and the plants alive, but it would be irresponsible to check on them now. He couldn't leave the children alone.

CHAPTER 9 –

Language is a Virus

It was early fall on Mars, 350 days after the accident. Porter was amazed at how quickly the children were learning to talk. When they had gotten over the shock of the new circumstances, some of the older children, particularly the girls, had demonstrated that they had surprising vocabularies. In the months since the accident, language had spread like a virus. Many of the children were talking in complete sentences now, and Porter spent time each day teaching them new words. The first things that occurred to him were words about their environment.

Table, food, water, potty, sleep, wall, floor, dirt, soup, cup, swing, rope, fire, and sand were tangible nouns describing things the children interacted with every day. He could easily point and announce what he was pointing at.

Some of the less tangible ideas were harder to communicate intentionally, but the children got them from context when he spoke to them. Pain, tired, hungry, thirsty, happy, sad, cold, hot … he could see them learning as he spoke and when they spoke to one another. He was glad they were figuring it out because he wasn't sure how to teach them.

Curly still didn't speak. He never played *with* the other children, although sometimes he played near them. He didn't seem interested in the others unless they disrupted what he was doing. He stacked bamboo cups, played in the sand, or made tiny structures with scraps. For their part, the other children mostly ignored him, although Helper always made sure to bring him his cup for meals.

Helper kept surprising Porter. Her initial interactions on those first days had endeared her to him, but there was more. She was obviously bright, although she wasn't more verbal than the other children. She was very observant, taking cues from Porter's examples that many adults might have missed. When Porter began an activity—meals, bathing, playtime, stories—Helper would often round up the children and provide assistance without being asked. The other children seemed to accept her "big sister" role much as they accepted Porter's role as a supporting adult.

Sniffles's development seemed to be lagging behind the other children; she was clearly the youngest, and she was also sickly and needed special attention. Most of the children insisted that they explore the world on their own, only allowing themselves to be carried as a special treat or if they were hurt. Sniffles seemed happy to ride the sling around Porter's neck, watching the world as he carried on with the day. He fed her pre-chewed scraps as she rode in the sling while he cooked, then fed her properly after the other children had been fed. She stretched out and slept for an hour or so after each meal but would then wake and whimper until he put her back in the sling. After dark when the other children slept, he carried her in the sling as he worked with the plants and gathered food and fuel. She watched silently, sometimes sleeping.

Porter's last chore before retiring was to build a fire in the barbeque and start the next day's soup. Once the water was boiling and he had chopped and stirred in tomorrow's ingredients, he would refuel the fire and head off to his sleeping table with Sniffles. The fire would die down within an hour, but the mass of the kettle and the lid on top helped keep the heat in and the soup would be ready by morning.

Porter usually went to sleep before midnight. He kept Sniffles with him to avoid disturbing the other children and to ensure she stayed warm. He would give her a small meal consisting of the remains of the previous day's soup, then wrap her in his old tee shirt and keep her nestled next to him while they both slept. She dozed off and on throughout the night but seemed content to be near him, rarely fussing. When he awoke, she was often already alert, observing Porter and the purple dawn spreading across the greenhouse, greeting them both with murmurs and coos.

The morning routine consisted of restarting the fire to warm the soup and warm the water for washing. Initially, Porter had awakened all the children in the morning for mealtime, but that meant thirteen young people who wanted food and attention all at once. After the first week, Porter learned that if he let them wake up on their own it was easier for everyone. The first arrivals got quick sponge baths, paying particular attention to children who had soiled themselves during the night. Then it was a quick dry by the fire and a cup of soup. The whole ritual took less than five minutes per child, but Porter chatted with them constantly about their bodies, and the soup, and what activities were in store for the day. It was individual time for most of the children, though Cisco and Pancho, and then the Things and Pigpen, were usually processed as groups.

When he spoke with the children, he referred to himself as "Porter," "Uncle," or "Uncle Porter," not wanting to usurp the children's fathers' roles. But he felt like more than an honorary uncle. As time passed, they became his children, and he loved them deeply. He was pleased that they seemed to be thriving. He was proud of their accomplishments. He was amazed that they seemed to be doing so well. The greenhouse was their home. This bizarre accommodation had become normal.

He spent quality time with the children that didn't involve feeding or cleaning them twice each day: once at midday when they would play games or sing songs or wrestle in the children's living area; then in the evening after dinner had settled, when he would tell them stories or teach them about plants and walk with them through Charlie.

He hadn't taken anyone but Sniffles into Delta. The unpleasant smell of decay was fading, but the construction debris and tools made it unsafe. He also didn't want them to observe him working the air lock—its counterpart on the far side of Delta opened into the Martian atmosphere and would be disastrous were a child to operate it.

Initially, Porter had half-heartedly and haphazardly begun developing Delta, more to keep busy and occupy his mind than out of a sense of need. He had set up a few grow tables and mixed the human waste with sand to start building crude soil organics in an effort to begin scrubbing carbon dioxide from Delta's atmosphere and breaking down the waste. The grasses he planted had initially thrived, then withered and died without producing seeds. Porter had turned the dead plants under and transplanted similar grass from Charlie, along with a layer of mature soil from the Charlie beds. This grass crop seemed to be doing better; he suspected a microbe deficiency might have been addressed with the soil transplant.

Mindful that rescue was months or years away, he became more methodical and slowed his efforts to a more deliberate pace. He didn't have seeds to spare, and the role of Delta shifted in his mind from an interesting dumpsite where he could scavenge supplies and perform tinkering experiments while awaiting rescue to an important future extension of their ecology. If he could get it fully operational, Delta would double the size of their livable world and might double their chances of survival.

Porter had once decided that it would take an Earth year or so for a rescue to be mounted, but October 39 had come and gone without a disruption to the routine. He had lain awake for weeks searching the dark night sky but saw nothing other than the occasional satellite and the two moons of Mars.

CHAPTER 10 –

Children of Mars

"Old McDonald had a farm," Porter sang with enthusiasm.

"Eee eye eee eye ooooh!" the chorus responded.

"And on this farm he had a..." Porter paused, pointing to Red.

"Cow!" Red shouted.

"Eee eye eee eye ooooh!" the chorus added.

"With a moo moo here and a moo moo there, here a moo, there a moo, everywhere a moo moo, Old McDonald had a farm, eee eye eee eye ooooh!"

The children never seemed to tire of the song. As it progressed, they went through an inventory of barnyard animals that the children had never known, mimicking approximations of the sounds that they made—chicken, dog, cat, goat, horse, sheep (which sounded like goat), and pig. The children were being immersed in an alien culture using oral traditions just as their ancestors had for countless generations.

At story time, Porter told them of three bears, and three little pigs, and the boy who cried wolf, although the nearest representatives of those species were about twenty light minutes or two hundred million miles away.

Porter also told stories of plants and animals. These were true stories. Porter told them how plants and animals so small that they couldn't be seen lived in and on everything in the greenhouse, even inside of their bodies. He told them of the roles that these small things played in digesting various other things, using them for fuel like the cooking fire used bamboo and twigs. He explained that these things ate one another and were eaten in turn by larger things like the worms and the bees. The children seemed more interested when he got to the scale where visual aids other than his crude drawings in the dirt were available. He talked about the role the worms played in preparing the soil and the bees in pollenating the plants. He talked about the part that the humans played, eating the plants that were digested by their intestines and by the microbes in their intestines, and pooping out stuff that was nutritious for the plants. He talked about the chemistry of life; how animals used oxygen to get rid of carbon and plants used the sun to extract the carbon from the carbon dioxide, producing oxygen as waste. He told them the importance of balance, making sure the plants thrived so that the humans could thrive. He taught them about the terrarium, a system closed to everything but sunlight that needed to have everything inside of it constantly cycling to keep things alive. He explained the magic of chemistry as best he could, describing the palette of elements that made up everything they could see in the terrarium, outside on Mars, and in the stars above them.

He told them about a distant place called Earth, a huge place where everything was heavier, with an atmosphere outside that they could breathe without artificial aid. A warm green and blue planet where liquid water covered 70 percent of the globe and ten billion people who looked like them had lived for millions of years. He told them about brave explorers hundreds of years ago who built water-going vessels and boldly sailed beyond the horizon to discover new lands. He told them of the great-great-great-grandchildren of those explorers who built ships that could fly into space to visit Earth's moon and then Mars. He told them of the adventurers who came here to settle Mars and build the greenhouses and the colony they could see out the window. He told them that these courageous colonists were their parents—that each of them carried the spark of those explorers inside them. He told them that they too would grow up to be adventurers, trying to survive and spread their seeds where they would thrive, just like the worms and the bees and plants and their parents.

The children were between four and six Earth years old now. They always had lots of questions, which Porter did his best to answer. It was challenging when their only context was the acre and a half of livable space enclosed by Charlie and Delta and the crude pictures and models he could make with sand or plant debris.

Sniffles, still smaller than the others, had rejoined the pack and no longer rode or slept with Porter, but she and Porter still shared a special bond. She was rarely more than a few steps away from Porter when she wasn't playing with the other children. Sometimes when she was sitting nearby, Porter would stroke her hair absently and lovingly as he had done since she was an infant.

The orange trees began to bear fruit.

Another Martian year passed.

They got their first crop from the breadfruit tree.

Two more Martian years passed.

That summer, a dust storm blotted out the sun. All they could see out the windows was a dark rusty sky with a light smudge where the sun should be. The sky was occasionally lit by huge streaks of lightning with no hint of thunder. The plants and solar panels were not getting enough light. Power reserves began to drop. Carbon dioxide levels began to rise. Knowing Martian dust storms could last months, Porter chose to sacrifice Delta a week into the storm. He and the children moved the plants and worms they could salvage to hastily prepared grow tables in Charlie and diverted all power to Charlie's grow lights, running them just enough to keep Charlie's air temperature above freezing. After a few days without heat, Delta cooled to -30° C, freezing and killing everything that hadn't been moved. The storm persisted for four weeks more, with carbon dioxide levels rising to dangerous levels before the dust began to slowly settle and sunlight gradually returned.

It took nearly another Martian year to restore what had been lost in Delta.

One summer day, the children were playing tag, with some of the children running and dodging among the grow tables and others climbing the ladder to escape the person who was "it," then leaping to a nearby grow table to escape if they were pursued up the ladder. Scar was trying to escape a determined Cisco, who could climb the ladder faster than any of the children, when he misjudged the leap and landed on the edge of the table, his forearm absorbing most of his momentum. His cries brought Porter at top hobbling speed from the far side of the greenhouse.

The scene was chaotic. Scar's arm was twisted at a sickening angle a dozen centimeters below his wrist, with bone sticking through the skin of his arm and a dramatic though modest amount of blood covering Scar and those trying to help him. All the children were talking at once; several were crying, and Scar was howling in pain. It was one of the few times Porter ever raised his voice to the children. "*Everyone be quiet*!" he barked.

The stunned children were silent, except for Scar, who continued to sniffle softly.

"Helper, you and Red go get the big first aid kit from my worktable," he commanded. He saw his two assignees wide-eyed and staring at him, immobile.

He softened his tone and took the two children gently by the arms, lowering himself to their eye level, and lowering his voice. "I need the first aid kit to help Scar. I want you guys to breathe. Take a deep breath…"

He waited.

They took a breath.

"If you are excited, it excites everyone else. Excited people don't listen well. I needed to calm down and I needed you to calm down. Now keep breathing and go get me the big first aid kit."

The two raced off.

Porter turned. "You too, Scar ... deep and slow breaths. They will help a bit with the pain. You are going to be okay. That arm looks pretty nasty, but bodies heal themselves with a little help." Porter wasn't sure who he was trying to assure more—Scar, the other children, or himself.

"You are probably going to have another scar here on your arm when this heals up, so your name will fit even better," Porter teased.

Scar smiled weakly and seemed to calm down. Helper and Red returned with the first aid kit. Porter was no doctor, but all of the colonists knew basic first aid. He was thankful that the kit included substantial narcotics. He had never set a broken arm before, let alone dealt with a compound fracture. He preferred that Scar was asleep during the process for both of their sakes.

After giving Scar a sedative and injecting the arm with painkillers, he made a show of slowly and gently cleaning near the site of the puncture with antiseptic while waiting for shock and the sedative to put Scar to sleep. Porter recruited Mary and Sniffles to assist him, explaining what he was doing in detail to stall while the others looked on. When he was sure that Scar was unconscious, he had Scooter, Red, and the Things hold Scar so that he couldn't wiggle if he woke, and Porter gently pulled Scar's hand and elbow in different directions to straighten and realign the bones. To everyone's relief, Scar didn't stir. Porter had Sniffles and Mary wipe the wound with antiseptic and tape the gash in Scar's forearm closed.

Next, he had Cisco fetch bamboo and the hand saw, and he improvised a splint to hold the bones as immobile as he could without cutting off circulation. Then he fashioned a crude sling. The ordeal lasted about an hour as the children looked on in fascination. Thereafter, Mary and Sniffles became the unofficial medics of the group, tutored by Porter as necessary.

The computer that monitored atmosphere in Charlie kept track of the Martian calendar. As April 38 came around again, Porter gathered everyone together to remember "Smoky Rescue Day," six Martian years earlier. The young Martians now ranged from about twelve to fourteen Earth years old. Porter again told them the story of the accident and Sumi fetching them from the nursery and Porter bringing them to Charlie. Although all had heard the story before, they listened with rapt attention.

"I think I remember," Mary offered. "I remember my mommy and daddy. I think I remember a big white place with toys and smoke and air that tasted funny and coughing. And a lady in a helmet saying something and carrying me ... but I can't remember what she said."

"I think I remember too," said Helper, "but in my memory I'm seeing Porter carrying me, and if he was carrying me, I couldn't see it."

"I don't remember any of that," Cisco added thoughtfully. "All of my memories are here with you, Uncle Porter. You and Pancho and everyone."

Pigpen seemed sad. "Uncle Porter, why don't I remember my parents? Should I have done something to remember?"

"Mary and Helper were older, Pigpen," Porter said gently. "Most people can't remember much before they are a few seasons old. Memories are also fragile things. Helper, I've told this story before and the picture in your mind when I tell the story merges with any old memories that you really have of Smoky Rescue Day. Even when I tell you what happened, I must be careful to remember it and tell it correctly. It was pretty confusing at the time and my mind tries to make sense of it when I retell it by changing the story."

"I wish we knew what happened to everyone," Thing1 ventured.

"I wish we could go inside the colony," Thing2 added. "Porter says that there is a bunch of stuff and seeds we have never seen before."

"I want to see the tool that lets us look at the little tiny plants and animals," said Sniffles. "I want to see what they look like."

"Is that all true?" asked Red. "Were you really a colonist, Porter? Over there?" He gestured toward the air lock.

"It's all true, Red. Unlike you all, I was not sprouted here on Mars. I sprouted and grew on Earth and came to Mars as one of the colonists. Because I have been alive longer, I'm bigger, just like the old bamboo is bigger than the seedlings. So, when Smoky Rescue Day came, I was grown up and when Sumi got you out of the fire, I brought you here."

"Why didn't you put out the fire, Uncle Porter?" asked Ginger.

"I couldn't, sweetie. My leg was hurt. Remember when Scar broke his arm last year jumping from the ladder to the table?"

Scar looked sheepish. Everyone remembered.

"Because my leg was hurt, I couldn't put on a suit so I could breathe and fight the fire. That's why we were so lucky Sumi and I could team up to get you out of danger." Porter looked around the group; even Curly was listening carefully. "We will go explore the colony as soon as some of you are big enough to wear an exo-suit safely. Then we can find a bunch of stuff and more seeds—and maybe some answers to your questions."

"I'm the biggest," said Scooter. She was nearly a meter and a half tall. "How much taller do I need to be?"

"How might we figure that out?" asked Porter, using the tone that suggested he wanted them to think about it.

"Try on a suit!" said Cisco. "Can we get one, Porter?" The air lock was strictly off limits without permission, one of Porter's few rules.

"Great idea, Cisco. You are in charge of the suit-fetching party. You, Curly, and Pancho go to the Charlie/Delta air lock and get two exo-suits. Handle them carefully, and make sure you close the air lock after you." Curly never spoke, but seemed bright and observant. Porter tried to include Curly in well-defined chores when he could. Porter trusted him to follow instructions. He also observed that Cisco seemed to get along with Curly and he cooperated with her. Pancho was timid, but very responsible. He thought the three would be a reliable team.

When the fetching team had run off, Porter asked the group, "How will we know if the suit fits well enough?"

"If Scooter can see out of the helmet?" offered Pigpen. She was very practical.

"That is a good start, Pigpen," said Porter. "What other tests should we do to make sure Scooter would be safe in the suit?"

"Why do you need Scooter?" asked Scar. "Why can't you go alone?"

Porter spoke slowly and solemnly for emphasis. "The most important rule of going outside Charlie and Delta is, *never go alone*. It isn't safe."

"But why isn't it safe, uncle?" Scar said. "What could happen that you would need Scooter along? She would have to be able to do that with the suit. Does she need to be able to carry you?"

"Carrying me would be ideal," responded Porter, "but I don't know if it is realistic." Porter thought the question was excellent, and realized that of all the children, stocky Scar was the only one who might be able to carry Porter, whose Martian weight was probably the equivalent of seventy kilos after twelve years on the greenhouse diet. He smiled, suspecting the boy was angling for a piece of the adventure.

"The buddy on an external walk has to be able to operate his or her own suit safely, walk across the surface safely, patch their own suit, patch their buddy's suit, and carry or drag their buddy to safety in case of emergency."

"What is 'pash'?" asked Scooter.

"Pat – ch," answered Porter with exaggerated enunciation. "The suits are pretty tough, but if a hole is torn in them the air will escape quickly. A patch is a bit of sticky material that you put over a hole or tear to stop it from leaking air. If you are wearing a suit that gets damaged, you might be able to patch a hole you can reach. Your buddy has to patch any holes you can't."

Cisco and the boys returned from their quest to the air lock. Cisco carried two helmets and Pancho and Curly each had two suits in their arms. "We weren't sure which suits to bring. There seemed to be different bigness." Cisco caught her breath after the short sprint. "They were labeled with letters XL, S, M, and L. What do the letters mean?"

"Those are sizes. 'S' is for small. 'M' is for medium. 'L' is for large. 'XL' is for extra-large. I had forgotten that there were sizes. It was a good idea for you to bring one of each. Let's try the 'S' suit for Scooter. Let me show you how to put it on. Helper, please bring me a pad. Scooter, hop up on this table."

As Helper went for the pad, the naked Scooter leapt up onto the table like a cat. She was wiry. Like the other children, she showed no signs of puberty. For convenience, because there were no combs or brushes, Porter generally kept the children's hair cropped short, above neck length, using pruning shears. Scooter was in need of a trim and her black hair hung straight to her shoulders. Porter removed the bulky gray and white suit from its package and examined it. It did not seem to have suffered from the passage of time. The fetching party did not know to bring an air canister, but Porter didn't think that was needed yet.

When Helper returned with the pad, Porter spread it on the grow table, then placed a barrel in the center upside down and instructed Scooter to sit. He placed the thick-soled boots under her legs and told her to step in. Her small feet swam a bit in the boots, but not as much as Porter had expected. He told her to stand and push her right arm into the suit, pushing the sleeve over her arm and the suit over her shoulder. The look of discomfort on Scooter's face suggested mild claustrophobia. Porter realized these were the first clothes she had worn in her memory.

"Are you okay?" asked Porter under his breath so only Scooter could hear.

"It's scratchy and uncomfortable," Scooter replied. "Are you sure you can breathe in one of these?"

"It will be less awkward when we get your other arm in, then you can catch your breath before we close it up," Porter assured her. He helped her get her other arm in, and adjusted the suit across her thin shoulders, tucking her hair inside.

"Colonists used to wear an additional thinner suit inside ... about as thick as three or four leaves. It acted like a pad between your body and the suit. That's probably why it seems scratchy."

"A suit inside a suit?" Scooter asked with surprise. "That sounds worse."

Porter smiled at her. "You get used to it. You'll see."

The other children looked on with fascination and envy as Porter partially zipped the suit up from Scooter's waist. He paused here so that the girl could get used to the suit and asked, "How are you doing, Scooter?"

She smiled bravely, but he noticed her rapid breathing. "I'm okay," she offered meekly.

"Let's pause here so you can get used to it." Turning to the other children, he said, "The purpose of the suit is to keep the air pressure inside comfortable so you can breathe. It also helps to keep you warm. It's like carrying the greenhouse with you."

"Are your feet getting hot?" Porter asked.

"Sweaty," Scooter said. "But not too hot."

"The bottom of the feet is where most of the heat will try to escape, because the ground outside is very cold. That's why the soles of the boots are thick. They also have a barrier of air in them to help keep heat in. Are you ready for the rest?" queried Porter. He saw that Scooter was determined to keep going, even before she nodded. He was proud of her and smiled. Porter swung the hoop-like collar forward over Scooter's head and zipped the suit the rest of the way, attaching the hoop to the collar. Even the small suit was a bit large for Scooter without underclothes and her chin was below the bottom of the hoop. Because she was sitting on the barrel on the table, the top of her head was all the other children could see.

"We won't worry about the helmet right now. Let's see how well you can walk around." He took Scooter's arm and braced her as she stood unsteadily and stepped toward the edge of the table.

"Hang on to my arm," Porter said as she stepped off the ledge. She dropped a meter and landed with a wobble, using Porter's arm to steady herself.

Helper clapped and cheered and laughed, quickly joined by the others who shouted their support for the suited adventurer. Encouraged, Scooter walked stiffly among the Martians with a huge smile that only Porter could see until she bent forward at the waist to see where she was going.

Porter began to reach for the XL suit and paused, then decided to try the large suit instead. He climbed up on the table where Scooter had been moments before and laid out his exo-suit. He had donned the suit solo hundreds of times during training and construction of *New Rome*, and while his mind hadn't contemplated the actions in several thousand days, his body remembered. Feet, then right arm, then twist and the mass of the left sleeve caused it to swing around. Left sleeve, then half zip and tuck the knees and bounce the hoop over your head, then finish the zip. It took thirty seconds with practice. The knee tuck gave him a jolt of pain from his impaired knee, but it quickly passed. All he would need to add were gloves and helmet—but not yet.

Porter glanced at the parade clustered around Scooter. He admired her grit; exo-suits were more constraining than he remembered. Scooter was right; the suits were also scratchier than he remembered without underclothes serving as a pad. He hopped off the table gracefully, landing with most of the weight on his good leg. Then he waded into the mass of people surrounding Scooter. "May I have this dance, young lady?" he asked, extending his hand high so that she could see it above the hoop.

Scooter wasn't sure about the meaning of his words, but his extended hand suggested his intentions and she followed his lead. She pushed back her sleeve with one hand so she could take Porter's hand with the other. Porter bowed and pranced toward her nimbly, then backed up a step. Scooter laughed and bowed awkwardly, using Porter's hand to steady her from falling over, then bounced forward and backward clumsily, leaning forward at the waist to see what Porter was doing from time to time.

The crowd formed a circle and watched the performance. After a few minutes, both Porter and Scooter were hot and winded. "Enough for today," Porter announced. "This is much more work than it seems, isn't it, Scooter?"

Scooter smiled. "It sure is! And I can't see anything below my waist."

"That would make patching my suit or dragging me to safety a difficult task. I love you and trust you would do your best, but I don't think we are ready yet. I think it is safe to say that the experiment was fun, but we will need a few more seasons before the suit fits well enough for someone to go outside with me. Shall we try again next Smoky Rescue Day?"

Curly looked thoughtful while the other children cheered in agreement.

Helper watched as Porter extracted Scooter from her exo-suit, admiring Porter's agility and grace in the bulky suit. She knew now that he must really have been a colonist. She imagined dozens of colonists prancing lightly over the Martian landscape beyond the greenhouse windows wearing the strange exo-suits. She longed for the treasures and mysteries of the colony and the answers that awaited them. She ached to explore the world beyond Charlie and Delta. She looked forward to the next Smoky Rescue Day. For the first time in her life that she could remember, the calendar mattered to her. *Only 687 days to go* she said to herself.

PART 2: MARTIAN SPROUTS

"For a seed to achieve its greatest expression, it must come completely undone. The shell cracks, its insides come out and everything changes. To someone who doesn't understand growth, it would look like complete destruction." - Cynthia Occelli

CHAPTER 11 – Scooter and Thing2

It seemed to Helper that the seventh Martian year since their rescue was crawling by. She was fourteen or fifteen Earth years old, but still shorter than most of the others. She had shared her dreams of venturing beyond the greenhouse with Scooter, envious of the taller Scooter's presumed role on the exploration party. To Helper's surprise, Scooter was looking forward to the trip in an abstract way but seemed oblivious to the inexorable drag of the days. Scooter was preoccupied.

Porter had assigned the care of the fifty-odd growing tables to the children in teams of two and three. Scooter and Thing2 were responsible for tending eleven tables. While Scooter enjoyed tending the orange trees and the soybeans that struggled to grow in their shade, she also enjoyed working with Thing2. She thought Thing2 the more handsome of the dark-skinned twins, and she was sure he was the cleverest and kindest of all the children. She liked being near Thing2. She liked the smell of him. He smelled of dirt and plants and sweat in a way that was different from the others. Sometimes when they were working together, she would brush her arm against him just so that she could savor his smell later when he wasn't around. His smell made her happy.

Thing2 liked to make things. Porter had showed him how to make four simple machines, mechanical devices that redirected or amplified force to make work easier. First, Porter had shown him the lever. It was magical to Thing2 that he could lift the much larger Porter using a couple of bamboo poles and a well-placed fulcrum. Porter had explained there were six "classic machines", but he could only remember four: the lever, the wheel and axle, the pulley, and the ramp. To Thing2, the beauty of these devices was how they let him move loads much heavier than he was. When Porter noticed Thing2's interest, he showed the twin how light and sound bounced.

When Thing2 and Scooter asked Porter why the beans under the orange trees were maturing so slowly, Porter had pointed out that the beans needed light to grow but were being shaded by the tree. Thing2's first thought had been to put grow lights into the orange tree. Porter had praised the idea but expressed concern that there was a scarcity of lights remaining to support their project.

"It's too bad the light isn't heavy, because I'll bet you could lift it from the floor and put it on the beans. If only there was a way to move the light," Porter mused in that "Porter way"—suggesting that there was an answer if they looked hard enough.

Thing2 had been running through his list of machines, trying to figure out which ones would help with the light when Scooter had said, "Could we redirect light underneath the tree here, '2, like Porter showed us how to reflect it off the shiny metal?"

Porter had smiled and walked away, saying, "That sounds like an interesting idea."

When their experiment resulted in better yields a month later, Porter showed everyone the result of the effort and said that they all needed to look for good ideas like this that helped grow food more efficiently.

Thing2 liked Scooter. She was taller than he was, and really smart. She defined problems well, and that gave him good ideas about stuff to build, like the table-moving device they created. Scooter had said it was too bad the grow tables hadn't been built on wheels so that they could be moved more easily. They had some wheels scavenged from some of the machines in Delta, but the full tables were too heavy to lift to put the wheels on. Thing2 had assembled a set of pulleys with Porter's help (Porter called the set a "blockentackle"). They fastened it to the movable ladder and used the blockentackle to lift one end of the table so that a small platform with wheels could be slid underneath. This let them adjust the position of the tables.

Thing2 enjoyed solving problems with Scooter. He also thought Scooter's straight black hair was pretty. He noticed how the light shined through it sometimes in the afternoon. He found it much more interesting than the tiny tight curls he and his brother shared. He noticed that Scooter was starting to grow tiny tight curls below her belly button and wondered if they had been spending so much time together that the hair on his head had gone to seed on her body. He saw he was getting tight tiny curls between his legs too. He meant to ask Porter about it but didn't want to embarrass Scooter; if she thought they were weeds she might want to pull them before anyone else noticed. He liked the idea of his curly hair growing on her; it made them seem more connected somehow. That made him smile.

CHAPTER 12 –

Pancho

Cisco, Pancho, and Curly were the most productive gardening team. This was disproportionately due to Curly's efforts. Curly didn't speak but was a very thorough worker. He could spot weeds that were invisible to others and could often find several bean pods among the greenery when everyone else thought they had all been picked. He was particular about how he worked. He liked to have all the tools cleaned before and after and didn't always respond to direction well, but once he was focused, he was the hardest worker on the team. Porter often commended the team for the quality of their work. Both Cisco and Pancho knew that Curly did more than his share, but they were comfortable sharing the credit because they had learned to accommodate Curly's quirks and work with him.

Pancho tolerated, more than liked, Curly. He was a difficult person to be close to. You couldn't have a conversation with him, and he didn't play and joke like the other children, keeping to himself and rarely interacting. Curly often didn't seem to be listening to what was going on around him, but Pancho noticed that later Curly would demonstrate that he had both heard and understood. Like the time years ago when Curly had made small models of grow tables out of bamboo. Curly liked to make models, and the tiny bamboo tables had been instantly recognizable. He had filled them with soil and bits of greenery and seemed quite content with his accomplishment. Red had seen them and made fun of Curly because the green and tan of the bamboo didn't match the black of the grow tables and the tables were square on the bottom and not rounded like his bamboo models. Red was like that—give him a delicious orange and Red would find fault in the seeds. Curly seemed oblivious to Red's criticism, but later had rubbed the models on the floor to square them and blackened the bamboo near the fire. The miniatures resulting from these refinements were better models. Sniffles had commended Curly for the likeness, and together she and Curly had made several more. Curly was talented, he was just ... different.

Pancho noticed that Cisco seemed particularly skilled at working with Curly and sensitive to his moods. When Pancho sensed resistance from Curly, he would defer to Cisco and she could often find the right approach or words to calm the situation down. This helped the team work together.

Pancho and Cisco were best friends and enjoyed working together. They shared everything. When Pancho confided to Cisco that he liked Ginger, Cisco had not teased him or revealed his secret. Thereafter, Cisco would initiate games with Ginger and some of the others and then casually include Pancho. She and Pancho were a great team.

Until two years ago, Delta had been off limits unless Porter accompanied them. One night, when it was still taboo, Cisco had suggested an adventure—a late-night exploration of Delta while Porter and the others slept. When everyone settled for the night, Pancho and Cisco waited for an hour, then quietly dropped to the floor and moved in the darkness through Charlie toward the forbidden air lock in the dim light. Pancho brought a bundle with a snack for an illicit picnic. They went through the forbidden air lock between Charlie and Delta and explored the big "off-limits" pile of dirt and sand at the back of the Delta greenhouse. Neither could figure out what was so special about the pile, but Porter had made it clear that this dirt pile, unlike all the other soil in the greenhouses, was to be left alone—which made it extremely interesting and dangerous.

They stood solemnly at the dirt pile and pledged an oath of friendship. Then Pancho opened his bag and produced a tomato (Cisco's favorite food) to celebrate their adventure. Pancho, with a twinkle in his eyes, then produced a bamboo bowl from the bag.

"Why did you bring your bowl?" Cisco inquired. "We can eat the tomato with our fingers."

"It isn't mine," Pancho said. He turned the bowl over to reveal Mary's name scratched on the bottom. "I took it after dinner."

Cisco beamed with delight. Mary was the oldest child; she and Cisco were often rivals. Pancho and Cisco secretly enjoyed tormenting her in harmless ways. This was perfect. Together, they buried Mary's bowl in the forbidden dirt pile, stifling laughter and mimicking Mary whining in the morning when she couldn't find it. Then they crept back through the air lock to their sleeping tables in Charlie, careful to leave no trace of their passage.

The next morning at breakfast, Mary was in a mood. "Who took my bowl? I can't find it anywhere!" she howled in frustration. "I know I left it right there!" She pointed to the shelf.

"I'm sure it will turn up, dear," Porter assured her. "There's no place for it to have gone. Here, use mine for breakfast."

"But I want MY bowl!" she persisted.

"We'll make you another later if yours doesn't turn up," Porter said.

Cisco and Pancho exchanged knowing glances but said nothing, trying not to smile at their private joke. Mary was not appeased, and each time she renewed her complaint, they smiled a little more. Eventually, they had to excuse themselves to avoid laughing. Cisco invited Curly to join them, and they went off to tend their grow tables, Curly quietly trailing behind.

CHAPTER 13 – Helper

As far back as Helper could remember, Porter had made a big kettle of soup each day. The children had two formal meals of the thick broth and could get more when they wished. The soup was hot in the morning and cold by midday. Last call was a couple of hours before bedtime and anyone who wished could eat his or her fill. Then the kettle was cleaned and prepared for the next day.

One day Helper was assisting Porter with some of the evening preparation chores for the next day's soup. Porter was stripping corn from the cob and mashing it with the mortar and pestle to put in the soup, and Helper ate some of the corn kernels that had fallen beside the mortar. It was wonderful! She experimented with the soybeans; they were a little boring but had a distinct flavor. She talked with Porter about the soup being a mix of all these flavors, and he told her about different flavors that existed on Earth and even in the station because they had more diverse ingredients—different plants and chemicals that affected the way that food tasted. He said that different foods and flavors were mixed in different proportions with care, like the soils, to emphasize different things. Porter said that some people specialized in cooking, mixing different flavors and serving foods that had flavors that contrasted in pleasing ways. Helper asked him if he would make some special food that had different flavors. Porter laughed and told her that he wasn't very good at it, but they could work together to make a special breakfast for everyone and try some different flavors if Helper was willing.

It was exciting! Porter dried some corn by the fire, ground it with some ashes and dried beans, and mixed it with water to make a paste. He set that aside and they went to Delta and the 3-D printer. Porter made a crude funnel with tripod legs that extended from the sides of the vessel to eight inches below its spout. He told Helper that this would help filter something called "honey."

They went to the beehive that was normally off limits because of the stings. Porter lit a small fire in a bucket and put some green leaves on the fire, then let the smoke filter up through the hive. Porter explained that this made the bees sleepy. After a few minutes, Porter pulled a frame from the hive, and gently brushed the bees away with some grass. Then he ran a knife around the edges of the frame, cutting out a dark and gooey rectangle he called a "honeycomb" and laying it on a sheet of graphene. He replaced the empty frame, closed the hive, and removed the smoke.

They took the honeycomb to Porter's workbench area. Porter explained that the bees made the wax of the honeycomb to store honey, and that honey was food their bodies made to store for later. Porter showed Helper how to crush the sticky honeycomb with a pestle, making a big wax and honey mess. When he was satisfied that the crushing was done, Porter handed the gooey pestle to Helper, suggesting that she lick it and see what she thought of the taste.

Helper was amazed; it was a sweet flavor she had never experienced before. She had a new respect for the bees. They did more than just help the plants make seeds—they made this wonderful sticky goo.

Porter put a handful of screws in the bottom of the funnel and scooped the sticky mess of the mashed honey and wax on top of the screws. He put a cup underneath the funnel and left it sitting near the fire where it would get warm. He explained to Helper that if they got it warm, but not so hot that the wax melted, the screws should hold back the wax but let the honey leak through the funnel.

He then halved some oranges and squeezed the juice into the cup beneath the funnel.

"What do you imagine this will taste like, Helper?" Porter asked.

"I think it will be an interesting combination—sweet and tart," Helper offered.

They watched the funnel expectantly and waited, but nothing happened.

"That's odd," Porter mused. "I would have expected the honey to be drooling down by now."

He looked into the funnel, then laughed. "This is the method used on Earth. Gravity pulls the honey away from the wax and through the filter. I don't think we have enough gravity to do it that way here, at least not quickly. Any ideas about how we can separate these?"

"You said we shouldn't melt the wax. What happens if we do? Would the wax combine with the honey and ruin it, or would they separate?" asked Helper. She was thinking about how some vegetables floated in the soup, and some sank to the bottom of the kettle.

"Interesting idea. Let's experiment."

Porter put a bit of the honeycomb into a stone bowl and placed it nearer the fire.

"I think we want to be careful not to get the honey too hot," Porter suggested.

"Does it burn?" asked Helper, thinking of a few times when the soup was cooked too hot for too long and tasted terrible.

"It might if we got things hot enough, but I think even getting it hot enough to boil changes it so that it won't keep as well. Honey is unique because it will keep forever without spoiling if you keep away extra moisture, but I seem to recall heating it might degrade this. I feel silly that we haven't harvested honey before this. It should add some variety to the food. I'm glad you asked about cooking, Helper."

After a few minutes, the wax began to dissolve. Porter poked his finger into the bowl, pulling it back quickly and putting it into his mouth. "Yikes ... pretty hot." He nudged the bowl away from the fire a bit.

They watched the wax soften to ooze.

"Do you suppose the wax goes to the top or sinks to the bottom?" asked Helper.

"I'm not sure, but I'll guess it rises to the top," said Porter. "We should save the wax. There are other uses for it."

"Can we eat it?" asked Helper.

"I don't think so, but it is liquid when heated, then solid when it cools so we can mold it to make stuff with it. Soft things. We can also make candles."

"What are candles?"

"They are devices for carrying a small bit of fire for light. Long ago they were used as portable lights before people figured out how to use electricity to make light."

"How will we get the wax out of the honey?"

"Once we heat it so that the wax melts, we should be able to let it cool and take the wax out in pieces."

"How did you learn about bees and honey?" asked Helper.

"Part of what I learned about plants, I learned in school. They taught us there about the science of plants and agriculture. Another part of what I learned was when I worked on a farm."

“Did you meet Old MacDonald?” asked Helper, impressed.

“No.” Porter smiled. “Old MacDonald is just in the song. I worked on a farm run by a nice lady named Mrs. Alvarado, in a place on Earth called California. She kept bees on the farm to pollinate some of the plants, just like we do here in the greenhouse. Her parents and grandparents had been farmers, and she taught me practical lessons about farming and caring for bees that I didn’t learn from my lessons at school. She was good at cooking too, and sometimes made special treats for those of us who worked on her farm that summer.”

“What kinds of treats?” Helper asked. She loved Porter, but he was a very predictable cook. The thought of variety intrigued her.

“She made something called tortillas from ground corn or wheat and ash and water. They are flat circles about the size of a plate that you could put meat and vegetables and beans on and then pick up with your hands and eat.” Porter was speaking wistfully and looking into the fire. “We used the tortillas to make tacos and burritos ... tacos were mostly meat on a tortilla folded like this.” Porter placed his hands flat in front of him, pinky fingers and sides of palm touching together, then folded his hands closed. “’Burritos were...”

“Folded like a person in a blanket?” interrupted Helper. She recalled Porter using the word during good night kisses when someone was cold. He would say, “Let’s fold you up like a burrito and keep you warm.”

Porter laughed. “Yes, like a baby in a blanket. Burritos usually have beans and other stuff in them. It’s a way of making food you can carry without a plate or bowl.”

“Are you making tortitos to put the honey on?” Helper wondered.

“Tor-tee-ahs,” corrected Porter slowly. “No, although I guess I’m using some of the same ingredients. Tortillas are very flat.” He held up his fingers with a narrow space between them. “Two or three leaves thick. That lets you fold them or roll them around what’s inside without breaking. What I’m hoping to do with the mixture we prepared over there is make something called pancakes.

Pancakes are thicker—about as thick as your little finger—if I can get them to work out right. Long ago, right after the accident, you asked me to make you some pancakes. You must have known what they were, and you weren't thrilled with my cooking."

The two shared a knowing smile.

"Probably just as well you guys don't remember my initial attempts, Helper. It was lucky for all of us that you kids were starving. Trust me, the soup is an improvement."

Porter peered into the bowl and saw the wax had melted. "Okay, let's let this cool now and see if it separates. If it does, we can do the same with the rest of the batch."

Porter stood and moved the bowl away from the fire to cool. He paused and stared through the air lock at the corridor beyond for a long moment before returning to Helper by the fire. She saw him do that sometimes. Just stare at the station. She assumed he must be thinking about the before time.

"Do you miss the station, Porter?" Helper asked.

"Yes, sweetie. I miss the people the most. There were lots of people. They were special people and I liked them; I miss my mate Julia most of all. We all went on this great adventure together, but now I'm the only one left—and you guys of course. You are all that is left of those people, like seeds of the plants from last season."

"What else do you miss?"

"Well ..." Porter looked thoughtful. "I guess I miss the connection to the past. In the last ten thousand years, our ancestors developed lots of machines and knowledge. It was easy to take for granted. Useful machines were everywhere, and you didn't have to know how to make them—I mean, someone had to know, but as an individual you didn't have to know how to build a computer or the chemistry of cooking or the details of electricity. We could enjoy the results of everyone cooperating, and what we contributed in terms of our work or information could be very specialized. The doctor studied bodies and knew how to fix my knee when I hurt it, but the doctor likely didn't know that corn is pollinated by wind or how to get honey from the bees. We needed each other, but we didn't realize how much. I miss some of the information that was so easily available. I had a device in my office that was about the size of a large tortilla. I could touch that device and find out almost anything that anyone knew or had ever known about a subject."

"Like what?" Helper asked. Porter didn't talk about the station this way during lessons. This was more like a conversation.

"Well, cooking, for example," Porter said. "There have been many really good cooking specialists. Different regions of Earth had various styles of cooking that favored different flavors because of the different local plants that were available. Many of them wrote instructions about good ways to make their favorite dishes—what ingredients to put in, how much of each, how to mix them and how to cook them. With my computer tablet, my 'magic tortilla,' I could request any of those to be shown to me. Then, if I followed the directions, I could create some wonderful different flavors that I might not have thought of myself."

"Will you teach me how to cook?" Helper asked.

"I think that is what we are doing today," Porter said. "And I think we are doing it together and in a more thoughtful way than I have in a long time. I'm not a very good cook, and you seem interested in the subject. Let's work on cooking together over the next few weeks. We'll get some other people to help with preparation and cleanup. I don't find cooking very interesting. If you do, perhaps we can share this job. I'm sure some of the others would appreciate a little variety."

"Except maybe Curly," Helper said.

"Except maybe Curly," Porter agreed.

When the small test bowl of honey cooled, the wax had coalesced at the top. They saved the wax for later and heated the balance of the honey/wax and let it separate, then cool. Porter mixed the resulting honey with orange juice to make a crude syrup. Then he placed a stone "skillet" he had made with the 3-D printer onto the fire and dolloped the corn and bean "batter" into little discs. The result didn't taste much like pancakes to Porter, but the children didn't know better. When the cakes were rolled and dipped into the honey-orange syrup, it was a big hit—even with Curly, when Cisco finally convinced him to try one.

A few weeks later, Helper had taken over cooking duties in the greenhouse. She was proud and excited. At first, she made soup as Porter had with minimal variation. As her confidence grew, she began experimenting with different ingredients and different proportions. Sometimes she cooked corn and served the kernels cut right from the cob. One time she hollowed out tomatoes and filled them with soybeans, then cooked them on the grill. She also varied the heat and the amount of time that things cooked. Her experiments were generally well received, and even in the worst case they were rarely as bad as Porter's soup.

Helper liked her special job. She liked being appreciated. She got to work with all the Martians as they took turns helping with cooking and cleanup duties.

Porter still consulted on menu planning, working to ensure that the children got a balanced diet and that nothing unhealthy was served (bamboo shoots were edible, bamboo was not), but he largely stayed away from cooking duties and was clearly pleased with the new arrangement.

Cisco suggested that Helper invite Curly to assist her when she wanted to try something new. Involving Curly in the process of food preparation, even if it was just having him stir the pot or tend the fire, seemed to decrease his surprise and improve his acceptance of the results. Although he never spoke, Curly was a thorough worker. Helper enjoyed working with him. When Curly seemed suspicious of a particular dish Helper was preparing, Helper would sometimes tease him, asking if he preferred soup. Curly never spoke, but the relief and appreciation on his face was clear.

Helper's favorite assistant was Scar. The dark-skinned boy with the straight black hair had beautiful white teeth and a surprising appetite. He was the largest and strongest of the boys, but he was quiet and shy. Helper thought Scar might like her. Scar often showed up to help with cleanup duties even when it wasn't his turn. She knew that she liked him.

When she wanted to try something new or different, Helper cooked small portions of new things and shared them with her kitchen helpers, especially Scar, to see if they liked them. Scar almost always said yes. She suspected that was for her benefit. He was very polite.

CHAPTER 14 –

Scar

Scar didn't much care for gardening. He loved the look and smell of the plants and the soil, and he enjoyed the buzzing of the bees as they flew among the flowers, but he found playing in the dirt unrewarding. He and Ginger tended some grow tables with peas and beans, but when he could, he preferred to do odd chores with Porter and aid Helper with kitchen duty. He liked the variety of Porter's tasks and enjoyed the extra time with Porter beyond the normal lessons. Porter seemed to know everything about plants and greenhouses and Scar was learning it in little bits over time.

Porter told him stories about Earth, Porter's huge home world that was closer to the sun. On Earth, all the air was breathable, and you could go outside without an exo-suit. There were huge puddles of water that stretched as far as the eye could see and water sometimes fell from the sky. There was only one moon, but it was huge, and its orbit had it march across the Earth's sky each day in a twenty-nine-day cycle. There was soil everywhere and plants grew wild. Porter said there were animals like in the stories— wolves and pigs and foxes and elephants. The variety of sizes and shapes and colors of the animals Porter described sounded fantastic, and Scar longed to see them. Sometimes

Scar wondered if Porter was making up the stories of animals and forests, but Porter didn't seem prone to exaggeration, and his stories were consistent about the smallest details. Scar thought it odd that with all those animals competing, humans were the dominant species. Porter said humans couldn't run as fast as most animals or fly like some of them could. Porter described some of them, like lions and bears, as ferocious predators several times the size of a person with big mouths full of large sharp teeth and claws like rakes. Some animals had thick hides that protected them that were tough like bamboo and difficult to pierce or tear. Scar had trouble imagining even a dozen men killing a fearsome beast like the ones in Porter's stories. Brains didn't seem like such a great advantage. Porter explained that with the development of tools, man had become superior. Scar couldn't figure out how humans lived long enough to invent tools.

The only world Scar had ever explored was the six thousand square meters of Charlie and Delta. He could look wistfully out of the greenhouse at the enticing red and tan rocks and sand of Mars which stretched as far as he could see into the horizon, but he couldn't walk among them. He could see the magic of the stars at night and watch the moons Phobos and Deimos sail across the sky, but he couldn't touch them. He could stare longingly at what Porter explained was the rest of the station, where the colonists had lived before the accident, but he couldn't go there. Porter told amazing stories about the station; there had been lots of other big people like Porter before the accident, but they were gone now, like leaves that had fallen. He said they left behind amazing machines that cooked food without fire and cleaned dishes. He said there were tools to fix machines and people. Scar would have thought these stories too fantastic to believe if he didn't trust Porter and had not seen what some of the amazing machines in Delta could do.

There was the electric tractor that lifted and moved heavy loads. There was the 3-D printer that made the pots and tools and tables and other implements from sand until it broke last season. Porter said the printers in the station could do more delicate work and make objects from metal, and that the computers in the station could make sounds and show visions of animals and other creatures from Earth. Scar hungered to see them.

Scar liked helping in the kitchen because he liked spending time with Helper. When he assisted her food prep and cleanup, she often made special food that just the two of them shared. Sharing food with Helper made him happy, a special joy in his small, bounded world.

CHAPTER 15 –
Pigpen

Pigpen had always been close to the Things. The twins were a unit, always full of energy and building something. When the other children made forts, they draped graphene sheets over tables and sat inside in the dark. When the Things built forts, Thing2 and Scooter used pulleys to move the heavy tables together and Thing1 and Pigpen used solar panels to run lights inside.

The twins enjoyed having Pigpen around; she was the pale third twin, and very clever. She observed, for example, that the solar cell wouldn't light the fort after dark, so she invited Scar to join them. This, she pointed out to the Things, had two advantages; one was that Scar was the strongest and could help put the tables in place, and the second was that if Scar agreed, Helper was more likely to join, and if Pigpen suggested that Helper bring one of her beeswax candles, they could light their fort at night. Helper, who often missed afternoon activities because of her cooking duties, was happy to be invited, and everyone knew that Scar and Helper liked each other, so the five of them (or six if Scooter came along) would have the best fort on Mars!

Pigpen understood the principles of the physical machines that Scooter and Thing2 built; the pulleys and levers made sense and clearly worked. She was less sure about Thing1's electrical creations, but she enjoyed working with him on them.

Porter had tried to explain how electricity worked but hadn't been very clear. He had admitted that he only vaguely understood the principles. He said electricity came in two parts, like the two wires coming out of the solar panel. He said the electricity "flowed" like water between the two parts and that this was good for three kinds of work.

The first was making heat and light. The bulb of the grow lamp was an example; the electricity made the lamp hot and bright. Porter said it was a reaction to the two kinds of electricity meeting in the hot part of the lamp.

The second was operating a motor. Porter didn't remember why an electric motor worked, but he showed Pigpen and Thing1 the "electric goat" tractor in Delta and pointed out the battery for storing electricity and the motor that went around when power was supplied to the two parts of the motor.

The third kind of work was computation. Porter said that there was a way for electricity to follow instructions inside something called a computer and do what the instructions told it to do. Porter had pointed out the environmental monitors in Charlie and Delta as examples of simple computers that listened to the monitors that were sampling the air, then did calculations and displayed them on the screens. He showed them how the 3-D printer was controlled by a computer to make what the computer told it to make.

The computation part was the most interesting to Pigpen, but they didn't have access to the tools needed to talk to the electricity and tell it what to do. She liked the idea of telling the electricity what to do. Porter warned her that it was frustrating because a computer did *exactly* what you told it to do, so you had to make your instructions very clear and specific, and most people found that very challenging. Pigpen thought she might be able to do it. She dreamed she could tell the computer to make Mars warm and have air so that they could go outside and explore.

Sometimes when Pigpen was alone, she sang to herself. Porter sang songs with the children, but they were silly songs about animals that didn't exist and railroads (whatever they were). Pigpen liked to sing her own songs. Songs about the red rocks of Mars and the green plants of Charlie and the fuzzy black manes of the Things and how much she longed to fly and see the station from above and the moons as they flew past. She sang these secret songs when she was happy, or sad, or excited, or sleepy. She dreamed that someday she would sing her songs, and everyone would hear them and like them, especially Thing1.

CHAPTER 16 –
Red and Sniffles

Red was restless. The other children had jobs they enjoyed or found something to enjoy in their jobs. Red thought his job was boring. He knew he was capable of more and didn't feel his contribution was appreciated. Sometimes Red fantasized about some terrible disaster befalling the greenhouse that only he could fix. Then they would appreciate him. Until then, his life was about corn.

Red and Sniffles tended all the grow tables for corn when she wasn't shirking her duties to work with Porter tending to this or that. To use the space efficiently, they also planted beans and squash in the tables once the corn had sprouted. Porter said that on Earth, ancient peoples had called corn, beans, and squash—"The Three Sisters"—and planted them together because the corn was tall and provided a firm foundation for the beans to climb, while the squash was low to the ground and its big leaves shaded the ground so that there were fewer weeds. Porter worked to help them vary the lighting and heat so that they got corn nearly year-round. Porter explained corn was vital to their diet because it had lots of calories, the energy that people get from food.

What Red liked about corn was that it made him important. He was sure Porter had given this job to Sniffles and him because it was crucial to their survival. More tables were dedicated to corn than any other crop, which made planting and harvest time busy for the team, but corn didn't require a lot of maintenance or nurturing in between other than varying the lights, so they had a secondary job of drying the stalks for cooking fuel and farming worms in the corn tables.

While he understood that the worms were important, Red preferred to let Sniffles manage the unglamorous worms. Red did what was necessary to tend the corn but took special pride in delivering it to Helper when it was harvested. He liked to make sure that everyone knew it was a result of his hard work (with minor assistance from Sniffles). It annoyed Red that the others didn't seem to appreciate him. Everyone acted like their jobs were important, even the people aiding Helper with the dishes.

Sniffles liked tending the worms. By the time the children were old enough to help, the soils in Charlie had been prepared and in production for years and the worm populations in each table were well established. Sniffles was fascinated by the little creatures. It surprised her how different they were from people: no eyes, no legs, no hands, no bones. She had trouble understanding how they could move above the dirt, let alone tunnel through it without arms. The worms were interesting partners. They helped the plants grow by making the soil better and by helping to digest the dead plant bits. Porter had taught them that the worms would take care of themselves if they had oxygen, warmth, food, and moisture.

Oxygen was easy. Porter said the worms needed less oxygen than people. Mostly, the gardeners just needed to avoid compacting the soil or saturating it so much that there wasn't room for air in it. Worms got oxygen through their skins from the dirt. They also dug tunnels, which increased the airflow through the soils, so even if the soil got packed a little too tightly, the worms would correct the problem over time.

Worms needed temperatures similar to those of humans, but they were more sensitive to extremes. Porter said that freezing would likely kill the worms, but that the soil was like a blanket; the worms would be fine provided the greenhouse didn't get too cold for too long.

Porter said worms mostly ate tiny bugs called "microbes" that were too small to see. He said these creatures lived in the soil and ate dead plants, so when the worms ate dead plants, they also ate the microbes. Porter had added microbes to the soil when he initially mixed it, so all Sniffles and Red had to do was dry and crush some of the plant debris and mix it into the soil before planting to keep the microbes happy, and the worms would have plenty of microbes to eat.

The worms needed moisture so that they didn't dry out, but not so much that they couldn't breathe. Porter supervised any significant changes to the watering schedule and the soil held water well, so keeping the worms moist wasn't a challenge except when they crawled out of the growing tables. Sometimes they found dry worms on the floor that had "escaped" from the table; Porter said that they probably froze to death lying on the floor and then dried out later.

Porter kept a special table dedicated to worms that was off limits to everyone. He called it his worm farm. He explained that worms were essential to their survival and that his worm farm was there in case some disaster befell the other worms. He had Thing1 set up a special grow light that was dedicated to keeping the worm farm warm, even when the temperature in Charlie got low in the winter. Porter explained that losing some of the worms would be okay but losing all of them would be a disaster for all the plants and people.

Sniffles thought it interesting that their survival depended on these strange little creatures. The worms seemed so helpless, but they had an important job tending and improving the soil so that the crops would grow. And the worms depended on microbes (and the humans, of course). It was a strange dependency that all the creatures had on one another. None of this would be happening here if the colonists hadn't brought the worms to Mars, and if Porter hadn't used other plants and sand and chemicals to make the soil. Sniffles was surprised that any of it worked. It seemed so complicated. Porter said it all occurred naturally on Earth, and that it took their ancestors a long time to figure out the relationships.

She wondered what else Porter's ancestors had learned. She dreamed of exploring the mysteries of the station. She sometimes sat alone looking out the north wall of Charlie at the station beckoning beyond. There were strange unmoving shadows that could be seen in some of the windows. What did those colonists hide in that station, just out of reach? Why had they come to Mars in the first place?

Sniffles and Red talked about the colony sometimes while they tended the corn. All the Martians were curious about the colony, but it seemed to Sniffles that she cared about it more than any of the rest. She hoped it could lead to an escape from Mars that would be more successful than the worms escaping the growing table.

"What do you think will be most interesting about the colony, Red?" she asked him one day, as they were bundling corn stalks to dry.

Red paused, then said, "I guess searching for stuff. I think I'll be the best searcher, finding more interesting things faster than anyone else."

"And what makes you think that?" Sniffles challenged.

"I just know it. Remember, I'm the one who found Porter's cup last winter. He said it had been tucked up under that grow table by one of us kids since the first Smoky Rescue Day. I found it. Porter said I was observant." He beamed.

"You probably put it there in the first place so you could get credit for finding it later," Sniffles chided.

"That would have been a good idea and I'm smart enough to do that, but I honestly don't remember hiding it," Red confessed. "What do you think will be most interesting about the colony, Sniffles?"

"It's hard to describe. Remember when we were little? There was Porter and all of us kids in Charlie, and that was everything. That was the whole world. Then as we got older, we could see out the windows to all of Mars outside the greenhouse and the colony. Porter taught us about the stars and Earth, and we could see them in the night sky—and then Charlie seemed to shrink from being a huge place to being a small place. Time passed and Porter taught us about the dirt and the worms and the microbes in our bodies and in the soil, and the elements in the air and how those elements flow through us and how in the end, all of it is powered by our distant sun star so far away—then Charlie seemed huge and complicated, like a whole world again, all fit into our greenhouse. I think the colony will be a much bigger world than Charlie. I think it will make Charlie seem small again. I think when we explore the colony it will be hard to think of Charlie as big, ever again."

"Of course the colony is bigger than Charlie," Red said, missing her point. "We can see that out the window."

"I don't mean size," Sniffles said. "I mean details … history … complexity. Imagine a worm, raised alone in a cup. All she knows about the world is that cup. Now imagine we put her in a grow table where all the other worms have died out. There are no other worms for her to meet, but she can see the evidence of their presence, the old holes the other worms had dug. Our little worm would never look at the cup the same again. It wouldn't just be about the size of the table compared to the cup. I think it will be a million times stranger when we get into the colony because there will be a million interesting things to find besides old worm trails."

"And I will discover more of the interesting stuff than anyone else when we get there," said Red with conviction. "Let's put these bundles next to the wall and get food. I itch from the little scratches. I want to wash up and I'm ready to be done for today."

Sniffles gave up. Red didn't understand what she was saying. She didn't think he was even trying to understand. She gave the colony a few last longing glances through the window as she tossed down the bundled husks. She was ready to rest and was getting itchy too. Cornhusks were scratchy.

CHAPTER 17 – Cisco

After dinner that evening, Sniffles sought out Cisco. With the sun low in the sky, the two girls walked to Delta. Sniffles admired Cisco as the girls walked. Cisco always seemed so confident. Cisco's blonde hair was cropped just below her ears and her blue eyes shone in the fading light. Sniffles recounted her earlier conversation with Red, her struggle to explain her feelings, and Red's failure to understand.

"Red doesn't think about stuff the way you do," Cisco said. "You think about interesting ways that things interact. Red thinks mostly about Red and how other people interact with him."

The girls laughed as they walked. Cisco was twenty centimeters taller than Sniffles and subtly slowed her gait so that Sniffles's shorter legs didn't have to hurry to keep up.

"I'm looking forward to getting to the colony, too," Cisco continued. "It will be an adventure. I'm curious about the colonists and what we will find. Porter says we may be able to use a machine in the station to communicate with Earth. Then the Earth people may send a ship and we might go there someday. Imagine being in a place where you can walk outside … walk as far in any direction as you want to go, without exo-suits or anything."

"What would you like to see on Earth?" Sniffles asked. "Of all the wonders Porter has told us about, what do you want to see first?"

"The big pools of water that stretch as far as you can see. I want to see them, and I want to walk in them. I bet it is weird having water around your feet. Imagine standing in the soup pot, but a thousand times bigger. What about you? What do you want to see first?"

"Cities," Sniffles replied. "Porter says there are places people live that are much bigger than the station, full of lots of people all doing different jobs. I'd like to see that."

"Maybe we can go together. We'll find a city by the waters and we can see both in the same day!" Cisco said.

The young women arrived at the air lock and passed through into Delta. Porter had recently given everyone permission to use this air lock to get to Delta, which was now officially part of their home. The only remaining areas off limits were the mysterious dirt pile, the air lock that led to the surface of Mars on the far side of Delta, and the beehives in Charlie and Delta.

They stopped so that Sniffles could fill a watering can. She and Red were sprouting corn on a few tables in Delta and Sniffles wanted to tend the sprouts. As they walked, they drank water from the can.

"These greenhouses get smaller all the time. I'm glad we can come to Delta whenever we want. It's so hard to get quiet time in Charlie."

"Maybe we are just getting bigger," suggested Sniffles, stopping to look Cisco up and down dramatically. "Some of us faster than others." She laughed.

Cisco smiled. "You're right. Porter says we all used to sleep sideways in one small part of a growing table. Now if we tried to sleep sideways everyone but you would find their heads and legs sticking over the side."

As Sniffles watered the corn seedlings, Cisco stared out the window to the south at the beautiful untouchable red and brown rocks and sand of Mars in the dwindling sunlight. White bits of ice here and there combined with shadows to accent the scene before her. Sudden movement caught her eye.

"Blowout!" she said excitedly, pointing through the window.

They watched the glorious plume of sand and dust shoot skyward from the shadows. The blowout was hundreds of meters away and shot high into the air. The bottom of the plume was in dusk, a dark brown streak reaching skyward. The top of the plume went high enough to catch the distant rays of the setting sun and glowed like purple fire.

"Porter says there are no blowouts on Earth," Sniffles said with a touch of sadness. "It may be the only thing I'll miss from Mars."

"Then we should appreciate them when they happen," Cisco said. "This one is particularly beautiful. I like the way the sun's light caught the top. I don't think I've seen one do that before."

They watched the plume slowly disperse as the sand and rocks fell back to the ground and the dust cloud spread and became indistinct in the growing gloom.

Cisco wanted to see Earth, but also wished to see more of Mars. The dusky shadows of the only world she had ever known called to her from beyond the glass. She wondered what other surprises were waiting just over the horizon.

She turned and looked at Sniffles, who was looking north again, toward the colony.

"I guess that is our next big adventure, eh, Sniff?"

"It's hard to be patient," Sniffles responded.

"You were talking about how Charlie seemed so big, and now it seems so little? I think time might work the same way. Remember when a growing season seemed to take forever? Now seasons come and seasons go before you know it.

I'll bet the next Smoky Rescue Day comes quickly and we can see who fits in the exo-suits and plan our exploration of the colony."

"Two hundred and thirty-five days," said Sniffles.

Cisco smiled. Cisco was now slightly taller than Scooter. She too was looking forward to Smoky Rescue Day with anticipation.

CHAPTER 18 – Puberty

"Porter, I'm bleeding!" Ginger held up her blood-covered fingers as proof. She was more surprised than distressed, because she wasn't in pain.

Porter looked startled, but quickly regained his composure. "What happened, Ginger? Did you cut yourself? Where?"

"I had a tummy ache, and then I started bleeding from my vagina."

"Oh. A lot, or a little?" said Porter, seeming relieved.

"Not too much, I guess. It just worried me."

"Wait here, sweetie. I think you are okay. Let me get some water."

Porter fetched and filled the watering can, then returned and rinsed off Ginger's hand, and then poured water on her belly so she could rinse her groin.

"You are going to be fine, Ginger. Your body is just changing. This is a normal part of growing up and I should have told you sooner that this would happen. How is that tummy ache?"

"Okay, I guess, mostly gone … but it felt strange."

"Your body is changing from a girl to a woman. It is an amazing transformation, and it happens all by itself. I think you may be the first woman who can say she was born on Mars. I imagine the other girls will join you soon enough. Don't worry, your body knows what to do."

Porter looked at his precious Ginger and realized that her breasts were beginning to bud. Her pubic hair was sparse, but present. He felt stupid. He hadn't prepared any of the girls for puberty—or the boys either, for that matter.

After dinner, when it was time for lessons, Porter told everyone that instead of math, they were going to talk about their bodies. Pancho was initially disappointed, but Porter piqued his curiosity when he said, "Something special happened to Ginger today and it reminded me of lessons I haven't taught you yet about your bodies. I feel foolish that I didn't tell you sooner.

"Do you recall how the leaves of seedlings are sometimes different from the leaves of the adult plant? That is because seedlings have different needs. Seedlings need to grow strong and tall quickly if they are going to survive, so their early leaves try to catch more sunlight to do that efficiently. If the plant survives and matures, the next set of leaves become like the mature plant. This transition makes sense if you think about it: the mature plant has different needs than the seedling.

"Now I need to tell you how human bodies change as they grow from children to adults. Remember we talked about pollinating the plants? How the pollen spores move from one part of a plant to another and bind there to fertilize and create seeds? With people and animals, it is a similar idea, but it works a little differently. Rather than have two parts of the same creature that can fertilize itself or others, people and other animals have only one of the two parts. Males have one part and females have the other."

"Is a penis the boy part?" asked Red.

"It's a part of the system, Red. It's kind of like the paintbrush we use to pollinate some flowers. A man's penis is a tool that helps deliver his part of the seeds into the body of the woman. Women keep their seeds safe inside their bodies.

"When two people believe it is time to make children, a man puts his penis into a woman's vagina and deposits his seeds. The woman's body may then choose one of the seeds to join with hers, and the combination makes a human seedling ... a baby.

"The baby grows safely inside the woman for about 280 days, from a speck too small to see, to a baby about this big." Porter held out his hands as if he were holding a large squash. "Then the baby comes out of the woman's vagina and into the world, ready to breathe air and eat and poop. Then, seven or eight Martian years later, they look like you."

He smiled and spread his arms wide to indicate his audience. The children knew there were differences between males and females, but this was the first time they had talked about human pollination.

"Human seedlings go through many changes while they are inside of their mothers. We can talk about that another time. There will probably be pictures I can show you when we get to the station. After they emerge, babies grow a lot and change a little—like when you lost your baby teeth—until they are about your age, and then they go through another special change." Porter looked at Ginger.

"What happens in males is that their bodies recognize it is time to change from boys to men. Your testes—" Porter pointed to his scrotum—"send a chemical signal to other parts of your body telling it to change. You start getting stronger and more muscular. Your voice changes and becomes deeper."

All eyes shifted to Scar, whose voice had been cracking lately, then back to Porter again.

"You boys will get more hair under your arms, in your groin, and eventually on your face."

Porter gestured to the curly short beard he had always worn. It was gray now. He kept it trimmed, but they couldn't remember seeing his chin. The girls looked at the boys for these telltale signs. Some boys looked under their arms. Those with it had already noticed early pubic hair.

"Inside your bodies, males begin making their part of the seed. These are microscopic creatures called sperm. Male sperm is half of what it takes to create a new human. Men's bodies make millions of these each day."

Porter paused for a moment. "There are also wondrous changes in the females. Their part of making a new human are tiny cells called eggs. Female bodies are born with thousands of eggs; they don't make their seed every day like males do. Female eggs aren't ripe when they are girls. When their bodies are ready—about as old as you are now—female bodies send chemical signals that begin to ripen their eggs. Unlike the orange tree where all the oranges become ripe about the same time, only one or two eggs each month become ripe inside a woman. The ripe egg has a brief period of time when the male sperm can pollinate it, only a few days. If the sperm and the egg combine during this time, it's called fertilization, and it becomes a special cell that can grow into a human. This cell is kept in a special place that a woman's body prepares fresh each month in case a sperm and egg combine. Think of it like very good soil. If the sperm and egg combine, the baby grows here." Porter pointed to Ginger's belly. "Over the next 280 days, if everything goes well, a woman's belly gets bigger and bigger as the cell grows and changes until she has a human baby inside her, then the woman's body pushes the baby out through her vagina. It's a pretty amazing process, and that's how all of us, you and me, came to be born. Thing1 and Thing2, you boys are special because sometimes the fertilized egg splits in a very special way and two babies grow at the same time inside of the mother. These babies are the result of the same sperm and egg combining, so they are very similar. These babies are called twins, and you boys are twins—that's why your bodies look alike. Your mother probably got an extra big tummy because there were two of you in there at the same time.

"Remember I said there was a special place prepared each month to receive the fertilized egg in case it was available? A woman's body prepares this area…" Porter stopped, struggling for a metaphor the children would understand. "Kind of like the soup pot. Fresh ingredients each month that will nourish the seedling human if it arrives. But if there is no seedling human, her body washes the pot out and prepares it again the next month. This is called a menstrual cycle. When her body cleans out the space each month, a woman will have some muscle contractions she might be able to feel and will have a small amount of blood mixed with special cells that flow from her vagina for a few days. This is her body cleaning out that special 'pot'. That's what happened to Ginger today; she had a slight flow of blood because her body is cleaning out that special place because there isn't a baby in there. This is probably her first menstrual cycle. It is a natural and normal process and I'm sorry that you were surprised, Ginger. I should have told you all sooner. Have any of you other girls noticed slight bleeding?"

"I think I have," said Pigpen. "I didn't hurt, and there wasn't much blood, so I didn't mention it."

"I might have," said Helper. "Only a little bit of blood, but a stomachache that lasted for a couple of days. But that was weeks ago and hasn't happened again."

"The first few cycles may not be as regular while your body is getting used to it," Porter said. "You girls may notice other changes too. The hair under your arms, on your legs, and between your legs gets thicker and coarse. These are visible signs of your body maturing."

"You will also notice that your breasts will grow and accumulate tissue behind your nipples. If you have a baby, a woman's breasts do a wonderful and special trick. The process of having a baby sends another chemical signal to your breasts and they produce a nutritious broth called 'milk' that the baby can drink right from your body by sucking on your nipples. Milk is specially designed to be the perfect food for seedling humans, and a woman's body makes it for the baby as long as the baby needs it, concentrating the nutrition from the food the mother eats to pass it to the baby. This is very helpful because babies don't have any teeth to chew food when they are born. Later, as the baby grows, it gets teeth and can start eating other kinds of food.

"This was one of the challenges that made it so hard for Sniffles on Smoky Rescue Day. Because she was the youngest, her body wasn't ready for any food besides milk, and there wasn't any milk to give her."

He turned and spoke directly to Sniffles, rubbing her hair fondly. "I did my best to chew food for you because you didn't have any teeth yet. I was worried you weren't going to make it, sweetie. You were so small and fragile. We were lucky and you were stubborn and I'm glad you survived." Porter's eyes were shining with tears of memory as he bent and kissed Sniffles on her head and whispered in her ear, "I love you." He stood up straight again.

"Now, I have a request for you all and I want you to listen to it carefully and think about it," Porter said. "Your bodies are maturing, and you are becoming adults. You will begin to feel that your bodies want to make children. It can be a powerful urge, more powerful than hunger. I ask you to refrain from pollinating one another until we can get established in the colony, even though your bodies may want you to do it sooner. Let me explain why.

"First, our limited diet here has not been as healthy as I would like. While Helper has improved greatly on Uncle Porter's famous soup—" Porter paused here for laughter that turned into appreciations for Helper and he smiled—"she has had a limited set of ingredients to work with. When we get to the colony, we will have access to some of the missing chemicals that your bodies need to function and grow properly. Because of our current diet, it could be dangerous for your female bodies to make children right now— dangerous for you and your children. Think of how poorly our plants do if the soils are not properly prepared for them. I want everyone to stay healthy. We should be able to remedy any deficiencies in our diet a few weeks after we get access to the colony.

"Second, I'm not sure how badly damaged the colony is, and it may be hard and dangerous work to reclaim it. A woman with a child inside her isn't fragile, but she and her unborn baby can be more susceptible to injury.

"Third, once we reclaim the colony, there will be much for you to learn that will be essential to all of our survival and possible rescue. The responsibility of caring for babies would be a distraction from that learning and might make it less likely that any of us will survive.

"Finally, I am proud of each of you in our family of survivors. You are smart and thoughtful. I think of you all as my children, although I didn't plant the seeds that made you. You are young. I'm almost four times older than you, and I can tell you there are many things for you to see and learn and do. Becoming parents is a big responsibility, and I encourage you to learn more about your own life and the life of someone you would have as a partner before you take the responsibility of making and caring for a child. Babies are a lot of work and a big responsibility and one you should make sure you are ready for before you undertake it.

"That is my request. Those are my reasons. Your bodies are yours and the decision is yours. I want to welcome you to the next phase of your life. You are no longer children. You are now young adults, seedlings no longer. I will be your guide for as long as I am able, and you are willing to have me as we face the future together. Always remember that I love you and will respect whatever you choose."

Porter asked if anyone had questions, and the flood of curiosity kept lessons going for two hours more. It was late when the lesson ended. It might have been the topic. It might have been the timing. It might have been that this lesson addressed questions that had been roiling in their minds for a while. The newly minted adults seemed to pay more attention to this evening's lesson from Porter than any of the "children" ever had.

CHAPTER 19 –

Ginger

After assisting Helper and Scar with kitchen cleanup and prep for the next day and sharing a late snack, Ginger went contentedly to bed. As she lay looking up at the stars through the glass, Ginger felt special. She was pleased to understand what was going on in her body. Proud that she was changing into a woman. Curious about what that would mean. She wondered if she would ever make a child. What would it be like to feel someone growing inside of you and depending upon your body for nourishment?

She wondered who she might choose to make a child with someday.

Scar was strong and helpful, but he was quiet and shy. He didn't seem interested in Ginger. Besides, Scar and Helper seemed to like each other. Probably not Scar.

Red was smart, but he was annoying and selfish and didn't seem to care about anyone but Red. Probably not Red.

Pancho was warm and friendly and nice to her. She liked Pancho very much, but Pancho and Cisco had always been inseparable, and Cisco was her best friend. Probably not Pancho, she thought sadly.

The Things were pretty and smart, but always seemed distracted by some project or other. Thing1 had always preferred the company of Pigpen and Thing2 seemed to spend all his time with Scooter. Probably neither Thing.

Curly was … different. She didn't think of Curly quite like anyone else. Because he never spoke, it was hard to know him, although he was nice in his way. Probably not Curly.

"Maybe someone from Earth I haven't met yet?" she thought, as she fell asleep.

She dreamed of hugging someone in the dark, their bodies intertwined. She didn't know who it was, but it was someone familiar and she felt delicious warmth and connection flow from the embrace. In her dream the luxurious hug made her body tingle in an indescribable way. She awoke to see the stars still above her and the twin moons low on the horizon. It was cool and quiet. The tingling thrill of her dream slowly faded. She wondered if this was a glimpse of the hunger that Porter had mentioned.

Ginger rolled over on her belly, raised her head, and looked to the north at the colony a few dozen meters beyond the glass. It had always been there, a curiosity. Now it had become a goal. The colony hadn't changed, but her perspective on it had. She lay her head down and went back to sleep. If she dreamed again, she didn't remember it.

The next morning after eating, Ginger got a special assignment from Porter. She and Sniffles and Curly were sent to Delta to harvest rice.

Sniffles was the smallest of the Martians. Although sickly as an infant, her health had generally improved as she grew. Still, she was frail and easily winded by hard labor. Tending rice was not easy, but it wasn't a strenuous workout, so working with Ginger and Curly on rice seemed like a natural assignment and a nice break from Red and the corn.

They had shifted bulk production of wheat, rice, and corn to Delta after a dust storm had forced them to let Delta freeze several years ago. Porter had explained that as long as they kept some seeds for the annuals safe in Charlie, they would only lose one season of growing if they needed to sacrifice Delta again. All perennials were grown in Charlie, with an assumption that Charlie would be the last refuge in an emergency, although some seeds for the perennials were stored in Delta, "just in case."

The tables for rice were constructed like those for the orange and breadfruit trees. These tables were the same height as the rest, but twice as deep. For the trees, this extra capacity was used for soil so that the tree roots could go deeper. For rice, this extra depth allowed the rice tables to be flooded.

Rice grew best in warm climates with lots of water, so the rice tables had dedicated grow lights and were kept with about ten centimeters of standing water above the soil. Rice liked temperatures in the mid-20s Celsius. From fall to spring, however, it wasn't warm enough and there wasn't enough solar power, so the rice tables were used for winter wheat, and Delta was cooled to the low teens to conserve power.

Sniffles spent the first hour filling plastic barrels with water from the two rice tables they planned to harvest and setting them on the ground so that Ginger and Curly could carry and dump the muddy liquid into an empty grow table nearby. As the team worked, they discussed Porter's biology lesson from the night before.

"Ginger, do you feel any different now that your body is changing?" asked Sniffles, setting a freshly filled plastic barrel on the ground.

"Not physically," Ginger replied. "Although it feels special to know that it is happening. I was glad to know I wasn't sick."

Curly paused and looked at Ginger thoughtfully, then picked up two more barrels and walked to dump them.

"What about you, Curly? Have you noticed your body changing?" Sniffles asked.

As he returned and deposited the empty barrels, Curly nodded and pointed to the hair that was growing in his groin and under his arms. Then he grabbed two more barrels and followed Ginger as she went to dump her load.

"What about you, Sniffles? You are the youngest, so you might see the changes last," Ginger said.

As she filled more barrels, Sniffles replied, "I have noticed my breasts being a little swollen and more tender, but I haven't seen any changes in my body hair or bleeding. I think that's about all the water we're gonna get out of here. I'm hot and I need a break. Can we sit for a minute before we start to harvest?"

"You go ahead of us, Sniffles. Let Curly and I dump these last barrels and we'll take a rest. Okay, Curly?"

Curly nodded, and he and Ginger carried and dumped the last of the full barrels. When they returned, Curly lined up the empty barrels precisely in three rows of four barrels each near where Sniffles was standing, then paused and handed an empty barrel to Sniffles and Ginger. Then, turning one over for himself, he sat.

"Thank you, Curly," said Sniffles as she sat. "I just need to catch my breath and cool off."

Ginger sat on her barrel. "It IS warm today. Particularly with these grow lights."

Curly stood up and gestured to Ginger and Sniffles to follow him. The two women looked at each other, puzzled, then stood and followed their olive-skinned companion. Curly walked to the table they had been filling with the water from the two tables they had emptied. He motioned toward the table expectantly. Ginger and Sniffles looked at him blankly.

"What is it, Curly?" Sniffles asked patiently. She knew Curly got frustrated easily when he wasn't understood.

Curly leapt up to stand in the water on the table, then crouched and sat down hard in the shallow pool, splashing them and giving a tentative, satisfied smile.

Ginger exclaimed, "Curly, what a great idea for a hot day!" She too vaulted into the table and, not bothering to land on her feet, landed with a splash on her backside, sloshing a wave of water over the side of the table toward Sniffles.

The water drenched Sniffles, who squealed with laughter as the muddy water ran from her face and hair. In a moment, she too launched herself into the air, landing in the pool between Ginger and Curly, splashing Ginger as much as she could in the process.

A brief splash fight ensued, cut short when an agitated Curly made clear he did *not* want his face wet.

When he calmed, Curly sat in the pool and watched his friends contentedly float on top of the cool shallow water in the table, their hair flowing out beside them.

"Thank you, Curly," Sniffles said as she bobbed. "This was a wonderful idea."

"Oh yes," Ginger added. "We need to tell the others about Curly's inspiration so they can share the fun. This is much nicer than showers from the watering can."

No further rice was harvested that day and "Curly's Pool" became the hit of the summer.

CHAPTER 20 –

Reading

Although Ginger and Scar usually tended peas and breadfruit trees together, today Scar was tending peas alone. It was Ginger's turn to assist Helper with tonight's meal, and for Scar, this meant a quiet afternoon and a chance to be alone with his thoughts. He was encouraging the pea plants to climb the tripods of dried bamboo in their grow tables. The trick was to keep one side of the tripod uncluttered by growth so that he and Ginger could easily reach the pea pods hanging on the inside when it was time for harvest.

As he trimmed and wrapped the climbing vine runners, he thought about the reading lessons that Porter had decided were now urgent. Everyone had learned to sing the ABC song long ago, and to recognize their names scribbled on their cups, but Porter had given up trying to teach everyone to read because the only writing in Charlie or Delta was in the books in the two emergency kits about treating injuries. Recently Porter had changed his mind and restarted the lessons, breaking the two identical books into bundles of pages that could be shared among his students to allow practice. Sounding the words out was challenging. There were a lot of different ways to spell the same sound that had different meanings, like "to" and "too" and "two," and a lot of different sounds from the same spelling, like "through" and "cough." The hardest part was the large number of unusual words in the first aid books—words none of them had ever used and had no idea what they meant or how to say them. They had to learn a whole new language while they were learning to read. It was a lot of work and many grumbled, but Porter insisted that gaining access to the wonders of the colony would involve lots of reading. That motivated Scar through the drudgery.

He initially found it hard to believe that reading was important, having lived all his remembered life in a building that had two copies of one book that only Porter could read. Someone—maybe Red—had suggested that perhaps Porter was worried about getting sick and wanted to make sure that everyone could read the book to make him well in case of emergency. First aid had seemed a pretty boring subject, until they had discovered the section of the book called "Labor and Delivery," which piqued everyone's interest after the baby discussion a few months ago. It was hard to imagine a baby as large as a squash coming out of an opening that seemed so small, but there it was in the book, complete with color pictures. Otherwise, the first aid book chapters had seemed tedious.

Although Scar's reading skills were better than most, he initially resisted the task—deciphering words you didn't understand seemed pointless. What the heck was an "appendix" and who cares? If it was hidden deep under your skin so you can never see it, why bother giving it a name? How could an organ protected so deeply in your body get sick anyway? He took his "appendix" frustration out on some runners, tearing off some stubborn tendrils that resisted his attempts to weave them where he wished them to go.

Porter said the knowledge accumulated by billions of people over five thousand years was stored in the colony waiting to be rediscovered. It all sounded fantastic. Porter had told him that the scar on his chest that gave him his name was likely a result of a part inside him being sick or broken when he was very little, before Smoky Rescue Day. Porter said one of the colonists who was a healer probably had to cut him open and fix something. Scar tucked his chin so he could see the dark smooth skin of his chest and the jagged discolored line of deformed flesh that ran from the base of his ribcage halfway to his navel. The thought that the colonists could cut him open like a tomato, fix something inside that wasn't working properly, and close him up again was evidence of their knowledge. Scar wanted to know more of their secrets.

He looked through the north wall at the colony, standing silent and unchanging fifty meters away. It was early November, less than two hundred days until the next anniversary of Smoky Rescue Day on April 38. Scooter was already a dozen centimeters taller than she had been. Scar was as tall as Scooter. Everyone was convinced the suit would fit the next time it was tried. Porter had been asked if more than one person might go with him and he had said, "We'll see," but also observed that there were several suits, and everyone had taken that as encouragement.

The lifeless windows stared back at him. The thought of standing inside the colony and looking out at Charlie seemed a fantastic dream. He looked at the red Martian soil of the ground two meters away outside the window. The thought of standing *there* and looking in Charlie's window seemed impossible. That was not part of the world he knew.

He had lived in Charlie and Delta forever. He had grown up here, tended by Porter like one of the plants. He had thrived in this space for over five thousand days. It seemed like the next two hundred would take an eternity, waiting for the event that would expand his world forever.

"Peas ready yet?" Red's question disrupted Scar's daydreaming.

"Not yet. I'm just training these vines to make them easier to harvest. If you want peas, there might be some young ones on the next table you could munch." He indicated the next table down which had more mature vines.

"Should I pick some for Helper to cook tonight, or just some for you and me?"

"I don't think there will be enough to share with Helper yet. They're ripening very slowly this time of year with the days so short."

"Yeah, the beans are ripening slowly too. Glad we dried some during summer."

Red walked to the next table and began poking around inside the tripod looking for tender young pods. "Who do you think will get to go with Porter?" Red asked. Perhaps he had seen Scar's wistful looks out the window at the colony? It seemed everyone was thinking about the station more and more these days.

"I don't know. Probably Scooter. Maybe Cisco—I'll bet Cisco is strong enough to pick Porter up and carry him. If several of us are big enough to fit the suits, how do you think Porter will decide?"

"We could vote," Red offered wryly. Red knew he wasn't very popular.

"I prefer he choose based upon dark skin color." Scar smiled, gently nudging his friend away from self-pity. "That would put the Things and me at the top of the list."

"Or red hair. That would ensure Ginger and me a place on the team. Although I don't think Pancho would like Ginger and me going on an adventure without him. I'd rather go with you, anyway. Maybe we should choose the roster in a fair and unbiased way, say … names in the order of the alphabet starting with Q. Let's see … no Q's, I'm the only R, and you would just beat Scooter. Red and Scar. What do you think?"

"Sounds good!" Scar enthused. Then he added, more seriously, "I'm hoping that reading skills might matter. I've been working at it hard. Except for the annoying words I don't know how to say, I'm getting pretty good."

"You are," Red agreed earnestly. "I don't understand why it's so important to Porter that we can make sense of those little squiggles. I mean, I'm sure it will matter later when we get access to the colony, but the first trips will be about being brave and smart." The conviction in Red's voice made it clear that he believed those were his best qualities.

"Porter says lots of stuff in the colony is like the air lock, with labels and instructions. He says the main computer in the colony is much smarter than our environmental monitor or the 3-D printer, and that we must be able to read to use it."

"I see how we need one person who can read, but I don't know why that couldn't just be Porter. He's an expert. He says he's read thousands of books, and he already knows how the station works." Red handed Scar a few tender pea pods as he chewed one absently. "Porter seems pretty serious about us being able to read."

Scar nodded and took the pods while thinking about Red's words. Red was prickly and arrogant, but also smart. Just the same, Scar was working harder than anyone else at reading. He imagined it was his best chance to be on the first adventure. He had to admit to himself that he was also begrudgingly learning about first aid. He thought about the strange effect of the written words in the book creating pictures in his mind to help him visualize objects and actions he had not observed and transmit knowledge gained from experiences he had not shared. The colonists certainly knew a lot. The words gave him access to that knowledge and he wanted more.

He looked at the empty station enticing him from beyond the greenhouse wall. He imagined again looking back out those dark windows through the greenhouse wall to the pea-covered tripods he was tending. The greenhouse that was the only world he ever knew grew smaller by the day.

CHAPTER 21 – Thing1

Electricity was amazing. Thing1 knew that the solar panels somehow turned light from the distant sun into the invisible substance called electricity. Porter had shown him that he could use electricity to power lights and create heat. The fact that the strange stuff could be stored in batteries for later use when the sun wasn't shining was miraculous.

Porter had said that the batteries used the electricity put into them to create a chemical change. Then when you took the power out, it undid the change, giving you back the power. He said storing electricity was like using energy to pull a rope with a pulley and lift a heavy load, high off the ground. When you took energy back out of the battery, it was like using the stored energy of the heavy load at the top of the pulley to do work.

Porter had helped Thing1 use the solar cell to charge the battery of the electric goat tractor in Delta, and they had driven it very slowly around the receiving area for a few minutes, lifting a few growing tables and creating excitement and enthusiasm among the spectators watching. The energy in the battery had not lasted long, even after days of charging. Porter said that when they were building the station, the goat could go for hours on a single charge; it might be that the battery now needed much more power than the single solar panel could provide, or it might be that the battery was getting too old and tired to hold a charge. Thing1 had suggested hooking the goat up to Delta's primary power system, but Porter didn't want to risk draining Delta's batteries, worried that a sudden dust storm could last for weeks and even months. He dared not drain the power.

Thing1 had tried charging the goat's battery for a longer period with his single solar cell and burned himself when he touched the wire leads while connecting it. A flash of light, a snapping sound, and his hand had jerked back before he could even think of what was happening, and then a painful burn and blister alongside his finger. The wires had melted. Porter said that Thing1 had been "shocked" when the electricity flowed through his body. Porter warned Thing1 that the main batteries for Charlie and Delta stored much more electricity than the goat, and that it would be very dangerous if that much electricity flowed through him. He also said that the electrical system in the colony carried much more electricity when it was working, and that when it was charged it would likely kill Thing1 if he were shocked by it. Porter showed Thing1 some of the insulated tools from the toolbox and explained how metal and water carried electricity, but plastic and cloth did not. Porter demonstrated that he could safely touch the battery while wearing the bulky gloves from the toolbox.

Thing1 tried hard not to think of the electricity as magic. He had learned about magic from stories that Porter told them after meals, magical doors that opened when you said special words, magical hats that contained an infinite number of white rabbits, magical carts and rugs that flew through the air. Porter said that there was really no magic. He said that magic was fun in stories and a way for people to imagine new things and how people explained phenomenon that they didn't understand, but that there was no magic. Everything worked according to principles that could often be discovered with study and experimentation.

Thing1 had marveled that light energy could be harnessed to do work. He knew that the plants in the greenhouse used light energy to grow, transforming the water and minerals from the ground and carbon dioxide from the air into plant material and oxygen. When his brother and Scooter had used reflectors to get additional light onto their beans, the results had been impressive.

It was hard to imagine that this light was coming from a star so very large and far away. He'd been taught that the Earth was about halfway between the sun and Mars, and that Earth's atmosphere had less dust than Mars, so sunlight was more plentiful and powerful and available for solar cells and plants. He imagined seeing the sun larger and clearer in the sky. Porter said the sun from Earth was about the size of his whole thumb held at arm's length.

Here on Mars, the sun was often blurred by dust clouds, giving a red glow to the sky at midday and a deep blue hue at twilight and dawn. Sometimes, when some of the dust settled out of the sky, the sun was a small, bright circle with a red halo … much bigger than either Martian moon, about the size of his fingernail if he held his arm out straight. On clear nights, you could see other stars too. Porter said these stars were millions of times farther away than the sun, and that there were billions of them, although only a few thousand of the brightest were visible in the dusty Martian sky except on the clearest night. Earth was sometimes visible too, a blue speck that didn't twinkle-twinkle like the stars in the song or the other stars in the sky. Jupiter was bright in the sky sometimes … bigger than Earth even though it was five times farther away.

Porter had described the view from the window of the big ship *Numa* that brought them to Mars. He said that space was mostly empty and deep black, with countless specks of brilliant stars in thick clusters, like looking at a bright sky through a black graphene sheet with a million tiny holes. He said it was breathtakingly beautiful and that the Earth was a huge blue and green and white ball that filled the ship's windows when they left. He said the Earth got smaller and smaller until it was just a bright blue-green spot, and then slowly and gradually the sun got a little smaller as the ship had crossed the vast gap between

Earth and Mars. Porter said he hadn't appreciated how large the sun was until they had been traveling for a month and the once-huge Earth was a small blue dot, but the sun wasn't noticeably smaller. As the months passed, the sun got slightly smaller and Mars got bigger and redder until it filled the window—big and red and huge with an impossibly thin layer of translucent red atmosphere faintly glowing around the whole planet, and the sun was still the largest object in the Martian sky, larger even than both Martian moons.

Thing1 ached to see Earth. To accomplish that, he would travel in space and see the sights that had taken Porter's breath away. To do that, they needed to communicate with Earth to request a ship to come get them. Before that, they needed to reclaim the colony. Thing1 felt as if his life were just about to begin. He felt like a battery that was charged and waiting for someone to connect the wires and flip the switch.

CHAPTER 22 – Mary

Mary was bored. Every day was the same; wake up, eat, work, eat, sleep. The others accepted this dull routine, but Mary was miserable. She didn't enjoy tending the squash, although the quick growth was gratifying. She didn't care about the worms. She took her first aid responsibilities seriously, but there wasn't much danger here in the greenhouses. She and Sniffles tended the minor cuts and scrapes that occurred from time to time, but she didn't feel compelled to read and reread the first aid book the way Sniffles did.

Mary's only interest was observing how the others interacted, particularly when their routines were disrupted. She noticed their alliances and felt left out. She didn't feel like she truly belonged in any of the groups.

People had drifted into teams that tended to work and play together. The Things and Pigpen and Scooter were a group. Cisco, Pancho, Ginger and Curly were another. Scar and Helper spent lots of time together. Sniffles and Red and sometimes Scar were a common grouping.

The rosters varied, but Mary wasn't a central member of any group.

Mary thought they were jealous of her because she was the oldest. Porter said she was about 17 Earth years old and was the first Martian. She was certainly smarter than they were, but she wasn't wasting her time applying it to trivial projects like the Things or using it to show off like Red. Mary was waiting. Waiting to get out of this confining dreadful greenhouse and off this dreary planet with these dull people.

She knew she wasn't tall enough to be part of the initial party; the only person in the greenhouse shorter than her was Sniffles. Either of them would be lost in the smallest exo-suit from the air lock. That was fine. She didn't crave adventure; she wanted the results of the adventure. She wanted to get away from Mars and never come back. She just hoped the initial party could accomplish that effectively.

Porter was nice enough, in his way—but the stories he told of the wonders of Earth confirmed to Mary that he was dull for ever leaving the excitement of that verdant world for this ruddy one. The thought of someone choosing to become an expert at plants and then choosing to come live on Mars astounded Mary. Porter was fond of reminding everyone that they had lots of choices to make in their lives, both now and in the future. Mary thought Porter's choices thus far didn't reflect well on him. She appreciated that the old fool had taken care of everyone to the best of his ability, but he was still a fool.

Her fellow Martians and their petty alliances and rivalries were a waste of time and energy. Tall and blonde Cisco thought she was a leader just because she could manipulate dimwitted Curly. Mary wasn't sure what Pancho saw in Cisco, but he was too stupid to see that Ginger liked him. What did Porter call stories with sad endings? "Tragedies?" Some tragedies were funnier than others.

Helper, always trying to please everyone, just wanted to be liked. Mary didn't care about being liked. She didn't care much about the others, provided they did their share of the work and left her alone.

Scar followed Porter like a shadow, trying to ingratiate himself so that he would be considered for the expedition. He also did extra dishes trying to gain favor with Helper so that he got more than his share of the food. His motives were so obvious.

Red was probably her only real friend, and that's because she took pity on him. He was nice enough, but he needed her leadership and he seemed to recognize that.

Smoky Rescue Day would come soon. The initial party would be formed. There would be more planning than necessary, and they would reclaim the station and there might be some amusements while they awaited rescue but getting away from Mars couldn't come fast enough for Mary.

CHAPTER 23 – Cooking Lessons

Sniffles and Ginger were assisting Helper with meal preparation. Sniffles had been harvesting winter wheat earlier in the day and was very tired, but it was her turn, and she didn't want to let Ginger and Helper down.

The day's menu was beans and rice mixed together with tomato sauce. Sniffles had been stirring the simmering tomatoes for an hour, and dinner was still two hours away. Her arm was tired, and she shifted the spoon to her left hand. Helper had said that it took a while to boil away the water in the tomatoes to thicken the sauce—but hours?

The good part about aiding Helper was that the kitchen crew ate well. The beans and rice had soaked and were ready to cook, so the only activity in the kitchen right now was Helper and Ginger cutting up orange wedges while the three of them talked. The current rate of consumption was about one orange slice consumed for every seven put into the serving bowl for later. As Sniffles's mouth watered in anticipation of her next wedge, it occurred to her that, except for cleaning the pot she was stirring after dinner, this was a good day to have kitchen duty. She enjoyed Ginger's company, and she adored Helper. Spending time with the two of them was a real treat, orange wedges or not.

"What do you think, Ginger?" Helper asked. "Who should go to the station first?"

Ginger pondered a moment, then said, "I'm curious, of course, but I'm not worried about who is in the first group. Let Porter decide. What's important is that we get access to the colony. Once we have access, trust me, I want to explore! I just don't much care who comprises the first group in. Honestly, I might not be the best choice. I might be just tall enough, but I'm not as strong as Scar or Cisco and I don't understand machines as well as the Things. I've been working hard on learning to read and I think that will serve me, but I'm surprised how worked up everyone is about who goes first."

"I'd like to go first," said Sniffles. "But, like you, I want to get in there and explore once we can. Those suits looked strange and uncomfortable. I'd get into one if I had to but would rather that we just get air into the station so we can walk around. What about you, Helper? You seem like you are in the 'oh my, I can't wait' group."

Helper smiled. Sniffles knew her well. "I want to go right now. These orange slices would serve me fine for dinner … to heck with dinner. I want to go and get into a suit and go through the air lock and put my footprints in the Martian dust. I want the adventure *right now*! I can't stand waiting. What surprises me is how patient the people who are likely in the first group are being. Scooter is certainly tall enough now, and some of the boys are taller than her. We have enough suits. I don't know why we are waiting for Smoky Rescue Day to choose … why don't we choose now and go tonight?" The excitement in her voice was partly, but not completely, exaggerated.

Sniffles and Ginger laughed.

"How much longer do I have to stir these tomatoes?" Sniffles asked, shifting the spoon back to her right hand. Steam continued rising from the pot, but the contents didn't seem to be much reduced from when she had started.

Helper stuck a few more bits of dried bamboo and corn stalk through the aperture into the coals of the cooker while saying, "You don't have to stir it constantly, just a few times per minute to keep it from burning and sticking to the bottom of the pot."

Sniffles sighed in relief, giving her right arm a bit of a break while she ate another bit of orange. "You could have told me that an hour ago," she scolded in mock indignation.

"Sorry, little sister," Helper replied. "As I learn about cooking, I forget to share the lessons unless someone asks. Maybe you should have asked an hour ago?"

Helper grinned, then picked up their earlier conversation. "What's the first thing you want to find when we get into the station, Ginger? What prize would make you happiest?"

Ginger thought for a moment. "I don't know where to start. I'm curious about the before time. I wonder about the accident, and the colonists that made me. I wonder what they were like. What did they look like? Mary's parents were the only ones Porter knew about. I wonder about my parents and I'm curious about what else we'll find, but I can't think of a particular thing. I don't know what to wish for. What about you, Helper?"

"Well, it might seem silly…"

Sniffles shifted the spoon back to her left hand and stirred with anticipation. "Come on, tell us," she begged with a smile.

"Well, I'd really like to get more information about cooking and the chemistry of food. Porter said that if we get into the station there are special machines that access all the knowledge that our ancestors developed. He called them 'magic tortillas'. I want to get one and learn more about food and how our bodies use it. Porter says that there are lots of different cooking ideas and different flavors in the tortillas too. He said that our diet here is pretty good, but that our bodies aren't getting all the chemicals that we need to grow healthy. I'd really like to know more about how I could cook healthier and tastier food."

"That doesn't sound silly to me," Sniffles offered. "One of the reasons Porter suggested we not make seedlings with the boys was that our diet wasn't as good as it might be. Fixing that sounds like a good idea."

"Did you have someone particular in mind to make seedlings with, Sniffles?" Ginger asked.

"No one in particular," she answered earnestly. "But the idea sounds exciting. I've been having these strange dreams. Have you had them? With a wonderful tickling feeling."

Helper nodded. "It started with dreams, but I've noticed that sometimes when I smell Scar, I get a little bit of that tickling while I'm awake. It's confusing ... sometimes I feel an urge to bite him—not to hurt him—but just to nibble him to let him know I like him."

Sniffles's face reddened. She felt the same confusion sometimes when she was near Curly, but she chose not to mention it.

"Nibble him?" Ginger said in mild surprise. "Hmmm ... I haven't felt the urge to nibble anyone, but I have had those dreams."

"Not just nibble him," Helper said. "Hold him. Smell his hair and his neck. Taste his skin. I don't know. I said it was confusing."

Sniffles shifted the spoon nervously to her other hand. "I wonder if the boys are having dreams," she said, to encourage a slight change in the direction of the conversation.

"I'll ask," said Helper, curious.

Sniffles admired Helper's direct approach. She looked forward to the answer.

CHAPTER 24 – Curly

Curly loved models, representations of objects he could observe in the world or imagine. When he was younger, he made physical models—representations of things in the greenhouse, plants, tables, people, cooking gear. When Porter began sharing the secrets of mathematics, Curly's love of models found new expression. The mathematical models of the world that Porter shared were so elegant, so perfect that Curly found their beauty staggering.

Counting and arithmetic had quickly become trivial. "I have five beans and you give me three more?" Eight beans. Memorization. Useful for the mundane tasks of children.

Multiplication and division were more helpful. How much soil was needed for a grow table? Multiply the width times the length times the depth of the table and you knew. The amazing part was that you could use any measure … centimeters, hand widths … it didn't matter. The answer would be correct in the cubic measure you selected.

Algebra had been the next natural step. It was a tidy and symmetrical language. Algebra was like the beautiful songs that Pigpen sang when she didn't think anyone else could hear her.

When Porter explained geometry, Curly's imagination buzzed with excitement. He and the Things and Pigpen and Sniffles seemed to enjoy it the most. Many of the children didn't appreciate geometry and Porter had made geometry beyond the basics optional. Only the five of them had cared enough to learn about postulates and theorems, building blocks for other knowledge. Porter could only remember a few of the theorems, but many more could be inferred from the rules. The system was magnificent. These relationships were tidy and perfect in every way. Best of all, he could show these concepts by using pictures drawn in the sand and models made of twigs or pebbles, so he never had to speak.

Curly sat sometimes, staring out the greenhouse wall, thinking about geometry. Infinite lines composed of infinite points. Infinite numbers of parallel lines forming infinite planes that shot flat through the whole of the universe that he could see or imagine.

When Porter told him that there were an infinite number of points in a sphere, Curly was sure Porter had made a mistake. How could there be an infinite number of points in a finite sphere like an orange? How could an orange compare to a plane that stretched to the ends of the universe?

Porter had seen Curly's interest and puzzled look and proceeded to amaze him with a few words and waves of his hand.

"Picture an infinite plane here on the floor, Curly," Porter had said. "Now picture a clear sphere one meter tall sitting on that plane." Porter held his hands to indicate the sphere. "The sphere touches the plane at exactly one tiny point right here." Porter pointed to a spot on the ground under the imagined sphere.

"Now imagine a line perpendicular to the plane, like an incredibly thin beam of light running straight up through the point where the sphere touches the plane, through the center of the sphere, and out through the top of the sphere here." Porter pointed to the top of the imaginary sphere. "We now have one point in the plane that maps to two points on the sphere. Can you picture that?"

Curly had nodded, not sure where Porter was leading him.

"Now, imagine the line is anchored to the point at the center of the sphere, but can rotate in any direction around that point. If I rotated the line to here—" Porter moved his imaginary line about forty-five degrees, using both hands so that everyone could picture the line—"where would it strike the plane of the floor?"

Curly had eyed the line and guessed a point on the floor a meter away from the touch point under the imaginary sphere. He touched the floor there and looked to Porter quizzically.

"Again, we have one point of the plane mapping to exactly two points of the sphere..." Porter had continued talking, but Curly wasn't listening. His mind was on fire and he was so happy he could burst. Any point on the floor would map to exactly two unique points in the sphere. Any point in the infinite plane ... a point a hundred kilometers from here or a million kilometers from here could be mapped to exactly two points in the sphere. In fact, there were two unique points in the sphere that described a line to any point in the infinite plane. The truth of it. The elegance. The joy. For days, Curly had imagined spheres of different sizes, from the smallest grain of sand to Mars itself, with bright blue lines extending through the center of the sphere and reaching out to other points in the universe. It was a perfect model, and it was all in his imagination.

He still had to count the number of bites he took when he ate (always a prime number). He still counted how many times he chewed each mouthful (always a multiple of two). He still had to organize barrels and cups and plants into carefully arrayed patterns. Sixteen cups were four rows of four, or he could stack them into two stacks of two wide and two deep and two tall (two stacks of two cubed). However, knowing this perfect fact—that there were twice as many points in a small sphere as there were in an infinite plane upon which the sphere sat—let Curly retreat into his mind when he felt compelled to practice some of his rituals. This lessened the compulsion a bit. When he was troubled by asymmetry, or his hands got sticky (he *hated* having sticky hands) he could think of his spheres or a proof of the Pythagorean theorem (he had been taught two and had deduced four more) to ease his anxiety while he dealt with the discomfort.

He still chose not to speak. It was a bother at times, but Porter, Cisco, and Sniffles in particular loved him and were very patient with him and he rarely needed to communicate ideas that he couldn't convey through other means. He didn't need to speak, yet.

Curly was safe. He had friends. He was loved. He had food to eat and water to drink. He had mathematics that filled him with joy. He had magnificent models in his head that were as big as the universe and they were so much more perfect and malleable than the models he could make with his hands that he could almost weep. Curly was happy.

Getting into the station had been Curly's dream ever since Porter told him about the books. Porter said that there were tens of thousands of mathematics books stored in the colony. Curly had calculated the area of the colony interior (excluding the greenhouses) at about sixty-two thousand square meters, with allowances for interior walls. If he assumed the books were distributed evenly through the structure, that meant when he got access to the colony, he should be able to find a math book every few steps. He knew it would take much of his life to read them all, but he loved to imagine tidy piles of books, stacked just so, using a Fibonacci sequence to order them according to his favorites:

- His favorite in a special spot by itself
- His next favorite also honored as a solo
- His next two favorites in a pile of two
- His next three favorites in a pile of three
- Then his next favorite five…

It would be glorious.

CHAPTER 25 –
Letting Go

Sniffles was following Porter as he made his rounds, helping with small tasks where she could. She adored him and loved to just follow him sometimes, watching him and talking to him. She had always had a special bond with Porter. She could sense his moods before any of the others could. She could tell when he was teasing and when he was serious. Where Curly's smell thrilled her, Porter's smell was very different; it made her feel safe and warm, like a nap in the sun after a big meal or a long comforting hug when she was sad or scared.

To Sniffles, Porter was defined by his calm demeanor. She couldn't remember ever seeing him angry. The few times he had seemed anxious were when someone was hurt or when the dust storm threatened the power supply and made them freeze Delta. He was anxious today, and she wondered why.

She watched Porter as he checked the condenser that pulled water from the air and placed it into the storage bladder. Porter was still taller than any of them, and more muscular with a fuller body. His torso was a rectangle atop his stout legs. His skin was a beautiful shiny dark brown-black like the rich dirt in the worm farm, darker than the Things but a little lighter than Scar. His hair and beard were fuzzy, like the Things, but speckled lately with increasing numbers of tiny white coils. His hair didn't cover the shiny black crown of his head and seemed to be retreating from his shiny forehead in the front. He was always quick to smile, showing a full mouth of impossibly white teeth, made whiter by the contrast of his full dark lips. His smiles had been fewer and shorter for the past few days. He was troubled.

"Uncle, you seem worried, is something wrong?"

Porter looked up from his task and gazed thoughtfully into Sniffles's eyes. He paused, then said quietly, "I am worried, sweetie. There is so much to do to prepare you guys for the station, and I feel like I have so little time."

"You've been preparing us all our lives. Teaching us to read, teaching us math, teaching us about growing plants and building things. Teaching us to think by answering our questions with 'Porter answers' that point us in a useful direction but don't lead us by the hand." She smiled.

"I have prepared you to live in the greenhouse. I suspect that if the greenhouse and the power supply and this technology—" he rapped on the condenser with the rag he was using to wipe down the coils—"lasted forever, you and your children and their children could survive here for a very long time. You know enough about your bodies to heal them if they don't get too sick. You know enough about the soil and plants and worms and bees to feed yourselves for generations.

"What I have come to realize, perhaps too late, is how little I have prepared you to leave the greenhouse. Mars is a hostile environment. It's hard for me to explain how dangerous it is. Our bodies weren't designed for it. Without the bits of technology and materials we brought with us from Earth to set up the colony, there is nothing here to eat. There is no air for us to breathe. The technology that allowed us to come here and live here is vast and complicated, the result of thousands of years of development by billions of people. I am the last survivor of over a hundred original colonists. We were carefully selected for this mission because of our specialized knowledge and skills. No one of us could operate the colony alone. Whatever happened inside the colony on Smoky Rescue Day so long ago killed over a hundred people who were specialists that were well trained to handle disasters."

He paused, then continued, "There is so much that I think I still need to teach you. There is so much that I don't know and can't teach you. The lessons I have shared with you guys over the last seven Martian years are tidbits of knowledge that I half remembered and thought you were ready for. I didn't have access to tools and information that would have helped me teach you. I'm worried that what I have done won't be enough—that perhaps nothing I could do would prepare you for the dangers of the station. I know we can't stay in the greenhouse forever, but I fear for your safety. Here, I knew just enough to keep you safe and alive, my precious little Sniffles." He smiled at her. "Over there—" Porter gestured toward the station—"over a hundred well-trained colonists who were experts in their fields and loved you as much as I do could not keep you safe."

There was a long silence as Sniffles considered Porter's words. She examined his furrowed brow, then asked, "This sounds like a puzzle: You wish to keep us safe, but you know we cannot stay here."

Porter nodded, looking into her eyes with mild surprise at her casually inquiring tone.

"Why did you come to Mars, Uncle?"

He pondered her question a moment, then slowly smiled and wistfully said, "For the adventure, and the challenge."

"Has it been an adventure and a challenge?"

Porter's brow unknotted and he laughed. "Yes, though not in the ways I expected."

"Are you glad that you came to Mars?"

Porter had gone back to wiping the condenser coils as he spoke, but this question caused him to stop again. He thought for another long moment. "I was so happy and excited when we were chosen for this mission. My wife Julia and I were sharing the biggest adventure we could imagine. We were very glad that we came. There were challenges and hardships, but it was a glorious undertaking, and we shared it. We were planning to have children and share these unique experiences with them. Then—the accident. I lost my wife. It is hard to explain to you how much she was a part of me. You may have a mate someday and it will make more sense to you then. For a while, I lost my purpose. My only reason for existing was you and the others. I knew that without me, you wouldn't survive. You became my purpose.

"Particularly *you*, my stubborn, youngest, littlest, I-refuse-to-eat-and-my-lungs-don't-work-right-and-I'm-always-cold girl." Porter said this with a chuckle and loving smile. "Do you know your feet hardly touched the ground for a year? I carried you everywhere in a sling around my shoulders so I could keep you warm and give you little bites of food and sips of water every few minutes. You were a real test of my dedication.

"My mission was to keep you and the others alive until help arrived. But help never came. You became the children that Julia and I wanted but didn't get to share. I had you all to myself. While you were growing up, I tried to honor your parents by never claiming that role for myself, but I felt like a parent. Parents want to keep their children safe and it's scary when their children grow up and want to have adventures of their own. You all are becoming adults. You want to explore your world and learn more than I can teach you and make your own mistakes. Mars is a terrible place to learn from your mistakes. Mistakes here are unforgiving." Porter began to look anxious again.

"So, you left the safety of Earth and came to Mars to explore and find adventure. What if we called the greenhouse 'Earth' and *New Rome* 'Mars'?" Sniffles said gently, then paused.

"We want what you wanted, Uncle," she continued. "We want to see the wonders of the unknown place. We want the adventure of exploration. We are the seedlings of explorers. We *are* your children. There may be dangers and joys and hardship. You said your purpose was to keep us alive until we were rescued.

You have always told us that *our* purpose was to thrive until we could get back into the station to pursue that rescue. You can help us prepare. You can guide us. You can help us avoid some mistakes—when we're smart enough to listen."

Porter bent and embraced Sniffles quietly for a long moment. She could feel his tears dripping onto her back. "I know you guys are smart. I'll try to be there to guide you. I'm just afraid for you, honey." He said this last part into her brown hair. "For all of you. I'm just afraid that I can't always keep you safe." She smelled him and felt safe and loved. His arms were like tree branches, strong and warm and stable around her.

He pulled slowly back from the hug and smiled softly, tears running down his face.

"You have time to prepare us," she repeated. "You can set the pace. Remember when we started helping with the plants? You gave us each a bamboo cup with a seedling."

"Wildflowers," he said.

"We started small. You didn't let us get overwhelmed. Pretty soon, we all had thriving plants, and we built from there, encouraged by our success."

"I replaced the ones you killed with fresh seedlings while you were sleeping." He chuckled.

"Well, it worked anyway," Sniffles said, undeterred. "We learned what we needed to learn and now we grow the crops and you help when there's trouble and keep the greenhouse running. We just need to think about how we can explore in small steps so we can learn as we go."

Porter was visibly less anxious. Sniffles was mildly surprised by the role reversal—always before, it was he who offered comfort. At the same time, she found this strangely unsettling. For the first time in her life, her beloved Uncle Porter, the only adult she had ever known, was just a man—a wonderful, kind man whom she truly loved—but also just a person, with fears and goals and worries and limitations. This realization was sobering. She knew his smell and his arms would always make her feel safe, but she now realized that "feeling safe" and "being safe" were two different things.

They continued their rounds of the greenhouse systems for another hour, Sniffles at Porter's side. They checked the worms and the bees. Porter checked and cleaned the condenser in Delta. The purple twilight prelude to the long January night lit their path as they walked, sharing a personable silence.

PART 3 – RUNNERS

"Animals are something invented by plants to move seeds around. An extremely yang solution to a peculiar problem which they faced." - Terence McKenna

CHAPTER 26 –

Planning

Helper and Scar finished the dinner dishes and walked to Porter's evening lesson hand in hand. They were the last to arrive, and Porter had been waiting for them. It was February 2.

In mid-January, after Porter's conversation with Sniffles, lessons had shifted to be more focused on the forthcoming trip to the colony and practical information needed for the excursion. He had demonstrated how to put on an exo-suit, including the helmet. In the process, he discovered that the batteries for the suits were dead and assigned Thing1 to figure out how to charge them. He had taught everyone how to patch the suits with the kits attached to them. He had taken a set of gloves and made each person perform simple tasks like manipulating twigs and husking corn while wearing them so that all had experience with the clumsy gear. He had inventoried the exo-suits and the air canisters, pleased to see that there were thirty-six canisters between the two air locks, all in apparent good condition. He showed the Martians how to swap air canisters. He told them the sobering story of the Carter tether, and why it was important to remain tethered together at all times on the surface outside the colony. He taught them radio communication protocols and simple hand signals in case the radios failed (come, stay, go, look, danger, okay, comm trouble, and help). He showed them how to operate the air locks when power was available as well as how to operate them manually to pressurize or depressurize if there was no power. One of the more exciting demonstrations was conducted at the Delta air lock.

The group had walked to the Delta air lock and Porter had filled a cup with water along the way. He opened the door and placed the cup on the bench inside, then sealed the air lock again. They had all crowded around to watch through the windows as Porter depressurized the air lock. The water boiled furiously within seconds as the pressure decreased. A film of ice developed on the water as it cooled, while still boiling. Drops splashed the window, and those drops also boiled and froze. Porter had warned them that there was about two hundred times more pressure inside the greenhouse than outside, and that it would be fatal to be outside without a suit, or with a compromised suit, for more than a few seconds. The demonstration made this abstract notion more real.

The practical preparations were exciting for everyone. The station had dominated conversations and daydreams all year; Porter was now preparing everyone for the colony in tangible ways.

The reading lessons continued, and the next portion of the aid books that Porter assigned was "Dealing with depressurization trauma." The reading lessons suddenly didn't seem nearly so theoretical.

Tonight's lesson had everyone clustered around Porter in the middle of the Charlie receiving area. Some sat on the floor. Another group stood behind. Helper and Scar climbed onto one of the grow tables for a better view. Porter had created a model of the station on the floor.

"Dinner was very good tonight, Helper," Porter said, acknowledging her arrival. "I've never been a big fan of squash, but it was quite nice roasted."

Helper smiled at the compliment. "I'm glad you liked it. Thank you for waiting for us, Uncle Porter. What is the lesson tonight?"

"Tonight," Porter addressed the assembled group, "I want to discuss a plan for our initial entry into the station tomorrow."

Everyone was silent. It was early February. Smoky Rescue Day was over a hundred days off. They watched with rapt attention as Porter continued. "Our ultimate goal is to reclaim as much of the station as we can, get as many of its systems working as we can, and make contact with Earth so you can see the home world of your ancestors.

"We are not going to be able to do all this at once. To be honest, I was feeling a little overwhelmed by the danger and difficulty of the whole undertaking, when Sniffles reminded me that we had to develop an approach and a pace." He paused and nodded to Sniffles, then continued. "That helped me break exploration down into more manageable parts."

Porter indicated a sketch of the station he had drawn in the dirt floor. "This is a crude model of the station. When the accident happened, I was in sick bay here." Porter pointed to the approximate position of sick bay at eight o'clock on the middle ring. "When I heard there was trouble in the nursery here—" he pointed to the nursery at four o'clock on the outer ring—"I took the middle ring to this corridor and went south to here." Porter indicated the corridor just outside the Charlie air lock on the model, then looked up and pointed to the corresponding air lock fifteen meters away in the Charlie receiving area. "Right there."

He paused for a moment to ensure everyone was oriented, then continued. "The smoke was pretty thick, and I didn't have a suit on so breathing was very difficult. I only got about twenty meters up the corridor, when I ran into the crewman who was pulling you all out of the nursery and trying to get you to safety, right about here." He indicated the place on the corridor. "I made several trips shuttling you guys from there to here, failing to close that air lock door on my last trip. When I woke up, the station had been depressurized. That is all the information I have for sure about the status of the colony just before and after the accident. What I was told while I was in sick bay was that there was a problem with the nuclear reactor here—" indicating the inner ring at ten-thirty—"and a fire somewhere here." He indicated vaguely the northeast quadrant. "It wasn't clear if or how the two problems were related."

Porter paused now, not so much for dramatic effect as to make sure they were following his words thus far. "So, I believe we had at least two problems in the station, fire and the reactor. You are all familiar with fire; it's a tool. We use it for heat and cooking, just like our ancestors did. Fire can also be very dangerous and destructive. One of the important ways it is dangerous—and I think the problem we had on Smoky Rescue Day—is smoke. When some materials burn, their smoke is poisonous. Depending upon what is burning, smoke can be irritating to your eyes and throat, or deadly toxic. Here's the good news. Seven years after the fire, particularly with the station decompressed, smoke won't be a threat to us. All we will likely have to contend with related to the fire is any damage that it caused, and perhaps the mess that smoke made. It shouldn't be able to hurt us.

"The nuclear reactor is technology that none of you are familiar with and it is more dangerous than you can imagine. The reactor is a bit like a controlled fire. It burns unbelievably hot and the heat was used to generate electrical power. Inside the reactor, it was hot enough to melt glass and metal. The heat was used to make steam, which turned a turbine … a motor in reverse. If you apply electrical power to a motor, the motor spins. If you spin a motor—with steam for example—you get electricity. The reactor was used in combination with the solar cells to generate power for the whole colony. It is very efficient and only needed fuel every ten years or so."

The Martians were stunned. They were used to adding fuel to their cooking fire every fifteen to twenty minutes with the light fuel of corn stalks and bamboo they had available.

"But the fuel it uses is extremely dangerous when handled carefully, and deadly if handled wrong. Just like a fire gives off heat and light, the nuclear reactor gives off heat and light as well as something very dangerous called radiation.

"If the reactor is properly shielded, the radiation is kept inside and isn't a problem. If the shielding that normally keeps the radiation inside is damaged, it can create a huge health risk and threat to us in two ways. First, the invisible radiation shines like a bright invisible light out of the reactor and damages the cells of any living thing it shines through. Unlike light, it shines through clothes and walls. It takes a meter of rock or a few centimeters of special metal shielding to stop the radiation.

"The second threat is that if the reactor is damaged, it may release tiny, very poisonous dust particles into the air."

"Like smoke?" asked Pigpen.

"Similar," Porter said, encouraged by her insight, "but different in an important way. Smoke is indeed particles, and you may have seen soot on the side of the cooker. The dangerous part of the smoke from the fire isn't usually so much about the particles; they just make the smoke visible. The dangerous part is the chemicals in the air with the smoke. Those gasses can be deadly. What's different about the nuclear radiation is that the particles themselves are terribly poisonous if you get them on your skin or inhale them."

"Won't the danger be less now after all this time?" asked Scar.

"That's the big danger. If the reactor was damaged and released particles, they will be poisonous for thousands of years. We won't be able to go near it without protection or else we risk an unpleasant death.

"This lesson about fire and radiation is intended to help you understand why I want to be very careful about how we explore the station. I want to have this adventure with you in little steps, so that we can acquire tools and skills to help us with later steps. Here's what I was thinking so far." Porter sighed. "Of all the things I regret, not closing the inner air lock door of Charlie on Smoky Rescue Day is near the top of the list. Because of my mistake, any expedition into the colony must go out the Delta air lock, across the surface of the planet, and into another functional air lock. Once we have the Charlie air lock working, we won't have to go outside and around to get into the colony. That means we don't have to worry about blowouts or Carter tethers. The trips will be shorter and less dangerous because we won't be as far from safety and won't consume as much air."

"If we want to avoid areas damaged by fire and possibly contaminated by the reactor, which air lock do we want to use?" Porter asked.

"The other greenhouses?" offered Red.

"I think you're right, Red." Porter nodded. "There may also be tools, plants, seeds and other things we can recover from those greenhouses that will help us here and help with our other exploration. Not only are those air locks farthest from the accident area, but also, like Charlie and Delta, the other greenhouses weren't integrated into the main ventilation system. That means they are less likely to have been damaged by smoke and less likely to have been subjected to radioactive dust if there was a problem with the reactor.

"So, the first stage of the plan to get back into the colony will be to move through the Bravo air lock to Alpha, then move through the Alpha air lock at nine o'clock on the outer ring, then come here to the Charlie air lock and close the stupid door that has been taunting me from the other side of that window since before most of you could walk."

The Martians, keyed up and listening attentively to the plan, laughed at Porter's outburst, taking some of the edge off their excitement.

"If all the air locks had power and were functional, this excursion would take about fifteen minutes. Exit at Delta, walk to Bravo…" He began tracing the route west from Delta to Bravo on the model, then stopped and waved at the imaginary party through the south wall. "Hi guys … be careful!"

More giggles.

He returned to the model and drew the remainder of the route to Bravo. "Through Bravo's air lock, through the greenhouse, through the shared air lock into Alpha—just like the one between Charlie and Delta—then into the colony through Alpha's air lock on the west side of the station. Then, take the outer ring to avoid the accident areas as much as possible, and back into Charlie. It might take an hour or more without power, depending upon what challenges we find along the way.

"Many of you have shared hopes and dreams of exploring the colony. There are many questions I want answered too. I want to encourage you to be patient. I propose we limit our first excursion to this simple route. Perhaps picking up useful supplies along the way in Bravo and Alpha. I also propose we do not wait for Smoky Rescue Day. I'm sure most of you are big enough to wear an exo-suit now. I can't think of a good reason to wait. I propose that we choose the members of the first party in the morning. We can fit and test the suits, and if all goes well, make our excursion at midday when the sun is high, so we have good light."

His audience sat in stunned silence for a moment. Then Cisco whooped with joy and soon everyone was cheering in celebration and anticipation.

CHAPTER 27 –

The Excursion Party

The next morning, chores were forgotten. The greenhouse was buzzing with conversation as the sun came up. Helper took her regular cooking duties seriously, but went with simple fare that was quickly made, consumed, and cleaned up after.

Porter fetched two small exo-suits from the air lock and had everyone line up according to their height. Sniffles accepted that she wouldn't be tall enough to go. She and Mary walked, resigned, to the short end of the line as everyone else began to do overtly what they had been doing covertly for months—comparing their heights. The tall end of the line was easy. Scar was skinny but had sprouted nearly as tall as Porter in the last few hundred days. Cisco was second, with Scooter running a close third. Next came Pancho and the Things, then Red, Ginger, Helper, Curly, and Pigpen.

Porter held up the small exo-suit and eyed the top of Thing1's head, muttering, "I think this will work." He turned to Thing2 and said, "Okay, Cinderella. Let's see if the slipper fits."

Thing2 beamed. "This will be way better than going to a party, fairy godmother! Will the suit vanish when the clock strikes twelve?"

"Let's see if it fits you first, dear." Porter mocked, smiling. He indicated a barrel that he had placed on a pad in the receiving area. "Have a seat, Cindy."

Thing2 sat on the barrel and looked at Porter expectantly.

"Feet first. Don't worry if the boots are a bit large; we can improvise some socks for you."

Thing2 lifted his feet in the air as Porter placed the open suit in front of him, then pushed his feet through the legs of the suit and into the boots.

"My feet feel fine," Thing2 said. "What are socks?"

"Cloth coverings for your feet. They serve as a cushion and barrier between your feet and footwear. If the boots were too small, that would be a harder problem. A little too big is okay. Okay, stand up and put your arms at your side."

Thing2 did as he was instructed.

"Okay, right arm in." Porter pushed the sleeve up and put the suit over Thing2's right shoulder. "Now left arm. Okay, let's get this even." The suit fit fairly well across Thing2's shoulders. "How does it feel?"

"A little scratchy," Thing2 said honestly, then hastily added, "but fine."

"Yeah, when we get into the station proper, I should probably get you guys some clothes. Normally you would wear a softer garment and the suit would go over that. Let's zip you up."

Porter zipped the suit halfway up Thing2's chest, flipped the collar hoop forward over his head, then zipped the suit the rest of the way up and secured the collar ring.

"We'll try the helmet in a bit. Walk around and see how it feels. I think you guys will fill out a suit fine when we get some undergarments for you," Porter said.

Five hundred days ago, everyone had watched with envy as Scooter had awkwardly donned the smallest suit. All they had seen of Scooter was the top of her head over the collar ring. The same-sized suit now fit Thing2 reasonably well.

Red was several centimeters shorter than the Things, about the same size as Ginger and Helper. The next people down in the size line were Curly, a couple of centimeters shorter than Helper, and Pigpen, slightly shorter than Curly.

Addressing the short end of the line, Porter said, "I don't think it will be much longer before you all will have exo-suits that fit. I honestly can't remember but think we must have some smaller suits in the station, or at least the ability to make them. All the adults in the colony had two exo-suits fitted to them individually, a primary and a spare. Those in the air locks were for emergencies and that's why our selection is limited."

Porter eyeballed Thing1 and Pancho. "I think this size suit will work for you two as well. '2, go stand by Cisco. I think she and Scooter may need larger suits."

When Thing2 and Scooter were side by side, Porter nodded. Even with the vapor barrier soles of the boots, Thing2 was five centimeters shorter than Cisco. "Helper, would you and Curly and Sniffles please go to the Delta air lock and get me two 'L' for 'large', two 'M' for 'medium' and another small exo-suit?"

Helper beamed a smile at Scar, pleased to help prepare him for his adventure, and trotted off with Curly and Sniffles.

Porter handed the other small suit to Thing1, and said, "'2, now that you are an expert, help your brother suit up. Scooter and Pancho, you help too. I want you guys to learn to do this alone at some point, but that can wait. Right now, I want you to get the feel of the suit and understand how it works. Don't force anything. If a zipper gets stuck or you aren't sure what to do, ask for help. It takes a little practice."

Thing1 was energized with anticipation. Where suiting up Thing2 was a slow, ceremonial reprise of Scooter's ritual from the year before, Thing1's excitement and the adrenaline of his brother, Pancho, and Scooter made short work of getting him into the suit. By the time Helper, Sniffles, and Curly returned, the Things were suited and prancing around laughing while Scooter, Cisco, Pancho, and Scar paced impatiently.

A few minutes later, Porter was leading a column of six exo-suited Martians followed closely by the other inhabitants of the greenhouse on an impromptu parade to the Charlie/Delta air lock.

Porter coached them as they walked. "Get used to walking. Pay attention to anywhere the suit is particularly scratchy or pinches and say something if your feet are sliding around in the boots. We will want to adjust before we leave so that you are comfortable and can walk without harming your feet." Porter knew all these years walking barefoot had toughened the soles of their feet but worried that their unfamiliarity with shoes might give them blisters on the top and sides of their feet quickly without socks.

When they arrived at the air lock, a pile of gloves and seven helmets lay on the ground awaiting them. Picking a helmet up, Porter raised the sunscreen and opened the faceplate to show how the latches operated. "When you know you're in a good atmosphere, you don't want to consume your suit's air and power, so you turn it off and open your faceplate. Remember we talked about the gasses we breathe, and that you need oxygen and that your body combines that with carbon so that you exhale carbon dioxide? If the suit remained closed without an air supply and you didn't open the faceplate to get fresh air, you would consume all the oxygen in the suit in a minute or two and the carbon dioxide would start to build up and poison you. We know the atmosphere in our greenhouse has oxygen, so here it is safe to put on your helmet and open the faceplate."

Porter's voice became serious. He pointed at the floor before him. "Scar, come stand here please."

Scar stepped forward, puzzled by Porter's sudden shift in tone. "In my official capacity as the oldest surviving colonist on Mars, I would like to crown you the *tallest male native Martian*!" The pronouncement was made in a formal, silly booming voice as Porter put the helmet over Scar's head, faceplate to the rear. Everyone laughed and Porter quickly corrected his "error." Scar was smiling broadly when his face became visible.

Porter said, "Okay, your majesty, you hold still and model this helmet while I show the others how to fasten it into the neck loop." He showed them the threads of the neck loop and how they lined up with the notches of the helmet at a thirty-degree twist to the right.

"Your turn, Cisco." Porter picked up another helmet. "Blah, blah, blah … *tallest female native Martian*!" Porter pronounced this quickly, mocking himself and placing the helmet over Cisco's head with the faceplate correctly positioned. "Scar, come see how it fits on here. The rest of you, grab a helmet. Try to put it on by yourself to get a feel for it. Get help from someone if you have trouble. Don't forget to open the faceplate. Experiment with opening and closing the faceplate and sun visor. The latches are a little knacky—uh—tricky. It will take practice. You will need to be able to do this with gloves on, so get comfortable with the task."

Porter recalled that Scooter was a little claustrophobic, and he came to her aid quickly when her first few attempts to open her faceplate failed. After opening her faceplate so she could catch her breath, he smoothly and quickly removed her helmet and reviewed the latching mechanism with her. Then he put the helmet on his own head, took her hand and placed it on the latch, and turned away from her so that she was behind him and couldn't see it. "Try it now," his muffled voice said from under the helmet. After a few successful attempts, he put the helmet back on her head and she seemed calmer and able to operate the faceplate.

"Okay, now gloves." Porter retrieved gloves of various sizes and helped the suited find an approximate fit. He showed them how the gloves locked onto the sleeves of the suits and had everyone practice putting the gloves on and taking them off, first in teams, and then individually.

"Now I want everyone to take a few deep breaths and relax," Porter instructed. "In a moment, with your gloves on, I want you to close and then open your faceplate, but before you do that, I want everyone to show me the hand signal for 'danger'."

About half of the suit wearers made one hand flat and began a chopping motion at their throats; the other half mimicked the gesture when reminded.

"If you have trouble operating your faceplate with your gloves on, give the danger sign and I will help you. Remember, you have a couple minute's worth of air in those suits, so relax. Ready? Go!"

Faceplates snapped closed. Gloved fingers fumbled with latches for a few moments. Porter's face was placid, but he was watching carefully. Scar opened his faceplate in about twenty seconds. Scooter and Pancho succeeded ten seconds later. Thing2, then Thing1, fifteen or twenty seconds after that. Everyone's faceplate was open but Cisco. She was obviously having difficulty operating the latch while wearing gloves but was stubbornly refusing to ask for help. A full minute after Thing1, Cisco calmly opened her faceplate.

"Gets kinda hot in there, doesn't it?" said Porter.

Cisco was breathing deeply. "Yes, but it makes you appreciate the cool air more." She smiled. There was no sign of panic or frustration on her face or in her voice.

"The first few times I tried to open the faceplate with gloves on, I couldn't do it. You did great, Cisco. You kept your cool. That is the secret to all the challenges we are going to face today. Keep your wits about you and think. Cisco, your gloved index finger is too long and bulky to easily flip the catch, so try with the side of your little finger or ring finger. That's usually easier."

Cisco snapped her faceplate shut, and the others followed suit. Scar was the first to get his open again, this time in about ten seconds. Cisco's faceplate opened a few seconds later. Everyone was breathing the greenhouse air within twenty seconds.

"All of this gets easier with practice." Porter fetched a suit for himself from the air lock and placed it on the ground in front of him, next to gloves and the remaining helmet. He stepped into the suit boots, then pulled it up to his hips and put his right arm into the sleeve in one smooth motion. He twisted his body to the right, causing the left arm of the suit to swing where he could catch it. He placed his left arm into the suit and squared it across his shoulders. Next, he zipped the suit up past his waist, and dipped his knees to flip the collar over his head. His bad knee protested the dip painfully, his muscle memory having not yet recorded and adjusted to his disability. They didn't see his grimace or hear his sharp intake of breath. He finished zipping up. He was out of practice; it took him forty-five seconds.

"I haven't done that for a while." He smiled. "But I had a *lot* of practice before that." He bent down and picked up his helmet and gloves. He pulled the gloves on and locked them to his sleeves before putting the helmet on his head and rotating it into place. Then he opened his own faceplate.

"We definitely need some underclothes as a priority," he said, aware of the rough suit against his skin. "But for now, we need to get some air canisters and test these suits. Follow me." Porter turned and walked through the Charlie/Delta air lock, picking up two air canisters as he went, then headed toward the air lock that exited Delta for the surface of Mars.

The parade of Martians followed him. He hoped events were moving too quickly for them to become overly anxious.

CHAPTER 28 – Egress

When they got to the air lock, Porter said, "Here's what we are going to do next. We need to ensure that your suit works and make sure you feel comfortable operating it. I'm going to go into the air lock with each of you one at a time. We are going to check communications. Then we will attach an air canister to you and slowly depressurize the air lock. Any issues with your suit should become apparent before the air lock is fully depressurized. If there are problems, we will repressurize the air lock and deal with them. If there are no problems, we are going to open the air lock and you are going to go outside with me and get a small rock—a token of your first walk on the surface of Mars. You will bring your rock back to the air lock; then you will manually repressurize the air lock using the auxiliary pump we would use if there were no power. Once the pressure is equalized, your turn is done, and the next person will go. The rest of you can take your gloves off but leave your helmets on and faceplates open. I want you monitoring communications. Don't speak, just listen. Does everyone understand?"

The helmets nodded.

"Scar, how about you first? You will officially be the first Martian who will touch the surface of the planet outside of the greenhouse. Turn on your suit." As Scar did so, Porter powered up his own suit as well, then clipped his Carter tether to Scar's and flipped his faceplate closed. "Close your faceplate, Scar," Porter said over the comm link.

As Scar complied, Porter looked at the rest of the crew and said, "If you can hear me, raise your hand."

Scar raised his hand, but no one else moved.

Porter looked through the visor at the assembled Martians and gave the hand signal for "comm trouble," tapping on the side of his helmet by his ears. Thing1 and Cisco quickly caught on and told the rest to turn on their communications links.

Porter saw them activate their comm links, and said again, "If you can hear me, raise your hand."

This time, the hands of everyone wearing a helmet went up.

"Watch how I insert the air canister into Scar's suit," Porter said. The crowd gathered around. He inserted the cylinder into the bracket on the chest of Scar's suit, seating it.

"Now, Scar, you insert my air canister. I want you to get the feel of it. You should feel it lock."

"I felt it," Scar's voice said in everyone's helmet.

"Good. Take this spare and put it on your belt. Always carry a spare. You can swap air canisters if you need to while we are outside. I checked before we started. See the blue numbers displayed on the lower right corner of your faceplate? It should say that you have about one hundred fifty minutes of air, do you see it?"

"Yes," said Scar.

"Good job charging the suits, '1," said Porter. "That number will fluctuate depending upon your air consumption. If you were exerting yourself, it would recalibrate to your current rate of consumption and predict how much air you have, assuming you continue at the current rate."

"What is the other number, the green ninety-nine percent?" asked Scar.

"That's how much power remains in your suit. Right now, power is only being consumed for communications, respiration, and to keep you cool. When we go outside, it will work harder to regulate your temperature so it will drain faster. There is also a headlight on your helmet, in case you need task lighting. You should be good for several hours with a full charge. When power reserves drop below thirty percent, the green number will become yellow to get your attention. When it drops below ten percent, it will become red and there will be an audible alarm. Without power, you will lose light, heat, and communications. For safety reasons you should never be outside when the power drops below about twenty-five percent. You understand?"

Scar nodded.

"If you are shaking your head, I can't hear it." Porter chuckled.

"I understand," said Scar.

"The rest of you understand?" Porter looked to the rest of the explorers.

There was a chorus of acknowledgement across the comm link.

"What do you see on the left side of your display, Scar?" asked Porter.

"The left side tells me the current air pressure is thirteen PSI, the temperature is 21 degrees Celsius, and the atmosphere is breathable."

"Good. That's the air pressure and temperature and atmosphere in the greenhouse. The display on the left is about your environment. The display on the right is about you. So, the suit's electronics seem to be working. It's been a couple of minutes and you aren't struggling for air, so the air circulation system seems to be working. You have also been breathing oxygen since we engaged your air canister, so take a couple of deep breaths and let's pressure test your suit."

Porter opened the air lock door to let Scar in, then followed him in and closed and sealed the door behind them.

"I'm going to depressurize using the electric pump, but I'm going to do it slowly. I want you to pay attention to how the feel of your suit changes as the pressure drops, okay? The pressure inside the suit will be greater than the pressure outside, so the flexible parts of the suit are going to expand as the external pressure drops."

Scar nodded.

"I can't hear you, Scar," Porter teased.

"Okay," Scar said.

The vacuum pump hummed as Porter decreased the interior pressure in the air lock. "What exterior pressure are you reading now, Scar?"

"Six point five PSI."

"Okay, that's about half of what we have in the greenhouse. Do you notice how the suit is more rigid and less scratchy?"

"Yes. It feels like it's filling with air."

"That's the pressure in your suit being higher than the pressure outside. Can you breathe okay?"

"Yes."

Porter decreased the interior pressure further. The hum of the vacuum dimmed and seemed far away. "What pressure are you reading now?"

"Three point two PSI."

"Do you guys outside see a similar reading on the exterior air lock display?" asked Porter.

Thing1 gave a thumbs-up through the window.

"Good hand signals, '1," said Porter. "How is your breathing, Scar?"

"Fine," Scar said, "but things sound strange."

"That's because there has to be a medium to carry sound. Air is the medium you are used to, but there is almost no air between us right now. Less air muffles and distorts sound. Shall we go the rest of the way?"

"Yes," said Scar, without hesitation.

Porter finished evacuating the air lock. "What is the current pressure, Scar?"

"Zero point zero eight four PSI."

Porter got in front of Scar and pointed at his own visor with two fingers, giving the sign for "look," then pointed at the equilibrium indicator in the air lock. Porter's voice crackled in Scar's ears. "That indicator means that we have the same pressure inside the air lock as we do outside. Are you ready to step out onto the surface of your home world, young Martian?"

"Yes!" said Scar eagerly. His voice sounded strange in his ears. It felt like his ears were stuffed up.

"Sun visor down. All the windows in your world till now have been tinted a bit to protect your eyes from the glare of the sun. On Earth, eye protection isn't required even though we are closer to the sun because Earth's thick atmosphere filters some of the harshness of the light. Dust storms do that sometimes on Mars, but in general, you want your sun visor down when you are outside during the day to protect your eyes."

Porter and Scar both lowered their sun visors, and Porter unlocked and swung open the air lock door. "Scar, let's go get you a rock."

CHAPTER 29 –

The First Rock

The only sound Scar heard was his breathing and the rustling of his suit against his body. As he stepped out of the air lock, he felt the gentle tug of the Carter tether feeding out from his belt. He could feel the spool of the tether vibrating, but he wasn't sure if he heard or imagined hearing it. He glanced back at Porter, perhaps three meters behind him, and beyond that he saw the air lock door. Porter had closed it.

"Is it okay if I walk around to the side of Delta?" Scar asked. "I'd like to see what it looks like from the outside."

"That sounds like a fine idea. I want to conserve air, so let's plan on heading back to the air lock in five minutes, okay? That will give everyone time to test their suits, then we can rest up and prepare for our adventure this afternoon."

Scar gave a thumbs-up and circled south around the end of Delta, then west a few meters and turned to look north at Delta's glass wall. Everyone was waving at him excitedly. They couldn't see through his sun visor, but he was beaming.

The clear portion of Delta's greenhouse wall started a meter above the foundation. The bottom part of the wall was opaque. Inside it appeared to be made of the same stuff as the greenhouse floor, but on the outside, it was dusty red rather than glassy black. Scar could also see the bank of solar panels that ran along Delta's southern wall. They shined black beneath a layer of red dust.

Scar realized that the whole greenhouse was covered in a layer of dust. The ground to the horizon was certainly red, but it was more vivid than he had ever seen it. The sun, still low, made the sky a beautiful shade of blue and purple and cast stark shadows on the ground.

He looked to the west, and for the first time in his life he saw Bravo clearly. From within Charlie, Bravo was barely visible because it only extended about fifty meters farther south than Charlie and it was about one hundred meters west. Attempts to see Bravo were normally like looking out of the corner of your eye because of the triple-paned glass of the greenhouse wall and the acute angle. Bravo was as tall as Delta, but the windows seemed black. He felt a shock of anticipation. Later today, they would be going there.

Elated, Scar bent down and selected a roughly square bit of stone the size of his open hand. With a grunt, he hurled the stone as far as he could toward the southern horizon. The limited mobility of his suit, the Carter tether, and the clumsy gloves constrained his throw to perhaps fifty meters, but Scar was pleased. He watched the clouds of dust that arose as the rock bounced and rolled across the terrain with satisfaction. He bent down and picked up a smaller stone half the size of his fist, then turned to Porter and said, "I have my rock. Let's go back in so we can get through with this testing."

As they circled back toward Delta's air lock, Scar circled wide and stopped, looking northwest at the colony. The detail of the colony was amazing. He realized he had been looking at it his whole life through dusty glass.

"Come on, Scar," Porter said gently. "I'm looking forward to this afternoon too."

They entered the air lock together and Porter sealed the door. "Okay, now I want you to repressurize the air lock manually, the way I showed you the other day." Porter began disconnecting their tethers.

Scar put his rock on the bench and adjusted the air lock controls as Porter had taught him and flipped down the foot-powered pump. He sat on the seat, adjusted the band around his back, and grabbed the hand holds. Then he began pedaling the pump with his feet to repressurize the air lock, pulling sips of the thin atmosphere of Mars into the air lock with each rotation.

Outside the air lock, his companions looked on.

After a few minutes, Porter said, "On Earth there is a wheeled device called a bicycle that uses energy like that pump does to move you around. There might be pictures of one in the colony."

"This is a lot of work," panted Scar.

"It's easier on Earth where you can use your weight to your advantage. Here it is mostly a matter of leg muscles. Take your time. Slow and steady should have the pressure up in another five minutes or so. Let your legs do the work. The pressure is already five PSI. You are a third of the way there."

When the indicator light informed them that pressure had been equalized between the greenhouse and the air lock, Porter said, "There you go, Scar. You can stop now. Check your display. What do you notice about the current environment?"

"Thirteen PSI… temperature minus four degrees… Atmosphere *toxic*? – ninety-five percent carbon dioxide!"

"So, taking off our helmets now would be a really bad idea?" Porter asked.

"What happened?" asked Scar. "Did I do something wrong?"

"No. When we entered the air lock to leave, it was filled with breathable air from the greenhouse. When you manually repressurize it, you take Martian air and compress it. Martian air doesn't have the oxygen we need, and Mars doesn't have the plants we have in the greenhouse to take the carbon dioxide out of the atmosphere. It won't support life for us—although the plants would think it's fine."

"Why is it so cold?" asked Scar.

"Did you notice the temperature outside was negative sixty?"

"No," said Scar, embarrassed. "I didn't."

"It's okay, Scar. Your first time out can be overwhelming. You will learn to monitor your surroundings. When you compressed the air, you warmed it slightly. You took all of the heat energy in that sixty degrees below zero air and compressed by a factor of two hundred, so we have this balmy negative-four degree room full of poisonous carbon dioxide."

"So, what do we do?"

"First, we tell everyone outside to back up out of the receiving area." He waved them back through the window even as he said this. "The volume of atmosphere in this air lock is very small in comparison to the whole of greenhouse Delta. When we open the door, it will quickly disperse. Carbon dioxide is only poisonous in this concentration; diluted, it is harmless. The cold air will mix with the warm air too; it shouldn't make a dent in the overall temperature of Delta."

Porter looked through the air lock window and saw that everyone had backed up out of Delta's receiving area. He opened the air lock door and stepped through, leaving the door open.

"Stay inside a minute, Scar, and watch your atmospheric readout."

"Wow. Carbon dioxide is dropping steadily… fifty percent ... twenty-five ... ten ... seven ... two … one … breathable now … point five … point two … point zero five… it looks like it's stable at point zero five."

"Carbon dioxide is a pretty heavy gas compared to oxygen. When I opened the door, you couldn't see it, but it spilled out like water and fresh air replaced it in the air lock. If we measured a few centimeters above the floor it might still be in high concentrations, but it will quickly mix with the other air in the greenhouse. I'm sure the plants will find it refreshing. Remind me when we are done testing and we will see what impact the environment sensors say six air lock cycles of carbon dioxide have on the overall carbon dioxide concentrations in Delta's atmosphere. Before you open your faceplate, always check the environmental sensor to ensure you are in a breathable atmosphere. Then open the faceplate, and power down your suit to save energy and air. Come on out. Welcome back."

Porter called to the spectators, "It's safe now … you may come and welcome home the first Martian-born explorer of Mars!"

Everyone cheered and came forward to congratulate Scar on his adventure. Helper smiled at Scar. He removed his helmet, then looked mildly panicked. "My rock!" He exclaimed and jogged back into the air lock to fetch it. He came out and proudly handed it to Helper with his gloved hand.

Helper looked at the stone with reverence and wonder for a moment, then shrieked in pain and dropped it, jamming her fingers into her mouth. "Ouch! It's hot!" she said in surprise. "It burned me."

Porter came over, drawn by her cry. "The rock isn't hot—it's extremely cold. It was very recently sixty degrees below zero." He reached down and picked up the stone with his gloved hand. Water vapor from the greenhouse was condensing on it in a thin layer of frost. "It should warm to room temperature in a little while. It isn't a very big rock."

Scar took the stone from Porter's hand and looked at it with interest.

Helper looked at the angry red marks on her fingers where she had held the frozen stone.

"It might blister, Helper, but you should be okay," Porter said. Then he turned and said, "Are you ready to get your rock, Scooter?"

CHAPTER 30 –
Preparations

The morning passed quickly. Manually repressurizing the air lock was time consuming, and Porter was tempted to reconsider that task in the interests of schedule, but it was important to him that everyone have first-hand experience because he doubted there would be power anywhere else in the station. He also thought the effort of operating the pump manually would help disperse some of the nervous energy evident in the young explorers.

After each returned from their outing, they removed their suits and stood by watching the excursions of their cohorts. As they watched Cisco through the greenhouse wall, Scar was telling Helper about the dust on the tinted greenhouse glass and how much clearer everything appeared outside of the air lock, when Scooter walked up naked and sweating from her recent foray.

"It's surprising how warm those suits are with it being so cold outside," Scooter offered. Scooter's black hair, which she had lately been growing longer, hung below her shoulders and was limp with sweat. Helper realized that Scooter and Scar now shared the bond of a common experience and it made her feel—angry—protective? She wasn't sure what that feeling was. Helper casually took a half step closer to Scar, taking his hand with her blistered one, determined not to flinch when she realized her mistake.

"And how much work it was to pressurize the air lock manually," Scar was saying, and he squeezed Helper's hand affectionately, oblivious to her pain.

They watched through the window as Cisco returned to the air lock with Porter and began repressurization.

"Let's check Delta's monitors to see if the carbon dioxide levels increase when they open the air lock," Scar said to Helper. She smiled and walked with him toward the display with a confusing satisfaction. Scar was hers. She smelled the sweat on his body and felt warm inside, her injured hand forgotten.

Curly overheard their conversation. He liked Scar, but thought he was being silly. The air volume of the greenhouse was over four million cubic meters; the air lock was about thirty. It was hard to imagine there would be any measurable difference. He began hunting for tomatoes idly on a nearby grow table. Curly liked tomatoes, as did Sniffles and Cisco. Breakfast had been a rushed affair. Curly was ready for more. He ate a small greenish-orange tomato as he continued his search for the ripe ones, so rare this time of year.

Cisco emerged from the air lock and removed her helmet. She was breathing heavily from the effort of pressurizing the air lock, but happy. She wasn't sure which of the Things took her place with Porter. It was hard to distinguish among the suited and helmeted explorers who wore the same sized exo-suits, although she did observe that Scooter walked differently than Scar. Cisco hadn't noticed that before. Porter closed the air lock door, and the process began again with whichever Thing was with him.

It took nearly two hours for the six explorers to get their turns outside the greenhouse. Their suits were piled neatly on the ground near the air lock with their gloves and helmets. Porter indicated he was going to take a nap and suggested everyone rest, eat, and evacuate and urinate in time for departure when the sun was high in the sky.

Scar worked with Helper to prepare an early meal. He was too excited to sleep. As she stoked the fire and put ingredients into the soup, she told Scar about her strange feelings earlier in the day when Scooter had approached. "I want you to be mine," she said quietly. "I like you. You are brave and strong and smart and thoughtful. I like the way that you smell."

Scar was pleased and surprised by Helper's confession. "I want you too, Helper," he said earnestly. "I have wanted to be near you for as long as I can remember. You are smart and kind and make me laugh and feed me well. When I'm with you, I am happy. When I am away from you, I think about the next time I will see you. I'm glad that you like me too."

They stopped what they were doing and looked at one another for a long moment. Scar smiled, put down the corn he had been peeling, and stepped toward Helper. He buried his face in her hair, filling his nose with her scent, bent down and gently licked the side of her neck. A thrill ran down Helper's back and her cheeks burned. She embraced him, holding him tightly against her. Soup could wait. For a few moments, there was nothing in the universe but Helper and Scar in one another's arms.

CHAPTER 31 – The Excursion

At noon, the excited party began to assemble. Not wanting to seem too anxious, they didn't don their suits right away, but instead loitered near Delta's air lock, exchanging stories about their adventures earlier in the day.

Porter arrived, carrying a graphene bundle that he laid out on the ground.

"We don't know what we are going to find, so I have assembled this kit," he said. "I wanted to show you what I had and see if you could think of anything else we should bring."

The bundle contained a hammer, a chisel, a metal water bottle, screwdrivers, wrenches, several exo-suit patches, seven air canisters, and elements of the first aid kit.

"Should we bring some wire and a solar cell?" asked Thing1. "All of the suits were fully charged this morning, but we might need power."

"Good idea, fetch them," Porter said. "Anything else?"

"What about a lever, Uncle Porter?" Thing2 offered. "In case we have to lift anything heavy. And maybe a rope and a blockentackle."

"Ah, clever!" said Porter with enthusiasm. "In the Charlie receiving area with the tools there is a breaker bar—a steel bar over a meter long with a pointy part at one end and a prying part at the other. That would help as a lever if we find stuck doors. Go fetch that and your ropes and pulleys, '2."

Thing2 jogged off, his black mass of hair vibrating with each stride.

"Should we bring a barrel or cart or bag to carry things we discover that we want to bring back?" asked Cisco.

"Excellent idea. That might be the best way to carry everything we want to take with us without encumbering our hands. Get the cart from the receiving area." Porter watched the tall blonde and smiled as she trotted away. He hadn't seen this much running since they were toddlers.

Scooter said, "I noticed when we were outside that the solar cells along the greenhouse wall were dusty. Should we wipe them off as we pass them, or should we do that another time?"

"I'm hoping we don't have to go this way again anytime soon, so taking a few moments to clean them is a good idea. I noticed that the batteries weren't charging as fast as they used to, and I assumed they were just getting old. I hadn't thought that dust might be reducing the efficiency of the solar cells. Let's each take a bit of graphene and wipe them as you suggest."

"What about the greenhouse itself, Uncle Porter?" Pancho asked. "Surely the dust blocks some of the sun needed for the plants. Should we wipe that off too while we are outside?"

"A good idea, Pancho, but I think that will take more time than we should invest right now. We should schedule maintenance out there soon, but doing that quickly and efficiently may take some planning. Let's focus on getting to Bravo for now. Spending a few minutes dusting off the solar cells as we pass is too big an opportunity to miss. Although taking a minute to dust off the lower panels of Delta and Charlie to improve the view for folks inside the greenhouse would be a good idea. Can you do that as we pass?"

"I will," said Pancho.

Scar felt embarrassed. Everyone had good ideas about what to bring, but he could think of nothing. "I'll help Pancho with that," he offered.

"Perfect," said Porter encouragingly. "You two can be a team. We should assign buddies anyway."

As the others returned, Porter assigned them to teams of two: Thing1 and Cisco, Thing2 and Scooter, Pancho and Scar.

"I want you each to tether to your buddy and be responsible for monitoring their status. This way no one gets lost in the excitement. Wait to tether until we get into the air lock, or we will be a tangled mess."

"What about you?" Cisco asked, realizing that they were a party of seven.

"I'll tether in with the cart. It is less likely to wander off, so I won't have to work as hard." Porter smiled.

The cart was soon loaded with gear. Thing2 elected to carry the breaker bar, since it was too large to fit easily in the cart. Each person was equipped with a fragment of graphene for wiping down the solar panels, and several fragments to wrap their feet before putting on their suits. While the expedition suited up, Porter went into the air lock and returned with two extra helmets. One, he placed in the cart. The other, he handed to Red, saying, "Red, you will be our home base monitor. You will be able to hear what we say on the radio and you can relay it to the others here in the greenhouse. I don't want you to talk unless there is an emergency here, but you can listen, and you all will know what is going on."

Red, who had been quite disappointed at being excluded from the day's excitement, was clearly pleased to have communication duty. He smiled at Porter and handed him his gloves and helmet after Porter donned his exo-suit.

The seven explorers checked their gear and stowed their extra air canisters. At Porter's example, they closed their faceplates and turned on their communications.

"Comm check. If you can hear me, raise your hand," Porter said in their ears. He looked to Red, whose hand was also in the air. "Okay, ladies and gentlemen, let's begin Phase 1—our journey to close the damn Charlie air lock door!" They shuffled into the air lock, pushing the cart with them.

"Tether up," said Porter as he sealed the air lock door. The air lock was near its capacity with seven exo-suited team members plus the cart. It reminded Porter why tethering was so unpopular.

"Beginning depressurization. I'll take it halfway and stop for a minute. Check your suit and check your buddy's suit. When I call your name, let me know you are okay. Pancho?"

"Okay."

"Scar?"

"Okay."

Three minutes later, the seven of them lowered their sun visors and emerged from the air lock. As he sealed the door, Pancho and Scar quickly wiped off the air lock windows. Then they turned, and the group circled right and hugged Delta's south wall. Porter pushed the cart slowly beside Delta while the Things, Scooter, and Cisco swept the dust from the solar panel array. Scar and Pancho brushed dust from the windows they could reach. The dust cleared quickly and easily, not slowing their pace as much as navigating the tethers among them seemed to.

The team traversed the hundred meters of Delta in ten minutes. Bravo loomed large ahead of them. Charlie went slightly faster, now that a routine had been established. All the while, faces peered at them smiling through the greenhouse windows, pacing them until they got to the windows outside the Charlie receiving area.

"Okay," laughed Porter, "our objective is about forty meters that way." He pointed north, through Charlie toward the air lock door. "But let's take the scenic route. Bravo, here we come!"

They walked beyond the view of their greenhouse spectators, everyone inside pressing against the glass to catch final glimpses of the exo-suited Martians as they continued on their way.

Bravo was a hundred meters west of their current position and extended fifty meters south. As they walked past the end of Charlie, they could now see what they had always imagined, but only Porter had seen before: the southwest portion of *New Rome* Station. Although they had grown up seeing the southeastern part of the station out of Charlie's north windows, seeing the station naked just a few steps away was a strange experience. Several of them had noticed how detailed the station was when it wasn't being observed through dusty polarized glass. Faint shadows could be seen within dark-tinted windows.

Porter noticed their pace slowing and appreciated what this might mean to them. "That is where you were born, just inside those walls. We have always been just a few steps away. Come on now—let me show you what it looks like from the inside."

Porter smiled, noting that the pace doubled.

It seemed silly. Although his charges wouldn't recognize it, they were only walking a little over a hundred meters farther. Even with the clumsy cart and the bulky suits slowing progress, it only took a minute or so to reach the Bravo air lock.

As they approached, Porter examined Bravo critically. From a construction perspective, Bravo was identical to Charlie and Delta. There were some minor modifications inside, but from the outside, they should have been identical. Where the glass of Charlie and Delta was slightly discolored by dust, the glass of Bravo appeared black with a patina of red dust. Something wasn't right.

The air lock appeared normal from the outside, and Porter was pleased to see that it was pressurized. He was not surprised, but disappointed to see that there was no power. He made a lesson of operating the air lock manually from the outside.

“The good news is that there is pressure inside, but that means we can’t open the door yet. Why?”

“Because we need to have the same pressure inside the lock as where we are coming from?” said Scooter tentatively.

“Very good. So now we unfortunately must vent the air lock. If there was power, we could save the atmosphere from inside by pumping it into the greenhouse like we did when we exited Delta. This is emergency operation of the air lock without power, so we have to waste some atmosphere.” Porter opened the valve and what looked like steam silently billowed out of the vent and dispersed. When the pressure had equalized, Porter closed the valve, unsealed the door, and swung it open so the group could enter.

“Good news!” Porter announced, pointing at a gauge on the far wall. “Bravo has pressure. Make room for Scar to manually repressurize the air lock. He wins the prize for doing it fastest this morning.”

As Scar got into position, Porter had a thought. “Cisco, this air lock should be fully stocked. Why don’t you grab seven more air canisters and give everyone an extra? The rest of you need to remember that there are air canisters, exo-suits, and a first aid kit here. I don’t want to fully deplete any of the air locks’ supplies, as they are stored here for emergencies—but I think we are in the middle of a long slow emergency right now, so we’ll take a few things that we might need later.”

Scooter and Thing2 were nearest the door between the air lock and Bravo.

“Scooter, can you see anything through the air lock window?” asked Porter.

“From the outside, it looked like the greenhouse glass was black, but from here it looks like a very dark green and black,” Scooter offered. “And there are strange patterns.”

“It looks like ice,” added Thing2, recalling the strange patterns they had observed in puddles of water seasons ago when they reentered Delta after letting it freeze.

"Ah… no power," thought Porter out loud. "No power, no heat."

"I don't remember seeing solar panels along the wall as we walked up," said Thing1.

"Bravo relied upon the main power grid," Porter said, remembering. "I think it might also get auxiliary power from the field of solar panels to the west, but it wasn't set up to be independent like Charlie and Delta. I asked the engineers to set up Charlie and Delta the way they were as an experiment. I wanted to prove that we could build and operate greenhouses independent of the power grid. I figured if I could demonstrate they could be independent most of the time, it would get me permission to build more greenhouses faster."

Scar was pedaling steadily. He couldn't tell if it got harder to pedal as the pressure increased, or if he was just getting tired. His labored breathing could be heard through the comm.

"Just a minute or so more," Porter observed. "I promise, we'll have someone else pressurize the next one."

Scar laughed. "Just as I'm getting good at it?"

When the pressure was equalized, Porter said dramatically, "Ladies and gentlemen, welcome to Bravo." As he said this, he unlocked the door and pushed against it, but the door didn't budge. He sealed it and unsealed it again. No movement. Nothing.

"This is strange," Porter said, puzzled.

"Should we use the lever?" asked Thing2, still carrying the breaker bar.

"I would hate to damage the air lock by forcing it," said Porter. "It might make it hard to seal in the future."

"Should we go around the station to the East air lock?" Scar asked.

"Let's go west and see if we can tell what might be blocking the door through the window. Probably should have done that before we came in," said

Porter. "We have been out about twenty minutes. Does everyone have at least one hundred minutes of air left?"

"I have seventy-eight minutes," Scar said.

"Ah… you were pedaling pretty hard. That predicted duration might increase a bit now that you aren't exerting yourself. You should have two spares, ones we came with and the one Cisco just passed out. Keep an eye on it. Anyone else below a hundred?" Porter paused for a response. Hearing none, he said, "Sorry, Scar, your work was apparently for nothing."

Porter sealed the inner air lock door and vented the pressure that Scar had worked so hard to build up, then he opened the outer air lock door and the group emerged into the glare of the midday sun. Once they were organized and their tethers clear, they swung right, heading clockwise around Bravo.

Dust and dirt were piled nearly two meters high along the west side of Bravo. There was no sign of a solar array in the dust field.

"The solar panels must have been buried," Porter said. He waved his arm across the flat expanse west of Bravo. "It was over there, if I remember correctly. Wait here. Let me see if I can find any signs of it." He took the breaker bar from Thing2 and moved tentatively forward into the smooth dust field.

They watched him move slowly west, probing the dust with the breaker bar, his calf-high white boots disappearing under the fine powder with each step.

Scooter looked at the steep pile of dust against the west wall and probed it with her glove. A cascade of powder responded to her touch, sliding away from the window and rolling down the two meter "slope."

"This pile isn't solid," she said, continuing to disturb the tallest parts of the heap. Then, with one sweep of her hand, a meter-wide section of the dust mound collapsed and cascaded down the pile.

"Look! The windows aren't as dark here," she said. "We can see inside."

Porter had stopped walking when she spoke and began heading back toward Bravo. "What can you see?" he asked.

Thing2 struggled to climb the mound in his bulky boots to take a look and sank quickly to his waist as the slope collapsed upon him and pushed him off balance and onto his bottom. "Hey!" he exclaimed in surprise.

Pancho and Scooter each grabbed an arm and lifted Thing2 from the mound. "This is no time to play," Pancho chided. The mound collapsed further as they pulled Thing2 from it.

"This is almost like snow," Porter said as he approached.

"What's 'snow'?" Scar asked.

"That stuff you 'dash through in a one coarse opens lay'," offered Cisco, remembering the song they sang before the New Year.

Porter chuckled. "On Earth, sometimes the water in the atmosphere freezes and falls from the sky as delicate white ice crystals. They are very light and if it stays cold enough, they can stack up very tall, but they are mostly air. If you try to step on them, like Thing2 did, you compress the air out of them, and they smash down a lot. Can you see anything through the window, Scooter?"

"The windows are dirty and it's hard to make it out, but I think—grow tables!" she said in recognition. "But it's really dark and it looks like the plants are dead. There's something dark green or black covering nearly all of the glass."

"But not as much on the glass where the dust was covering the windows," Scar observed.

Porter walked up to the wall. "It looks like moss and maybe mold took over Bravo. Mosses are a kind of plant that we don't eat. I had a lot of different plant species in Bravo. When I stopped tending it, the mosses must have overpowered everything else."

"What is that gray stuff on the floor by the air lock?" asked Scooter.

"It looks like a big gray slab. Funny, no moss or mold on it. It's ICE!" said Porter with excitement. "That's why we couldn't open the door. There is a sheet of ice covering the floor. It must be holding the door closed."

"So, we are back to needing power," said Thing1. "If we turn on the power, are there grow lamps in Bravo that will warm it?"

"There should be, if they are still working," Porter answered.

"That brings us back to the solar array. Even if we find it, how can we remove the dust from it?" asked Pancho. "How big is the array?"

"It was a large array, about four times the size of the one south of Delta. It was a series of metal frames with the panels attached. There were probably a dozen frames with a dozen panels each. It looks like they are under a lot of dust. Even if the dust is very light, it's hard to imagine how we can remove it all."

"Maybe if we can find the frames, we could lift them out of the dust?" asked Cisco.

"I'm afraid it took several men and an electric goat to put the arrays in place," Porter began, but then interrupted himself. "And we have seven of us, and Thing2's lever. We can probably do this. We just need to find the structures."

"How were they cabled to the station?" asked Thing1. "If we can find the cable, it should lead us to the array."

"Good idea, '1. I don't remember, exactly," said Porter. "I don't think the array was in place when they built Alpha. That's the one you can see just down there." He pointed further down the structure that was Bravo. Bravo was the size of Charlie and Delta, about one hundred meters long, and covered with dark glass. Beyond one hundred meters the opaque glass ended and clear glass began. From here, Alpha appeared about half the length of Bravo.

"I noticed that the solar array south of Delta went through Delta's wall near the connection with Charlie," Thing1 said. "Maybe we could start looking there?"

Without warning, it suddenly became distinctly darker.

"Blowout!" said Cisco, pointing to the west, where a huge column of dust and debris was silently and violently headed skyward and beginning to block out the sun. The blowout was only forty meters from where they stood. She could feel the rumbling through the soles of her boots. Cisco had never seen a blowout this close. It was beautiful.

"Everyone move to your buddy! Grab him if you can!" yelled Porter.

The massive rising cloud of dust and debris began to decelerate. The more solid chunks began to fall back toward the ground. The large rocks—some as big as the cart—fell first, landing near the mouth of the blowout and raising their own clouds of dust as they struck. Then the rock strikes began moving outward from the blowout, coming toward them, followed closely by a thick expanding dust cloud. As the circle of falling debris moved closer, the rocks got smaller, soon becoming the size of helmets, slamming silently into the dust. When the maelstrom reached them, the largest rocks were the size of oranges and the dust from the blowout and the dust raised by the falling rock combined to reduce visibility to zero. It was as if they were submerged in muddy brown water with only dim light filtering from above as rocks and gravel pummeled them.

Scooter and Thing2 had been side by side when Cisco called out. When Porter yelled, they crouched with their backs to Bravo's wall as dust covered them and rocks made irregular sounds—*tik… CRACK… tik… tik… THUMP*—against their helmets and pounded their bodies through their exo-suits.

Cisco had been ten meters from Thing1 when she had seen the blowout from the corner of her eye and turned, fascinated to watch the rising column. When she registered Porter's shouted instructions, she turned and closed the distance to Thing1 in a few bounds. Her momentum knocked them both from their feet and onto the ground in a tangle.

Scar had been walking toward Alpha when the ominous shadow cast its shade. When Cisco called out, he turned and watched in silent wonder at the mass of dust and rock being thrown silently skyward. When his awestruck brain processed Porter's command and he turned to look for Pancho, but wasn't sure which of the exo-suited companions in the swirling dust was his buddy. An instant later the cloud of debris engulfed him, rocks pelting him and bouncing off of his helmet. He fought back rising panic from the disorienting chaos obscuring his vision. In vain he turned left and right, hoping for better visibility. He stumbled and fell forward into the powder, smashing his chest hard into something under the dust.

A cacophonous mix of voices and cries came over the comm link, punctuated and made further indecipherable by the clatter of rocks against helmets being broadcast through microphones.

CHAPTER 32 –

Confusion in Charlie

Red had been monitoring the transmissions from Charlie, self-importantly relaying the group's progress to the others through the open faceplate of the helmet. Suddenly, he went silent, a puzzled look on his face that bloomed into panic.

"What is it, Red?" Helper asked.

Red didn't seem to hear her and started yelling into the comm link, fear cracking his voice. "Is everyone okay? What happened? What's going on? Is everyone all right? Do you need help? What happened? *Are you okay*?"

He paused briefly and strained to listen but couldn't make out anything in the jumble of sound.

"*Red*!" Helper snapped, grabbing his shoulders and placing herself in the center of his field of vision. "Tell us what is going on."

"They were looking under some dust for the solar array that feeds Bravo, then Cisco yelled 'blowout' and Porter said they should grab their buddies and now everyone is screaming and there's a bunch of noises…" Red said breathlessly.

Helper had never seen Red so afraid. The thought of something happening to the party had seemed abstract.

Red yelled, "Porter, are you okay? Anyone? Are you all right? Someone say something!"

Helper realized that the most important thing she could do now was to calm Red. "Red, take a breath," she said. She looked into Red's eyes, trying to show him a calm she wasn't sure she believed herself.

Red resisted her ministrations for a moment, resenting her composure. Then he realized he was contributing to the confusion. He nodded at Helper, then took a breath and listened.

Helper turned to the group. "Mary and Curly, go get two small suits from the air lock in case they need help."

Red's anxiety had been contagious. Everyone had been watching in nervous silence. Curly jumped up and bolted toward the air lock. It took Mary a moment longer to register Helper's instructions, then she turned and ran to catch up with Curly.

Helper turned back to Red. "Any word?"

CHAPTER 33 –
Man Down

"QUIET!" Porter boomed.

The cacophony of voices on the comm subsided, but the staccato clatter of rocks and debris against helmets still cluttered the channel.

"Porter! Is everyone okay?" Red implored. "We were so worried!"

"Red, I need you to be quiet too," Porter said in a normal voice. "None of us can see right now. We are in the middle of a dust cloud. Be quiet and listen. I'll let you know if we need anything from you.

"If you are with your buddy, find their hand and squeeze it once if you are okay," Porter said. He paused a few seconds, then asked, "Is anyone *not* touching their buddy? If you aren't touching your buddy, say your name."

"Scar."

"Pancho."

"So, your buddy is accounted for, you guys just aren't together. Are you both okay?" Porter asked.

"I'm okay," said Pancho. "Just a little beat up by the rocks."

"I got my foot stuck and fell," said Scar. "I hurt my ankle, but I'm... *wait*! My helmet display says I'm out of air!"

"Don't panic, Scar. Pancho, follow your tether to Scar and be careful not to trip over him. Scar, check your suit pressure. Is it stable or dropping?"

"Pressure is stable."

"Okay. I suspect your air canister was damaged or dislodged. Remember, you have enough air in your suit for a couple of minutes. Relax. Breathe slowly. I want you to lie down on your back and wait for Pancho. We have plenty of time. Don't panic."

"How about the rest of you—report and keep it short. Cisco, are you and Thing1 okay?"

"Yes."

"Scooter, you and Thing2?"

"Yes."

"Check your helmet displays. Only answer if you have a problem. Does anyone else have less than sixty minutes of air or are you losing pressure?"

Silence.

"Okay, I'm hoping this dust will disperse in a minute and we will be able to see again. Everyone but Pancho, stay where you are. I don't want you to move until we can see and get oriented. I don't want you to wander into the blowout area like I almost did."

Pancho was listening to Porter while struggling to follow the tether to Scar. It was hard to feel the cord through his thick gloves and the dark brown dust made vision useless. The tether played out easily from the spool at his belt, so there was little tension. He thought to wrap the cord around one of his hands to eliminate the play from his own spool, but it was still hard to figure out what direction the cord went. He hoped he wasn't heading for the blowout. He tried to use his other hand to feel which way the tether went but had no success. Then he had an idea. "Scar, grab your tether and pull me to you."

A minute later, Pancho announced, "I've found him!"

"Feel his chest where the air canister should be," Porter instructed. "If it's there, remove it. If it's not there, you are going to replace it."

"I don't feel it," Pancho said.

"Okay. Remember we all have a couple of spares. Take one of your spares and hold it firmly. This is a little challenging to do in the dark, but the important thing is not to drop it. Don't stress. You have backups. How are you doing, Scar?"

"I'm okay. I'm trying to breathe slowly, but my body wants to breathe faster."

"Stay calm, Scar. You will be okay. Pancho, find the brackets that hold the air canister, and make sure you can feel the top and bottom bracket. Let me know when you find them."

"Okay, I've got the top of the bracket … I can't find—oh, wait, there it is. Okay, I've found the brackets."

"The canister has a seam around its middle. Slide your glove along the canister to the seam. The canister on one side of the seam is bigger than the other, do you remember? The big side is the top of the canister and it goes into the bracket closest to Scar's head, then you rotate the bottom of the canister into the bottom bracket. You do that now and ask me if you have any questions."

"I don't feel the seam!" Pancho said anxiously.

"You will, Pancho. Be patient. It's not quite halfway."

Scar's labored panting was audible over the comm link.

"I think I have it!" Pancho announced. "Top first, right?"

"That's right. Top first, then it swivels into the bottom bracket and locks," Porter assured him. "Hang in there, Scar. You have several minutes you can pant before this gets serious. Try to stay calm."

No sound but panting. Seconds passed.

"I think that got it," said Pancho. "How are you doing, Scar?"

In between pants, Scar said, "Helmet says… one hundred fifty … minutes of … oxygen."

"Give it a minute to circulate. You are going to be fine. Good work, Pancho. That's hard to do in the dark without practice."

"We are going to wait for this dust to settle, then continue. Everyone take a minute and review your status. I'll check in with you one by one."

CHAPTER 34 –

Taking Stock

Scooter and Thing2 sat silently with their backs to the dust mounds against Bravo's west wall. They were still holding hands, periodically squeezing or moving their gloved fingers to remind one another that they weren't alone. Neither could see anything. The combination of bruises from the rocks, scratchy uncomfortable exo-suits, and complete lack of vision through the faceplates of their helmets was terrifying. Their only comfort was that they were together. They both seemed to sense this, and the limited contact through their gloves was reassuring.

Listening to Scar's ordeal, particularly his panting before it subsided, made Scooter acutely aware of her own breathing. She was drawing deep and slow breaths. Her knee had been struck sharply in the darkness. With her free hand she tried to explore the injury, but the bulky gloves and the thick fabric of the pressurized suit made blunt tools for probing and all she could do was confirm that it hurt. Gingerly, she tried to extend her leg. She felt pain, but thought it was probably manageable.

Thing2 squeezed Scooter's right hand with his left. His right hand was damaged; it had been smashed by something—probably a rock—as he sat next to the wall. His fingers throbbed. He didn't think he could move them. He pictured himself back in Charlie, outside of this oppressive suit in the cool air, still holding Scooter's hand. He gave her hand a squeeze, meaning to say, "I'm right here. I'm still here. I'm glad you're here with me."

Cisco had collided hard with Thing1. When they stopped rolling, she felt numerous small painful strikes and two significant blows as heavy debris struck the back of her thigh and the left side of her torso from behind. She thought her thigh was probably just bruised. The back of her ribs hurt when she breathed deeply. When the confusion began to abate, she realized she was on top of Thing1. She rolled off him, surprised that he had not tried harder to wriggle out from under. When she found his hand and squeezed, she was pleased that he squeezed back, but his response was delayed and weak. She wanted to ask if he was okay but knew to wait until Pancho and Scar had sorted out their emergency.

The violent collision with Cisco completely knocked the air out of Thing1. As they tumbled, her shoulder or knee had struck him with force just below his rib cage. He couldn't speak or breathe for several moments. Combined with the cries and rumble of clutter on the comm link, Thing1 thought everyone was dying. He wanted to call out but had nothing in his lungs to expel and couldn't make a sound. Initially, Cisco's body pinned his weakly writhing frame to the ground, and he spent about a minute disoriented, claustrophobic, panicked, in agony, and unable to breathe. As he slowly regained the ability to pull small puffs of air, Cisco had rolled off and found his hand and squeezed it as Porter instructed. In his world of pain and fear and darkness, her squeeze was the only indication that there was anything beyond the dark brown void of his helmet. It took him a beat to register that, and another to be reassured by it—then he belatedly offered her the same reassurance. As Porter directed Pancho to Scar's assistance, Thing1 slowly recovered both physically and mentally from the trauma. He interlaced his gloved fingers with Cisco so that he could better feel her presence and struggled through the receding ache in his chest to breathe more deeply and evenly. Maybe he wasn't going to die.

"How are you doing, Pancho?" came Porter's voice over the comm.

"I'm okay. I don't like this darkness. I can't see anything, not even the outline of the sun from where I am." The shaking in Pancho's voice underscored his discomfort.

"How about you, Scar?" Porter asked.

"Breathing is fine. I might have found the solar array; I think that's what I tripped over when I hurt my ankle. Thing1 said the cable might be a clue and I walked a few steps toward Alpha to see if I could spot the cable coming out of Bravo. When Cisco called the blowout, I turned to look but didn't stop walking. I wedged my boot under something and fell. I think my ankle is okay. I can wiggle it a bit. It hurts but it doesn't hurt like a broken bone." Scar recalled the pain of his broken arm from years before quite vividly. His ankle was annoying but wasn't screaming messages to his brain like his arm had.

"Good job finding the array." Porter chuckled over the comm link. "Be careful with that ankle. Broken bones have different severities based on the size of the bone and how badly it is broken, from cracked to shattered. Your arm a couple years back was particularly spectacular, the way it poked through the skin and all. Ugh. You know, of all the messes you guys made when you were little that I had to clean up, setting and dressing that arm of yours was the hardest thing I ever had to do. I was elated when Mary and Sniffles took over most of the doctoring. I don't much care for blood."

"Cisco?"

"I took a hard hit to my back and it hurts when I breathe deeply, but I think I'm okay," she answered.

"Thing1?"

"Okay now," Thing1 whispered weakly. "When Cisco tackled me, something hit me under my ribs. I couldn't breathe at all for a while, but I'm getting better."

"Sounds like you got hit in the solar plexus, a bundle of nerves at the base of the diaphragm muscles that work your lungs. That's happened to me before and it is not fun. Incapacitating blow—kind of like getting kicked in the testicles. Glad you are recovering."

"Thing2?"

"I'm with Pancho. I don't like this darkness. Something smashed my right hand and some of my fingers aren't working right now. Hand is throbbing. Otherwise, I guess I'm okay."

"Does your hand feel wet?" Porter asked. "If you have bones sticking through the skin, young man, I will definitely make Mary and Sniffles tend to you!" His tone said he was only partly serious about the last.

"Not wet. You probably don't have anything to worry about, uncle," Thing2 said.

"How about you, Scooter?" Porter asked.

"Something hit my knee, but I can still bend it. I think I'm okay," she replied.

There was a moment of silence, then Cisco asked, "What about you, Uncle Porter? Are you okay?"

"A little battered by falling rocks, but it sounds like you guys got the worst of it," Porter answered. "I'm sure glad Scooter called me over to look in Bravo's window. If I had kept walking towards that spot where the blowout happened, it would have been bad news. I feel silly that I didn't recognize the signs. The piles of dust should have been a clue. Can anyone see the outline of the sun from where you are?"

"We have our backs to the walls of Bravo," said Scooter. "We can't see the sun, but we can make out the shadow of Bravo behind us."

"Try raising your sun visor," Porter said. "Maybe getting rid of the filter will help."

Scooter began laughing, joined a moment later by Thing2. "Our visors were covered with dust. There's still a dust cloud, but we can see through the haze without our sun visors down."

Moments later, the expedition had regrouped. They had been separated by no more than thirty meters. Everyone and everything were covered with red dust. Clouds of red still swirled around them. Scar and Scooter were limping. Thing1 had taken the breaker bar from his brother, who was instinctively holding his right hand close to his body.

Scar had indeed found the leading edge of the solar array. Thing1 found the cable leading from the array to a box on the wall with a metal cover where Bravo joined Alpha. Inside were several dark indicator lights and switches that controlled whether power was routed toward the main station power grid, or Bravo's battery bank, or neither. Currently, the switches were set to route power to the main grid. Thing1 conferred with Porter, and they changed the switches to route power to Bravo, hoping the batteries would take the charge. They spent several minutes clearing dust away from a few solar panels, while Cisco monitored the power indicators for signs of life. The dust cloud was finally settling. When they had cleared half a dozen panels, Cisco announced that the panels were generating measurable amounts of power.

Porter polled the group and, apart from Scar with his fresh canister, they each had about an hour of air left. "Let's clear a dozen more panels and call it a day," Porter suggested. "Hopefully that will generate enough power over a few days to begin raising the temperature in Bravo. Meanwhile, we can head back home with stories to tell."

No one disagreed with Porter's proposal. They attacked the dusty panels with renewed enthusiasm despite their various injuries. A few minutes later the dust-covered, bedraggled expedition was limping east toward Delta, Porter in the rear still pushing the cart laden with the booty from Bravo's air lock.

CHAPTER 35 – Aftermath

Upon their return, everyone gathered to hear the story of the excursion to Bravo and the blowout retold from each adventurer's perspective. During his turn, Porter commended Pancho for his calmness under pressure in helping Scar. Mary and Sniffles did their best to administer first aid to the injured while the stories were told, but the wounds weren't like the scrapes and cuts they were used to treating, so assistance was mostly limited to gentle hands and kind words.

When the retelling was done, Porter suggested they wait a week to give the wounded explorers a chance to heal and see if their ministrations to the solar array might yet allow them to access the station through Bravo. He said if there were no signs of progress in heating Bravo after a week, the next expedition would try to get into the station through the East air lock, near the area affected by the fire.

The group dispersed while Helper made final preparations for dinner, the weary adventurers nursing physical and emotional trauma and seeking solace where it could be found.

Cisco knew she couldn't be part of the next expedition when she needed help getting out of her exo-suit. The blow to Cisco's back appeared to have cracked or broken at least one of her ribs. Several dark blue bruises were revealed as they carefully removed the suit, with a particularly large and nasty one on the left side of her back. She complained that deep breathing hurt, and she didn't like having her bruise touched even by Sniffles's tender probing hands. The first aid book said there wasn't much to be done but protect the area from further damage and seek medical help immediately. Sniffles and Mary found the instructions amusing.

Mary insisted that Porter relieve Cisco of work duties while she mended, and Porter agreed over Cisco's protestations. Pancho assured Cisco that he and Curly could manage their daily chores without her for a while, leaving Cisco to take it easy and spend time with Helper. Cisco tried to be stoic, but she was bitterly disappointed by her disability. Helper reminded her that everyone had wanted to go with the first group to share the adventure, and everyone wanted to go on the second expedition as well. "The difference for you is that you know what we will be missing."

Cisco sighed and nodded. "It probably wasn't as wonderful as you all imagine, but it was pretty amazing."

Helper brushed Cisco's hair back from her sad eyes and smiled. "Well, I expect you to tell me about it in detail so I can share the experience—without the bruises, thank you."

Thing2's hand was sore and swollen, but not serious. The lighter skin on the palm side of his dark fingers plainly showed bruising from the trauma. Mobility began returning soon after they got back to Delta, and his focus quickly shifted to Scooter's discomfort. Scooter's knee had a lump the size of an orange and a nasty dark bruise under her light brown skin. Porter suggested Thing2 team up with Pancho and gather cold rocks from outside Delta's air lock to fashion a cold compress to cool Scooter's knee and relieve some of her pain and swelling. The bond between Thing2 and Scooter had been deepened by their shared experience during the expedition, and he was pleased to have a way to offer her comfort.

They added layers of insulating dirt to the graphene bundle of cold rocks to avoid burning Scooter with the cold, and then slowly removed insulating layers as the rocks warmed. Thing2 held the bundle gently against Scooter's leg, shifting from side to top to side every few minutes to avoid freezing her flesh. Scooter enjoyed the relief offered by the cold nearly as much as she appreciated the attention from Thing2. After a few hours, the swelling had subsided a bit, and Thing2 alternated between gently massaging Scooter's knee and applying cold.

Scar walked with a bit of a limp from his twisted ankle, but his gait was steadily improving. He felt foolish that he had fallen and was the only person who had required help. He hoped that it wouldn't disqualify him from the next expedition to check Bravo.

Red tried to cheer him up. "I was listening to the whole thing. I think you did great. You kept calm. I don't know if I could have done so well, particularly when you started panting. That was scary. It isn't your fault that your air got knocked away. I'm just glad no one got hurt worse."

Scar had been surprised when he learned that Helper had been poised to launch a rescue effort and encouraged that the others were prepared to act so swiftly in the face of so much chaos and uncertainty. "You didn't think we were going to leave you out there, did you?" Helper teased. "You're mine now. I can't have you putting down roots outside the greenhouse without me."

Pancho felt fortunate to have escaped the ordeal unscathed. He assumed that he would be part of the next party because he had no wounds to heal. When he explained the confusion in the dark and how difficult it was to feel the tether and follow it to Scar, Ginger said, “It was clever of you to have Scar pull you to him. That was keeping your head in an emergency.”

Mary, however, was unimpressed. “I think any of us would have done the same, Ginger.”

“Why can’t you ever appreciate it when someone else does something smart?” Ginger snarled. “You are quick to criticize, but never seem to appreciate hard work or insights! If Pancho hadn’t kept his cool under pressure, Scar might have been in real trouble.”

Mary looked shocked at the rebuke. She stood speechless for a moment, then stormed away.

Pancho was surprised how quickly Ginger had come to his defense. “Thank you,” he said meekly.

“I’m sorry if I hurt her feelings, but she deserved it. I’ll let her pout a bit, then find her and apologize. She can be such a pain.”

Pancho smiled and nodded.

Thing1 explained to Pigpen that while lying on top of him after the blowout, Cisco had shielded his body from the falling debris that had injured her. He was relieved and grateful that his injury had been temporary but felt guilty that Cisco had borne the brunt of the damage. He confided the panic he had felt: “I couldn’t breathe. I thought my suit was broken and it was the vacuum killing me. I was confused and afraid; I thought everyone was going to die. I was worried I would never see anyone again. Never see you again. It was terrible.”

They were sitting on the ground in Charlie, away from the others near the gently buzzing beehive. Tears welled in Thing1's eyes and sadness came over him as he relived the terror of the moment, and he began to sob softly and shiver. Pigpen pulled him to her and put his head on her lap. She soothed his fuzzy hair, gently rocking him and singing the song Porter used to comfort them when they were hurt or afraid. "Baby, baby, baby…" she cooed repeatedly, soothing music to Thing1's ears. Soon, his tears stopped. The sadness left him. He became calm. Peaceful. Lost in her crooning. Then he was asleep, breathing slowly and evenly while Pigpen continued her gentle lullaby and stroked his head.

CHAPTER 36 –
The Second Expedition

"Porter! Everyone! The lights are on in Bravo!"

It was past sundown on the evening of the first excursion, and Thing2 was lumbering into the Charlie receiving area in an exo-suit without a helmet. He explained excitedly as he approached, "Pancho and I were getting more rocks for Scooter's knee and we could see a glow through the dark glass in Bravo. Little bits of light poking through."

"Excellent news, '2," said Porter. "We'll give Scooter's knee a few more days to heal, and Bravo's grow lights and heaters a few more days to warm up Bravo and melt the ice, then we will make another attempt."

The days crawled.

Four days later, the swelling in Scooter's knee had subsided and her limp was barely noticeable. Thing2 and Pancho stopped going through the air lock to get rocks, but Thing2 continued to massage Scooter's knee regularly.

Finally, the big day arrived. With a disappointed Cisco looking on bravely, the remaining six explorers again donned their exo-suits.

"If we can get into Bravo, that's great," said Porter. "If we can't, we will come back around and try the East air lock." He pointed out the window toward the station to the northwest. "I can't think of a good reason to make two trips, assuming we can avoid getting pelted by rocks this time."

As before, Porter pushed the cart and Thing2 had his breaker bar. Apart from the missing Cisco, the only other difference was that Thing1 was now tethered to Porter. They entered the air lock, checked their equipment one last time, and the second expedition began.

The second expedition moved more efficiently. Being outside of Delta wasn't a novelty. The group moved purposefully toward Bravo, past the solar panels and windows they had dusted a week earlier. It took less than three minutes to cover the three hundred meters to Bravo.

"Good news, Scar! There's power for the air lock," Porter announced as he scanned the display. "Would you do the honors and pressurize it? You guys get in; we'll be back in a minute. '1, let's peek at the solar array first."

As the others filed into the air lock, Porter and Thing1 walked to the west side of Bravo, the scene of their drama a week earlier.

"I still see our footprints in the dust," said Porter. "It doesn't look like there has been much activity. From here the solar panels still look clean as we left them. We were just lucky about timing, I guess. Or maybe tromping around on the ground here spurred the blowout." At Porter's words, Thing1 turned and nimbly scuttled back toward the air lock. Porter smiled and followed.

Porter and Thing1 entered the air lock dragging the cart behind them and sealed the door. "Go for it, Scar," said Porter.

As Scar pressurized the air lock, Porter said, "You guys keep your helmets on until I say it's okay. I'm not sure what kind of chemical processes might have been going on in here before things froze up. The air might not be breathable. Our helmets should warn us if there is a problem, but I want to be extra careful."

When the pressure was stabilized, Porter unlocked and tried to open the inner air lock door to Bravo. It didn't budge.

"Perhaps the ice hasn't all melted?" Scooter offered.

"There might be crud sealing the door shut," said Porter. "I don't know how long there was standing water in Bravo before it froze."

"What about this lever?" said Thing2, offering the breaker bar.

"That's a last resort, '2," said Porter. "If we damage the door, we might not be able to repair it."

"Let's all push," said Scar. "Get in a line and shove."

"Worth a try," Porter agreed.

The six of them lined up closely near the door.

"At the count of three, we all push. Ready?" Bodies swayed in time as Scar counted, "One … two … *three*!"

The mass of bodies crashed into the door and it shifted open a few centimeters, then stopped.

"Yeah!"

"Not through yet," Porter exhorted. "One … two … *three*!"

The door opened a centimeter more.

"Another big push," said Scar. "One … two … *three*!"

This time, there was a dull cracking sound and the door swung wide, depositing their bodies in a heap on the floor in five centimeters of slime-filled standing water and ice.

Laughter filled the comm channel as they flailed to untangle themselves and got their first look at Bravo. Then they were silent.

The disorienting scene in Bravo was strangely familiar, yet very different. As they had learned from looking through the windows on the previous expedition, the glass walls of Bravo were covered with black and green sludge that blocked the sun. Here and there, slivers of light peeked through the darkly covered glass. The gloomy room was also dimly illuminated by grow lights whose radiance was muted by a covering of slime. The water on the floor had chunks of the sludge and ice floating in it.

While the whole of Bravo was the same size as Charlie—a hundred meters long and thirty meters wide—it had been divided into a series of smaller rooms by plastic "walls" that hung from the ceiling with a zippered "door" in the middle of each. The plastic walls were as opaque as the glass walls of the greenhouse. A pile of debris at the base of the nearest plastic wall served as an impromptu dam, forming the shallow pool they were laying, kneeling, and standing in. The grow tables were familiar, but there was nothing growing here … only soil and the remains of dead plants. The plants didn't resemble anything the Martians had seen before. Several stalks reached two or three meters toward the ceiling, roughly surfaced poles as big around as Porter's leg. They had no limbs and ended in clumps of dead broad leaves sticking out from the end.

"This portion of Bravo was set up as a tropical zone." Porter closed the air lock door. "I used it to grow plants that required warm and wet conditions. These palm trees grow in tropical climates on Earth. Let me check the atmosphere."

Porter turned toward the air lock to review the climate monitor, but it was covered in black goo. "It must get warm enough each summer for these molds and mosses to grow without extra heat. They get a growing season and then freeze up and go dormant. Looks like there was enough humidity for them to thrive here." He pawed at the goo on the monitor with his gloves but couldn't make out the display underneath. "The heating and freezing cycle combined with the moisture was probably pretty hard on the electronics. Okay, we have pressure. My helmet says it's okay, but let me confirm this is breathable. You guys stand by."

Porter took a deep breath, exhaled, and opened the faceplate of his helmet. The others watched him closely as he sniffed the air, took a small breath and smiled. "Smells like rotten vegetables but doesn't seem too bad. Give me a minute to ensure there are no bad effects."

Porter took a couple of deep breaths. "I wonder if the monitors in the other rooms are as damaged as this one?" he mused. "You can open your helmets but pay attention. If you start getting dizzy or sleepy, say something."

As they opened their faceplates, Porter said, "Now you know what a swamp smells like—although it's warmer air than this and there's some greenery smells that mix with the decay, so a real swamp is more pleasant."

New smells were a rarity. Apart from Helper's occasional failed food experiments, most everything in Charlie and Delta smelled like ... Charlie and Delta. Scooter saw Thing2 wrinkle his nose and laughed. "It is... *different*," she said.

"There are four rooms. Each was a different climate zone for different kinds of plants. This was the wettest. Let's move to Alpha. I doubt anything survived the cold but keep an eye open for anything green. Grab any tools you see and put them into the cart. I don't imagine we will find much of anything until we get to the receiving area by the Alpha air lock. I try to keep a tidy greenhouse."

"That may have been your intention," said Scar, picking up a bucket and putting it into Thing1's cart, "but there may be useful stuff here just the same."

Porter smiled and nodded. The group moved through the first zippered door into the second chamber. The dead plants were less alien, and the floor was damp, but it had little standing water. The smell of decay was less overpowering. A bit more light got through the moss-caked glass. Scooter put a coiled hose into the cart. Scar added a trowel and a coffee cup.

The third room was like the second, but less plant matter caked on the glass meant more light shone through. The light was still dreary, but it might have been enough to read by even without the artificial lights. Treasures recovered here included pruning shears and a moldy pair of gloves.

When they reached the door to the last room, Porter paused. "There should be tools and seeds we can recover here. If we are lucky, the air lock will be working so we can go into Alpha."

Porter unzipped the door and the team moved through. The receiving area resembled Charlie. Grow tables covered the first two thirds of the room, ending in a work bench with a sink, barrels of chemicals for soil formation, and cabinets.

The glass of the walls and ceiling were darkly streaked with mold and some moss but allowed more light than the prior rooms. The red cast to the light made it apparent that some of the diffusion was probably caused by dust on the glass of the greenhouse.

The air lock had power and the environmental monitor, though covered with dust, seemed to be working. Porter reviewed it.

"The power must have been off for a long time; the computer has forgotten what day it is. The atmosphere here is breathable—but without live plants pulling the carbon dioxide out, it would become toxic to us eventually if we stayed here. If we are going to reclaim this area, we will need to get some plants in here and clean off the glass so they can get sunlight."

Turning his attention to the cabinet, Porter mused, "In my imagination, every tool and seed I've longed for was left in here. Memory is a fragile thing and easily fooled. Let's see what we have…"

The cabinet, like the first meter of the greenhouse walls and the grow tables, had been created from Martian sand by a 3-D printer. Porter opened the bulky doors and took a step back.

Bravo had been his first real office on Mars. He had a work space as soon as the *Numa* had landed, but it was cramped and there was no reason to unpack his gear and his precious seeds because there was no place to plant them. Alpha was nominally a greenhouse, and he'd briefly had a small area to nurse some of his cuttings, but Alpha had been primarily used for aquaculture and water recycling. Bravo was the first real greenhouse and Porter had joyfully begun setting up shop as soon as it was pressurized. He had brought a few yards of soil from Earth so that he could start seedlings right away while he perfected soil development with the inorganic materials of Mars. They had joked that his was the most expensive dirt in the solar system, with a shipment cost that far exceeded its weight in gold. The colonists had brought bulk seeds for staples: corn, rice, wheat, squash, beans, soy, and hundreds of smaller samples and cuttings for a variety of diverse plants so that Porter could determine what would grow best in the Martian environment.

The cuttings were long dead. Many died on the voyage, some failed to root, and the rest were represented by the debris in the growing tables they had walked past this afternoon. The seeds were a different story. Half of the cabinet was filled with carefully packaged and indexed vials of seeds. Porter wondered which of these might have survived the extreme cold and the years.

"I suppose it is unlikely that any of these will grow after so much time, but it should be an interesting experiment. Let me grab a few handfuls we can try to foster in Charlie. The rest will be here when we come back."

Porter thought for a moment, and selected a few vials, reading the labels aloud as he put them into a small box. "Jalapeño pepper, white onion, yellow onion, garlic, mustard, cumin, rosemary, grapes. If we can sprout some of these, we will make Helper a very happy lady, and in turn you will all be in for tasty treats."

Elsewhere in the cabinet was a cup filled with pencils, a magnifying glass, a framed photograph, a computer tablet, vials of seeds, and assorted gardening paraphernalia.

"Leave this stuff for now," Porter said quietly. "We can get it later." He put the box with the selected seed vials, the framed picture of a younger Porter and a woman holding hands, the magnifying glass, and the computer tablet into the canvas bag, and put the bag gently into the cart. "Please be careful not to damage these; they are fragile." Porter sounded sad and distant. A moment passed. Porter closed the cabinet, and with forced enthusiasm said, "Well, then, let's get along to Alpha!"

The air lock was pressurized and the door into it opened easily. Red-tinged daylight came from the window in the far door of the air lock. The group filed in and closed the door behind them.

"There's no pressure in Alpha," Scooter said, looking at a gauge on the wall. Peering through the window, she added, "And it looks like there is red dust on this window."

"Close your helmets. When everyone is thumbs-up, go ahead and depressurize the air lock, '2," Porter instructed.

Once the air was gone from the air lock, the door swung open easily into Alpha. After the gloom of Bravo, the bright glare of unfiltered sunlight made them squint while their vision adjusted to take in the collection of strange, dust-covered objects that cluttered the room. One by one they closed their sun visors to better see what was before them.

Alpha was half the length of Bravo. There were rows of translucent enclosures four meters wide and two meters high that ran the length of Alpha on the west side, away from the station. Between the enclosures were rows of tanks two meters in diameter and five meters high with pipes running between them and the enclosures. The west side and center of Alpha established an expectation of order, but the symmetry was shattered by chaos on the east side near the station.

The roof was gone from most of the east side and sunlight glared through the ragged opening above. The floor on the east had a rough oval hole twenty meters long and four meters wide that started about a third of the way from the far wall and stretched to about the halfway point. The hole was surrounded by what appeared to be broken remnants of greenhouse ceiling and the same types of tanks and enclosures found on the west. The nearest edge of the hole was raised up nearly a meter, as if a giant poked a stick through the roof and into the floor at an angle. Where the floor was visible between the nearest edge of the hole and the wall behind them, it was broken and deeply cracked, littered with shattered slabs of translucent glass and shards of tanks in various sizes from pebbles to chunks larger than Porter. Martian soil could be seen a meter below the hole in the floor.

There was enough debris between the nearest end of the hole and the wall with the air lock to suggest that the east side had once matched the west, before the giant's stick had violently rearranged that side of the room. Everything was covered with a thick layer of red dust.

"Wow. What happened here?" asked Scar. "Is this what caused the accident on Smoky Rescue Day?"

"I don't think so," Porter said as he moved cautiously toward the hole for a better look. "My guess would be a meteorite."

"How big would a falling rock have to be to make a hole this big?" asked Thing2, closing the air lock door behind them.

"Not very big if it were traveling fast enough," said Porter. "Remember we talked about kinetic energy being a product of mass and velocity? With so little atmosphere to slow it down, whatever hit here could have been traveling several kilometers per second. It could have been the size of your fist. It must have been something to see. These tanks were all filled with water and water plants and fish. Without power, it would have been frozen. As soon as the roof depressurized, the water in the ice would have slowly boiled away."

The party swung left around the debris and moved toward Alpha's receiving area.

Beyond the empty enclosures along the east wall forty meters ahead they could see another air lock. It went at a right angle into the station, like the

Charlie air lock. Debris covered much of the floor, and Porter and Thing1 fell behind the group as they struggled to maneuver the small cart through the mess.

"Colonists!" exclaimed Scooter, as they got closer to the receiving area. She pointed to where several bodies lay on the floor, near the air lock.

"I'm surprised there was anyone here," said Porter, his voice troubled. "'1, grab the other end of this cart and let's carry it." They hefted the cart awkwardly and moved to catch up with the rest of the group.

"Maybe they sought refuge here like you did with us in Charlie, Uncle Porter," said Pancho.

"Their skin is all shriveled up like an old squash," Scar observed. "Their exo-suits are very thin, and I don't see any helmets. It looks like their suits have been torn or burned away."

"The bodies!" Porter said with dawning recognition. "These were some of the first people who died on Smoky Rescue Day. When I was with the doctor, they brought in several people who were dead, and the doctor's room was getting crowded with bodies. I had some of the crewmen bring the bodies here so that they would be out of the way."

Porter and Thing1 had navigated past the debris and set the cart down, joining the others. "Yes. These aren't exo-suits, just clothes. See how they are burned here?" Porter pointed at the charred and dust-covered cloth on a mummified body. "You haven't seen clothes, let alone burned cloth, so you wouldn't recognize it."

Thing2 picked up several buckets that were nested in a stack and put them into the cart. Scar found a toolbox and added it to the cart.

"Should we bring these containers?" asked Scooter, pointing to small plastic barrels lining a shelf. "What do you think is in them?"

"Those are probably chemicals for use by the aqua culturists," Porter guessed.

"What about these drawers?" Scar pointed to a cabinet.

"The cart is pretty full. We can come back for more another time. Let's get into the station and back to Charlie," Porter suggested.

Porter worried that the morgue crew might have left the air lock door open in haste and was relieved to see that the air lock door into the station was closed—then realized that since Alpha was depressurized, it wouldn't have mattered. He released the pressure in the air lock and the group entered the Alpha air lock and closed the door. Scar offered to pressurize the lock, but Porter reminded him that there was no pressure on the other side; all they had to do was open the door. Scar swung the door open.

For Porter, getting inside Bravo was a significant milestone marking his return to *New Rome*. For the Martians, there was a special significance to entering the long-forbidden station proper. Everyone paused before exiting the air lock. There was a reverent silence.

It was dark beyond the door, the only light coming through the air lock windows behind them. As they emerged from the air lock, they were in a corridor junction that was blocked by airtight doors in all directions

Porter turned on the headlamp of his helmet, and the clean gray walls were suddenly illuminated. He turned to the right. "We are at the two hundred seventy-degree position of the circle—nine o'clock. The Charlie air lock is at one hundred eighty degrees—six o'clock. We are almost home."

Porter opened the airtight door and Thing1 held it for the others. Porter's tether to Thing1 played out as he walked past. When all were through, Thing1 caught up, and the group continued along the slowly curving corridor. Doors appeared on their left and right, but Porter pressed forward without investigation.

Then another airtight door came into view. They opened it and emerged into light filtering from the Charlie air lock windows. Porter bent down and picked up the helmet that he had used to prop open the air lock door so long ago and put it into the cart.

Faces pressed against the other side of the Charlie air lock's glass walls. The Martians looked at the group as they filed into the air lock and closed the door. Scooter pressurized the air lock, and they were home. Helmets came off and everyone was laughing and cheering and happy. The second expedition had been successful. The air lock from Charlie to *New Rome* had been reclaimed.

CHAPTER 37 – Lessons

After a quick meal, everyone gathered to hear details of the second excursion and the adventurers shared their recovered treasures. The utilitarian gear—buckets and tools and hoses—were known to the Martians, although the novelty of "new" items, like the stack of shiny buckets Thing2 had collected, were appreciated. Most of the plastic buckets in Charlie had worn out or cracked years ago and been replaced by cruder and heavier "stone" buckets fashioned with the 3-D printer before it had given out.

The toolbox Pancho acquired in Alpha contained unfamiliar specialized plumbing and electrical tools in addition to the familiar wrenches, mallets, and screwdrivers similar to those the construction crews had left behind in Delta so long ago. It also contained some wire and power connectors that Thing1 prized.

The audience was particularly interested in details about the bodies of the dead colonists found in Alpha. Porter was initially surprised by this interest, thinking the meteorite that had struck Alpha more noteworthy. As he listened to the tone of the questions and answers, he realized that "colonists" had taken on mythical dimensions for the Martians, but because they had never known an intact Alpha, they were less impressed by the catastrophe.

As the session wound down, Porter removed the computer tablet from his canvas bag, and passed it to Thing1 with ceremonial gravity, saying "If this still works and you can charge it, I may be able to show you all some very interesting things tomorrow."

Thing1 accepted the tablet and the challenge with interest. "It looks like a standard connector. Shall we use Delta's battery power or would you rather I wait and charge it with solar?"

"It shouldn't draw much power," answered Porter, pleased at the thinking behind Thing1's question. "You should be able to use Delta's cells without fear of draining the reserves."

As Pigpen and Thing1 disappeared in the direction of Delta, Porter walked to the Charlie air lock and stared through the glass at the pressure indicator. Soon, he hoped, there might be answers to the questions that had long haunted him.

The next morning at breakfast, Thing1 and Pigpen presented Porter with his charged computer tablet. Porter suggested light duties for the day to allow a longer lesson to start at midday. The Martians scrambled off to their chores with enthusiasm, except Cisco, who was still nursing her ribs.

"What's the lesson today, Uncle Porter?" She looked curiously at the tablet.

Catching her glance, Porter smiled. "Good guess, Cisco." He held up the tablet. "This is a connection to the past and I wanted to give people a glimpse of that past to prepare them for what's ahead."

"Can you give me a hint?"

"Tell me something that you would like to know. I don't have all of the colony's information on this device, but I have a fair bit. This tablet has a bunch of data I amassed before the Mars mission as well as some I got from my grandfather that he had accumulated when he was alive. It's one of my only personal links to the past."

"What kinds of things does it contain?"

"Movies … er … stories, music, books, pictures … things that are true, and stories that are made up. Information about how to cook, how to build things, history, chemistry, math, poetry, lots of things," Porter said with enthusiasm. "What is something you would like to see?"

"The big waters of Earth. Oceans, you called them."

Porter touched the device and the screen was illuminated. "Siri, show me pictures of the Earth from space."

The device spoke crisply with a strangely accented woman's voice. "Showing thumbnails of Earth from space. You may further refine your search by specifying a continent or latitude and longitude and an approximate distance from Earth."

A grid comprising circles colored in patterns of blue and green and white and brown appeared on the tablet. Porter touched the grid with his finger and scrolled through the images. Cisco came closer as Porter stopped scrolling and selected one of the circles. The circle expanded to fill the screen.

"Think of Earth like a bumpy sphere covered with water. The green and brown and white parts here are where the land sticks out of the water. When the bits of land are relatively small, we call them islands. When they are really big, we call them continents. There are seven continents on Earth. The one in this picture is called South America. Its surface area is about … hmm … maybe ten percent of the surface area of Mars? The waters to the right are called the Atlantic Ocean and the waters to the left are called the Pacific Ocean. There are five oceans on Earth that surround the continents. The Pacific is the biggest. If I remember correctly, the surface area of the Pacific Ocean is about the same as the surface area of Mars."

"The whole planet Mars?" Cisco asked, astonished.

"I think that's right," said Porter. "Siri, what is the difference between the surface area of the Pacific Ocean and the surface area of the planet Mars?"

"The surface area of the Pacific Ocean is 165.2 million square kilometers. The surface area of planet Mars is 144.8 million square kilometers. The surface area of the Pacific Ocean is 20.4 million square kilometers larger than the surface of planet Mars. Expressed as a ratio, the surface area of the Pacific Ocean is approximately 1.14 times the surface area of planet Mars."

"How deep is the water?" Cisco asked, staring at the picture of the ocean partially obscured by clouds.

"Siri, how deep is the Pacific Ocean?" Porter relayed.

"The deepest point in the Pacific Ocean is Challenger Deep in the Mariana Trench at 10,915 meters average tidal depth," the strange voice answered. "The average depth of the Pacific Ocean is 4,280 meters."

"Thousands of *meters* deep?" Cisco asked, incredulous.

"The deep parts are far offshore," Porter explained. "It's beautiful, Cisco, let me show you. Siri, show me pictures of the California coast near Montara on a clear sunny day."

A new palette of small images appeared, and Porter selected one. The caption said, "Gray Whale Cove State Beach, Montara, California." The top third of the image was the blue sky of Earth. The foreground showed low grassy hills. Peering beyond the hills, the Pacific Ocean was on the left side of the screen and white-capped waves washed from left to right onto a sandy beach in the middle of the picture. Beyond the beach, a brown and rust bluff rose to meet the sky.

"The sky looks strange … so blue. The water is blue too. Very pretty," Cisco mused.

"I grew up near here," Porter said wistfully. "I used to beg my mom to take us to the ocean so we could play in the water, but the water was so cold I couldn't stay in it for long. I could sit on the bluffs and watch the ocean for hours. Waves washing into the shore made a beautiful sound that was so peaceful…"

"I wish I could hear it." Cisco sighed.

"Siri, play the sound of ocean waves," Porter said, pleased.

"Please specify distance from shore, wave height, weather conditions, beach or cliff," the voice replied.

"Siri, play ocean waves, ten meters from shore, wave height one meter, light winds, beach."

A symphony of white noise punctuated by gentle waves breaking and washing out to sea erupted from the tablet. Cisco closed her eyes and listened, mesmerized.

They sat together in silence for several minutes, then Porter said, "Wait, open your eyes, Cisco! I've been silly. Siri, show video Hawaiian Honeymoon June 2034, body surfing lessons."

The screen abruptly changed to pictures of a younger Porter and a beautiful brown-skinned woman. They were laughing and playing in light blue waves crashing onto a sandy beach.

"We rented a photographic drone when we went on our honeymoon. A honeymoon is a ceremonial trip that lovers sometimes take after they officially become mates. Julia had just finished a very long and challenging part of her schooling and we celebrated by getting married and going to Hawaii for our honeymoon trip. Hawaii is a group of islands about thirty-five hundred kilometers southwest of Montara and the water is warm … you can play in it all day." Porter's voice grew distant. "You could rent these drones that took video as you went places and did things. They hovered nearby. It seemed like a good idea, but we ended up with days of video, lots of it boring. I liked this part and saved it. We played in the surf for hours. We both got terrible sunburns. It was a wonderful trip."

The figures in the video embraced and kissed. Porter looked on longingly and smiled.

"What are you doing there?" Cisco asked.

"Kissing. It's a sensual interaction with someone you … love," Porter responded wistfully. His last word was choked off and he looked away out the windows toward *New Rome.*

"I thought it was just a good-night snuggle for children," Cisco said, choosing not to notice the tears in Porter's eyes. "It looks … interesting. I'll have to try it."

"It's pretty fun with a special friend. Tasting them. Breathing their breath. Not as much fun as rubbing bodies together, but a nice start."

"Thank you for showing me the big waters, Uncle." Cisco touched his shoulder lovingly. "I feel special for getting this first look. I will see you at lessons."

Cisco walked away to leave Porter to his thoughts, marveling at the notion of vast expanses of blue water extending beyond the horizon and thousands of meters deep. She looked out the window at the dusty haze of the red and tan Martian horizon and imagined it covered in water. She was curious too about the tender passion she had seen in the lovers' kiss and wanted to explore that further.

She found Pancho tending the worm beds. "Hey, Pancho, I want to try an experiment."

Pancho looked up from his task, smiling. "Sure. What's up, Cisco?"

"Porter showed me a picture of adults kissing in a loving way. It looked way more fun than good-night kisses. I wanted to try it out to see what it was like with you. If you like it, maybe you can share it with Ginger."

Pancho nodded. "What do we do?" He and Cisco had a special bond, different than his feelings for Ginger. There was nothing he wouldn't do for Cisco, and if this was fun, he would welcome the chance to share it with Ginger.

Cisco embraced Pancho and pressed her lips to his for several moments, then her tongue tentatively darted into his mouth. Pancho's eyes widened in surprise. He returned the kiss, touching her tongue with his for a moment, embraced her, then pulled away, elated and perplexed. "Wow!" he said.

"Was it—weird?" Cisco asked, her usual confidence shaken.

"No, it was … wonderful! I felt a thrill through my whole body. It was a little confusing. It made me wish you were Ginger. I don't know how to explain it. I can't wait to show her. Thanks, Cisco!" Pancho smiled excitedly and went off to find Ginger.

Cisco was pleased for her friend. It *was* a delicious thrill. She felt it too. It made her body ache with joy and expectation.

Helper made a quick and easy stew for the midday meal, assuming that people would be eating throughout lessons and the pot could serve as both lunch and dinner. She sat next to Scar and waited for Porter to begin. Pancho and Ginger were sitting near them, and Helper noticed that they seemed particularly cuddly today, holding hands and exchanging knowing glances. She moved closer to Scar so that the sides of their legs were touching and quietly sniffed his "Scar scent" with satisfaction.

Porter began by thanking Helper for the tasty stew and then produced his tablet.

"I'm not sure where to begin," he said. "There is so much to share. This device has some of the information that our ancestors have accumulated. Not as much as the computers on the station, but more than I could share in a lifetime. What kinds of things do you want to know first?"

The Martians sat, thoughtful for a moment.

"I want to know about the colonists," said Red. "How did they come to be here?"

"Siri, please play the public relations summary of the *New Rome* mission."

The tablet began to play music and show images of the *Numa* sitting in the space dock with Earth slowly spinning below it. A narrator intoned, "Since the beginning of recorded history, humans looked longingly at the heavens without the means to explore them. Envious of birds' natural flying ability, mankind could only marvel at the mysteries of flight."

The picture shifted to birds soaring above the terrestrial landscape.

"Beginning two millennia ago, the Chinese developed unmanned hot air balloons and kites, learning to defy the gravity that kept mankind harnessed to the earth. Legends tell of manned kite flights in China and Japan in the sixteenth and seventeenth centuries."

Old drawings of early kites and balloons filled the screen as the narrator continued, "By the eighteenth century, French inventors had demonstrated manned balloon flight, giving humanity a view of their earth that could previously only be imagined." Drawings of the ground from a balloon showed roads and patches of farmland extending off to the horizon.

"Less than one hundred years later, in 1902, the American Wright brothers succeeded in flying a human in a glider. A year later, they successfully added an engine and achieved powered flight."

Jerky black-and-white video images of early flight accompanied the narration. The Martians sat in rapt attention as a montage of airplane evolution gave way to video of primitive rockets.

"The first rocket that was capable of reaching space was the German V2, invented in 1942. Fifteen years later in 1957, the Russian Sputnik became the first artificial satellite carried into space. Two years after that, in 1959, the Russian mission Luna 2 placed the first human-made object on Earth's moon, a quarter of a million miles above the Earth's surface."

Historical black-and-white footage from these missions went by quickly as they were mentioned.

"Humanity's quest for the sky accelerated, and two years later in 1961, Russian Yuri Gagarin became the first human launched into space, his Vostok I capsule orbiting the earth at an altitude of two hundred three miles before returning to Earth."

Grainy video of the smiling Russian waving and still photographs of Vostok I gave way to color pictures of the Saturn V rocket launches of Apollo.

"Less than ten years after Gagarin's historic flight, American Neil Armstrong became the first human to set foot on Earth's moon, in 1969."

Black-and-white video of the lunar module descending onto the lunar surface and the announcement that "The Eagle has landed" were followed by Armstrong descending the Apollo 11 lunar module ladder and poor-quality audio of his historic words: "That's one small step for man, one giant leap for mankind." Next, a sequence of still photographs in dazzling color of Earth's moon, ending with the famous "Earthrise" photograph, showing the earth above a barren lunar landscape, half in light, and half in shadow.

"Having explored its nearest neighbor the moon, humanity raised its sights to a more ambitious target, sister planet Mars. Mars is about four hundred times farther from Earth than Earth's moon, and Mars orbits the sun independently, creating a technology challenge that wasn't mastered until 1971 with the unmanned Soviet Mars 2 probe crashing onto the red planet.

"Allowing humans to cross the great distance proved a much more formidable challenge. It took over sixty years before India's Ravi Verma became the first human to set foot on Mars, piloting his Ramachandran IV vehicle on a one-way mission to Earth's nearest habitable planetary neighbor."

The video now showed brilliant color images of a smiling, helmeted Verma waving at the camera with his saucer-shaped lander in the background on a barren red-and-brown landscape that looked quite familiar to Porter's audience.

Verma's voice came from the tablet: "I stand here humbly, on the shoulders of the giants who came before. I hope my contribution can help humanity work together in peace to further explore the cosmos."

The narrator continued, "Landing on Mars in 2032 and surviving for 122 days on the hostile Martian surface, Verma gathered essential information about the challenges future colonists would face and laid the foundation for mankind's next great adventure: establishing a permanent colony on another world."

The images now shifted back to the *Numa* floating in space dock above Earth.

"Seven years after Verma's voyage, the United Nations will launch a mission to establish the first permanent extraterrestrial colony on Mars, *New Rome*. Slated to leave Earth orbit in 2039 carrying 127 colonists, the spaceship *Numa* will travel over 200 million kilometers to land on Mars at the colony site where unmanned ships have been caching supplies for the past three years. These brave colonists will establish a self-sustaining outpost for humanity that will serve as a way station for exploration of the outer planets."

The tablet now displayed computer-generated animation of *Numa* landing amid the pre-positioned supply ships and *New Rome* being constructed in time lapse. The mines to the north were excavated in seconds. Alpha, Bravo, Charlie and Delta grew like bean sprouts from the main station.

"Living and working here, the colonists will give birth to the first generation of humanity that has never touched the Earth. These brave pioneers represent the next step of man's exploration of the cosmos."

Porter paused the video. The Martians who, apart from Cisco, had never seen video before, stared at the frozen and now silent screen, entranced.

"And that," Porter said, "is how the colonists—including me—came to be here."

“That explorer Ravi, he came to Mars before the colonists?” asked Mary. “He told them what to expect, he died here after a hundred days, and they came anyway?”

“Ravi was a great pioneer and scientist. His sacrifice helped us understand what challenges we would face so that we could come better prepared for them,” Porter answered.

Mary looked disappointed and said nothing more.

“What were the sounds while the man was talking?” asked Pigpen.

“What sounds, Piggy? The rockets?” asked Porter.

“Can you show it again?” Pigpen asked.

Porter touched the screen and the video replayed. The music began to swell…

“That!” said Pigpen excitedly. “What is that sound?”

Porter stopped the video. “Ah, you mean the music! Music is sounds made by different instruments or … eh … tools. Siri, display musical instruments.”

Dozens of small images filled the screen in tidy rows. Porter selected some and enlarged them.

“This is a drum. It is an instrument by itself and sets the pace for other instruments.” He touched the screen and a rhythmic drum riff played.

Porter touched the screen and the tidy rows reappeared. He selected another image.

“This is a guitar. It is one of several stringed instruments. When the strings are touched, they vibrate and make sounds of different pitches depending upon the frequency of vibration. This is controlled by the thickness and length of the strings. A player can pinch the string along this part, called the neck, to change the length of the string and make different sounds. When these instruments are played together, the sounds can be very enjoyable. Siri, play B.B. King, ‘The Thrill is Gone’.”

A brief drum introduction was followed by electric and bass guitars playing a passionate prelude before the singer began his sad song of dying love.

The Martians stared wide-eyed and listened intently.

"That was so beautiful," said Pigpen. "His voice was strange and ... rough, but it sounded so good with that music."

"Groups of people singing together can make beautiful sounds. Siri, play 'A Million Ways' by Carbonite Vacation".

As the harmonies began, Porter whispered, "This is called 'a cappella'. There are no instruments but the human voice. I saw these guys live at a concert in San Francisco in 2032. It was one of my first dates with Julia. They sang a bunch of beautiful old songs."

The short love song reminded Porter of a different time. He noticed that Helper and Scar were holding hands and looking at one another as the music wove its tale of devotion.

As the song ended, Porter thought it best to move away from the love theme among a group of hormone-charged young adults.

"Not all music has singing," Porter said. "Would you like to hear some different kinds of music?"

"Yes please!" said Pigpen, before anyone else could answer.

Porter smiled. "There is so much I want to share with you. Siri, play Mason Williams, 'Classical Gas'."

"Guitar only, or the orchestral version?" the tablet asked.

"Both. Guitar only first," Porter replied. To the young Martians, he said, "My grandfather played this for me when I was young. Both versions are beautiful. The first is simpler."

The guitar version introduced a pretty melody, slowly at first, then growing in complexity and tempo. Porter's eyes glazed as he heard the tune again. His smile grew and he nodded his head in time. The Martians sat in awe.

As the first tune wound down, Porter said, "That version was with one guitar. This next version has several other instruments join in playing the same tune with different complexity."

The second version sounded the same as the first for thirty seconds or so, then a drum gently joined in. The sound continued to grow in complexity and pace. Moments later, other instruments joined, and the sound grew richer and fuller and bigger … but still the same pretty melody. Porter smiled broadly. "I always enjoyed listening to music, but I never played an instrument. My musical friends said that there were lots of mathematical relationships between the different sounds."

"Mo please," said Curly quietly.

Everyone turned to look at Curly.

"Mo please," Curly repeated.

Porter paused, surprised, then continued. "There is something very special I would like to share with you in honor of your request, Curly. There was a famous composer—er, music inventor—several hundred Earth years ago that created some beautiful music. People say he was a genius. They say that one of the last things he wrote was particularly special because he never heard it played. His ears stopped working as he got older, so he couldn't hear the music—only imagine what the music he was writing would sound like. This is called 'Ode to Joy'. It's a beautiful and complex piece of music. Siri, play Beethoven's 'Ninth Symphony'.

"This music has a lot of different instruments cooperating," Porter added. "It is one of my favorites. You will notice several different patterns get explored and combined."

As the music played, Sniffles found her interest in the patterns of music waning and waxing as it changed. Sometimes the sounds seemed repetitive but pretty—then they would shift and excite her, then they would lull her again. She looked around the group to see the reaction that others were having.

Helper and Scar leaned next to one another, their eyes closed, sharing the moment and seeming lost in the listening.

Thing2 and Scooter held hands and listened intently. He stroked her knee gently to the pace of the sounds. Thing2's eyes were closed, but Scooter was looking at him with warmth and affection.

Pancho sat between Cisco and Ginger. Cisco's eyes were half closed. She looked happy and peaceful. Pancho was listening to the music and watching Ginger's reaction to it. Ginger seemed happy, periodically closing her eyes as the music played, sometimes opening them and seeing Pancho's glance and smiling.

Behind Sniffles, Thing1 stared at Porter's strange device in amazement, wondering how such wonderful sounds could be made with electricity.

Pigpen sat next to Thing1, slowly swaying to the rhythm and smiling. "He captured happiness and put it into sound," she whispered with admiration. The rise and fall of the music enchanted her.

At the back of the group, Mary stood quietly, swaying to the sounds with her eyes closed.

Red, also on the periphery, watched Mary with interest. Usually, she was aloof and unengaged—but this seemed to inspire her. He listened to the sounds and considered her movements in their context. It added a dimension to the experience that surprised him. He didn't stand still but swayed with the music also. He noticed that there were different choices about which parts of the sound you would move to.

As the music continued, Curly sat perfectly still, his eyes closed, listening intently. He could imagine the colors of the different sounds arranging themselves all around him and pulsing with the cadence of the beat—layers and layers of beautiful colors, shifting and not quite repeating a pattern, but instead repeating a variation of a pattern. Usually, this asymmetry would trouble him, but this was different—it was … awe-inspiring. The sound was so big and complex and wonderful that Curly cried silent joyful tears as the sounds washed over him and swept him away. He was no longer sitting with the others. He was no longer in Charlie. He was no longer on Mars. He imagined himself in deep dark space, with the colors pulsing during the sound parts and blackness taking over during the quiet parts. He was floating in space among the patterns woven by a long-dead genius and brought to life by a crop of instruments and a hive of anonymous humans. It was bliss.

Later, when the Beethoven had finished, Porter suggested they take a break. Curly opened his tearful eyes, devastation and longing on his face.

"Again?" Porter asked.

Curly looked relieved and nodded his head imploringly.

As the other Martians drifted away, Porter touched the tablet so that it would replay Beethoven and left the tablet with Curly, bending to kiss the dark curls on top of his head as he did so. Curly took the tablet in his arms and held it tightly to his chest, slowly rocking back and forth as the string section again began to play.

CHAPTER 38 – Postlude

Cisco was glad that she and Pancho could share experiencing the music with Ginger. She was pleased to see her friends so happy.

When Porter called the break, Sniffles headed toward Delta. Cisco caught up with her and asked, "What did you think of the sounds?"

"It was pretty amazing, and a little overwhelming," Sniffles replied.

Cisco nodded, "It was pretty. That last part went on too long for me … but the others seemed to enjoy it."

"Yes. It was beautiful, but there were so many different sounds. Cisco, you work with Curly the most. I've never heard him speak before, have you?"

"Never. I didn't know he could. I was as surprised as anyone. The music seemed to—touch him in a special way." Cisco mused, thinking of Curly's tears. She couldn't remember him ever crying, either.

"There is so much to learn about the colonists … the people from Earth. They have so much history. Porter's device is … surprising … amazing … I don't have words," Sniffles said, looking up at Cisco. "This is going to be stranger than I ever imagined."

Cisco nodded.

CHAPTER 39 – More Lessons

The following weeks were an immersion in Earth culture, history, science, and engineering. After chores were done, Porter would lead a lesson for everyone, they would discuss what they had learned, and then smaller groups would take turns exploring different things that interested them on the tablet. Everyone quickly shifted from their long-established routine of rising with the sun and going to bed a few hours after sundown to shifts of sleeping at different times to allow them to maximize their availability for Porter's magical device.

The Martians had been shocked to learn about the long history of war among their ancestors, unable to imagine organizing to harm, displace, or subjugate different people. Porter had explained that the violent and territorial nature of the human animal had been hard to unlearn, and that "different" was often mistakenly equated with "bad" or "inferior." He had also explained that groups claimed territories for their farms and livestock and then resisted "incursion" by adjacent groups.

Religion was another strange concept to explain. Porter had never been religious or talked much about religion with the young Martians as they grew. He had shared stories of Greco-Roman mythology at bedtime when they were young, explaining that these were the beliefs of primitive peoples trying to understand their world—but he had shied away from discussing more contemporary religious traditions out of respect for their parents.

"What do *you* believe, Uncle?" Sniffles asked when they discussed that Earth peoples still had numerous religions, each seeking to guide their followers to live in a way that pleased their concept of "god" or "gods".

"I think that the core principles of many religions have value. Most can be summarized by the rules I tried to teach you: treat each other kindly, fairly, and with compassion. I find many of the details and rituals confusing and sometimes silly. I like the idea of treating other people kindly and fairly because that's how I want to be treated, not because I believe there are invisible beings who reward or punish me if they approve or disapprove of my behavior. As much as it would be comforting to imagine that when I die, I will see my wife Julia again, I don't believe that will happen. I've certainly never understood the friction and sometimes hostility between different religions. I encourage you all to explore the different ways of thinking about this for yourselves. You may find that some belief systems appeal to you. Your parents may have had beliefs that will interest you."

Periodically, Porter put the tablet away and encouraged people to share what they had learned or seen. He had soon realized that it was important to explain and emphasize the difference between fiction and non-fiction, and for the Martians to understand whether they were learning facts and science versus art and speculation. These sessions helped him guide the learning.

The interests of the Martians had taken expected as well as surprising turns.

Mary and Sniffles, as the de facto healers of the group, immediately began researching human biology to better understand how bodies worked. This required study of biochemistry, which led back to a broader view of biology that integrated much of what they had learned about plant biology from Porter as they were growing up. When they began to learn about the chemistry of nutrition, they worked with Helper to adjust her cooking with the new knowledge. When they learned about surgical remedies to common conditions, they shared the information with Scar. Secretly, Sniffles wondered whether her constant shortness of breath was caused by some congenital defect, damage she had incurred on Smoky Rescue Day, or something else. She wondered how she might gain further insights, but without some of the sophisticated equipment referred to in the tablet that allowed a doctor to look inside a body without cutting it open, she couldn't think of a way to discover the difference.

Thing1 and Pancho wanted to better understand electricity, which led to an interest in physics and mathematics beyond what Porter had been able to share previously. Together they built and demonstrated an electromagnet to see the principles in action.

Curly, Ginger, Scooter, and Pigpen often studied with Thing1 and Pancho and enjoyed watching the experiments, but they seemed less interested in working with electricity and more interested in the math. They also studied the physics of acoustics and sound, which led them to study and listen to a wide variety of music. They did a demonstration of the speed of sound for the other Martians at one of the sharing sessions, with Scooter standing at the far end of Charlie and banging two rocks together with exaggerated motion so that all could observe the sound taking longer to reach their ears than the light of the event to reach their eyes.

"How do you know that it doesn't just take longer for our ears to process the sound?" Red asked. "Maybe our eyes are more efficient and do it quicker?"

Pigpen thought for a moment, then had Scooter move from the far end of Charlie to the middle and repeat the experiment. The delay between sight and sound was still observable, but smaller. Red agreed that was a good test and was impressed by how quickly Pigpen had refined the demonstration to address his question.

One day Ginger surprised Porter by suggesting everyone listen to the music of "Peter and the Wolf" as part of the common lesson. She had discovered it on the tablet while reading an introduction to music. Porter hadn't remembered that he possessed it on the device. The piece highlighted the participation of different orchestral instruments and included narration to call out the sounds that they made.

Pigpen had been particularly engaged by learning modules that explained how electricity could do work, called "programming," and after a few false starts, was able to program the tablet to generate tones with different frequencies and durations. Soon she could write programs that played simple tunes with patterns Ginger and Scooter had found and decoded.

```
Begin                          /* song "My Old Steam Boat" */

    Playtone(523.251,0.25)     /* play "C" for .25 sec "Putt" */
    Playtone(0,0.25)           /* .25 seconds of silence */
    Playtone(523.251,0.25)     /* play "C" for .25 sec "Putt" */
    Playtone(0,0.25)           /* .25 seconds of silence */
    Playtone(523.251,0.25)     /* play "C" for .25 sec "Putt" */
    Playtone(0,0.25)           /* .25 seconds of silence */
    Playtone(523.251,0.25)     /* play "C" for .25 sec "Putt" */
    Playtone(0,0.25)           /* .25 seconds of silence */
    Playtone(523.251,0.25)     /* play "C" for .25 sec "Putt" */
    Playtone(0,0.25)           /* .25 seconds of silence */
    Playtone(523.251,0.25)     /* play "C" for .25 sec "Putt" */
    Playtone(0,0.25)           /* .25 seconds of silence */
    Playtone(523.251,0.25)     /* play "C" for .25 sec "Putt" */
    Playtone(0,0.5)            /* 0.5 seconds of silence */

    Playtone(523.251,0.25)     /* play "C" for .25 sec "Goes" */
    Playtone(0,0.25)           /* .25 seconds of silence */
    Playtone(587.330,0.25)     /* play "D" for 0.25 sec "my" */
    Playtone(0,0.25)           /* .25 seconds of silence */
```

```
    Playtone(659.225,0.25)      /* play "E" for 0.25 sec "old" */
    Playtone(0,0.25)            /* .25 seconds of silence */
    Playtone(587.330,0.25)      /* play "D" for 0.25 sec "steam" */
    Playtone(0,0.25)            /* .25 seconds of silence */
    Playtone(523.251,0.25)      /* play "C" for .25 sec "Boat" */
    Playtone(0,0.5)             /* 0.5 seconds of silence */

    Playtone(523.251,0.25)      /* play "C" for .25 sec "Putt" */
    Playtone(0,0.25)            /* .25 seconds of silence */
    Playtone(523.251,0.25)      /* play "C" for .25 sec "Putt" */
    Playtone(0,0.25)            /* .25 seconds of silence */
    Playtone(523.251,0.25)      /* play "C" for .25 sec "Putt" */
    Playtone(0,0.25)            /* .25 seconds of silence */
    Playtone(523.251,0.25)      /* play "C" for .25 sec "Putt" */
    Playtone(0,0.25)            /* .25 seconds of silence */
    Playtone(523.251,0.25)      /* play "C" for .25 sec "Putt" */
    Playtone(0,0.25)            /* .25 seconds of silence */
    Playtone(523.251,0.25)      /* play "C" for .25 sec "Putt" */
    Playtone(0,0.25)            /* .25 seconds of silence */
    Playtone(523.251,0.25)      /* play "C" for .25 sec "Putt" */
    Playtone(0,0.5)             /* 0.5 seconds of silence */

    Playtone(523.251,0.25)      /* play "C" for .25 sec "on" */
    Playtone(0,0.25)            /* .25 seconds of silence */
    Playtone(587.330,0.25)      /* play "D" for 0.25 sec "the" */
    Playtone(0,0.25)            /* .25 seconds of silence */
    Playtone(659.225,0.25)      /* play "E" for 0.25 sec "same" */
    Playtone(0,0.25)            /* .25 seconds of silence */
    Playtone(587.330,0.25)      /* play "D" for 0.25 sec "old" */
    Playtone(0,0.25)            /* .25 seconds of silence */
    Playtone(523.251,0.25)      /* play "C" for .25 sec "note" */
    Playtone(0,1.0)             /* 1.0 seconds of silence */

End
```

Pigpen proudly demonstrated her original program, and later versions she built that included a loop for the repetitive parts. Later, she assigned the note frequencies to variables with meaningful names so that she could play music without needing to look up the frequencies.

Curly found a series of video lectures by a physicist named Richard Feynman who, though he spoke with a strange accent, explained mechanics, heat, gravity, and celestial dynamics very economically and well. Feynman used a special black wall to illustrate important points, making white marks on the wall to draw models that explained key concepts. Scooter and Curly watched them several times. They were as entertaining as they were educational.

Thing1 discovered a tutorial on the power systems planned for the station among a briefing package that Porter had received during preparations for the mission. The station was powered by nuclear power from a primary thorium reactor, supplemented by solar arrays. The goal had been for the station to build toward self-sufficiency using solar in combination with fuel cells to store the energy, but the dust storms expected on Mars could block the sun for months at a time, so the nuclear reactor was expected to provide a consistent and reliable source of power. This led Thing1, Ginger, and Curly to learning about the basics of nuclear power generation. While the forces involved could be dangerous if mishandled, the amount of power generated was inconceivable when compared to the energy of a fire or the energy of a solar cell.

Red, Scar, Cisco, and Mary had found common interest in history, learning as much as they could about the twenty-first century. They also discovered video of people dancing over the last hundred years. They marveled at the different styles of dress and movement and music through time. They also discovered that their skin pigments indicated that their ancestors were from different parts of the world—Mary's from east Asia, Scar's from west Asia, and Red's from Europe. At one of the lessons, they showed pictures of different people from different places and the Martians marveled that regional differences and evolutionary adaptations could account for such diversity. This led to a discussion of what future generations of Martians might look like. Porter said he wasn't sure, but that evolution worked over long periods of time.

Porter explained, "The next few generations would likely be a stew of what everyone here looked like. If Scar and Helper had a child, it would likely be darker skinned than Helper and lighter skinned than Scar. It might have Helper's small nose, or Scar's big ears, or have features similar to one of Scar's or Helper's ancestors. My sister's sons looked a lot like me," he added, "but because my sister's mate had ancestors from China, they had pretty, oval-shaped eyes like Mary and her ancestors, and they were lighter skinned than me. Where my hair is dark and very curly and Mary's ancestors' hair is dark and very straight, my nephews had dark wavy hair like Curly."

Porter brought up an image of the earth. "This is a picture of land masses called Africa and Europe, seen from space. Indications are that all our ancestors originated in Africa—this big mass here—millions of years ago. They probably all looked a lot like me then, dark skin and kinky dark hair, attributes that helped humans survive in the hot and sunny environment of Africa. See this thin sliver of atmosphere? The atmosphere filters some of the ultraviolet light from the sun before it gets to the planet. Remember how I told you that some plants need more light than others, and some are harmed if they get too much? Near the equator here in Africa, the sun goes straight through the atmosphere, so not much ultraviolet light gets filtered. Imagine the atmosphere is like the skin of an orange. At the equator, the faraway sun goes straight through, like a stick. It doesn't have far to travel. Some ultraviolet light is good—like plants, we need it. Too much damages cells, so my ancestors evolved with dark skin like me when they were near the equator in Africa, the extra pigment filtering some of the light to protect the cells. As for you paler people," he said, pointing to Helper, Red, Ginger, and Cisco, "as some of your ancestors migrated up into this place called Europe over thousands of years, the sun was going through the atmosphere at more of an angle, and the atmosphere was filtering more of the light. Your ancestors didn't need dark skin to protect them; in fact, they needed lighter skin, less pigment, to let more of the ultraviolet light that they needed through. I suspect your more recent ancestors were from here—that's where a lot of light-skinned tribes originated.

"As for Mars, it might be that over time, people with darker skin would flourish on Mars because the denser pigment decreases the amount of solar radiation that penetrates deeply. On the other hand, it might be that people with lighter skin are more likely to survive because their skin can produce vitamin D more efficiently from the light of the distant sun. It might be your descendants would emerge with lovely green skin and purple hair for some reason we can't guess. Remember, you are all the product of millions of years of natural selection for a completely different environment. None of us are well suited to live out there." Porter motioned toward the glass wall that separated them from the rocks, ice, and dust of Mars.

Scar, Thing2, Cisco, and Pigpen were interested in the construction and manufacture of things and materials, particularly those used to build the station. Disappointingly, there weren't detailed plans for the station in the tablet, instead just a discussion of proposed methods and materials. Porter said the details of the station construction were in the main computer.

"The information on my tablet is from the mission briefing," he speculated. "After we had some experience building here, we refined many of the suggested techniques and developed some of our own."

As the weeks passed, Cisco's ribs healed, and she became restless. The lessons provided glimpses of the colonists and the larger world that tormented her. Charlie and Delta seemed to get smaller each day. After a night of tossing and turning, she approached Porter early one morning. "I think I'm healed and ready. When can we explore more?"

She noticed a flicker of guilt as he confessed, "I guess the novelty of the lessons is probably wearing off?" He paused. "I think I was stalling, Cisco. I spoke with Sniffles a few months ago and confided to her that I was worried about exposing you all to the dangers beyond the walls. She reminded me that I couldn't keep you guys safe forever. Her nudge is what encouraged the excursions. I think the distraction of everyone exploring the wonders of the tablet let me get a little complacent again." He smiled. "Time for more action?"

Cisco nodded and smiled back. "What next, Uncle?"

"I was thinking we should restart farming in Bravo. It will be hard work to get it cleaned and ready, but you guys have experience with most of the tasks from when we had to restart Delta after that dust storm a few years ago. Is that enough adventure to start?" he asked. "This will give more time for lessons before we are exposed to the dangers and novelty of further exploration of the station."

Cisco was delighted. "When can we go and look? What needs to happen? Can I organize the work?"

"Get Helper and Red together and we can head over after breakfast. The small exo-suits will still be a little large for them, but we can go through the station now so the sloppy fit shouldn't be a safety problem. The shorter ones need some adventure too. Besides, we need to get everyone familiar with the suits."

After breakfast, Porter, Cisco, Red, and Helper suited up and met at Charlie's air lock. Porter initiated Red and Helper as he had the others, ensuring they knew how to operate their suits and could manually operate the air lock. The slightly oversized suits made operating the foot pedals of the manual air pump challenging, but their excitement helped them work through the discomfort. After the orientation, they exited toward the station and went left in the corridor toward Alpha. It took less than five minutes to traverse to the Alpha/Bravo air lock. Soon, helmet visors open, they were breathing the dank Bravo air and touring the four chambers of greenhouse Bravo. Porter stopped them when they reached the far air lock.

"You may notice from your helmet displays that carbon dioxide levels are ten times higher here than in Charlie," Porter said. "About half a percent here, compared to about point-oh-five percent there."

"No plant life!" Helper injected enthusiastically. "The oxygen we breathe in gets transformed into carbon dioxide in our lungs, but there are no plants doing photosynthesis to extract the carbon again."

"Exactly," Porter said with a pleased smile. "If we stayed in here for an extended period without living plants doing their part, the carbon dioxide would build up until it became poisonous. Whatever we do here, we need to monitor carbon dioxide and oxygen levels closely to make sure we stay safe. So, what should we do first?"

"The grow lights are working," said Red, pointing at the nearly opaque mildew covered glass of the Bravo greenhouse. "So as much as we have a lot of cleanup to do, we don't have to clean the glass before we can plant."

"Good thinking, Red," Porter said. "What needs to happen before we can plant?"

"You prepared these soils long ago. Can we use them without further treatment?" Cisco asked.

"Good question, Cisco." Porter smiled. "Bravo never lost pressure, but it probably got very cold for a long time. What would that mean?"

"No worms. No microbes," Helper said.

"You are probably right about the worms," Porter ventured. "I'm not sure about the microbes. Some of them can survive freezing for a while."

"We can bring both live soil and some worms from Charlie," offered Red. "Now that it's warm, there should be plenty of plant debris for them to eat."

"What about bees?" Helper wondered.

"Excellent idea," Porter said. "We will need pollinators eventually. It will be an interesting challenge starting up another bee colony. I think we can worry about bees later, once Bravo is up and operating. Cisco, this is your team. I want you to take the lead. What needs to happen?"

Cisco thought a moment. "We need to get soil, worms, and some plants started to keep the air breathable. Then we let the plants and grow lights do their job for a while. We can pollinate by hand for the first few generations. Once we have some sustainable plant growth and the oxygen and carbon dioxide levels are stable, we can take on the larger chore of cleaning up the mess."

Cisco looked at the dingy glass and the mildew covering most surfaces. Her smile glowed.

Porter's tone became serious. "Before you start this project, let's agree to some ground rules. First, check carbon dioxide levels every day. If carbon dioxide ever gets above two-thirds of a percent, let me know immediately. At that level you will feel headaches, drowsiness, and irritability. Second, no one *ever* travels between here and Charlie alone. Not for a minute. Always have a buddy. Third, no exploring without me. You are allowed to move directly between Charlie and Bravo air locks only for now. The rest of the station is full of things that look harmless but might be dangerous, not because you are foolish, but because you don't know what they are and how they work. We will get to them in time, but no independent exploration. Fourth, Cisco is the team leader and what she says, goes. You can debate and discuss as long as she is willing to tolerate it, but her say is final. Cisco, you have a smart team, you shouldn't need to be too bossy. Can you all agree to those rules?"

The import of Porter's words became clear. Bravo was theirs to colonize. The group excitedly assented.

"You can recruit others to help you, but they must agree to the same rules." Porter looked around and began to move back toward the Alpha air lock. "You guys have a lot of work to do. Let me know if you need help or have questions. Now let's go so that Helper can make lunch."

The group followed him briskly. Mars's gravity seemed even lighter as they splashed through the puddles on Bravo's floor.

CHAPTER 40 –
Bravo

The Bravo team had some initial challenges: How to carry soils and worms from Charlie to Bravo without exposing them to the near vacuum and chilling cold of the Martian atmosphere. Rather than consulting with Porter with their first puzzle, they talked it through. Red suggested they could put dirt and worms into their gloves for the short trip. And so it was that several dozen worms and a few cups of viable soil made the trek to Bravo as stowaways in the left gloves of several Martians' space suits.

Cisco and the team discussed what they should plant first and found merit in diversity, hardiness, and fast growth. They decided to start with three grow tables. One would be devoted to wildflowers, one to squash, and one to bamboo. They prepared the soil of each table over a week by spading it up with hand trowels to turn under the existing debris and add air to the soil, watering it, and mixing in soils from Charlie. They also established a toilet in Bravo, mixing the waste so that it accumulated with soils to add living organic materials. When the soil seemed to be uniform, they added a dozen or so worms to each table and let things sit for a week, then brought in seeds for the wildflowers and squash, and bamboo seedlings—all carried between greenhouses within exo-suits. After the planting, there was little to do but wait.

The carbon dioxide level was 0.53 percent when they set the timers to run the grow lights around the clock over their three new tables, and left Bravo to let time and the plants do their work.

Two weeks later, small green plants were sprouting in the tables. In the wildflower and squash tables the baby "seedling" leaves had given way to broader leaves to soak up as much of the grow light energy as possible. Bamboo stalks were sprouting leaves and nearly twenty centimeters high. The carbon dioxide level had crept up slightly. Porter pointed out that some of the decomposition being performed by the soil bacteria would release carbon dioxide and might be offsetting the modest greenery.

After two more weeks, the grow tables were thriving, and the carbon dioxide level was 0.59 percent. The team repeated their process to prepare six more grow tables, balance the soils, and introduce bacteria and worms.

Two weeks later, they introduced corn, soy, and beans setting a course to establish Bravo as a supplement to their food supply and a "lifeboat" of plant life in case anything happened to Charlie and Delta. The carbon dioxide level was 0.52 percent.

Twelve weeks after the start of their efforts, the carbon dioxide levels had fallen to 0.32 percent and Cisco began to rotate teams through to perform the tedious task of scrubbing and scraping the mildew from the glass of Bravo's walls and roof. She made a point of consulting with Porter to involve the shorter Martians. The novelty of leaving Charlie and Delta thrilled Sniffles and engaged Mary sufficiently to mute her complaining.

As always, Curly was a meticulous worker who never grumbled. He had spoken so rarely since his first words asking for more music that it was easy for Cisco to think that she was misremembering the event, but occasionally now he did say "please" or "thank you." Scooter told Cisco that sometimes when she and Curly were alone he would ask her questions about the physics that they were studying, but Scooter admitted that if Curly didn't understand it, she often didn't know either, so they would search for the answers together.

The second crop of squash was just getting its flowers, the broad leaves gathering light and carbon dioxide around the clock. The squash and wildflowers were being pollinated by hand with brushes. The bamboo was growing furiously and was over two meters tall.

By week twenty, Cisco felt proud of her team and their achievement. She reflected on their cooperation and realized there had been little of the petty bickering she would have expected a year earlier. Even dour Mary seemed to share a sense of accomplishment as the first crops began to ripen.

Cisco savored the moment as she surveyed Bravo. They were making progress cleaning the glass and it was transparent in some places and translucent in most. Thing1, Thing2, and Scooter had repaired the water recovery and sprinkler systems. There was no more standing water on Bravo's floor. Apart from some stubborn discoloration on the floor, walls and ceiling, Bravo looked like Charlie. The plastic walls that had separated Bravo into four climactic zones had been carefully taken down to facilitate cleaning. Without the plastic walls, the tall arching ladder could move freely the entire length of Bravo to attack the rest of the mold and mildew. Bravo still smelled strange, but Cisco had been unable to identify a specific source. Pollination was still being done by hand. Porter said that he would need some special equipment to split the hive and carry bees to Bravo, and that he thought that could wait until after they had made more progress getting into the station itself.

Cisco reflected that this must be how Porter had felt when Bravo had been initially established, and again when he had set Charlie into production. She realized what she and the team had done was restorative—Porter's achievement had been more pioneering. Still, it made her smile to think that she and Porter might share that sense of accomplishment. Thinking of Porter made her realize something else: for the past twenty weeks she and her team had been busy, and the lessons had continued—but no one had made further progress toward reclaiming the station.

As she closed her visor and headed with Curly back to Charlie, the question on her mind for Porter was, "What next?"

PART 4 – BRANCHING OUT

"Seeds of great discoveries are constantly floating around us, but they only take root in minds well prepared to receive them." - Joseph Henry

CHAPTER 41 –

Scavenger Hunt

When they gathered for lessons, Porter made an announcement. "I spoke with Cisco earlier, and we have agreed that Bravo is now officially settled and ready to be part of our food supply. The carbon dioxide levels have stabilized, crops are thriving, and the first Bravo squash should be in Helper's pot any day now. Great work to all of you, and a special thanks to Cisco for coordinating the effort." He began a round of applause and the group joined in. Cisco beamed.

Porter continued, "Not content with that accomplishment, Cisco then asked me a tough question: What next? I have shared with some of you my concerns about the dangers of the station. Not just the obvious dangers of radiation and whatever caused the decompression, but also the many everyday things in the station that you haven't encountered before that could be dangerous. I'm reminded of the time Thing2 shocked himself by touching the wires of the electric goat—not because he was careless, but because he didn't know any better—foolish Uncle Porter failed to warn him. Now that he understands electricity better, he probably realizes that if he had been standing in salty water when that happened, it could have been much more serious.

"I think what we can do next is explore the crew quarters in the outer ring between nine o'clock at the Alpha air lock and six o'clock." He pointed to the Charlie air lock. "Crew quarters are less likely to have any dangerous machinery and they are a chance for you all to learn more about the station. If I remember correctly, all these rooms should follow the same approximate pattern for crew quarters.

"First, there's a main room where people spent their waking hours. It has a small eating and food preparation area, a table that folds out from the wall, and a bed suspended from the ceiling. Then there are two small auxiliary rooms on one side that might be used as an office or storage room; and a small bathroom that is shared with the adjacent quarters."

Porter sketched the layout in the dirt. "This is approximately to scale, though some of the rooms will be flipped around right to left. The whole apartment is about six meters wide and four meters deep."

He continued, "I want to suggest we explore in teams of four—three of you and me. I'll lead the team as we initially explore your team's room and make sure it is safe, and then you and your partners can work alone to salvage things that you think are interesting or useful. Don't feel like you need to take everything and try not to break anything. I'm hopeful that we can move into these apartments if we can restore pressure to the station.

"The quarters on the outside of the ring will have windows, so there will be some natural light. Those on the inside may have skylights, er … translucent windows in the ceiling that let in some light, but we will probably need helmet lights. Thing1, please make sure all the exo-suits are charged and ready in the morning. Any questions?"

Porter paused. There were no questions, but the excitement was palpable. Thing1 stood up and touched Pigpen's shoulder. They left together to charge the suits.

The team exited the Charlie air lock and turned left through the airtight door of the outer corridor. The airtight door closed behind them, leaving them in darkness apart from their helmet lights bobbing along the wall. The first door they came to on the left had a sign that read **O 06:35**. Porter paused and tried the handle. Without power, locking mechanisms were deactivated for safety. Sunlight spilled from the room and into the corridor as he pushed the door inward. Red, Sniffles, and Mary followed him as Porter entered. Indicating the two doors on the left wall, Porter said, "Those are the auxiliary rooms—storage or office or whatever. You might find those interesting."

He pointed to the right side of the window in the opposite wall. "That is the food preparation area. Most meals were taken in the cafeteria—a common area at the center of the station—but as soon as we started moving into quarters, we realized the value of being able to prepare and eat some food privately."

Pointing to the door on the right wall, he said, "That door should lead to a shared bathroom with the quarters next door. The closet to the left of the door likely has clothes. Why don't you guys look around and see what you find? I'll watch and be available to answer any questions you have."

Red went to the closest door on the left wall and opened it. It was dim inside. The only light came from the translucent wall to his right and his headlamp. The lights from his helmet were focused beams as he turned his head to illuminate a simple desk and chair. A computer tablet sat on the desk next to a stack of what looked like pages from a book. A set of shelves against the wall held a collection of rocks in various colors from gray to red to brown to black. Small labels by each rock had numbers written on them. Beneath the rock shelf was a collection of rectangles with pictures on them. A smiling man with light skin and close-cropped brown hair was standing between two smiling people with wrinkled skin and gray hair. Most of their bodies were covered with patterns and colors, only their heads and hands exposed. In another rectangle, the same smiling man was standing with a brown-skinned woman with straight black hair that hung down below her shoulders. He was taller than she was. Her covering was a light blue triangle that exposed her arms and neck. Red thought she looked pretty. The next rectangle was a picture of the same man and woman. This time his covering was mostly black, and her covering was white—a much bigger triangle that only exposed her arms from the elbows down. She also had white mesh on her head and flowers in her hand. The next shelf had three books, and several piles of something that looked like folded graphene in a variety of different colors and patterns. Red decided against disturbing the rocks. He picked up the computer tablet and the books and a few of the folded things and left the room.

Mary was exasperated that Red had darted ahead of her. She paused, then moved to the remaining door on the left wall and opened it. The window on the right wall illuminated the room and the shelves along the translucent left wall. The room was dominated by what looked like a small low grow table with rods extending the sides up and supporting a mesh. It reminded her of soil sieves, but it was soft and pliable. Next to the table was an oversized chair. There was a fuzzy doll, perhaps a representation of an animal in the small grow table. The doll was white with black stripes and was partially hidden by a square of material that looked to be a meter on a side. The shelves held other dolls, as well as stacks and stacks of colorful material. Plastic boxes stacked against another wall resembled those Porter used to store chemicals in Charlie. Looking inside the boxes, Mary found strange objects that were flat and hard on one end, then rose like a deformed cone of softer material that was pliable. Several colors were represented, and they seemed to come in sets of two that were nearly identical. Another box contained cartons of round colored balls with bent wires sticking out and bundles of green wires with what looked like glass fragments of different colors sticking out, spaced every fifteen to twenty centimeters. Mary wasn't sure what she was hoping to find, but she was disappointed. She grabbed the material from the grow table, and put the doll, a box of the round balls, one of the bundles of wire, and two sets of the deformed cones into it; then she pulled the material at its corners to contain her loot and left the room.

Sniffles was thrilled to be on the first team to explore the crew quarters. When Red and Mary went for the doors to the left, Sniffles decided to explore the main room and the cooking area. The main room was dominated by things that appeared to be for sitting and a low table that extended from the wall. There was a ladder by the wall that climbed to what Porter had said was the sleeping area suspended above. Sniffles climbed a few rungs and found layers of a strange, thick substance snarled and twirled on a large soft flat surface. Touching it with her thick gloves, she found it was supple. "Porter, what is this stuff in the sleeping area?"

"What did you find, honey?" Porter asked, standing on a chair to gain sufficient height to see the top of the sleeping platform.

Sniffles held up the supple white and green layers. "They are like small tarps but seem more pliable and thicker."

Porter laughed. "Those are sheets and blankets, Sniff. They help regulate your temperature while you sleep. They are much better than tarps or those scratchy pads we've been using for that purpose. Anything else up there catch your eye?"

"What are these?" she said, holding aloft a thick chunk of something soft and flexible.

"Those are called pillows. You rest your head on them when you sleep. You guys are used to forming dirt to rest your head on, but these are a specialized improvement on that. I'll take these so we can show the others. Anything else up here?" Porter pulled the sheets and blankets from the bed and put the pillows in the cart.

"Nope," said Sniffles as she dropped from the ladder to the floor and landed lightly on her boots. She next moved to the food preparation area. There was a sink like the one in the Charlie work area, but smaller. In the sink were delicate cups and white plates. There was also a small container the size of a corncob and a strange conical thing the size of her thumb that ended in a round base that looked like it might screw onto the end of the container.

The work area was covered in what seemed to be small brown gravel or soil. There was a plastic container on the counter that was half full of those same rocks. The rocks were very light. What appeared to be the container's lid was on the counter under more of the gravel.

One cabinet contained dozens of little containers and boxes and bottles. Many of the bottles were broken and some of the boxes appeared to have spilled their powdery contents. Another cabinet contained more of the delicate cups and plates, plus bowls of various sizes. The drawers had trays with more metallic implements that appeared to be small spoons and knives as well as larger spoons and spoons with small slots carved into them.

Sniffles took a big bowl and grabbed a sampling of the unbroken bottles and boxes from the cabinet. She added some of the metal implements and two of the cups, as well as the corncob container and the strange lid. She put the top on the container of brown gravel and added it to her bowl. As she did, Red emerged into the room, carrying his treasures. Mary came out a moment later.

The three of them looked at Porter.

"Shall we head back and share what we found with the others?" he asked.

Each of the Martians put their prizes into the cart, Sniffles last. Her over-filled bowl balanced atop the other things scavenged.

They had been in the room less than ten minutes when they turned to leave.

Sniffles's container of gravel imploded when they repressurized the air lock. Sealed at near vacuum, the increasing pressure crushed the plastic container until the seal broke and the atmosphere rushed in. The air currents sprayed most of the ground coffee throughout the air lock, to the surprise and then delight of the occupants.

"That was a relatively inexpensive lesson," Porter offered as he realized what had happened. "We will need to be careful about bringing sealed things into the air lock, whether they were sealed with pressure or without. The differential is too great for most containers to bear."

The Martians had been awaiting the group's return and gathered in the receiving area as the first "crew quarters exploration party" removed their exo-suits. Mindful of Helper's hand being burned by the Martian rock after Scar's first excursion, Porter suggested they wait until after lunch before unpacking the cart.

When the group reconvened, each adventurer told their story and said what they had seen, then revealed the things they brought back to the group. Porter added context and answered questions as they came up.

Sniffles's prizes were on top of the cart. "I started exploring the sleeping area. What I found there is on the bottom of my pile. I'll show you that in a minute. Then I explored the food preparation area." She described the sink, counter, drawers, and cabinet, revealing her found items as she did.

"The mess you found among the packages was likely made when the station decompressed," Porter said. "Sealed packages would likely burst. Sealed bottles might burst or might have waited until they froze, then burst. The coffee—the brown gravel you found—probably sprayed out of the container on the counter with the decompression, much like it sprayed out of the container when we got into the air lock."

"What seems to be intact is…" Sniffles read the label of a small bottle with a narrow neck. "Van–il-la extract." She looked to Porter.

Porter extended his hand and Sniffles gave him the bottle. He scanned the label curiously. "Ah, the extract contains alcohol. Alcohol freezes at a lower temperature than water and doesn't expand when it freezes the way water does. Still, a pretty sturdy bottle." He opened the lid carefully and smelled the contents, then looked up. "Wait—I'm setting a bad example for you all. I should tell you that I know what vanilla extract is; it's for cooking and I know it is safe to smell this. I don't want any of you smelling the contents of any bottles or powders you find until you know what they are. Some could be very dangerous. This smells like it's supposed to. I'll pass it around so you can smell it too. You can taste it too—the slightest bit of wet on your finger, just a small fraction of a drop—but you probably won't like it. It's very strong. It gets diluted in cooking to a pleasant flavor. Vanilla is a kind of bean that we aren't growing. Dried and crushed and mixed with alcohol and water, it gets a sweet flavor that is added to cooking." He passed the bottle around for the others to smell. Despite his warning, everyone elected to taste a bit of the vanilla as well. Most made faces at the taste. All seemed to find the smell interesting.

Sniffles held up a small red jar. "Chip-otel?" she puzzled, handing the jar to Porter.

"Chi-pot-lay!" He beamed. "This is a wonderful dry spice made by smoking some spicy peppers called jalapeños and grinding them into a powder. We can make chili! This is another spice where a little goes a long way … just a few grains on your tongue or it will burn your mouth. You probably want to be careful when you smell it as well. You don't want to get any of the powder into your nose. Smell from a distance." As Porter said this, he tried to turn the lid on the jar. It appeared to be stuck. He tried again and there was a POP sound as the lid came off and red powder exploded from the jar and sprayed into the air. Porter gasped for air, coughed, laughed, and cried, "Ooh!"

Scar was sitting near Porter and got a face full of the red powder. He sputtered in surprise and shock, then howled, "My eyes! Aaah! It burns!"

The other Martians scattered away from the dusty red cloud.

"Get water!" Porter gasped, laughing and coughing. "Is that you, Scar? You will be okay, but you will be miserable for a while. Wash it off with water as best you can. Guys, take Scar to rinse his face. Try not to rub it into your eyes,

Scar. Damn! I hope I didn't waste it all..." Porter's voice trailed off into fits of laughing and coughing.

Cisco, Red, and Ginger worked with Helper to lead Scar to the cooking area where Helper quickly filled a pot with water and used it to wash Scar's face. His eyes were red and swollen and he was clearly in a great deal of pain. Her fingers quickly became covered with the red sludge and she realized she was smearing it around rather than wiping it away. Without thinking, she licked her fingers to clean them. She briefly tasted a strange smoky flavor—then it felt like her tongue caught fire. She stopped tending Scar and scraped her tongue on her teeth and spit. The burning spread and her lips began to sting. She scooped water from the pot Scar was using to wash his face and drank it quickly, trying to douse the flame, but the water had a film of the dark red dust on top of it and swishing it in her mouth only spread the torment. Helper coughed and spit. Scar continued to splash water on his face hoping to soothe his eyes, unaware of what had happened to Helper.

"Get fresh water!" Helper gasped, looking desperately at Ginger, who grabbed two bowls and ran for the nearest hose.

By the time Ginger returned with the bowls of fresh water, Helper was through the worst of her pain and had begun assisting Scar again. She laid Scar on his side and poured the water across his eyes in a small stream from the bowls while Ginger ran to fetch more water. Scar's eyes were bright red and swollen, but after a few minutes the pain diminished to something he could manage, and he calmed down and began to laugh, much to the relief of those looking on and particularly Helper. Helper looked frustrated and confused, then began laughing as well. She looked to Porter and said incredulously, "That fiery powder is for cooking?"

Porter smiled. "Remember how I said a little goes a long way?" He handed her the jar with what remained of the red powder. "When you are ready, I'll show you how to make chili. You may be surprised at how flavorful a little bit of this is if you add it to a large kettle of chili. You do want to be careful though—it's not recommended for the eyes."

When the group reconvened half an hour later, Porter said, "I think what happened was that the seal on the jar had leaked over the course of the years, but it must have been a small leak. The pressure didn't have time to equalize before I removed the lid. There may be many dangers in the station like that. We must be extra careful whenever we transport sealed containers. Sorry, Scar." He smiled at Scar, whose eyes remained red and swollen and whose nose was running freely. Scar smiled back sheepishly.

Porter continued, "I believe Sniffles was sharing her finds with us when we were interrupted?" He nodded to Sniffles.

Sniffles produced a carton labeled "Tea" from her bowl and passed it to Porter. "I found this in the cabinet as well.

Porter held the box dramatically at arm's length and winced as he snapped opened the flap of the box. The Martians drew back, and he smiled playfully. "I'm just teasing. Tea is the dried leaves from a special tree that are soaked in boiling water to make a beverage. I had started a couple of tea trees in Bravo, but they have been lost. I should check to see if I have any tea seeds left, although I don't have high hopes for germinating many of the remaining seeds given the repeated freezing that they have endured. We can make some tea after dinner so you all can have a taste. With a little honey, it is quite nice. What else did you find, Sniff?"

"I found these delicate tiny metal spoons and dull knives and a strange bent rake." She held the cutlery out for all to see.

"Those are tools for eating," Porter said. "The bent rake is called a fork."

"How are they used?" asked Cisco. "The spoon would work for soup, I guess, but it would be slower than drinking from a cup or bowl. Our teeth already do a better job than a dull knife. If the knife were sharp, why not make it bigger to help with food preparation—and what's the purpose of the bent rake?"

"Very small plants?" Red offered sarcastically.

Porter smiled and held the fork, pantomiming eating. "Different cultures use different tools. We didn't have any forks and we did have bamboo, so you all grew up using chopsticks. None of you have ever had a thick steak. Knives and forks have their place. I'll show you how to use them later. What else you got, Sniffles?"

Sniffles held up the cups. To the Martians, who had only seen Porter's large ceramic mug and the individual cups that had been fashioned from bamboo, these delicate and shiny white cups were a real curiosity.

"What are they made from?" asked Pancho. "May I touch them?"

Sniffles handed one of the cups to Pancho who took it gently from her. "It's pretty, and so light!" he said.

Porter took the other cup, thumped the side with his finger, then passed it along for others to examine. "I think it is probably a kind of opaque glass. On Earth it could also be made from fine clay that is cooked in an oven, but it is unlikely that anyone used their limited weight allowance to bring porcelain cups from Earth. I suspect these were fabricated from Martian sand. Sniffles?"

Sniffles held up the plastic box with the remains of the brown gravel. She explained what had happened in the air lock. One or two handfuls of the light gravel remained in the box after the implosion had scattered the contents.

"May I?" Porter asked, reaching out his hand. Sniffles passed the box to Porter, who opened it and put one of the brown nuggets into his mouth. "Coffee. Terrible coffee after being exposed to the paltry Martian atmosphere for a dozen years to have all the vitality sucked out of it, but coffee all the same. This is also used to make a hot beverage that is bitter and wonderful. Like tea,

I had a couple of coffee plants in Bravo that have been lost. We can experiment with this tonight too. Most humans develop a preference for coffee or tea. We will have a tasting and you can decide which you like. Anything else to share, Sniffles?"

"I found this container and strange lid." Sniffles held up the corncob-sized container, which was blue, and then the cone-shaped cap. The rigid base of the cone was white and clearly was meant to attach to the top of the container with a twist. The conical portion was brown, pliable, translucent, and rounded at the end.

Porter laughed. "That was exactly what you and the other infants needed right after the accident, Sniff. That is a baby bottle. You put nutritious liquid in the bottle, put the top on, and then you can use this to feed a very young human. They don't have any teeth, but they can suck on the end of the bottle and little sips of the liquid will come out. We should keep this safe. Some of you may need it sooner or later."

Sniffles held up the bowl she had carried her smaller treasures in. It was as big as a helmet, but not as deep. The walls were very thin compared to the crude kettle and bowls Porter had fashioned using the 3-D printer. "I got this for Helper." She presented it ceremoniously. "Thank you for taking over the cooking duties. I'll keep looking for tools to make your job easier." Sniffles beamed.

Helper took the bowl and smiled at Sniffles.

Sniffles then reached down and picked up the bundle of sheets and blankets and pillows, passing them around the group. "Porter says these are for sleeping. The colonists slept on soft squares suspended from the ceiling. They put their heads on those..." She pointed and looked to Porter.

"Pillows," he replied.

"And they wrapped themselves in those..."

"Sheets and blankets," Porter added. "A sheet was placed on the sleeping area, then another sheet was placed on it, then thicker, warmer blankets were placed on top of that. People slept between the sheets. Sheets were comfortable against the skin and protected the bed and blankets from the oils and sweat and such that come from people's bodies. This way you could wash the sheets every week or so and not have to wash the blankets or bed. We had a few soft blankets like this after the accident, but they wore out when you were still toddlers. This should be a real improvement over the thick pads and tarps we are using now."

The Martians marveled at the soft, pliable fabric—much thicker than leaves, but nearly as flexible as graphene. "I'm looking forward to experimenting with them tonight," said Sniffles.

"Thank you, Sniffles," said Porter. "You stumbled upon some fine treasures. Mary, tell us about your discoveries."

Mary felt awkward. There had been no exciting drama when they had gone through the air lock with her scavenged goods. Likely none of them were edible. She wished that she had gone before Sniffles because she felt her finds wouldn't be as interesting. Sniffles had always been Porter's favorite anyway—but it was her time, so she showed what she had found. "The room I was in was pretty boring. There was a strange low grow table with poles sticking up and netting around. Inside there was this bit of material and this fuzzy doll." She held up the material and the doll.

"That makes sense," Porter said. "The low table was probably a bed for the infant that used the bottle Sniffles found. What you have there is a smaller version of a blanket and a toy zebra. What else did you find, Mary?"

Mary told them about the plastic boxes and held up the colored balls and bundles of green wire with the glass fragments. "These were pretty, but I don't think we can eat them."

Porter laughed. "Those look like Christmas decorations, Mary. Christmas is a holiday that many cultures on Earth celebrate. One way to celebrate the holiday is to decorate with colored balls and lights. Sometimes they are used to decorate a tree. Those plastic boxes that hold the chemicals are a standard issue. We brought many of them on our journey from Earth. Some held essential supplies, like the chemicals we used to treat and enrich the soil. When the contents were consumed, colonists often repurposed the boxes for general storage. There's no telling what you might find in storage boxes. What else do you have there?"

Mary held up the strange, lopsided cones. "Several of these in different shapes and sizes, always occurring in twos."

"Those, my dear, are shoes. They are coverings for feet. They help protect your feet from things on the ground. They come in different sizes because people have different sized feet. They come in different colors because it makes them look interesting."

"And if they were made of glass and exactly fit on your size feet, a prince will marry you?" Thing2 asked with false enthusiasm.

"Exactly!" Porter approved. "Between your foot and the shoes, you would usually have a cloth covering. As I've told you, they are called socks. They act as a pad or cushion. Remember the graphene we wrapped around your feet before you put them into the boots of the exo-suits? Socks are fabric that better serves that purpose. Anything else to share, Mary?"

Mary shook her head and sat down quietly.

Red stood and told of the room that he had searched. Conferring with Porter earlier, he had determined that he was likely exploring space dedicated to working and studying. Porter said it was called an office. Red triumphantly held up what he was sure was his big find—the computer tablet. It resembled Porter's but was larger and thinner. The Martians were visibly excited, and Red was proud. There was never enough time available on Porter's tablet. A second would relieve some of the contention.

There was no sign of life when the power button was pushed. Porter said that Thing1 would need to put electricity into the device to charge its batteries before it would work.

Red next held up the books that he had found. "These were stacked on a shelf with some rectangle images of people. I know that we were all hoping for some books to do with something besides first aid, so I grabbed these without looking at them." He spread the books on the ground and opened them.

The books were a collection of still pictures, with no words other than sometimes names and dates and places. One book had the word "DuFresne" imprinted on its thin cover. Inside were pictures of people of various sizes in strange places. Rooms with walls. Near trees covered with lights and balls like Mary had found. In all the pictures, people were wearing strange-colored coverings on their skin. When asked about the coverings, Porter explained that on Earth, as well as in the station, people often wore thin coverings like fitted blankets on their skin to keep them warm and protect them from the sun. As with the shoes Mary had found, the colors generally had no significance other than being pretty. As they flipped toward the end of the book, Red recognized the smiling man from the rectangles on the shelf. Seeing that the dates were getting later and later as they went through the book, Red recognized that some of the earlier pictures were of the smiling man when he was younger. From the names, they determined the smiling man was named John. Porter said that this was likely a "photograph album" of John's time growing up on Earth. These collections of pictures were used to help people remember the past. The other people in the pictures were probably his friends and family.

The second book was titled "Garcia-Sanchez" and had pictures of a darker-skinned and dark-haired family with three boys and a girl. Now that they understood what they were seeing, it was more apparent that as the pages turned, the children grew older. This book had no words or dates, just pages of pictures of a family growing up. Some of the pictures showed the family among trees that were impossibly tall. Others showed them standing by a huge body of water with trees and huge rocks in the background. As she aged, it was clear even through her clothes that the girl's body was changing from the straight lines of a child to the curvy lines of a woman. Red confirmed that the woman the girl became was also in the rectangle on the shelf.

The third book was titled "DuFresne-Garcia." After a few pictures of the man and woman together in different clothing and places, there was a clump with many similar pictures of the smiling man and the shorter dark-haired woman. In these, he wore black, and she wore fluffy white clothes with a bit of white netting in her hair. Porter said these were "wedding pictures." He explained that a wedding was a ceremony in which a man and woman chose to commit their lives to one another. It was a special gathering of friends and family that usually included feasting and music to celebrate the occasion. The clothes they wore were traditional for weddings in some cultures. Later pages showed the smiling man in an exo-suit without a helmet. Porter recognized the scene from the background and told them this was from mission training on Earth.

A few pages later when Porter saw a picture of the dark-haired woman in an exo-suit without a helmet, he exclaimed, "That's Maria! She was the aquaculture specialist. She helped set up the fisheries in Alpha. She was a very smart lady. I didn't work with her much, but I took a couple of classes with her while we were preparing for the mission."

Later pictures were looking out of a window at a huge Earth. These were labeled "Launch Day." Then there were a few pictures of the couple floating in the air. "That was probably while we were on the *Numa*," Porter said. Later pictures showed people in exo-suits laboring to establish the foundation and walls of what would later become greenhouse Alpha. There were also pictures of an excavation in the red Martian surface with equipment carrying rocks of various colors and sizes. Porter explained that these were the mines north of the station where minerals were extracted for use in building the station and its contents.

Red said, "There was a shelf that had a bunch of rocks of different colors that were labeled in a strange way. I didn't want to disturb them. Perhaps John DuFresne worked in the mines?"

"Good guesswork, Red. We should leave those rocks alone until we understand what the labels mean. It might be valuable information."

A later series of pictures showed Maria standing in front of a wall naked and turned to the side. As the series progressed, her belly began to distend, and her breasts grew larger.

"She's growing a baby inside her!" Mary exclaimed.

Porter nodded.

The pregnancy series ended with a picture of three people. It was labeled, "John, Maria, and Madison." Now there was a flurry of pictures of a growing baby. She began a small being with wisps of black hair that flew straight away from her head, dark eyes, and a thin mouth. Initially she was propped up among pillows and staring vacantly. In subsequent pictures the eyes focused and the initially toothless grin became a smile with more teeth. In the last pictures, the child was sitting on the floor and her straight black hair hung to her neck. Red read the caption on the last pictures aloud: "13 months and still no crawling, but Madison gets around fine scooting on her behind."

Everyone looked at Scooter, whose eyes went wide. Though Porter had told them the origins of their names long ago, the Martians had mostly forgotten, but with that hint, they knew who Madison had become.

CHAPTER 42 –
More Treasures

Over the next few days, Scooter considered changing her name, but rejected the idea. She had been "Scooter" as long as she could remember, and "Madison" seemed foreign. She studied the fuzzy zebra intently, trying to force or coax herself to remember it, but she detected no special significance. The people in the photographs were her parents; they seemed vaguely familiar, but she couldn't be sure. Still, it was intriguing to glimpse her lost past. She was the seedling of colonists. She had known that in an abstract sense, but now it seemed more real. Madison DuFresne-Garcia, descended from two Earthling families, the only surviving member of those families on Mars.

The photo albums were the only things from the initial trip that Scooter felt strongly about possessing. Porter suggested that Scooter should have first claim to any personal items found in the DuFresne quarters and recommended that Scooter be put on that team so that she could explore for herself. Mary gladly swapped with Scooter, hoping that she could find more interesting things elsewhere.

Scooter had high hopes about getting more information about her history and family from the tablet, but despite Thing1's charging activities, the power button generated no response. Porter said that the temperature variation may have hurt the electronics over time and suggested that Scooter keep the tablet in hopes that it might be repaired, or the data stored on it salvaged someday.

The Martians had been excited and energized by the first excursion, and it was followed by several more in rapid succession. Porter encouraged them to do short trips and debrief afterward so that all could learn something of the alien culture of the station.

They soon discovered that the sleeping areas were very similar. Soon all the Martians were using scavenged pillows and blankets and sheets in their dirt-filled sleeping tables. The blankets helped regulate temperature much better than the tarps and pads they had grown up with.

Helper's kitchen supplies were quickly enhanced by an assortment of bowls, cups, plates, and cutlery. She was happy to experiment with the few recovered spices. She and Porter made a bean and corn stew seasoned with chipotle that half of the Martians loved, and the rest found too spicy to eat. To Helper's surprise, Curly was among those who enjoyed it—he even returned for seconds.

Clothes began to accumulate, initially in one big pile, then sorted by type and size as the Martians began to wear them. Porter quickly adopted the habit of wearing pants. The Martians had been naked since a few months after Smoky Rescue Day and nakedness was normal. Porter explained that clothes served as a comfortable pad between their bodies and the exo-suits, and this information prompted successful experiments and rapid adoption of the practice of wearing clothes under exo-suits. Red discovered that wearing clothing while tending the corn resulted in fewer scratches, and he passed that information to Sniffles. Sniffles mentioned it to Helper, who observed that clothes protected her skin from cooking fire embers and splashes of hot food. Thing2 discovered that pockets gave him a place to store tools and small parts when he was fixing things. Soon many Martians were partially clothed most of the time.

Within a week they discovered that clothes needed to be washed periodically or they began to smell unpleasant, and a new chore was born. Without soap, soaking in a pot of hot water was the best way to clean the clothes. Because that involved spending time near the cooking fire (and Helper), Scar volunteered for laundry duty. Soon clothes lines were strung among the rungs of the ladder and draped with all manner of clothing, sheets, and blankets.

Six more tablets were discovered. Four hadn't survived. One of the remaining two required a password. The remaining functional tablet had belonged to someone interested in mathematics, electronics, and computer programming, judging by the books it contained. It also had interesting histories and music and literature from Asia. It quickly became the favored device for Pigpen, Curly, Thing1, Mary, and Red.

The Martians found a handful of books made of paper that Porter said were probably prized personal property. Porter explained that physical books were a rarity on the station apart from first aid books and emergency procedures to be used when computers might not be available, since electronic books were essentially weightless and free to transport.

Curly was bitterly disappointed by the implications of this on his stacks of mathematics books fantasy but encouraged that it might mean there were more books in the station than he had imagined.

Real books brought from Earth were rare treasures and included an early edition of "The Origin of Species" by Charles Darwin, a book of essays and letters by Albert Einstein, a mathematics book by Stephen Hawking, a book about architecture by Christopher Alexander, a fictional book called "The Martian" by Andy Weir (signed by the author), a thin paperback book of poetry by E.E. Cummings, a worn paperback called "the Prophet" by Kahlil Gibran, a small Bible, and a Quran. The Martians devoured most of them, although many found the stilted prose of Darwin, the Bible, and the Quran off-putting.

The three dozen crews' quarters of the outer ring between the Alpha and Charlie air locks had been thoroughly searched within a few days.

Although cribs and other evidence of children had been found in five of the rooms searched, there were no further clues as to which if any of the Martians might have lived there before Smoky Rescue Day.

Cisco continued to lead development of Bravo. Porter and Thing1 successfully replaced the Bravo environmental monitor that had been overcome by moisture and mold with one of the monitors from Alpha. Bravo was now self-sufficient and getting greener every day. A third of the tables were now productively growing bamboo and food and keeping carbon dioxide levels manageable.

During the initial foray to Bravo, Porter had selected a few of his old Earth-origin seeds for careful husbandry, including peppers, onions, garlic, mustard, cumin, rosemary, and grapes. Although his initial heirloom seed stock was the best Earth had to offer, carefully selected and meticulously packed, he was pessimistic about seed viability. Of the hundreds of seeds he soaked and carefully tried to grow, he was surprised and elated that several dozen germinated. None of the grape seeds survived, but a few hardy sprouts of the other plants were soon peeking out of the soil in a Charlie grow table. Encouraged, Porter had emptied his old Bravo seed cache and set up small pots in two grow tables in Bravo and two in Charlie to attempt sprouting all his remaining Earth origin seeds. He adjusted the pH in the pots to accommodate the seedlings and recruited Ginger and Pancho to monitor these tables for signs of growth.

A few weeks later, Ginger and Pancho proudly showed a pleased Porter that more of the old seeds had sprouted. He helped the pair differentiate the leaf patterns from the weeds and turned over care of the seedlings to them. His priority was to get fresh seeds from this generation preserved and stored in all three greenhouses as a hedge against disaster. His second priority was to expand the variety of growing plants, so the Martians weren't so dependent upon a limited variety of flora for their food and oxygen. His last priority, less pragmatic but more satisfying, was to expand Helper's inventory of cooking ingredients.

CHAPTER 43 –

A Sense of Urgency

Red's arms were tired. He had been scrubbing for hours trying to remove the last of the mold stains from his section of Bravo's glass ceiling. It was tedious work. He and Cisco were near the top of the maintenance ladder that stretched from one side of Bravo to the other, arching in the middle to match the contour of the ceiling thirty meters above the floor. The ladder was a meter wide and had a meter of clearance between itself and the wall/ceiling. This meant Cisco and Red were crouched at the top of the arc, not quite standing as they scrubbed. Ginger and Pancho were cleaning the walls from positions lower on the ladder, chatting as they worked. Sniffles, Mary, and Curly were tending plants below.

"My arms are tired. Ready to call it a day, Cisco?" Red asked.

"I am! We need to make the ladder taller or the roof lower so we can lie on our backs and do this. My knees don't like bending this way." In a louder voice, Cisco called, "You guys ready to be done?"

Murmurs of agreement rose from below.

"Give me five more minutes," Mary said. "I want to finish this row." She had been pollinating flowers by hand. Sniffles grabbed a brush and began to help her, eager to get back to Charlie and dinner.

"Race you, Cisco!" Red barked, as he left his bucket tethered where he had been working and vaulted over the side of the ladder.

As they had gained experience cleaning the ceiling, they had become impatient with the time required to navigate up and down the scaffold and the traffic that inevitably occurred when you had to move past someone. Red had tied a rope to the center of the arc, to allow buckets of water or other gear to be easily raised and lowered at the center of the span without needing to maneuver past others on the ladder. It didn't take long to realize that climbing the rope was much faster than climbing the ladder, particularly to get down. Red caught the top of the ladder with his hand as he went past, swung underneath, and grabbed the rope and quickly began to descend.

Cisco yelled with mock indignation, "No fair! You gave yourself a head start." She launched after him, trying hard to catch up so that she could "accidentally" hit him with her feet, but he was too far ahead. He had covered the thirty meters to the ground before she reached the halfway point, and he stood at the base of the rope, smiling.

It had been a long day. Cisco was pleased with their progress. Half of Bravo's glass, from where they were standing to the Alpha air lock, was as clear as Charlie now. Fifty meters finished, fifty to go. Months ago, they had started at the air lock and made a quick pass of all the glass to scrape the mold and mildew and let some light in. This was a more rigorous cleaning pass. Each day they moved the ladder another meter away from the Alpha air lock and cleaned another sixty or so square meters. In another forty to fifty days, they would be done.

The group donned their exo-suits and moved toward the Alpha air lock, helmets in hand. As they approached the air lock, helmets went on, visors went down, and Cisco did a quick comm check as they filed into the air lock proper and sealed the door. As thumbs went up, Red spoke, "Cisco, my air is low. I've got nineteen minutes, but I need a new canister soon."

"Me too," Pancho offered. "I've got twenty-three minutes, but I'll need a new can also."

Cisco glanced at the amber numerals of her helmet display: seventeen minutes. The numbers of the display turned red at ten minutes left. "Everyone has a spare in case of emergency, right?" she asked.

The response was a chorus of thumbs.

They cycled the air lock and moved to Charlie.

"Porter, we have a problem."

Porter looked up from the seedlings he was tending to see Cisco in her exo-suit, helmet in hand. She looked troubled. "What's up, Cisco?"

"We are running out of air canisters. We have three that haven't been used in each of the six air locks we have explored. Apart from those eighteen, all our other canisters—there are about eighty—just have a little air left, most less than thirty minutes."

As her words registered, Porter looked shocked. "How could I let this happen?" he asked, frustration apparent. "I was treating it like there was an unlimited supply and you guys didn't know any better. There is equipment in the station to recharge the canisters, but we haven't gotten to it yet. We have been depleting the emergency stores from the air locks for our excursions. The exterior air locks started with two dozen canisters and the secondary interior air locks have a dozen each. You said there are eighteen fresh ones remaining?"

Cisco nodded.

Porter said gravely, "We need to pick up the pace of reclaiming the station, or we won't be able to."

That afternoon, Porter organized an excursion to go into the station and fetch the air canisters from the East air lock. He assembled everyone after lunch and briefed them over a map of the station drawn in the dirt.

"We have been going too slowly. I wanted everyone to get used to the suits and the station and wanting you to have experience before we encountered anything too dangerous. Until now, we have limited our exploration to Bravo and the outer ring from nine o'clock to six o'clock." He pointed to the outer ring of the station on his model. "I was trying to avoid the east side because I believed the fire was somewhere in the northeast and I wanted to stay clear of that."

Porter looked around at the faces of the Martians. "We need to make faster progress. What I want to do now is take a small group and go to the East air lock to retrieve some additional air canisters. Then we will go west to the cafeteria along the three o' clock spoke, then come south. Our priority is to gather air canisters and assess the damage to the station that we can see. This will be a quick trip, consuming as little air as possible. I want to bring a small team, me plus three. Who should come?"

Cisco said, "Scar is the strongest."

Thing1 added,"'2 is the most mechanical. If things are damaged and you need to move debris, his lever and breaker bar would be helpful."

"Cisco is healthy now, she should go," Helper offered. Everyone knew Cisco had organized the effort that reclaimed Bravo. Whether she realized it or not, everyone assumed Cisco was the Martians' leader.

"Let's each bring a fresh air canister as a backup, but let's use up some of the partials," Porter said. "We'll leave in half an hour. '2, grab the breaker bar and some rope. Scar, get the cart. Cisco, you make sure the suits are charged and get the air canisters we'll need. Pancho, make sure your helmet is charged, too. You'll be our comm link back to Charlie."

As the team split up to prepare, Porter walked over to the clothes piles and searched for a tunic and socks.

CHAPTER 44 –
The East Air Lock

"There may be more bodies," Porter told the team. "We don't have time to deal with them right now. Keep an eye open for air canisters. Take any you see, but don't touch anything you don't recognize. Everyone ready?"

The team gave a thumbs-up and put their helmets on. A few moments later, they were moving counterclockwise along the gently curving outer ring from the Charlie air lock toward the East air lock. The task lights on their helmets illuminated the dark corridor. They came upon a cart sitting in the hallway that resembled the one they were pushing.

"I left that on the last trip on Smoky Rescue Day," Porter said. "I crawled back to the air lock from here." He took the newly acquired cart and continued down the corridor.

The doors to crew quarters along the outer wall were like the ones they were familiar with until the four o'clock position. There, a door marked "Nursery" stood ajar.

Porter hesitated. *No*, he thought, *not right now*. He moved on determinedly. He noticed smoke stains on the corridor wall. When they had passed the nursery, he said, "That was where you guys were on Smoky Rescue Day. Sumi pulled you from there and gave you to me in the outer ring. I brought you to Charlie."

An airtight door closed the corridor ahead. Porter noticed smoke stains on the wall, but none that suggested the door had leaked. He pulled the door open and held it for the others. Light streamed through the opening. Across the spacious East air lock receiving area were another pair of airtight doors, but they were offset twenty meters to the left, combining the middle and outer ring in the northwest quadrant. Beyond those doors the center ring would continue and arc to the left. To their immediate left was another set of double airtight doors; beyond those, the three o'clock spoke would lead to the cafeteria. To the left of those doors were the doors to the middle ring that would lead back to the six o'clock spoke. To their right was the East air lock and the ruddy daylight of Mars through the windows of the big double air lock doors. Porter moved to the air lock and peered inside.

The North and East air locks were the largest on the station, big enough for two vehicles to pass. North was the primary, and East the backup. Other than a six-wheeled emergency vehicle gleaming in the sun, the air lock appeared empty.

"I hate to vent so much atmosphere, but we have no choice," Porter said wearily. "Do it, Cisco."

Cisco operated the valve and the air noiselessly escaped. It took several minutes to vent the air lock.

"Is that a cart, Uncle Porter?" Scar asked. "It's huge!"

"That's a vehicle for emergencies," Porter explained. "It's like the electric goat in Delta, but big enough for a small crew and a few passengers. If someone got hurt while they were outside the station, this vehicle was designed to go and get them and bring them back. It has medical supplies and its own little air lock. If you look at the side, it can also dock with the other exterior air locks at Delta and Bravo."

As they opened the air lock door and moved inside, Porter said, "This large air lock should have more supplies than the others. Leave four air canisters here in case of emergency. Gather up the rest and put them in the cart. Let's secure the air lock and move to the cafeteria."

"If that vehicle is for emergencies, it probably has air canisters too," said Thing2. "We should take it. This would be a way to get things from Delta to Bravo that don't fit into an exo-suit."

"Good thinking, '2," Cisco offered. "Maybe that's how we could move some bees. What do you think, Uncle Porter?"

"I can't imagine the batteries have any juice left, but if Thing1 can figure out how to charge it, it would be very useful," Porter said.

"It has wheels," Scar observed. "We might be able to push it or pull it. Maybe we could use the goat."

"All good ideas, but let's stay focused. Leave it intact for now, with whatever air canisters it has."

The team made quick work of the supply cabinet. They found forty-eight air canisters and loaded forty-four into the cart. Then they moved back into the corridor, closing the air lock behind them.

The doorway ahead of them was four meters wide. Rather than the single doors they had seen thus far, a pair of airtight doors blocked the three o'clock spoke. Cisco opened the right door, and they moved past. Beyond lay the three o'clock spoke and twilight dimming to darkness as it progressed west. They moved ahead, closing the airtight door behind them. As their eyes slowly adjusted to the light from their helmets, Scar said, "Okay, my current air canister is close to zero. Hold on a second while I swap in another."

As Scar pulled a partially spent canister from his pocket, Porter scanned the walls, again seeing signs of smoke. "I don't see how the smoke managed to get everywhere. The ventilation system should have isolated the station into a lot of independent compartments when the airtight doors closed. But the smoke seems to have had no trouble spreading. You can see the smoke stains here and here." Porter gestured at the stains high on the wall.

"The stains are heavier by this grate." Thing2 pointed at a vent by the floor.

Porter knelt to look. "You're right, '2! Your eyes must be better than mine. I didn't notice till you pointed it out. The ventilation system must have been compromised—which explains a lot—but the ventilation system was designed to prevent that from happening. We'll have to inspect it and see what we can find. We need to fix the ventilation system before we can move back into the station."

"I'm ready," Scar said, fumbling with gloved hands to put away his spent air canister.

Soon they came upon another pair of airtight doors. Porter pointed. "To our left and right should be the inner ring. Would you please get the door, '2?"

Thing2 opened the right side of the paired doors, and the team moved through. Airtight doors sealed the entrances to the inner ring on either side. Double doors again barred the westbound path along the three o'clock spoke. There were two exo-suit clad bodies on the floor. They did not have helmets.

Cisco retrieved air canisters from the dead colonists' suits, fascinated by the desiccated faces. Traces of dried brown blood colored the withered faces and the floor. Scar moved to the far doors and opened the right side.

The wide corridor continued to another pair of airtight doors thirty meters ahead. As in previous spoke segments, there were no doors on the sides of the corridor, just smooth smoke-stained walls.

"Beyond is the cafeteria," Porter said.

"Is the corridor this wide so that the cart can get through?" Cisco asked.

"Yes," Porter answered. "The twelve o'clock and three o'clock spokes are about four meters wide, where the other spokes and the rings are only two meters. This made it easier to bring materials into the station in bulk."

They reached the doors, and Cisco stepped up and pushed open the door on the right. It swung a few centimeters and stopped. She looked through the gap, her helmet illuminating the dark.

"Oh," she said quietly. "There are bodies blocking the door."

"Try the left door?" Porter asked.

Cisco shook her head. "Bodies there too. Help me push."

Scar and Thing2 stepped beside Cisco. Porter unlatched the left and prepared to push on that side.

Cisco saw everyone was in place and said, "Push on three, ready? One... two ... three."

The left door slowly opened ten centimeters and then stopped. The right door slowly opened, sliding or pushing whatever was behind it, until it too came to a halt.

"Can you fit through?" Porter asked.

"'2 and I probably can. C'mon, '2," Cisco replied.

Cisco slipped between the doors. Thing2 followed.

Over the comm link, Scar and Porter heard Cisco say, "Let's move these to this side."

Grunting and heavy breathing came over the comm. Thirty seconds later, the right door opened wide. The scene beyond was chaotic. The floor was strewn with bodies, half of them in exo-suits. A few helmets were scattered on the ground here and there. The door opened into a clear space on the floor, but the stack of bodies blocking the left door was almost a meter high.

"Can we get these canisters later?" Cisco asked. "There are probably more than will fit in the cart anyway."

"Sounds good, Cisco," Porter answered. "We need to clear a path for the carts."

Scar strode forward and began clearing a path along the right wall by stacking bodies along the left. Cisco and Thing2 joined him, with Porter dragging both carts awkwardly behind.

The cafeteria was a large open space, roughly twenty meters across. Most tables and chairs appeared to have been pushed sloppily to one side. The few that remained near the center of the room were covered with blankets and bodies and medical supplies. There were thirty or forty bodies on the floor. None wore helmets, although dozens of helmets were on the floor or stacked haphazardly on counters and tables.

"Decompression must have been sudden," Porter said. "Catching everyone by surprise."

Glancing around the room, the airtight doors to the twelve o'clock spoke were open, blocked by bodies. The single doors to the nine o'clock and six o'clock spokes were closed.

"I need to swap out my air," Thing2 said.

Porter's gaze swept the room. As he turned his head, the harsh light from his helmet cut the darkness. That was probably the doctor, near the medical tables. Here and there were the husks of nameless and faceless fellow colonists. His light and vision paused briefly on each, then moved on. He wasn't sure if he wanted to find Julia among them, but still he searched. He would find her eventually.

"What's back here?" Scar pointed to the door behind the counter near the southwest wall of the cafeteria.

"That's the kitchen," Porter replied, distracted from his search. "Let's grab some foodstuffs and utensils for Helper and head home."

The small industrial kitchen was unlike anything the Martians had ever seen. Surfaces for food preparation. Stacks of bowls and plates. Knives and spoons of various sizes and shapes. Rows of metal pans and lids hanging from hooks. Racks of bulk items in tidy containers: flour, sugar, beans, rice, powdered milk, pasta, and vegetable oil. Gleaming metal cabinets lined the far wall.

Porter took a large pot from the hooks and put it in the cart, then nested several smaller pots inside. He took corresponding lids and added them to the cart. He placed flour, sugar, and oil into the cart, then added knives, spoons, and several spatulas. He went to a rack near the large stove and grabbed several containers of spices and vitamin supplements that he added to the cart. Both carts were filled to overflowing in less than ten minutes as the Martians surveyed the kitchen in awe.

"You guys make a path for the carts and let's get out of here," Porter said.

The path home on the six o'clock spoke was uneventful and they were soon in the Charlie air lock. When they emerged, the rest of the Martians were full of questions. Cisco, Scar, and Thing2 seemed excited by the novelty of adventure. Porter was subdued. He left the cart and walked to Delta while the rest of the team debriefed those who had remained behind.

CHAPTER 45 –

Morgue Patrol

It was clear to Cisco that they needed to dispose of the bodies. Her first instinct was to bring them to Bravo or Charlie, reclaim their clothes, cut them up, and churn them into the soil to recycle their biomass and minerals. She discussed this with Helper and Porter. Porter observed that different cultures had different death/funeral rituals and it might be more respectful to determine and address those individually. Cisco was frustrated by the inefficiency this implied but recognized his point.

While Porter might have been correct, determining the various cultural requirements didn't seem like a priority to Cisco. She sought Red's ideas, and he suggested moving the bodies to Alpha to get them out of the station proper for now. Red pointed out that there were already colonist bodies in Alpha and that repressurizing the station was a priority, but fixing and reclaiming Alpha was not.

"If we move the bodies there, they will be out of our way and we can deal with them later," Red said.

Cisco liked the idea of getting the bodies out of the way and dealing with cultural sensitivity at their leisure, so she quickly organized what Porter dubbed the "Morgue Patrol." She had Thing1 charge the goat and Thing2 and Scooter rig one of the carts so it could be towed by the goat. She assigned Ginger to operate the goat and Scar and Pancho to load the bodies.

After a quick recon of the nine o'clock spoke with Red to ensure there were no surprises or obstructions between the cafeteria and Alpha, Cisco had the Morgue Patrol clear the bodies from the cafeteria and the three o'clock spoke, cautioning them not to venture beyond the airtight doors of the twelve o'clock spoke from the cafeteria.

The goat was slow and steady. The "trailer" could hold half a dozen stacked bodies. The bodies were light and easy to stack. The morgue crew accomplished their task in a little over an hour, recovering air canisters from the bodies wearing exo-suits. That evening, when Cisco went to Bravo to oversee the cleanup crew's efforts, she found seventy-three bodies stacked neatly along Alpha's west wall. *Yes*, she thought, *there had been colonists. They were not three meters tall. They were human—and clearly mortal.*

CHAPTER 46 –
A Special Breakfast

Porter got up early the next morning and headed straight for the cooking fire. Helper was getting the kindling started and looked up, surprised, to see Porter in what was now her domain.

"Good morning, Helper," Porter said with a smile. "I was hoping I could catch you before you made breakfast. I have something special in mind."

"Scar said you seemed to raid the central kitchen with a purpose." Helper gestured toward the items recovered in yesterday's foray to the cafeteria, stacked near the other supplies.

"Let me show you a recipe that we haven't had the stuff for, assuming it hasn't gone bad with time."

Porter decided that the flour tasted a little off but didn't mention it to Helper. He set to work as Helper looked on. An hour later they presented a surprise to everyone gathered for breakfast. Porter lifted the lid from a warming pan with great fanfare, saying that, at last, he had discharged his promise to Helper after all these years. The warming pan contained four dozen real pancakes, made with powdered milk, flour, sugar, cooking oil, baking powder, salt, and vanilla. There was even artificial maple syrup with artificial butter-like flavor.

Whether the Martians enjoyed the pancakes of their own accord, appreciated them for the novelty, or simply wanted to humor Porter, who was obviously proud of his effort, the pancake feast was well received, and the cakes quickly devoured.

CHAPTER 47 – An Impromptu Ritual

"Porter?" It was unusual for him to sleep late. Helper gently touched his shoulder. It was cold.

"Porter!" she said more loudly and shook him. He was stiff. The blanket fell away from his face. It was peaceful, but still.

"Cisco!" Helper yelled. "*Cisco*!"

She caught herself and checked for a pulse. Nothing. She put an ear to his mouth. Nothing. Helper couldn't believe what her senses were telling her. Porter was gone.

Cisco came at a run. "What's wrong, Helper?" She stopped short. Whether she could deduce the situation from Porter's still figure or the sad shocked look on Helper's face, she knew in a moment what had happened. She hugged Helper, who began sobbing.

Others came shortly after, drawn by the commotion. Word spread quickly and soon all were assembled. They had seen corpses before—the desiccated corpses of the colonists in Alpha—but this was different. This was Porter, the only colonist, the only parent, that they had known.

For a long while they sat quietly in a haphazard circle around Porter's sleeping table, trying to imagine life without him.

Finally, Ginger stood and spoke. "Thank you, Uncle Porter, for saving us on Smoky Rescue Day." She bent over and kissed Porter's cheek, then sat down.

A few moments later, Red stood. "Thank you, Uncle, for keeping us safe." He leaned and kissed Porter's forehead, then sat, tears silently rolling down his cheek.

Thing2 stood. "Thank you, Porter, for asking us 'Porter questions' that taught us to think and explore." Thing2 laid his head against Porter's chest for a long moment and then returned to his seat.

Scar stood. "Thank you, Porter, for feeding us when we were young…" Then with a twinkle in his eye he added, "…and turning cooking duty over to Helper as soon as you could." Everyone laughed. He reached over the grow table and hugged Porter. Then he sat down next to Helper as she stood.

Eyes gleaming, Helper kissed Porter's lips. "The pancakes yesterday were pretty good though..." Her voice cracked on the last word, and she sat down crying quietly in Scar's arms.

Sniffles stood. "Thank you for taking care of me and carrying me. With the seedlings, you taught us to weed out the small and weak ones. I'm glad you had different rules for Martians." She put her hands on his face and kissed the top of his head. "You always made me feel safe and special. I love you, Uncle Porter." Sniffles sat down, trying to be brave. Curly was sitting next to her and comforted her as best he could. Sniffles nestled into his arms. He rocked her slowly and gently while she shed silent tears.

Pancho stood. "Thank you for showing us the station." He paused, struggling for words, then added, "You made the world bigger." He sat next to Ginger.

Cisco and Mary each started to rise at the same time. Cisco sat, nodding to Mary. Mary said, "You kept us alive and taught us to survive. I guess that was the best you could do to get us off this desolate planet. It's up to us now. We may succeed or fail, but we wouldn't have had a chance without you." She stroked the fuzzy hair on his head for a moment, and then sat down, silently mouthing, "Thank you."

Cisco rose. "Porter showed me the ocean. It was a special thing that he shared with me. And he let me lead the Bravo cleanup crew when I got hurt and was feeling sorry for myself. Thank you for showing us how to make one another feel special." Cisco smiled sadly, then sat.

Scooter stood and touched Porter's cheek thoughtfully for a long moment, then smiled and sat down again.

Curly comforted Sniffles, stroking her hair and rocking her until she was cried out. Then he stood and jogged toward the receiving area, leaving Sniffles weary and confused.

Thing1 stood. "We will always remember you, Uncle Porter. I remember reading a story that said, 'A man is not gone as long as someone speaks his name.' I will speak your name to my children. You are not gone; you live on in our memories." Thing1 kissed Porter's nose and sat down.

Pigpen stood. She sang a song of strange and pretty words that no one could understand. It was a sad song. It began quietly—just above a whisper—but grew into a full-throated ballad whose melody spoke of love and loss while the words danced in a strange rhythm. When the song ended, she sat down quietly next to Thing1.

Helper slowly rose again and moved to where Porter lay. She stroked his fuzzy hair and bent to smell him one last time. She lingered a moment, then wordlessly returned to her seat.

As Helper sat down, Curly returned with Porter's tablet. He touched the controls and soon Albert King's "Blues Power" issued forth, slowly at first, then building. He placed the tablet on Porter's chest, then backed up and stood, eyes closed, swaying to the music. Soon the others too were standing. Some moved with the music, while others seemed lost in reflection. The engaging guitar of a long-dead blues master celebrated the life of their friend, parent, and mentor.

People stayed for a while after the music stopped, and then began drifting away in ones and twos. Cisco was the last to leave. With the other colonists, it was unclear what cultural rituals might apply, but Porter had taught them about the circle of life. Cisco removed Porter's clothes, struggling to remove his tunic from his rigid arms. She removed the blanket and pillow and the tarp that separated him from the soil that made his bed. Then she filled his grow table with soil to cover him, watered it, added worms, and sprinkled the top with wildflower and grass seeds. She knew that the worms would grow fat and the flowers that bloomed would be lovely.

CHAPTER 48 –

Priorities

Later that night at dinner, Cisco addressed them all. "We need to figure out what to do next. Porter said the power source might be the cause of the trouble on Smoky Rescue Day. He also said it could be more dangerous that we could imagine. I think we need to learn more about it before we go farther north in the station. Who has been learning the most about physics and energy?"

Thing1 said, "Pancho and I learned a bunch about electricity. Curly, Ginger, Scooter, and Pigpen studied physics beyond that."

Pigpen demurred. "Scooter and I really focused on sound. I think Ginger and Curly got more deeply into atomics and energy."

Ginger smiled. "The math was really pretty and a little scary. It's amazing how much energy is released under the right circumstances. We didn't study nuclear power exactly, though."

Curly listened to Ginger, nodding his head in agreement.

Cisco said, "It sounds like you two are the best prepared to learn more about the subject. I need you to focus your attention on power generation and things that can go wrong. Do we have enough material to support that?"

"What we have found so far is pretty basic," Ginger said. "Where can we get more information about the actual power plant in *New Rome*?"

"Sounds like that is a priority before we go farther north," Cisco responded. "Anyone have an idea?"

Pigpen spoke. "Porter said there was a computer system with information about how the station operated and training materials and technical manuals. If we could locate that system and get it working, we would know a lot more."

"If we can't find that computer, there is always a chance we could find other tablets in the other crew quarters or other parts of the station," Red suggested.

"I suggest we do this," Cisco said. "Let's do a quick search of the station from the cafeteria south. There's a fifty-fifty chance the computer is located there. While we are searching, we need to be careful of things we haven't seen before and be on the lookout for computers, tablets, and any instructional manuals. We need to stay focused and avoid toys and curiosities for the time being. The only things we collect are tablets, computers, books, and air canisters. Are we agreed?" Cisco paused and looked at each of them.

"Porter put you in charge of Bravo cleanup, not *everything*!" Mary said.

"Do you have a different plan, or do you have concerns about this one?" Cisco asked patiently.

"No, but why do you have to be so bossy?" Mary complained.

"Mary, you have made clear that you—more than any of us—want to get away from Mars. To do that, we need to reclaim the station and figure out how to communicate with Earth. If you have suggestions for how we can do that faster or more safely, please offer them. If you don't, then help us plan and support the plans we agree to," Cisco said in an even tone.

Everyone was silent. The Martians all looked at Mary. Mary looked away and sat down.

Cisco addressed the group again. "Are we agreed?"

Pancho spoke first. "Sounds good to me. What size teams are you thinking?"

"I was thinking teams of four to start with. It should make the searching go faster without sacrificing safety. It took all four of us to force the airtight door on the three o'clock spoke," Cisco said.

Red said, "Cisco, with the limited air, maybe teams of two would be more efficient. If they run into anything they can't move, or a door they can't open, they can move on and come back later for help."

Scar agreed. "I think Red has a point. Teams of two should be able to do a preliminary search quickly. We should have a much better idea of what's going on in the station after we have visited the south half of it."

"Okay, teams of two for exploring the south part of the station—probably three or four person teams for the north to address safety. Should we start now, or wait till morning? There are no lights in the station other than our helmets, so daylight isn't relevant."

The group had eaten dinner in a subdued silence. Porter had been their first intimate experience with human death. The adventure of exploration had reenergized the group. They decided to begin right away.

Cisco had drawn a map in the dirt on the floor:

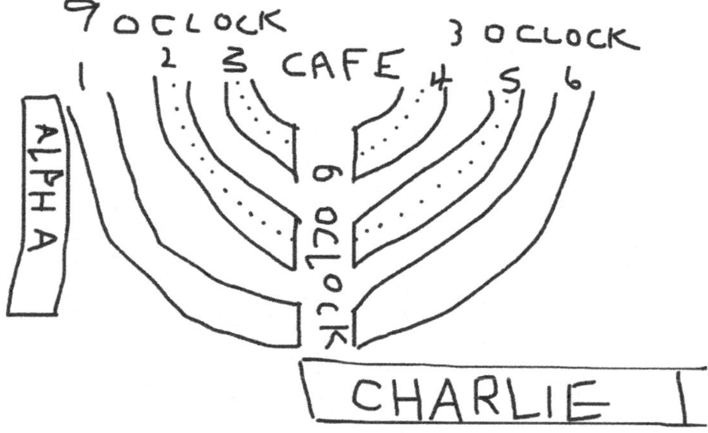

"We have three rings to explore: outer, middle, inner. We are focusing on the south side of the station. The southern half of the rings are split by the six o'clock spoke into a southwest side and a southeast side. Let's number the quarter rings from left to right.

"We have already explored the outer southwest ring—ring 1. Those were crew quarters. Porter said that ring 6 was also mostly crew quarters. Let's have the first teams explore ring 6, the outside of ring 2, and the outside of ring 5. We have traveled those corridors and know they are clear, so Red's point about teams of two probably being safe should apply. That makes three areas to explore. Let's assign one person in the station to serve as communications coordinator for each of the three teams so we can monitor them, so it will really be teams of three—two in the station and one here in Charlie on comm. Who are the teams?"

Scooter said, "Thing2 and I can be an exploring team. We will take outer ring 2. Sniffles, will you coordinate comm for us?"

Sniffles nodded, happy to be included.

"Ginger and I can be a team. We'll do ring 6. Will you cover comm, Helper?" Pancho offered.

Helper smiled and nodded.

"Scar and I can be the third team," said Red. "Outer ring 5. Mary, will you be our comm?"

Red's question hung in the air for a moment. Mary was looking down. Cisco appreciated Red trying to involve her and normalize things after her earlier complaining, but it would only help if Mary accepted the invitation.

A beat later, Mary acquiesced. "I guess so, sure."

Cisco was pleased by the enthusiasm. "Okay, let's meet at the air lock suited and ready to go in fifteen minutes."

The sun was low in the sky as they assembled at the air lock, casting long shadows and giving everything a deep blue-purple glow. All the teams were early. *I guess we really are descended from explorers*, Cisco thought. Everyone seemed energized.

"Should we all be on the same channel, or should we use three separate ones?" Helper inquired.

"What do you guys think?" Cisco asked.

"Separate channels," Red suggested. "We each have independent comm help and we are going for speed. Too much chatter with different teams exploring different areas. We can change to a common channel later if necessary."

Thing2 nodded.

The teams adjusted their communicators, lowered their visors and did a comm check. Sniffles, Helper, and Mary sat in a circle without exo-suits, helmets on and visors up. Curly, Thing1 and Pigpen sat with them. Cisco watched the teams exit the air lock, then moved to sit with the others.

Exiting the air lock, Scooter and Thing2 went left, the other teams went right, the beams of their headlamps bobbing on the wall and then diverging.

The first door Scooter and Thing2 came to was labeled **O 06:32 – Utility Access**. Opening the door, they found a hatch in the floor. Thing2 lifted the hatch, revealing a ladder going down.

"Hey, Sniffles. Check the tablet and find out what 'Utility Access' means," Scooter said.

"Hmmm … 'Utility' has a couple of definitions. 'Useful for a purpose … a limited function computer program … a service such as electricity or water that is provided to the public,'" Sniffles read aloud.

"This could be interesting. I'm betting power and water, maybe air. Let's explore quick, '2," said Scooter. "Sniffles, let Cisco know we are going down the ladder behind the Utility Access door."

Thing2 stepped down onto the ladder, grabbing the sides of the ladder loosely with his gloved hands and dropped into the hole, braking with his hands to control his speed. The crash of him hitting the floor could be heard through his comm channel as landed in a heap at the bottom of the ladder. "Yeow! Floor down here is slippery. Careful, Scooter."

Scooter descended the ladder cautiously, the light of her headlamp shimmering and scattering in a thousand directions as it bounced off the translucent floor. She stopped at the last rung and tested the footing. "Wow. *Very* slippery."

"I think it's frozen water. Look here. This pipe is broken." Thing2 pointed to a fractured pipe the size of his leg.

Scooter looked around the room. It was a vast open space with a low ceiling. Pillars ran from floor to ceiling every ten meters or so. Neatly bundled cables and a collection of pipes of varying diameters were affixed to the ceiling and the pillars and seemed to run everywhere. Several of the pipes were burst, as if something inside them had grown large and escaped.

Thing2 was moving tentatively and carefully north from the ladder, his boots clearly sliding without purchase over the floor.

"There appear to be two or three other ladders," he said. "I can see them on the outer rings at three o'clock and nine o'clock. I'm guessing there's also one at twelve o'clock, but it's dark and there is some structure near the center that blocks my view. Look how thick this layer of frozen water on the floor is!" Thing2 pointed at a mass emerging from the floor.

Scooter didn't recognize what she was seeing at first. Then she noticed the tops of the wheels barely visible above the layer of frozen water on floor and realized it was a tool cart, like the electric goat kept in Delta. "That's why the ceiling seems so low. The ice must be nearly half a meter thick."

"Okay, guys, sounds interesting, but 'computers, books and air canisters' are the priority," Sniffles chided gently.

"Right, Sniff," Thing2 responded. "We *will* need to explore this more later. There's water to reclaim and the ventilation system may be down here. I'm sure '1 would love to follow these cables and figure out what goes to what."

Scooter swept her headlamp one last time around the huge dark space, and then ascended the ladder. Thing2 followed her up. They closed the hatch, closed the door and continued clockwise around the outer ring.

The next door was labeled **O 06:34 – Laundry**. There was a transparent panel in the top half of the door. Beyond the door was a room three meters wide and four meters deep. Inside they found six metal cabinets sitting on the floor along one wall and a table along the other partially covered with clothes, some folded and some thrown haphazardly into a plastic storage box.

"Look, '2!" Scooter exclaimed, pointing. A computer tablet lay on the table beyond the plastic box full of clothes.

"We found a tablet!" Thing2 announced, as Scooter retrieved the treasure.

The next door was labeled **O 06:38 – Gym**. It was a room twice the size of the laundry. Inside were several strange machines, but none that looked immediately useful.

Door **O 07:00 – Facilities Office** was next. It was a small room with two desks. On one wall was a large diagram of the main floor of the station as seen from above with tidy hand-drawn notes. The other walls held pictures of the station in various stages of construction: several angles of the vacant Martian landscape, some with *Numa* appearing in the background; several images of a progressively excavated hole that probably corresponded to the utility space they had seen below their feet when they went down the ladder; a layer of rock or cement lining the now-completed excavation that would serve as the bottom of the station's pressure vessel; the mesh floor of the main level being built on top of the Utility Access space, supported by pillars from below; the walls of the concentric rings of the station emerging, as if they had grown up from the floor; the roof appearing in stages, obscuring the finishing work below; and finally, pictures of various rooms and air locks, including one picture of the Alpha greenhouse that showed its symmetry before the meteorite destroyed its eastern side.

Most of the pictures showed exo-suited workers actively engaged in construction, giving a constant sense of scale to the endeavor.

"This is amazing," Thing2 said reverently. "I'm tempted to bring these images back. What do you think, Scooter?"

"We can come back with a tablet and copy the images of construction so we can show the others. Let's take the big diagram back so we can study it. Do you think we can get it off the wall without harming it?"

"I think so," Thing2 said, examining and then touching the image. "It appears to be resting against this wall, but I don't understand why it remains suspended at this height."

He pulled the bottom of the image slightly away from the wall and peered awkwardly behind it with his bulky helmet. "It seems to be attached at the—"

The picture fell away from the wall and twisted from his gloved grasp, crashing noiselessly into the desk and breaking the frame at the bottom. The image appeared unharmed.

"I figured out how to get it off the wall," Thing2 said sheepishly.

Scooter laughed. "You know, your problem solving skills are one of the reasons you are my favorite."

Scooter searched the rest of the room. She found a toolbox in a cabinet, and another tablet in a desk drawer. She also found some large and flat drawers that contained detailed drawings of the station with strange notes on them. She stacked the drawings on top of the large image from the wall for ease of carrying.

"This was quite the room," Scooter said with satisfaction. "We found another tablet and some great pictures of the station to help with our exploration. We have a couple of rooms to go, Sniffles, and then—"

"*Wait*!" Sniffles said, her voice on edge.

"What's up, Sniff—" Thing2 began.

"*Quiet*!" she interrupted. "There is a problem—Ginger is hurt! Come back to the air lock, *now*!"

Scooter and Thing2 left the images stacked on the desk, grabbed the two tablets they had found, then quickly ran toward the air lock.

CHAPTER 49 –

Fish Out of Water

Pancho and Ginger were exploring the crew quarters on the outer ring to Charlie's east. The layout was similar to those they had explored to the west months before: the apartments consisted of a main living quarter with two small rooms to one side and closets and a door to a shared bath on the opposite wall. Unlike their prior explorations, minimal light filtered through the exterior windows because the sun was nearly down. They could see the lights of Charlie through the windows glowing ever more brightly as the sun set and it gave them pause. It was a perspective both of them had imagined but never seen.

"It's beautiful." Ginger sighed. "I look forward to showing this to you, Helper. The grow lights illuminate the greenery, and a little bit spills out of the greenhouse window and lights up the ground beside the greenhouse. The shadows seem to devour the light. Hey, stand up and we might be able to see you."

They were in the third apartment counterclockwise from the six o'clock spoke; the sun was now just a suggestion of blue light below the horizon. They saw Helper's helmet pop up perhaps twenty meters away and Pancho and Ginger trained their helmet lamps in her direction. Helper waved.

"I see you!" Helper laughed. "How many times have I stared at those dark windows wondering what was inside!"

"I suspect your imagination was more interesting that what we are finding, Helper," Pancho offered. "Unless you imagined a bunch of furniture, blankets, and clothes. We did find an air canister in a closet and some more jars and bottles, but no tablets, computers, or books."

"You guys have been gone for fifteen minutes and you've only found one air canister? Scooter and '2 have found a tablet and a whole different area of the station that we didn't know about. You better get exploring!" Helper teased.

The next apartment they entered was labeled **O 4:20 – Captain Lee**. The room was twice the size of the others. The floor plan was unique. The main room was dominated by a round table composed of two halves. A dozen chairs surrounded the table. The window was larger than those found in the other quarters, the greenery of Charlie filling their view and stray streaks of light peeking through the window to make strange shapes on the table. A large dark computer screen dominated the wall containing the entry door. A keyboard and stylus lay on the table. There was a small sitting area in one corner with a few stuffed chairs and a small clear table. Several books were arrayed along a high shelf near the ceiling.

Exploring the two auxiliary rooms revealed one to be a kitchen with a small table for two, and the other to be sleeping quarters. Apparently, the captain preferred his bed firmly on the ground rather than suspended from the ceiling as the others had been. He also appeared to enjoy a private bathroom.

There was no sign of a tablet.

"Looks like the books are our only treasure, Ginger," Pancho sighed. "I can't reach. I'll lift you up so you can get them."

Ginger climbed up on the little clear table and beckoned Pancho over. "I'll get on your shoulders."

As Pancho approached and began to turn, Ginger shifted her weight to the center of the table and the glass surface fractured. Her leg went through the table surface, the glass shards ripping her exo-suit. Mist sprayed in all directions as her suit lost pressure.

The audible alarm of the suit said, "Suit integrity compromised..." The electronic voice trailed off.

Ginger said, "Oooh!" and then made a gurgling whoosh sound that quickly diminished to silence.

It took Pancho a moment to figure out what had happened. "Are you all right, Ginger?" he called.

No response.

Then he noticed the mist and blood streaming from the slices in the leg of her suit.

"Helper! Ginger's suit is damaged. I'm bringing her to the air lock. I'll need help."

It took a moment to extricate Ginger's leg from the shattered table, then Pancho picked her up and hurried from the room.

Red and Scar met Pancho in the hallway and helped carry Ginger. Red wrapped his hands around her calf as tightly as he could and her suit began to inflate, but he could not hold the seal and mist and blood repeatedly sprayed out beneath his grasp.

When they reached the air lock, Scooter was holding the door open and Thing2 was standing by the controls. They rushed Ginger through the door and Scooter closed it. "Sealed, '2!" she yelled.

It had been forty-seven seconds since Ginger stepped through the glass tabletop when the air lock began to repressurize.

CHAPTER 50 – Emergency

"Get her helmet off!" yelled Mary.

Helmets were designed to be put on and taken off by the wearer, it was awkward for Pancho to do it bent over Ginger's prone figure. When it did come away, he was horrified. Her face was swollen, and deep red. Blood trickled from her closed eyes and nose and ears. She had vomited in her helmet.

"Oh no!" he cried. "Ginger!"

"No time for that now. Get her out of this suit! Be careful of that leg, it looks like she still has glass in it." Mary called to mind what she and Sniffles had seen in the first aid videos, A-B-C-D.

Airway. Mary turned Ginger's head to the side and pushed her fingers into Ginger's mouth, quickly scooping away as much of the vomit as she could.

Breathing. Ginger coughed weakly, bits of vomit spraying from her throat. Sniffles ran up with a tank of oxygen and the bulky first aid kit. "Is she breathing?" At Mary's nod, Sniffles held the mask to Ginger's face and opened the valve on the tank. She then put the elastic band of the mask around Ginger's head.

Control shock. "Get blankets!" Mary cried. "Get her out of this suit, cut it if you have to." As they removed the suit and cut away her clothes, it became clear that Ginger's body had been traumatized. The suit contained blood and urine. Ginger's skin was angry red all over. "Put the bundle of clothes under her feet to elevate them."

Dress the wound. "Get me some water and clean rags!" Mary said. She began to remove the pieces of glass from Ginger's calf and clean the wound with disinfectant while Sniffles washed the rest of Ginger's body.

Sniffles observed that removing the glass worsened the bleeding.

"Leave the glass alone, Mary," Sniffles said. It wasn't an order, but it wasn't a question.

Mary paused, scowling.

Sniffles could see that Ginger had lost a lot of blood, and her wounds were still bleeding freely. She took a rubber hose from the first aid kit and wrapped it tightly several times around Ginger's leg just below the knee to constrict circulation. The bleeding continued but slowed. "Removing the glass is increasing the bleeding. She has lost a lot of blood and I think we need to get an IV of replacement blood started right away," Sniffles said.

Mary looked at Sniffles with surprise. An IV? That might be what the book said, but they had never…

"I don't remember the dosage, but we should probably give her some epinephrine as soon as we get the drip set up. It should restore blood pressure and help her heart. Mary, as I recall dosage is done by Earth weight. It's about 2.5 times Mars weight. Ginger is probably seventeen or eighteen kilos… so what … fifty kilos?"

Mary hesitated a moment and then realized that Sniffles was in charge. Sniffles had clearly advanced beyond her in their medical studies. Mary was taken aback, and a little hurt, but she put that aside. *No time for that now,* she thought. She grabbed the first aid kit and searched for the artificial blood and epinephrine.

Pancho was distraught. Ginger was red and swollen all over. Blood still flowed from the gashes on her leg. He didn't know what to do. He was trembling. He felt powerless.

Sniffles was trying to figure out the business end of the IV, aware of Pancho's panic. "Pancho, hold this bag by the end, chest high." She handed him the IV bag. He took it wordlessly, numbly following her instructions.

Sniffles wrapped rubber tubing around Ginger's arm to help find a vein. It took several stabs to get the IV properly placed, but then she taped it down and injected the epinephrine syringe Mary handed her into the IV port.

"Okay, we need to get the glass out of that wound, clean it up, bandage it, then release the pressure on that cord," Sniffles said.

The other Martians looked on in stunned silence as Mary and Sniffles attended to Ginger. It had been less than twelve hours since they had said goodbye to Porter. Porter seemed asleep. His death had been quiet and tidy. Ginger had clearly been grievously wounded—a visceral reminder of the mortality that they knew intellectually, but only barely understood.

Ginger lay covered by a blanket, her face and exposed arm bright red and puffy, her legs elevated above an expanding puddle of her own blood. Her body had been mostly wiped clean, but the bloody rags and gauze pads used for the task were nearby and bore witness to her ordeal. The Martians stood by helpless and worried for the health of their beloved Ginger, watching Mary and Sniffles stitch her wounds closed.

"We need to move her to a bed where she can rest comfortably," Sniffles finally said. "It will be warmer than the ground."

"I'll prep her sleeping table," said Cisco, running off.

"How can we move her?" asked Pancho.

"Graphene sheet," said Scar. "Like Porter used to move dirt and vegetables. Put it under her and we can lift from the sides without jostling her too much."

Soon, Ginger's prone body was being gently conveyed by half a dozen Martians to her sleeping table. An anxious Pancho walked beside her, the IV bag held high over his head.

CHAPTER 51 –

Tasteless

Sniffles took the first turn watching Ginger. There wasn't much to see or do. The first IV of artificial blood took about an hour to administer. When Ginger's pulse was stable, Sniffles slowed the flow of the second IV, watched and waited.

Pancho brought Sniffles some broth and an apple as the first hint of sun began to roll back the gloom of night. Sniffles stifled a yawn, thanked Pancho, and devoured the offering.

"Why don't you sleep, Sniff? You could climb into the table with her. I'll keep watch and let you know if she wakes up or if there are any changes."

Sniffles resisted for a moment, but she was very tired. She showed Pancho how to take Ginger's pulse and check her breathing and made him promise to wake her if there were any significant changes. She knew that Pancho needed a way to be helpful and the look on his face said he wouldn't sleep any time soon. Ten minutes later, Sniffles was snoring softly near Ginger's feet, and Pancho's vigil began.

Pancho listened with relief to Ginger's steady, wheezing breath. He checked her pulse every hour or so, finding it weak but stable. He was becoming concerned about the IV bag nearly being empty and was preparing to wake Sniffles when Mary arrived.

The three of them took turns of several hours each. Day faded to night. Night became day again. Martians came to check on Ginger and bring her caretakers food and water.

Day faded to night again. Sniffles was watching Ginger while Pancho slept by her feet when Ginger emitted a croaking sigh.

"Hey, sweetie, how are you feeling?" Sniffles asked, hearing an echo of Porter in her own voice.

"So … I'm not dead?" Ginger rasped weakly. When she opened her eyes, they were a shocking blood red.

"You tried, but we weren't ready to let you go."

"Your voice sounds muffled and far away. My head hurts—my whole body hurts. My throat is so dry. Can I have some water?"

"Sure, but go slow, you have been asleep for a couple of days." Sniffles offered the cup of water.

"Days?" Ginger lifted her head slightly to sip the water and made a face. "This tastes wrong."

Sniffles took the cup and sampled it. "Tastes okay to me."

"Feels like I have dirt on my tongue. Got anything I can eat?"

"Here's some pancakes and hummus. The hummus is pretty good. Helper put some of the new garlic in it. See what you think." Sniffles spread the hummus on the cake and rolled it into a tube. "It's a little spicy, but good."

Ginger took a small bite. "I don't taste anything. I can feel the pancake on my tongue, but I get no flavor at all."

"Well, chew it well and drink some water. Maybe you forget how to taste things after a couple of days. I don't think we have ever gone two days without eating before. I'll check the first aid book and see what I can find out. How does your leg feel?"

"Like fire, now that you mention it," Ginger replied.

Sniffles put her hand gently on Ginger's forehead. "You probably have an infection. The wounds on your leg were pretty nasty." She fumbled with the first aid kit for a moment and emerged with a vial of antibiotics. Removing the lid from the bottle, she wrinkled her nose. "If this tastes anything like it smells, you may be happy you can't taste anything right now."

Ginger did little but eat and sleep for several days. On the fourth day after she awakened, her sense of taste began to slowly return. Sniffles's research discovered that a temporary loss of taste was a strange side effect of vacuum exposure, reported by the few people who had survived it. As she explained it to Ginger, "Maybe saliva boiling off your tongue kills or shocks your taste buds."

The infection in Ginger's leg was slow to retreat, even with the antibiotics. On the eighth day after the accident, Sniffles and Mary decided to reopen and clean two of the more serious-looking lacerations. Fortunately, the first aid kit had both anesthetic and tranquilizers. Ginger was able to abide the procedure with only minor discomfort. Two days later, Ginger's fever broke. She still reported difficulty hearing; everything was muffled. Her bloodshot eyes transitioned from bright red to pink as the days passed, then faded to white as they gradually returned to normal. Her "vacuum bruise," which had initially caused her skin to swell to an angry red, turned brown and dark blue, and then faded through green, and eventually went away.

Twelve days after her accident, to everyone's relief, Ginger resumed her studies of nuclear physics with Curly and was hobbling around Charlie, asking people to speak louder.

CHAPTER 52 –
New Rome

While Ginger was recovering, exploration of *New Rome* continued.

The detailed map that Scooter and Thing2 recovered from the facilities room helped focus the expedition. According to the map, the south side of the station was primarily concerned with the colonists:

- Living quarters
- Laundry
- Medical facility
- Gym
- Group cooking facility
- Childcare
- Classrooms
- Social spaces
- Meeting rooms

The north side was where most of the station's business was performed:

- Processing ore from the mine
- Garage for building, storing, and repairing vehicles
- Power generation
- Heating and ventilation control
- Pressure maintenance
- Carbon dioxide scrubbers and oxygen plant to keep the air breathable
- Raw material storage
- Chemistry, physics, and biology labs
- Manufacture and repair of clothing, tools, electronics, furniture and parts
- Communications and central station operations
- Computer systems
- Water generation

Spaceship *Numa* had been integrated into the northwest corner of the station and served as backup communication, storage, and offices.

Thing1 and Thing2 returned to the Utility Access area below the station and explored it more fully. Many of the pipes had burst. Thing2 speculated that the designers had assumed the area would always be heated and might not have anticipated water freezing in the pipes. The Utility Access area was responsible for water, air, heat, data, and power distribution throughout the station. There was a ruptured storage tank on the west side labeled "water." Pipes appeared to run between that tank and Alpha. The space was also used for bulk storage and they discovered an elevator for moving bulk freight between the basement and the cafeteria.

The main computer systems were located on the inner ring at ten o'clock. There was no specific mention on the station map of where the air canisters might be refreshed, but Scar suggested that, based on his understanding of chemistry, it would likely be with the carbon dioxide scrubber or associated with the chemistry lab, both of which were in the northeast between one and three o'clock. This area was where Porter believed the fire had occurred and he was worried it would be dangerous, so Cisco suggested they try to get to the computer systems first to get additional information about the station before venturing further.

After Ginger's accident, the search teams were more cautious. They had done a preliminary search of the southern half of the station, finding a total of three computer tablets; one was password protected, the second dead, and a third that proved to be a trove of music, literature, and movies. Nonfiction offerings included books about computer algorithms, evolutionary biology, psychology, and chemistry, though none of these works had information specific to the station.

The "real" books that they recovered from the captain's room included a book about maritime law, a book of Earth history, a picture book of historical ships, and a book about navigation using the sun and stars. Apart from picture books for children, and three volumes of detailed medical texts, no other physical books had been found.

The teams discovered seventeen air canisters scattered throughout the crew quarters, most with at least 50 percent of their capacity remaining. They also found several more exo-suits. All the Martians now possessed a suit that fit them.

CHAPTER 53 –

I 10:17

The team moved west from the cafeteria toward the airtight door leading to the nine o'clock spoke. It had been four weeks since Ginger's accident. Headlamps made bobbing circles of light amid the shadows of the floor, tables, and walls. All the bodies had been moved to Alpha, but debris remained on the floor: cups, plates, helmets, bandages, tools, clothing, and many bits and piles of nondescript remnants of unknown origin. Thing2 operated the door to open it, and the other three Martians moved through and into the corridor beyond.

"If these airtight doors worked, it's hard to understand how the station could decompress quickly," Scooter observed as she walked through. She ran her gloved hand along the door's seal. "It doesn't appear to be damaged."

"Porter suspected it was a problem with the ventilation system," Thing2 reminded her. "The doors were designed to close in case of fire or decompression, and they appear to have closed. I imagine there would have to be a similar device operating in the air circulation system; otherwise the doors would close but the air would quickly escape through the vents."

"I wondered if it might have been a power problem," Thing1 said. "But I read that these doors were held open by electromagnets." He pointed his helmet's lamps toward the device mounted on the wall and the corresponding post on the airtight door. "Without power, they would snap closed with force."

"I doubt it behaved the way they planned," said Pigpen. "Porter said they hadn't hooked the ventilation system up to the greenhouses yet and that may be why we are alive."

Twenty meters of hallway led to the next door. Thing2 again operated it, letting his companions through to the chamber beyond. This group of four airtight doors was the nexus of the inner ring and the nine o'clock spoke. The group turned north to follow the inner ring. Pigpen operated this door. This was the Martians' first foray into the north half of the station. It swung open into darkness broken only by their helmet lights.

More bodies—bodies in doorways, bodies in the hallway—six in all. Some wore exo-suits; none wore helmets. The party began moving the bodies to the left side of the hallway, clearing a path for the cart Thing2 pushed.

"Having seen what happened to Ginger in a few moments of vacuum, I feel differently about these bodies than I did before," Thing1 mused. "Before, they were just things to be moved, like a box or a bundle of corn stalks. Now, I realize the colonists were people—like Ginger—but no one was here to rescue them."

The group worked in thoughtful silence for several moments.

"Ginger said she didn't remember much. She said her leg hurt from getting stabbed and the air was knocked out of her and her ears hurt, and her tongue was bubbling, and she couldn't breathe, then she didn't remember any more," Scooter said. "It doesn't sound like it hurt too much until she woke up again."

"I 09:47 – Communications," Thing1 read the sign as he walked past the door. "This will be important later when we figure out how to power up and use the gear."

"I 10:17 – Computer Room," Scooter said. "Let's see what we have." She swung the door open. The room was large, perhaps two meters on either side of the door. Inside the room were two chairs and a table with a large display and keyboard. Beyond the table in the middle of the room were six racks about fifty centimeters wide and two meters tall. The racks were filled with computer components similar to the one that ran the 3-D printer. It looked like a rack might hold twenty or more of those components. Bundles of cables of varying colors ran among the units. Some disappeared into the floor.

A shelf against the wall behind them had boxes filled with cables and components that didn't seem to be connected to anything. The bottom shelf was cluttered with books.

The wall to their left had a shiny white surface covered with drawings in different colors.

"How do we move this?" Thing2 wondered.

"If we take this apart, we will never get it back together again," Thing1 said.

"There must be a purpose to this configuration of wires and such," Pigpen said encouragingly. "Let's take images of all this, take the books, and go back to Charlie and see what sense we can make of it."

"Good thinking, Piggy," Scooter said. She reached into the cart and handed Thing2 Porter's tablet so he could capture the images, then began loading the books from the bottom shelf into the cart.

"What do you think, Cisco?" Thing1 said.

Cisco had been monitoring them from Charlie and replied over their helmet comm, "Sounds like a good idea to me. I look forward to seeing the images."

"It's not as exciting as I expected," Thing1 said, taking a last look at the snarl of colored wires running among the cabinets. "In a scary complex way."

CHAPTER 54 –

Emergency Recovery

Thing1, Pigpen, Thing2, and Scooter pored for days over the books recovered from the computer room. Some identified the different modules in the racks: processors, storage, power conditioners, and network components, and described how they were physically configured in terms of power and cabling. These books did not explain how the modules did what they did. The group was getting discouraged, when Scooter found something called "Disaster Recovery Plan." It described how to restore the station's computer systems to a different computer in the event that the primary systems were damaged. Unlike the other books, these instructions were relatively easy to understand and walked through the process step-by-step.

According to the plan, all data in the station was written to two storage systems—one in the computer room, and a redundant "backup" storage system housed in the *Numa*. The plan described two levels of recovery from disaster: Full Recovery, which would reload and replicate the full configuration and network that existed in the computer room; and Emergency Recovery, which would provide access to all station data from a single device. To the Martians, the Emergency Recovery looked like a viable path to gaining access that didn't involve recreating the tangle of wires and devices they had found in the computer room. The documentation suggested that what was required was a trip to *Numa* to get the backup storage device and a computer and cables stored there for emergency recovery purposes.

The challenge was that *Numa* was attached to *New Rome* near the nuclear power plant at the northwest corner. It was unexplored territory and Porter had specifically warned the Martians about the extreme danger if the reactor had malfunctioned.

Ginger and Curly had narrowed and accelerated their studies of nuclear physics but had no specific information about the functioning of the station's reactor. They told Cisco that while nuclear power had grown safer over the years, the energy potential exceeded anything in their experience and a malfunctioning or leaking reactor could be deadly.

"So, this byproduct, radiation, is invisible and damages tissue?" Cisco asked.

"Yes, radiation is like heat from a nuclear reaction." Ginger said. "Materials in the container keep the radiation from escaping. If the failure broke the container, it makes two problems. First, the nuclear material inside is very poisonous. Even small amounts picked up like dust on boots, if inhaled, could kill us. Second, if the reaction is still occurring, it will give off rays that travel through space and can damage cells. Beta rays can travel meters and penetrate a few millimeters of skin. Beta rays cause damage based on their strength and the duration of exposure. Gamma radiation is the harder one to defend against. It travels like light and can go a long distance from the source. But unlike light, gamma radiation can penetrate most materials. Remember when Porter taught us 'The ABC Song' and 'X was for X-ray'? An X-ray machine uses low doses of gamma radiation to image bones inside a body. The image is built because gamma radiation going through flesh encounters less resistance than through denser bone, so the difference detected on the other side of the radiation source can be used to 'see' the bone. At higher doses, gamma radiation destroys cells as it passes through."

"Hmm. If it's hard to defend against, what *can* we do?" asked Cisco.

"If radiation is present, stay away. If we can't stay away, limit exposure to as few people as possible for as little time as possible. Also, avoid any contact with the source and dispose of any gear that gets contaminated." Ginger said. Curly nodded in agreement.

"If the power plant container was broken open and the poisonous dust escaped, might it have been pumped throughout the station?" Cisco suggested. "Perhaps that's what killed the colonists! We assumed it was a loss of pressure."

Ginger looked at Curly. He shook his head. Ginger turned to Cisco and said, "Radiation poisoning is a relatively slow process. The cells in our bodies are constantly dying and being replaced. Gamma radiation damages cells so that they can't reproduce. At low exposure levels, people might recover. At moderate levels, they might live for months. At high levels, they might live hours or days. The bodies we found seemed as if they fell where they were standing. That's not consistent with the descriptions of radiation poisoning we've read."

Curly listened to Ginger thoughtfully, and then looked to Cisco and nodded agreement.

"Then our next task is to recover the computer storage device and spare computer from the *Numa,*" Cisco said. "As quickly and with as small a team as possible."

"Ready to go?" Cisco's voice sounded metallic, amplified by the comm system in her helmet. The three-person team preparing to recover the emergency backup equipment was about to enter the Charlie air lock. The plan was to go clockwise around the outer ring to the *Numa*. It was noon and the sun was high in the sky but dimmed by a dust storm that had been raging for days.

Pigpen and Thing2 answered, "Yes" in unison while giving thumbs-up.

"Are you with us, Red? We are entering the Charlie air lock."

Red was their communication relay. "I'm here. You guys stay safe."

A few moments later the team was by the Alpha air lock looking at the airtight door that would lead them north through an unexplored corridor toward the *Numa*.

Cisco opened the door and Pigpen moved beyond it to illuminate the darkness with her helmet lamps. Thing2 followed, pushing the cart, the breaker bar sticking out at an angle. There was a single desiccated body beyond the door. It wore clothes, but no exo-suit. Pigpen flipped the stiff corpse against the right wall of the corridor to clear a path for Thing2's cart. Cisco moved past Pigpen, down the curving outer ring corridor.

"O 10:30 – Power Station." Cisco pointed to a door along the right wall. "The door is closed. Maybe that is a good sign."

"This must be *Numa*," Thing2 said, indicating the unusual doors on the left wall ahead. It looked like a double air lock. The nearest doors were propped open. Beyond these were another set of open doors. There were familiar air lock controls in the small interior chamber.

Before they entered, Pigpen pointed her headlamp farther down the outer ring corridor. "Look."

Where they would expect an airtight door at the twelve o'clock spoke, instead there was only darkness and debris. The airtight door wasn't there—or more accurately, wasn't whole. The twisted wreckage of the door and doorframe were a few meters to the side of the frame. A thin layer of red Martian dust was visible on the floor at their feet, getting deeper on the floor of the corridor nearer the door frame.

"Red, we are about to enter *Numa*. Further up the corridor the airtight door appears seriously damaged. We are not investigating right now." Cisco turned and entered the open air lock, walking past the open doors.

Beyond the familiar air lock, connected by a short ramp enclosed by a translucent tube, was a second air lock. It too had both sets of doors propped open. This air lock was unlike anything they had seen.

Numa had not been built on Mars. Whether it was the architecture or the building materials that made that evident, it was too obvious to require comment. The rhythm and consistency of the station was by now a familiar pattern to the explorers. Doors were spaced just so. The spoke corridors were level and straight and the ring corridors were arcs, but the walls were vertical and had ninety-degree angles to the floor and ceiling.

Numa was like a huge segment of bamboo, a cylinder they entered from the side. They went up the short ramp and stepped through a doorway and air lock in the curved side of the ship. Beyond the air lock was a small room with passageways immediately to the left and right. A similar pair of passageways could be seen on the other side of the room. In the center of the room a ladder ran between holes in the low ceiling and the floor. Shining their headlamps down the corridors to the left and right they saw walls covered with white fabric. Metallic hand holds ringed the passage every meter or so. There were small doors on either side of the curving corridor as far as they could see.

"This is a little ... close," Thing2 observed.

"Can you imagine spending months in these narrow halls?" Cisco asked.

Pigpen laughed. "It's probably almost as big as Charlie—this narrow corridor just seems strange. I'll bet there are windows in some of the exterior rooms."

"Where do you think we might find the backup storage device?" Cisco wondered.

"My guess would be some remote corner of the ship," Pigpen offered. "You wouldn't expect that you would need it very often."

"I would imagine it would be clearly labeled," Thing2 said. "You wouldn't want to hide emergency equipment."

"Okay, let's assume you are right about labeling. Remember we are going for speed. Let's stay together and clear this corridor. Piggy, you take the right side and I'll take the left. '2, see if you can keep up with that cart of yours."

The corridor was almost too narrow for Cisco and Pigpen to walk abreast comfortably in their exo-suits. Pigpen took the lead and began scanning the signs stenciled on the doors in bold black letters, reading aloud as she went. "Crew 28, crew 26, crew 24…"

Cisco started a similar chant. "Crew 27, crew 25 … wait! Pigpen, look at the small signs by the door handles. This one says Food Storage 2. The small signs must be how they repurposed the original ship after it landed."

"Good catch, Cisco." Pigpen backed up and examined the smaller signs. "Export Minerals 1, Export Minerals 3, Food Storage 1."

At the end of the corridor was another ladder leading to the level above and the level below, as well as several doors in the fore bulkhead labeled "Lavatory."

"Let's leave the cart here," suggested Thing2. He retrieved the breaker bar and followed Cisco and Pigpen up the ladder.

The next level up had slightly wider corridors. The doors here were larger and spread farther apart. The fore bulkhead had a substantial door labeled "Bridge."

Here they found compartments labeled food services, gym, observation lounge, and game room. These did not appear to have been repurposed. Perhaps they had still served those purposes for *New Rome*?

Then they reached the door labeled "Computer Systems – Authorized Personnel only".

They tried the door, but it was locked.

"I thought the doors on the station unlocked in case of power failure, for safety?" Pigpen said.

"Maybe these locks were not as fancy." Thing2 looked for purchase for the breaker bar. He found that he could slip the breaker bar through a hand hold, then use the hand hold as the fulcrum of a lever to push the door. When the three of them pulled on the bar it was clear that something had to give, either the door or the handrail. The small latch in the door never had a chance. The door buckled inward. Thing2 positioned the breaker bar to open the damaged door, and with another push the way was clear.

Inside the room, they found a metal rack filled with computer equipment, and a shelf with a double tall component labeled "Emergency Recovery Data." A single cable ran from the rack to that device. Next to the device was a red bag labeled "Emergency Recovery Computer." Inside the bag they found printed instructions, cables, and a computer component.

"I think we got what we came for," Cisco said. "Let's go home."

CHAPTER 55 – Hello World

When the team returned to Charlie, the Martians were waiting. Thing1 had already run a power cable from the battery array and was standing by. Scooter and Ginger had been reviewing the restoration procedures from the disaster recovery book and cleared a space for the computer and the storage device on the grow table where their meals were normally served.

Thing2 pushed the cart forward triumphantly, his helmet now sitting atop the computer equipment inside the cart. Thing1 reached into the cart to move the helmet, then dropped the helmet on the ground recoiling in pain. "Yikes! Cold."

The Martians laughed. At some time or another, most had experienced touching something that had been outside the greenhouse without allowing it time to absorb some heat. The burns weren't lasting if you were smart enough to let go quickly.

"We should probably let this gear warm up before we apply power," Ginger said, disappointment clear in her voice. "We don't want to cook any of the parts."

"First thing after breakfast then?" said Cisco, trying to set an example of patience, but not feeling it herself.

The long-sought information on the station computer would have to wait a little longer.

The morning sun wasn't distinctly visible through the dust of the lingering storm, but the sky glowed a little brighter where the sun should be on the horizon.

Helper made a quick meal of corn mush, rice, beans, and berries and then the Martians gathered around Scooter and the still recovering Ginger as they talked through the emergency recovery procedure. Scooter connected the storage device with the cables provided and attached power to the computer module and connected a keyboard and display, then hit the power button and waited.

Half of the electronics that they had recovered from the station thus far had not survived the extreme Martian temperature swings. The average temperature on the surface of Mars at night was about -75°C, while daytime highs could range from -18°C in the winter to 15°C or 20°C during the summer. Porter had speculated that his tablet might have survived in Alpha because it had been insulated by the seed cabinet that inhibited the temperature swings. Scooter hoped that *Numa* had sufficiently insulated the computer equipment as they waited for some indication that it might still be alive.

The computer beeped and a green light near the power button began glowing. The Martians cheered. The screen flickered and displayed the message: "Initiating Emergency Recovery Procedure, hit 'Y' to confirm or 'N' to cancel."

Scooter looked at Cisco who nodded, and then pressed "Y."

Next the screen displayed the message: "Internal clock error. Please enter the current Mars Standard Date and Time."

Red ran to the temperature control panel and called out, "Coordinated Mars Time is 09:14, September 37, Martian Year 55."

Scooter entered the date and time.

A strangely accented woman's voice emerged from the computer. "Last recorded log date is April 38, Martian Year 47. The date you have entered is 8.5 Martian years in the future. Please confirm discrepancy."

Scooter confirmed.

The voice continued, "This system is in emergency recovery mode. You may:

A. Review Station Log
B. Access Station Data
C. Initiate data communications with Earth
D. Change system configuration parameters
E. Shut down the system."

The computer screen mirrored the question. Scooter looked to Cisco.

"Let's contact Earth," Cisco said.

Scooter entered the selection on the keyboard.

"I'm sorry, data communications do not appear to be functional. Please ensure the communications array is functional and connected to port five. For more information, see the data communications equipment primer in the system library of the Station Data."

The voice repeated the options.

"Let's review the station log and find out what happened." Cisco suggested.

Scooter entered the selection.

The voice returned, "Please specify log data to review:

A. Commander's Log
B. Biological Log of Station Personnel

C. Video Log

D. Environmental Log

E. Communications Log

F. Data Log."

"What do you think? Commander's Log?" Cisco asked.

Amid nods of approval, Scooter made the selection.

A list of log entries was presented. The last two were from April 38, Martian Year 47, one at 15:21, one at 21:47.

Scooter selected the first. A talking image of a man with brown skin, a square jaw, almond-shaped eyes, and grey hair appeared. It was captioned April 38, Martian Year 47, 15:21.

"Commander's log, routine:

- "Mine production issues have been addressed and mine production is returning to expected levels.
- "Water production is exceeding expectations and additional water storage is being brought online over the next few weeks.
- "Chemical extraction and synthesis continue to run significantly behind the expected pace. We are still trying to determine whether this is a performance problem or if the predictive models were too aggressive.
- "Construction of greenhouse Delta is ahead of schedule and we expect to officially transfer responsibility for Delta to our chief agronomist so he can begin production by the end of next week.
- "Agricultural production is on schedule and we are on pace to be calorie self-sufficient within five hundred sols if we can sustain this trend.
- "Consumption of food stores remains slightly below predicted levels, giving us a safety margin of over three hundred days rations and growing.

- "Crew morale appears good and has been steadily improving since the completion of crew quarters in *New Rome* and the move out of the *Numa*. The sight of toddlers in the hallways and in common areas also seems good for morale." The brown-skinned man's face broke into a smile. "Earth children may have two parents, but Martian children appear to have over a hundred."
- "Crew health is good. The crewman treated for breast cancer appears to be recovering with no lingering effects. One accident to report—earlier today a crewman caught his leg in a ladder in greenhouse Charlie and fell, damaging his knee. See medical report for specifics. Doc says the crewman will likely be off duty for a few days and on light duty for a few weeks. Accident prevention awareness will be part of tomorrow's daily commander's message."

The next log entry was briefer. The brown-skinned man reappeared. It was captioned April 38, Martian Year 47, 21:47.

"Commander's log, emergency SITREP: A fire broke out in the chemical lab at 21:06. Fire suppression teams are working to contain the problem and report continuing success. We considered decompressing that part of the station in response, but fire suppression efforts appear to be sufficient. We have nineteen reported dead, twenty-seven injured.

"The fire has exposed a serious problem with the ventilation system. The airtight doors designed to seal the station operated as expected, but smoke from the fire continues to circulate in the station. The chief engineer's preliminary report is that there is previously undetected damage to the valves in the ducting that are supposed to isolate the ventilation system in case of fire or decompression. These components are not functional. We have isolated the ventilation system manually for the inner ring. I will have a full report in a few hours when the fire is extinguished and the damage to the station has been assessed.

"There was an erroneous report that the station's thorium power plant had been somehow compromised or damaged as part of the fire. The power plant was shut down as a precautionary measure until the fire is extinguished and a full inspection is complete. Sending this now … will provide an update when I have more information. Things are chaotic right now but seem to be calming down as the fire threat is contained. Commander Lee, out."

There were no other log entries.

"The reactor wasn't damaged! That means no radiation threat *and* we might be able to restart the reactor!" Pigpen said excitedly.

"We still don't know what happened to the colonists," Scar said. "Now it will be safer to explore and find out."

"Well, we saw that the airtight door between the outer ring and the twelve o'clock spoke was damaged," Thing2 said. "Did the fire do that or was it something else, I wonder?"

Mary interrupted, "If Pigpen is right and there is no radiation threat, then the next priority should be communication with Earth so they can get us out of here. We don't *need* to know what happened to the colonists. We don't *need* power. We don't *need* to explore the station beyond locating the communication equipment that needs to be plugged into 'Port 5' or whatever."

She looked at Ginger and continued, "We don't *need* to risk any more lives."

She shifted her gaze to Cisco. "We don't *need* to find books or tablets or air canisters!"

Tears glistened in Mary's eyes and her voice cracked. "We just *need* to get away from here!" She turned and stalked away.

There was a long moment of silence. The Martians looked at one another, and then at Cisco.

"Perhaps she is right that communication should be a priority," Cisco suggested quietly. "But that doesn't mean it's the only thing we pursue. While

I hope we can contact the Earth people and that they will come—they haven't for eight years. We need to be prepared for the fact that they might not. We might not be able to get communication working. They may not hear us. They might never come."

CHAPTER 56 –

The Storm

While they studied the communication system and the power systems, the dust storm persisted. It had been getting worse for two weeks and seemed to be trending darker. Visibility out the window was limited to twenty meters at ground level, but it was hard to tell whether this was a result of particulates, or the lack of sun caused by dust in the upper atmosphere. The dark sky was occasionally broken by impressive flashes of lightning.

"Power reserves have dropped to thirty-two percent in Charlie, thirty-seven percent in Delta, and fifty-seven percent in Bravo," Thing1 reported over breakfast. "Power is now dropping about three percent per day in Charlie, slightly less in Delta and Bravo."

"Why do you suppose Bravo has more reserves?" asked Pigpen.

"I would guess we are consuming less power there because we haven't finished planting, and fewer grow lights are running," offered Thing1. "It also has a dedicated solar array that is larger than what we have for Charlie and Delta."

"Should we plan on abandoning Delta?" Helper asked, recalling Porter's response to a significant storm years earlier.

"Most of what is in Delta are annuals," Cisco said. "I think Porter planned to keep Delta expendable in an emergency. What would we lose if we cut power to Delta right now?"

"We'd lose everything but beans and maybe a little squash," Scar said. "Soy and green beans are coming in nicely. First pickings were this week and we could get most of the crop over the next couple of days. Next rice is about four weeks away. We just planted the second squash crop. Tomatoes went in a couple of weeks ago and won't be ready for eight weeks or so. The first squash is almost ready for harvest, starting to come in now; we can get more if we wait a week. Corn is ten weeks off. We could harvest all the bamboo and move the worm beds in a day or two. Everything else would be lost."

"What if we lowered the power to keep it just above freezing?" Sniffles asked.

"If we knew how long this storm would last, that would be attractive," Red mused. "But if it goes on for more than a week, we would have to sacrifice Delta anyway, and we might not have enough power to keep Charlie going."

Scar said, "We have made good progress with Bravo, but we aren't relying on it for production yet. What about sacrificing Bravo and moving its solar array to Charlie?"

Scooter shook her head. "That array is pretty big. It would be hard to move."

"Maybe we could use that vehicle we found in the East air lock to move it?" Thing2 asked.

"Good idea, and I would love to operate that machine, but we probably would need to charge it, and I suspect it would consume a lot of our power reserves to do that," observed Thing1.

"What if we sacrificed Bravo and ran a cable from there to here—move the power, not the array?" Pigpen suggested.

"What would that take?" Cisco asked. "A hundred meters of cable, maybe one fifty?"

Scooter thought for a quiet moment, then had an inspiration. "There might already be cabling in the Utility Access! There were wires running everywhere. Might have to make a few new connections and disconnect the rest of the station from that circuit, but I think we could connect Bravo's batteries to the main station, then connect Charlie to the same small circuit and we would have access to Bravo's batteries *and* the larger array."

Cisco was disappointed that their hard work in Bravo might have to be sacrificed, but the danger was clear. "Okay. Pigpen and '1, figure out if you can do the cabling. That will give us information about what we can do with Bravo. Scar, you organize everyone else to harvest what we can from Delta. Let's assume that we turn off the lights and transfer power from Delta to Charlie tomorrow night if this storm isn't showing signs of weakening."

"What about communication?" asked Mary. "I thought you all agreed that was a priority?"

"Our power reserves are low, Mary," Cisco said. "If we can't survive this storm, communication won't help."

"It looks like this is the power connector from Alpha to the station," said Pigpen. She was examining the inside of a metal box on the west wall of the Utility Access room, the lights of her helmet glaring off the shiny metal of the box. "I don't see a coupling for Bravo. Do you think they were run in series?"

"Good thinking, Piggy," said Thing1. "There was a switch on the west side of Bravo that determined whether the array went to Bravo or the main. If we can't find a Bravo connection, we could flip that and see if Alpha—this connector—gets power."

"That might not give us access to the battery power in Bravo," Pigpen said.

"Maybe we could disconnect the batteries and move them to Charlie?" Thing1 suggested.

"Let's see if the cabling works," Pigpen suggested. "If it does, then we can either try to figure out how to connect through the batteries or move them."

The Martians were frantically harvesting what they could from Delta. It was a sobering experience. The three thousand square meters of the greenhouse was two-thirds filled with grow tables. Staggering the harvest throughout the year regardless of season meant that much of the hard work cultivating plant life in Delta that wasn't ready for harvest was about to be sacrificed.

Scar had one team harvesting all the soy and green beans they could find, while another team cut all bamboo that was more than three centimeters thick and moved it to Charlie. Red took responsibility for exporting the Delta worm farm, pouring a mixture of water and lime into the bed and putting the worms that wriggled to the surface into the cart with soil for transport.

At the end of the second day, the dark red brown beyond the windows of the greenhouse gave no hint about the location of the setting sun. They gathered some squash ready for harvest, turned off the grow lights, transferred all of Delta's power to Charlie, closed the air lock, and left Delta to freeze.

"We have connected the Bravo solar array to Charlie," Pigpen said. "We couldn't easily run the power through the batteries, so we brought the batteries here and rigged them up with Charlie's batteries. The combined power system now has reserves of forty-one percent power. Over the last day, the reserves have dropped about two percent. At this rate, we have about twenty days."

"Let's let Bravo go tomorrow night," Cisco said sadly. "The only crops ready there are squash and I think we have more than enough of that. We'll take what we can get tomorrow. Make sure we have a half dozen seedlings in Charlie for any of the spices or other crops we started there."

The next evening, they let the lights go out in Bravo. Charlie power reserves were now 38 percent and falling.

The additional solar array and Bravo's batteries had provided enough power to slow power consumption to 1 percent per day initially, but as the days passed and the sky drew darker the solar arrays stopped contributing much to the batteries. Two weeks later, power reserves had dropped to 18 percent.

"Maybe we should dust the arrays," suggested Scar, his breath misting in the cold. Power reserves were falling faster than expected now, almost 3 percent per day. They had lowered the temperature to just above freezing two days ago. Everyone was wearing layers of clothes and taking turns standing near the fire pit for warmth.

"Good idea. With all that dust swirling around, some is sure to have settled on the arrays," Cisco said hopefully—trying to encourage herself as much as the others.

It was noon and the view out the windows was nearly the color of soil, a rich dark red brown. There was still no hint of the sun's position on the horizon. The darkness was broken every few minutes by flashes of lightning—dull bursts of glowing brown hues when distant, spectacular webs of white and silver when close.

Later that day, a party went through the air lock and wiped away the thin layer of dust that had accumulated on the solar collectors outside Charlie and Bravo. The effect on energy production was minimal. The next morning, power reserves were at 16 percent. With the reduced use of the grow lights and the lack of sunlight, carbon dioxide concentrations in Charlie's atmosphere were now approaching 0.25 percent.

Three days later, power reserves had fallen to 9 percent. Carbon dioxide levels were approaching 0.66 percent and headaches were becoming the norm. The Martians had begun sleeping huddled in groups of two and three for warmth. Everyone's clothes and Charlie's air smelled of stale smoke. They had a day or two before the grow lights and heat would no longer function. The fire could keep them warm a while longer, but without photosynthesis cleaning the carbon dioxide from Charlie's air, their choice would soon be to freeze to death or suffocate.

Helper made a thick stew for dinner and the Martians consumed it heartily, as much for the nutrition as the warmth and comfort it provided.

As they sat quietly around the fire, Ginger mused, "I wonder if we could figure out how to restart the nuclear reactor? The man in the log video suggested it wasn't damaged."

Thing1 brightened at the idea. "It sounded pretty complicated, but we don't have much to lose at this point. The computer doesn't draw much power. Let's see what we can find out."

After a short flurry of activity, the Martians were trying to read technical manuals and watch videos on the computer screen that were either designed for experts and difficult to follow or designed for novices to explain concepts and not helpful in a practical way.

The concepts seemed straightforward. The thorium reaction occurred in a slurry of molten fluoride salt catalyzed by Uranium-233 that flowed around in a reaction chamber and heated gas in pipes that ran a turbine to generate power. At the bottom of the molten salt reaction vessel was a "plug" of frozen salt, refrigerated by the power system. In the event of accident or shut down, the power cooling this plug was disengaged and the molten salt melted the plug, allowing the salt and thorium to drain into a holding vessel containing a chemical that inhibited and stopped the reaction. To restart, a new plug would have to be inserted and kept cool, then fresh thorium laden salt and fuel would need to be loaded into the reaction chamber.

Mary was in a mood. "Why are you worried about these stupid manuals? Let's hook up the communications equipment and see if the Earthians can help us with the reactor."

Mary's tone was annoying, but Cisco realized she had a point. "We can do *both*!" she said. "Ginger, Curly, and Thing1, make a trip to look at the reactor and see what sense you can make of it. Take one of the tablets so that you can capture pictures of what you see, then come back here and work with the manuals and see if you can figure out how to get the power going. Meanwhile, Red, '2, Scooter, and Pigpen, see what you can figure out about getting the communication cables connected. Like Mary said, maybe we can ask Earth for help. Good idea, Mary."

Despite the gloom, Cisco's instructions generated a flurry of enthusiasm and activity. In addition to the two groups specifically tasked, the remaining Martians ran errands, prepared exo-suits, and did whatever they could to support their two last hopes for survival.

The reactor room, though larger than most, didn't look particularly special. Their helmet lamps illuminated a metal box three meters wide, a meter tall, and two meters deep that was perched on a pedestal. A cluster of colored pipes rose from the floor, entered the box at one side, and exited on the other, disappearing back into the floor. There was a console of sorts on the side of the box—a bank of dials, valves, and switches. Under the box was a metal tank. A large pipe connected the box above to the tank below through what must have been a hole in the pedestal.

Elsewhere in the room were a small desk, a round table, and several chairs. A bookcase along the wall held several books and what looked like a model of the equipment before them. Two strange exo-suits hung from the wall, bulkier than those they had seen elsewhere.

As they surveyed the room, Ginger pointed to the soot stains climbing the wall and on the ceiling. "Did it burn?" she asked.

Looking behind and under the device, Thing1 said, "I don't think so. No signs of damage. The smoke seems to originate from the vent in the floor under here."

"Let's take the books and the model. Curly, would you take images?" Ginger said, turning to look at him. Curly was already on his hands and knees taking pictures of the device from several angles. He gave Ginger a thumbs-up, then resumed his efforts.

The Communications room was smallish, two by three meters. Two video monitors sat on a small desk, cabled into a computer rack that stood alone in the center of the room. A thick bundle of brightly colored cables descended from the ceiling into the rack. Another bundle of cables attached to the rack disappeared into the floor.

Red took images with a tablet but had no idea what he was looking at or for. He had hoped that there would be a single cable, ideally labeled "Plug me into the computer to establish communication with Earth." Instead, this looked like a color-coded tangle of creepers from a beanstalk.

Scooter found a book in the desk drawer that might describe the cabling scheme. She suggested, "Take the pictures and let's get back. This may be helpful when we have time to study it. It's hard to read through my helmet."

Pigpen observed, "These cables appear to have labels of some kind, letters and numbers. Make sure and get images of these, Red. The characters are so small I'm having trouble reading them."

Thing2 found a toolbox in the corner and boxes of colored cable. "These tools look like they are specially designed to cut and join cables. '1 might find them interesting." He put both the books and the toolbox into the cart.

In ten minutes, they were heading back to the air lock.

An hour later, the teams were showing what they had found and explaining what they had learned.

Scooter explained what they had learned about the communication system. "According to these documents, there is a device on the roof of the station that communicates with several satellites in synchronous orbit—that means they orbit Mars at a speed that matches the planet's rotation so that it is always at the same place in the sky. Those satellites relay signals to others that orbit Mars and they send signals to Earth. The good news is that this means we don't have to try to correctly aim our signal at Earth. The scary part is that the routing is complicated and hasn't been used in eight years. We also have no reason to expect that anyone will be listening."

She continued, "We think we know which cables need to be attached to the emergency recovery computer, but we need to figure out how to get power to the communications computer and the transmission system. Thing1 thinks we could take one of the batteries we recovered from Bravo to the Communications room and wire it in, but we don't know if that is the only thing that must be powered. We don't know how we would test the signal. The computer might be able to tell us if the system is working, but if it isn't, we aren't sure where we would start."

Cisco mused, "So, again, it comes back to power. Do we have any idea how much power the communication system needs? We don't have much left in the batteries, and everything we consume decreases the amount of time we can survive."

Cisco looked out the window at the void of night in the dust storm. There were no stars, there was no horizon, nothing could be seen but the dust particles near the glass reflecting stray firelight from Charlie, and the Martian terrain that vanished into mist and shadows just outside the window, interrupted periodically by lightning.

Ginger looked defeated. "We know what needs to happen in theory to reset and restart the reactor, but the details are complex and assume a good deal of training and experience. There are also special precautions and equipment necessary. It seems as if, done properly, it is a relatively safe and simple procedure—but we are still trying to puzzle out how to do it. Even if we get the reactor started, it only generates heat … there is a whole other component that appears to exist in the Utility Access that turns that heat into electricity. We know that some of the pipes in the Utility Access have burst. We don't yet know if the generation system is intact and we haven't found instructions for it. We have a guess where it is, but we haven't yet gone looking. Apparently, the system that turns heat into electricity was considered separate from the reactor that served as a heat source. They are independent modules and perhaps were treated as independent specialties, sort of like one team tending the fire while another managed the cooking."

"How do they make electricity from heat?" Cisco asked.

"It has to do with motion in magnetic fields," Thing1 answered. "It's the opposite principle as the motor in the electric goat. There, you put in power and you get rotation, but in the case of a generator, you put in rotation and get power. The heated gas is used to turn a wheel or turbine; the circular motion generates electricity."

"How much power do we need to keep Charlie going?" Cisco asked.

"Normally we can get by with about two hundred fifty kilowatts per hour because the sun helps out during the day," Thing1 replied. "In this storm without the sun, we have been consuming double that just to keep from freezing."

"Is that a lot?" Cisco hadn't been as interested in electricity or physics as some of the others.

"I read an article a while back that talked about human-powered generators, something like the device we use when we manually pressurize the air locks. Healthy humans working hard can generate between one hundred and two hundred watts per hour. So, if there were twenty-five hundred of us..." Thing1 grinned.

"A simple, 'yes, that's a lot' would do," Cisco said, cutting him off. "How much power can the reactor generate?"

"A lot," Thing1 said, smiling. "At full power the generator was rated at ten megawatts."

"It can generate as much power as—one hundred thousand people!" Cisco's shock was apparent as she did the math.

"Remember, our ancestors built machines that lifted and flew most of the things here ten light minutes from Earth," Thing1 chided.

"Well, what do you guys think we should do? We don't have much time and we don't have much power," Cisco asked.

Red spoke up. "I think Mary had a good point about the importance of communication, and your decision to pursue both was sound. We don't have to choose between the two options; we can keep trying to do both. Since the reactor is complex and dangerous, let's keep researching that while we try to contact Earth to get help. If we can't get communication to work, we do the best we can with the reactor. None of this is going to matter in a day or so if we can't figure something out. Let's take the battery to the communication station and see if we can get it going."

Two hours later, one of the bulky Bravo battery packs so recently moved to Charlie had been moved again to the Communications room. Thing1 hoped that powering the freezing components wouldn't break them. He connected the power and the computers and the monitors thankfully glowed to life. The monitors displayed some diagnostic information that they didn't understand, then displayed the message "Ready."

Beneath his feet, Pigpen and Scooter were in the Utility Access area, identifying what they believed was the primary network connection to the communication array. The blue cable marked "A5" descended from the ceiling above their heads and went into a network junction box. Scooter unplugged the cable from the box and plugged it into a long extension of Charlie's network cable that Pigpen had run across the floor.

"Cable is in place," Scooter said.

"Let's see if that's all it takes," Thing1 said.

Back in Charlie, once the network cables were in place, Scooter initiated the emergency backup computer as everyone else looked on.

The accented computer voice said, "This system is in emergency recovery mode. You may:

A. Review Station Log
B. Access Station Data
C. Initiate data communications with Earth
D. Change system configuration parameters
E. Shutdown the system"

Scooter selected "C" on the keyboard expectantly.

"I'm sorry," said the voice. "Data communications do not appear to be functional. Please ensure the communications array is functional and connected to port five. For more information, see the data communications equipment primer in the system library of the Station Data."

Scooter hesitated a long moment, disappointed, then said determinedly, "Ginger and '1, review this equipment primer with me again. What are we missing?" She pulled up the primer on station communication system and began going through it again while Ginger and Thing1 looked over her shoulder.

Curly was reading the technical manuals for the thorium reactor carefully. He could picture what needed to happen but wasn't clear how to turn the knowledge into action. He also wasn't sure how much power would be needed to initiate the system.

The log suggested that the reactor had been shut down. Curly could see the switch on the console labeled "Emergency Shut Down." He decided to set aside the manuals about the reactor and go instead to the schematics for the console. Perhaps if he could figure out exactly what happened when the system was shut down it would give him a better understanding of the system's current state.

"The emergency computer doesn't seem to think that a working cable is plugged into port five," Scooter mused. "That might mean a problem with the cable, or a problem with the communication array. What can we do to test the cable?"

"We could plug some other devices into either end of the cable and see if they can talk," Pigpen said. "If they can, then we know the cable is okay."

Thing1 nodded. "Good idea. There are network cable ports on some of the working tablets we have recovered. Let's see if we can get them to talk with one of the small cables we have here, then we can take one to the Communications room and plug it into the cable we are trying to connect to confirm that the cable is good."

Two hours later, they determined that there was a problem with the cable that ran from the Communications room to Charlie.

They replaced the cable and successfully tested the connections. Then they tried using the emergency backup computer again.

"I'm sorry," said the voice. "Data communications do not appear to be functional. Please ensure the communications array is functional and connected to port five. For more information, see the data communications equipment primer in the system library of the Station Data."

"Well, now we know the problem is in the Communications Room," said Scooter.

"Or beyond," Pigpen added sadly.

"Let's go through the configuration and set up instructions again," said Thing1.

Curly was excited. The schematics for the power plant control panel showed him how the emergency shutdown switch cut power to the cooling system that held the plug intact. This led him to a description of how to repair the cooling system and that described the process for replacing the plug. It required safety gear, probably the odd exo-suits they had seen in the reactor room, and a new plug. The directions made it sound like there were several plugs on hand. It was now a matter of finding one and installing it, then replacing the fuel.

There were also instructions for installing the heating crucible that prepared the fluoride salt and thorium by melting them before they went into the reaction chamber. Curly believed that if they could find a replacement plug and get enough power to operate the crucible, they should be able to restart the reactor.

It was late. He went looking for Ginger in the darkness to show her what he had found. As he approached her sleeping table, he heard hard breathing and rustling of the blankets. She was not alone. He stopped, unsure of what to do next.

He felt what he had to share was important, but something told him this was not the time to interrupt. A few moments later, Ginger moaned gently, another voice growled softly, and the rustling subsided. Curly took the ensuing silence as an invitation and walked the last few steps to where Ginger lay under the blankets, whispering to Pancho beside her.

In the dark, Curly thought he saw a slight smile as Ginger looked up and said, "Hi Curly."

He tugged gently at her arm.

She sat up. "Did you find something?"

Curly nodded.

"Let's go!" She quickly kissed Pancho and fumbled with her clothes, pulling them on as she dropped over the side of her sleeping table.

"So, replacement plugs and fuel should exist somewhere. If we can find one and replace the plug, then we think we know how to reload the reactor." Ginger was explaining Curly's find to Cisco over an early breakfast. Helper listened in as she finished the cooking. Curly looked on, chewing thoughtfully and nodding.

"What about the cooking part?" Helper asked. "You said before that the reactor generated heat, and the power was generated by a different system."

"We haven't considered that yet," Ginger admitted. "We figured if we couldn't get the fire started, there was no point in worrying about cooking."

"Time to worry about the cooking, too," Cisco said, "while the rest of us hunt for those plugs. Power reserves are at four percent."

"I can't find anywhere that says where the plugs are stored." Ginger had just finished unsuccessfully searching the document library of the emergency backup computer.

"You would think that you would want them near the reactor itself. Why store them anywhere else?" Scar asked.

"They might be radioactive, and you would want to store them safely. Probably near the fuel—" Ginger jumped up excitedly. "That's it! They are probably stored with the fuel." Ginger dove back into the computer documents with a refined focus.

"The fuel is stored in a facility outside the station?" Cisco said. "How far away?"

"About a kilometer to the northwest," Ginger explained. "Apparently the fuel was staged here by a dedicated supply ship. It landed slightly away from the site of *New Rome* in case there was any problem with the landing so that it wouldn't contaminate the other stores and equipment. For safety reasons, they just left the fuel stored there."

Cisco nodded. "Take Thing2, Scar, and Red. Encourage Curly and Thing1 to keep working on the 'cooking' problem."

CHAPTER 57 –
Going North

The hastily assembled fuel recovery group decided to leave from the East air lock. The plan was to turn northwest and observe but not explore the north side of the station as they moved past. The dust storm dashed their hopes of catching a glimpse of the north side of the station during their trip without altering their route.

They expected to be buffeted by the winds that blew the dust, but they felt no pressure against their suits. Despite the fact it was midday, visibility was severely limited. The dust-blotted sun offered only the dim light of late Martian twilight and their headlamps merely created glowing beams of glare in the swirling dust. Visibility was ten meters at best. The position indicators in their helmets helped them navigate, but the dust clouds made it challenging.

Thing2 operated the electric goat as he walked beside it. He was tethered to Ginger, who walked to his left, trying to stay out of his way and keep their tether from tangling with the goat. Ahead to the right and left, Scar and Red walked abreast, separated by about eight meters. Even with the limited visibility, everyone could see two other people, and Scar and Red could see a combined twenty-five meters wide to the front to help them navigate around obstacles.

The dust had drifted thick in some places, and they were unable to travel in a straight line, weaving among boulders and dust bowls that were barriers to the goat.

"If there was a trail here, the years have covered it," Red observed, as they swung wide around a rock formation that blocked their way.

"I think we need to go a little more to the left," Ginger offered, monitoring their course as they corrected. "It shouldn't be too much farther, maybe a couple hundred meters."

They had passed the remains of several transport ships. The hulls were not intact, likely scavenged for metal. They slowed, worried about debris, but under the dust, the ground seemed clear of obstructions.

"We may have found the path," said Red. "It makes sense that they would have a clear route to these ships to get supplies and parts."

"The goat is going well over this smooth terrain," said Thing2. "I wonder if we can find our way back from here?"

"We can probably follow our footprints," said Scar. "They don't seem to be filling in very quickly, and—"

"I think I see it!" interrupted Red. "I think we are here."

A tall dark shadow emerged and loomed over them as Scar, Thing2, and Ginger moved toward Red. This was no wreck and there were no signs of salvage. The structure was roughly dome shaped and four meters tall, with a skirt of metal and eight engines positioned evenly around it. A ramp two meters wide rose to a closed door above the metal skirt. The ramp was covered with dust, but as they walked up, the textured metal beneath the dust was exposed and provided solid footing.

The door was unlike any they had seen before. Their helmet lamps revealed words written in yellow block letters "TURN CLOCKWISE TO OPEN" and an arrow pointed to a recessed compartment. Red reached in and fumbled with the mechanism. In short order, he had unfolded a crank, which he operated with some satisfaction.

Silently the doors parted, and the party ventured inside. The utilitarian and dense assortment of shipping containers made clear that this compartment was not intended for human transport. There was little mystery to the box contents, which were written in block letters beneath a large yellow circle half-filled with three black triangles. Apart from the part numbers, which seemed to increment by ones, the label read:

RADIATION WARNING - AUTHORIZED PERSONNEL ONLY

RELOAD PART TR-24-002

CONTAINS:

31 each THORIUM/FLUORIDE FUEL FOR TR-24 THORIUM REACTOR

1 each U233 URANIUM CATALYST FOR TR-24 THORIUM REACTOR

1 each DRAIN BASIN PLUG FOR TR-24 THORIUM REACTOR

WEIGHT: 1020 KG

"A thousand kilos!" Thing2 exclaimed. "That box doesn't look big enough to weigh a thousand kilos."

"Probably Earth weight," ventured Ginger. "Still, even four hundred kilos would be a lot. Can we lift it?"

Red and Scar approached the box and tried unsuccessfully to move it.

"Maybe we could open it and load the contents onto the goat a little at a time?" Thing2 suggested.

Red examined the shipping container for a moment, then flipped a latch and opened it. Inside were nearly three dozen half-meter-long hexagonal metal bottles the size of his calf nestled in padding and a metal box at the center the size of a pumpkin. All but one of the canisters was silver. The odd canister was black with a red top. Red picked up one of the silver bottles and handed it to Thing2. "Wow—these are surprisingly heavy. That might have been Mars weight."

Thing2 walked down the ramp and loaded the bottle onto the goat.

Scar handed a container to Ginger and she walked halfway down the ramp and handed it to '2 for loading. Red handed the next canister to Scar, who handed it to Ginger, who passed it to Thing2. In a moment, the human chain had loaded about a dozen of the heavy canisters, when the goat silently collapsed in a small cloud of dust.

"Aaargh!" yelled Thing2 over the comm link. "My foot! Get it off!"

In the background, they could hear the pressure warning from his suit quietly competing with his voice on the radio channel: "Suit integrity compromised. Suit is losing pressure. Apply patch or move to a pressurized area immediately. Suit integrity compromised. Suit is losing pressure. Apply patch or move to a pressurized area immediately."

Ginger tried unsuccessfully to lift the wounded goat. It didn't budge.

"Guys, unload the goat, quick," Ginger barked. "It's too heavy to lift."

Scar and Red leapt down the ramp and began to unload the goat while Ginger took out an emergency patch and set it on top of one of the front wheels. "Hang on, '2. It will just be a few seconds more and we will have you patched up."

"I think we broke the back axle," Thing2 hissed. "We will need to walk."

"We can head back with you, the plug, and a few bottles. That will give Curly something to work on," Ginger said soothingly. "How bad is your foot?"

"Can't tell," Thing2 gasped through clenched teeth. "I think I feel wetness."

Ginger grabbed the breaker bar from the back of the goat and jammed it under the goat's frame.

"Ready, guys? Lift on three," Ginger said. "One … two … three!"

Scar, Ginger, and Red lifted the broken goat off of Thing2's foot. Even with limited light and thick swirling dust, they could see the jet of white mist spraying from his punctured boot.

Ginger dropped the breaker bar and grabbed the patch, removing the backing and applying it to the puncture.

"This little hole in your boot isn't nearly as dramatic as when I sliced up my exo-suit," Ginger teased. "I probably could have used a smaller patch, or maybe saved the patch and just had you walk back with it blowing the dust out of the way." More earnestly she asked, "How are you doing, '2?"

"I think my foot is not good for walking, but the patch stopped the leak. Pressure returning to normal," Thing2 answered. The audible alarm in his suit repeated a few more times on the radio channel, then was quiet. "That alarm is sure annoying. I got the message the first twenty times."

"Have Pigpen show you how to turn it off," Red said. "She was reading up on the exo-suit controls to help us navigate here and there is lots of stuff you can customize on the display and the alarms."

"I'll carry '2," Ginger said. "You guys grab a couple of bottles and the plug and we'll head back."

Scar and Red grabbed the box with the plug. It weighed more than Red. They carried it to the ramp, put it down and Red cranked the door closed. Then they picked up their burdens and trudged down the ramp.

"This is heavy," Scar said. "How can we get it back?"

"I wish we had some rope," Red said.

"What about the breaker bar? If we put it through the carrying handles and each grab an end?" Scar suggested.

A few moments later, Scar and Red were at either end of the breaker bar with the plug and two fuel bottles hanging from the bar between them, walking for spurts of twenty to thirty meters, then stopping to rest. Ginger had Thing2 slung uncomfortably across her back and was trudging through the dust beside them. Fortunately, Scar had been right—even in the poor light they were able to easily follow their tracks back to the East air lock.

Within an hour, Sniffles had bandaged Thing2's crushed foot and Pancho had replaced him on the expedition. Cisco took Ginger's place so that Ginger could help Curly with his studies of the reactor, and the reconstituted party was off again. No goat this trip. Instead, they took sheets of graphene and rope to make bundles of the bottles. They found that each of them could carry two bottles slung around their necks, one on each side. In a few trips, they had everything stored in the reactor room, waiting for Curly and Ginger.

Power reserves were now at three and a half percent.

CHAPTER 58 –
Acquisition

Scooter, Pigpen, and Thing1 were poring over the technical manuals for the communications system. The jargon in the manuals was maddening. They had given up trying to understand the strange words from the context in which they appeared and were taking turns looking up unfamiliar words.

"It seems like the computer in the Communications room is responsible for acquiring and maintaining a signal with satellites in orbit," Thing1 said.

"But all the monitor says is 'Ready'," said Scooter in frustration.

"Maybe there is a program we need to run or a command we need to give?" Pigpen wondered aloud.

"Where would that be described?" Scooter asked.

"The power system has a user's guide, and the electric goat had an operator's guide. Maybe search for a guide?" Thing1 suggested.

Scooter searched, muttering to herself. After several minutes she exclaimed, "Communication Console Operations Guide! It isn't stored in the same area as the technical manuals—it's in a file area for training."

She opened the file and they looked over her shoulder. It displayed pictures of a computer console that filled the screen and showed the status of the various satellites.

"But the screen doesn't look like that!" Thing1 said, his frustration evident.

"I'll bet we need to start an application on the computer," Pigpen said. "Search the document for 'start' and 'initiate' Scooter."

Scooter laughed. "Here it is. We need to type 'Run 3xD234.f'."

"Well, we weren't going to accidentally stumble on *that*. Let's go see if it works."

Fifteen minutes later, the three of them were in the Communications room. Scooter entered the command on the console keyboard and the display they recognized from the operation's guide burst forth on the console monitor. It showed not satellites, but rather a small rectangle at the bottom of the screen displaying the words "Acquiring… Acquiring…" repeatedly.

Slowly, the display began to change. A small blob labeled "MarsComm-4" appeared, followed by a second labeled "MarsComm-7" with a green line between the two. In a few moments, a total of five blobs were displayed. All had green lines to one or more of the others. The small place at the bottom showed four messages: "Unable to acquire MarsComm-1"; "Unable to acquire MarsComm-5"; "Unable to acquire MarsComm-6"; and "Unable to acquire MarsComm-8."

"Let's hope this is enough," Scooter said. "We should head back."

Power reserves were at two and a half percent.

Scooter tried again to initiate communications with Earth from the emergency backup computer.

The computer voice said, "This system is in emergency recovery mode. You may:

A. Review Station Log
B. Access Station Data
C. Initiate data communications with Earth
D. Change system configuration parameters
E. Shutdown the system"

Scooter selected "C" on the keyboard expectantly.

"Do you want to send data or text message?" the computer voice asked.

The assembled Martians cheered.

Scooter selected "text" and turned to Cisco. "What do we want to say?"

Cisco thought for a moment and said, "Let's keep it short. How about: Help. Dust storm blocked solar array. Batteries almost depleted. Need detailed instructions to restart reactor. We have fuel and plug.'"

Scooter pecked out the message on the keyboard.

"Communication sent," said the computer voice.

They waited anxiously for half an hour. There was no reply. Their enthusiasm plummeted with their prospects for communication. Finally, they turned the computer off and shifted focus to their last hope—restarting the reactor.

Power reserves were at two percent and carbon dioxide levels were slowly rising into the toxic range as the Martians discussed their options over dinner. Everyone had a headache, and most were irritable. Sniffles explained that these were early symptoms of carbon dioxide poisoning.

"Curly and I think we should try to start the reactor," Ginger said. "At this point, we have very little to lose. It will consume the last of our power, and that may not be enough, but I think it's our only hope at this point."

"What about the power generation side of the problem?" asked Cisco.

"Our only hope is that it is intact. There's no reason to believe otherwise. We have enough power for a day at best. The storm shows no sign of letting up. Without power, we either freeze or suffocate in a couple days."

"What do you all think?" Cisco asked.

Cisco looked around the table at the Martians. One by one, they nodded their head in agreement with Ginger.

"Do it then. Thing1, you have the generator hooked up to provide power to Charlie?"

"Yes. I bypassed everything else in the station. If the solution is even partially successful, we should see power here—none of it would be wasted anywhere else. The only things hooked up are the reactor, which uses a bit of power to operate and monitor itself, and us."

"Let's do it," said Cisco gravely.

Ginger and Curly took the last three full air canisters and headed for the reactor room. Thing1 wired the last of the Bravo battery packs into the power system so that Curly could use them to heat the thorium salts, cool the drain plug, and initiate the reaction.

When they arrived, Ginger saw that Curly had already opened the top of the reactor. "So, you think we just pour the thorium fluoride salts into here, add uranium and apply power to melt it, and then power generation starts?"

Curly gave a thumbs-up.

"What about the plug?" Ginger asked.

Curly pointed a gloved finger at the empty box on the floor that had contained the plug, then indicated the compartment beneath the pedestal where the plug would be inserted.

"Already done, then?"

Another thumbs-up from Curly.

Curly took the chair from the console and placed it by the reactor so that he could reach the top. Then he pointed at the hexagonal canisters. Ginger handed one of the heavy silver canisters up. Curly removed the top and poured the amber and black granules into the port at the top of the reactor. He carefully replaced the top of the canister and exchanged the empty canister for a full one Ginger offered. In time, all thirty-one canisters had been loaded. Then they took the heavy black canister with the red top and poured its blue pellets into the port. Finally, Curly sealed the top of the reservoir, and stepped down from the chair.

Curly turned to look at Ginger, pointing to a switch at the top of the console marked "Power." Ginger flipped the switch, and they waited.

The display on the console showed the temperature within the reactor: **-73**.

Then the display began to change rapidly: **-54 … -31 … 0 … 43 … 75 … 101 …**

"It's working! The temperature is rising… one fifty-seven … two twenty-eight … The temperature we need for self-sustaining operation is about five hundred, right, Curly?" Ginger asked.

Curly nodded.

The display began to change more slowly. **283 … 322 … 375 …**

The display went dark.

Curly and Ginger looked at each other for a long moment.

"What's happening?" asked Cisco over the comm.

"The display went dark," replied Ginger. "Give us a minute."

They waited several minutes.

Curly turned to leave.

"I guess that's it, Cisco," Ginger said over the comm, solemnly. "We didn't have enough power to melt the salt and start the reaction. We'll be back soon."

Ginger followed Curly and Thing1 to the Charlie air lock in silence.

Helper had decided a feast was in order whether the generator could be started or not. With the last of the power gone, there was no light other than candles and the fire. They stoked the fire for warmth and Helper laid out a grand meal. Scar had helped her harvest honey and they had generous portions of pancakes and stew.

When they finished the meal, Hungry looked at the mess in the cooking area and laughed. "Maybe we don't need to clean up tonight. You all have the night off from cleanup duty." She turned to Scar and suggested they turn in for the night. Scar smiled and hugged Helper, smelling deeply of her smoke scented hair. They lingered for a moment, then turned and walked away from the firelight.

Red got one of the tablets to play music and the remaining Martians danced around the fire, as much for warmth as recreation. Mary shared some music she had discovered. Then Red took another turn. Pigpen put on some folk tunes she had found and sang along as others danced.

When the dancing concluded, Ginger took Pancho by the hand, said good night to the crowd, and led him away.

A few minutes later, Scooter and Thing2 left, Thing2 hobbling and leaning on Scooter's shoulder for support while holding his bandaged foot off the ground.

Thing1 and Pigpen exchanged knowing glances and left the circle.

The remaining Martians—Red, Mary, Sniffles, Curly, and Cisco—sat by the fire for another half hour. Then Sniffles turned to Curly and said, "I have always thought that you smelled good. You are smart and brave, and kind. Will you join me?"

Sniffles held out her hand and Curly took it. They walked away together to the shadows beyond the flickering firelight.

Five more minutes passed.

Cisco looked at Red and Mary and shrugged her shoulders. "I guess we are the odd ones out." Turning to face Mary, she said, "I owe you an apology. Seasons ago, when your bowl was lost … Pancho and I had taken it and buried it in the forbidden dirt pile. We thought it was funny, but it was mean. I'm sorry."

She was silent for a moment. Then Mary said, "That was mean. As long as I can remember, I have wanted nothing but to leave Mars. I thought the rest of you were stupid for living your lives here. I had fantasies about leaving and going to Earth and mating with an Earth man—and now, this is it? I wasted my life planning for a tomorrow that will never come. I know I haven't always been the easiest person to get along with. I…" Mary broke down sobbing.

Red reached out to comfort Mary and she melted into his arms. Cisco wrapped her arms and a blanket around them and the three of them huddled by the fire.

Mary composed herself and said, "Thank you, Red." Then she looked up into Cisco's eyes. "I forgive you—and Pancho too." A slight smile tugged at the corners of her mouth.

"I had dreamed of mating with an Earther, too," Cisco confessed, "and seeing the big waters of Earth."

"I wanted to see Earth … but more than anything, I wanted to see space. I wanted to see the whole of Mars from space and float like Porter said we would without gravity during the journey," Red offered. "But this has been a good adventure. We did well, even without Porter for a while. He always said we weren't designed to live here, but he was always hopeful."

The three of them sat by the fire, nestled under the blanket and staring at the embers. After a time, Cisco offered, "You know, we would be warmer sleeping together than alone…"

Mary stood and kissed Cisco's cheek and mouthed a silent "thank you," then turned to Red. "Let's stoke the fire, go to bed, and see what happens."

Red nodded.

They put more bamboo into the fire and retreated to Cisco's sleeping table, leaving the lonely fire burning and crackling with the fresh fuel.

CHAPTER 59 –
The Morning After

Cisco was sleeping peacefully, nestled naked between Mary and Red, when a blinding light cut through the darkness, assaulting her eyes. Shielding her face with her hand, she looked around to see that grow lights had come on all across Charlie.

"Power!" Cisco yelled. "You did it!"

Sleep tables around her were discharging their occupants—naked Martians with frosty breath muttering and searching for warm clothes.

The sky beyond the window remained dark brownish red.

"It must have been just enough to start the reaction," Ginger said. "The first power would go toward operating the reactor. Once it was up and running, it had enough power to share."

"You and Curly should go look and make sure there's nothing else we need to do," Cisco said.

Ginger and Curly scrambled toward the air lock, gathering clothes and exo-suits as they went.

"Look at this cooking area! It's a mess," laughed Helper. "Breakfast will be leftover stew—and no whining."

Thing1 was examining Charlie's monitor. "Batteries are at point two percent and climbing! Temperature is just below freezing. Carbon dioxide remains near dangerous levels. Let's put out the fire to conserve oxygen and turn on the heat. Hopefully the plants aren't all dead."

A flurry of activity persisted throughout the morning as the Martians celebrated their good fortune and tried to salvage what they could from the cold.

Ginger and Curly returned from the reactor room to report that everything seemed normal and they had throttled the reactor down to produce just one megawatt per hour for the time being.

By the afternoon, Thing1 and Scooter had routed power to the Communications room, eager to make another attempt at contacting Earth.

When they started the communications console on the emergency backup computer, an indicator showed they had messages waiting. Everyone gathered around as Scooter read them aloud.

"2317 HELLO MARS! THRILLED TO KNOW YOU ARE ALIVE. WE THOUGHT ENTIRE COLONY WIPED OUT. ATTACHED FILE DESCRIBES REACTOR RESTART PROTOCOL. PLEASE SEND STATUS AS SOON AS POSSIBLE."

"0030 HELLO MARS. PLEASE ACKNOWLEDGE RECEIPT OF REACTOR RESTART PROTOCOL. SENDING AGAIN IN CASE LOST IN TRANSIT."

"0130 HELLO MARS. PLEASE RESPOND."

"0230 HELLO MARS. PLEASE RESPOND."

"0330 HELLO MARS. PLEASE RESPOND."

"0430 HELLO MARS. PLEASE RESPOND."

"0530 HELLO MARS. PLEASE RESPOND."

"0630 HELLO MARS. PLEASE RESPOND."

"0730 HELLO MARS. PLEASE RESPOND."

"0830 HELLO MARS. PLEASE RESPOND."

"0930 HELLO MARS. PLEASE RESPOND."

"1030 HELLO MARS. PLEASE RESPOND."

"1130 HELLO MARS. PLEASE RESPOND."

"1230 HELLO MARS. PLEASE RESPOND."

"1330 HELLO MARS. PLEASE RESPOND."

"1430 HELLO MARS. PLEASE RESPOND."

"Let's look at their protocol and see if we forgot anything," Ginger said.

Scooter opened the file, called "TR-24 RELOAD PROTOCOL," muttering, "Well, isn't *that* a useful name. I'm surprised we couldn't guess it."

Ginger and Curly scrolled through the instructions, discovering that, apart from some safety steps, they seemed to have performed the restart correctly.

"What should we send as our status?" Scooter asked.

"How about: 'We have successfully restarted the reactor and believe we can now recover from the dust storm. We would welcome a visit from you and look forward to visiting the world of our ancestors.'" Cisco asked. She looked around the group. They nodded their approval.

Scooter typed awkwardly on the keyboard.

"Communication sent," said the computer voice.

They waited. Thirty-five minutes later, a reply arrived.

"1532 HELLO MARS. HOW MANY SURVIVORS? WHAT IS NEW ROME STATUS?"

Cisco said, "Tell them, 'Fourteen survivors of the disaster. One original colonist, Porter, and thirteen of the colonists' children. Porter died four weeks ago. Greenhouses Bravo, Charlie, and Delta are pressurized. Remainder of station decompressed. We believe problem was northeast side of station. We have not yet explored site of fire.'"

Scooter painstakingly sought the keys on the keyboard to compose the message, complaining about the keyboard layout as she typed.

"Communication sent," said the computer voice.

The reply came thirty-two minutes later.

"GLAD TO HEAR YOU ARE OK. WORKING OUT DETAILS OF RESCUE MISSION ON THIS END. BEST GUESS 24-36 MONTHS BEFORE ARRIVAL. WILL PROVIDE AN UPDATED ESTIMATE IN 72 HOURS."

Shortly after that, a clarification.

"OOPS. TIME ESTIMATED IN EARTH MONTHS … FOR YOU 700-1000 MARTIAN DAYS/SOLS."

Cisco looked around the gathered circle. "Tell them we will be waiting."

The Martians cheered. Each began to imagine what it would be like to see Earth. Their universe had just gotten much bigger.

CHAPTER 60 – Bad Air

Earth was organizing an expedition to the station. It would take longer than initially imagined. The ideal time to launch—when the distance between Earth and Mars would be optimal—was fall of 2060 on Earth, twenty-one Earth years after the *Numa* had initially left Earth's orbit. The trip would take one hundred seventy-four Earth days, with a tentative arrival date of April 15, 2061 (Earth standard) or April 51, Martian Year 57. In Martian terms, this put the arrival of the ship about nine hundred Martian days after the restart of the reactor. When the ship from Earth arrived, they planned to repair and reclaim the station and generate fuel for the return trip. They expected it would take one hundred to three hundred days on Mars before they could depart, depending on the extent of the damage to the station and how long it would take to distill sufficient fuel.

When the celebration ended, the Martians faced a sobering reality—they might not live to meet the expedition from Earth. Carbon dioxide levels in Charlie remained near toxic levels and the cold had severely damaged the plants that had not been killed outright. The Martians in Charlie were beginning to feel the urge to pant involuntarily because of the toxic levels of carbon dioxide.

Their heads ached. Cisco worried that there wasn't enough living greenery in Charlie to clear the carbon dioxide from the air before it killed them.

Pancho saved them from asphyxiation. Delta had frozen hard, killing all of its plants, worms, and bees. While surveying the crop devastation in icy Delta, Pancho noticed that in spite of the cold, he could breathe more easily. Checking Delta's environmental monitor, he saw that although the temperature was well below freezing, Delta's carbon dioxide and oxygen levels were normal. Delta had been shut down to save power before the carbon dioxide levels had begun to climb and the air lock had been sealed to keep Charlie warm. This had preserved breathable air in Delta. Lots of it. Everyone bundled up and quickly relocated to Delta. They gladly accepted the bitter cold in exchange for breathable air and an end to the headaches.

Although Porter had taught them to tune the duration of the grow lights in the greenhouses to mimic days and seasons on Earth so that crops ripened at different times, Pigpen suggested they temporarily abandon that practice for Charlie and Delta, running the grow lights night and day to speed up warming, encourage faster growth, and maximize photosynthesis.

Ginger observed that transit between Charlie and Delta didn't involve cycling the air lock—just opening and closing the air lock doors—which could be done quickly. This meant that an exo-suit sealed at the last moment in the Delta air lock could hold enough air in the suit to last for one or two minutes of working comfortably in Charlie before the wearer had to exit for fresh air. This avoided consumption of the precious few remaining air canisters. Consequently, the initial rehabilitation of Charlie was done with countless short trips and focused initially on the plants and tables nearest the Charlie/Delta air lock.

Most of the annuals in Charlie had perished in the cold. As the temperature warmed, they turned brown and limp. The orange tree leaves seemed unfazed initially, but after a few days many of the leaves became brown and droopy. The bamboo stalks remained green, but the leaves were brown and wilted. The cold appeared to have killed the evergreen breadfruit trees outright. Charlie's pine trees alone seemed untroubled by the freezing. Most of the bees and a few of the worms had thankfully survived.

Even with the grow lights and heat running constantly, it took days to warm Delta above freezing. Despite the cold, the Martians decided to refrain from fire in Delta until Charlie's carbon dioxide levels returned to normal. If they used up the breathable air in Delta before they could safely move back to Charlie, they were doomed. With unexpended air canisters in very short supply, it would be much harder for them to repeat the trick and relocate to Bravo while continuing to rehabilitate Charlie. Transit from Bravo to Charlie was time consuming because it involved cycling two air locks and walking about two hundred meters. It would take air canisters to pull that off—air canisters they didn't have to spare.

When the temperature in Delta finally did rise above freezing and the water in the storage bladders began to return to liquid form, restarting Delta's grow tables to make breathable air was a priority. Replanting and nurturing seedlings consumed all of their available time. They transferred worms and bacteria-rich soil from Charlie. Most of Delta's newly planted tables were dedicated to growing squash and bamboo, some of the hardiest and fastest growing plants available. Pigpen suggested they move some of the pine saplings from Charlie as well, and several tables were dedicated to pine and wildflowers.

The Martians worked tirelessly and watched anxiously over the next few weeks as the carbon dioxide level in their new Delta home began to climb faster than the level in Charlie was coming down. Delta's carbon dioxide finally plateaued at 1.25 percent. Ten days later comparable levels were reached in Charlie. Levels then began to slowly decline in both greenhouses.

In ten weeks, carbon dioxide levels had dropped to 0.50 percent and cooking fires were lit again. Helper's hot food seemed to improve everyone's spirits and signaled a return to normalcy.

A few weeks later, there was enough squash ripening in Delta to feed them for a year, and they began methodically replacing the squash and bamboo with a variety of plants from the seed stores Porter had insisted they accumulate. The grow lights were trimmed to simulate the Earth seasons the plants were accustomed to, and more normal crop rotations and growing cycles resumed.

With the crisis passed, Thing1 and Ginger made an excursion to replace Bravo's batteries and reroute power to Bravo both from the reactor and from Bravo's solar array. They waited a week to allow Bravo to warm. Then Scar and Mary made a trip to begin planting there, only to discover that they had forgotten to turn the heat and lights on. They reset the light program to warm the greenhouse and returned to Charlie, waiting another ten days before returning with worms and soil to plant wildflowers and squash to begin bringing Bravo back to life.

About eighty days after the power plant had been restarted, the dust storm seemed to begin fading. Lightning was less frequent. The dimly glowing disk of the sun could be recognized again through the brown haze beyond the greenhouse wall. It seemed the Martians might survive to see Earth after all.

CHAPTER 61 – The North Air Lock

Initially, the Earthers had lots of questions and the Martians had done their best to respond, but the questions were incessant and the delay between question and answer made "conversations" awkward and time consuming. The Earthers sometimes used words that the Martians didn't understand, and getting clarification was agonizingly slow. Finally, Cisco suggested they limit themselves to one hour per day from 1800-1900 hours Martian time, because of the urgency of rehabilitating Charlie and Delta. This usually meant that a series of text messages from Earth had accumulated which were read at 1800, discussed by the group, and responded to. These brief restricted exchanges continued until the air situation stabilized in Charlie and Delta.

Typing on the awkward keyboard made creating responses painfully slow at first, but with the Earthers' assistance, Thing1 and Ginger were able to move files from the tablet to the communications computer. Thereafter they recorded their responses as little videos on the tablet and exchanged files with Earth. This made communication much easier.

Once the audio/visual exchange was established, the face of Earth communication was primarily a man named Scott. Scott had weathered pale skin and an easy smile, with no hair on top of his head and short gray whiskers on his lip and chin. He seemed cheerful and focused, with a deep, strangely accented and modulated voice that made words longer. "What parts of *New Rome* have you explored? We're sending a map. Which rooms and corridors have you been to and what did you see? Have you been outside the station? Where did you go and what did you see?"

While they did their best to respond, Earth had many questions about the station and the accident that the Martians could not answer. Once that was clear, Scott's questions turned to the surviving Martians and their immediate environment.

"Who are the survivors? Please send a file with names, age, gender, height and weight. How is your health? What does your diet consist of? Are there any health issues we can assist you with? Please send the environmental information from the Bravo, Charlie, and Delta monitors—temperature, humidity, pressure, and atmospheric chemistry."

Cisco had questions as well. One priority was learning how they could refill the air canisters. They were down to three partial canisters, plus the few kept in air locks for emergencies at Porter's direction. Scott responded by introducing a woman named Shash. Shash had dark skin and straight hair like Scar and spoke formally in crisp melodic tones. She had a very different accent from Scott. She explained that the air canisters didn't really hold much air; rather, they held a chemical that pulled carbon out of carbon dioxide and released the oxygen back into the system for breathing. As the chemical in the canister filled with carbon, it became less effective. Shash said there should be a machine in the chemistry lab that would use electricity to heat the chemical in the canisters and release the carbon as carbon dioxide. Then the canisters would be "fresh" again. She showed a picture of the machine and described its operation, encouraging them to ask any questions they had about using it.

Cisco thought that getting the machine before the last of their canisters was depleted might constitute a "Porter emergency" and suggested that a four-person party retrieve the machine, using four of the last fresh air canisters they had in reserve in the Charlie and Delta air locks. The Martians agreed and Thing2, Thing1, Scooter, and Ginger set out with a cart to fetch the machine. They exited the Charlie air lock into the station and went counterclockwise around the outer ring past the East air lock to the airtight doors that led north to the middle ring. This was the first time they had tried to go north past the three o'clock spoke, and the airtight doors wouldn't budge.

"They are bent," Thing2 observed over the comm, pointing to signs of distressed and bulging metal where the doors latched at the ceiling.

"What about your pry bar, '2?" Scooter suggested as she took the steel bar from the cart and offered it to him. Thing2 tried to wedge the bar between the doors but couldn't get purchase.

"Maybe at the top where it's bent already?" asked Ginger. "If not, we could go around."

"Good idea, Ginger. Let's try at the top." Thing1 turned the cart on its side and braced it to give his brother a place to stand. Ginger and Scooter steadied Thing2 as he climbed onto the cart and shoved the breaker bar into the small gap between the doors by the ceiling where the door had buckled slightly. The tip of the bar took hold and Thing2 tried to pry open the doors, but they didn't move.

"Porter said that these should have all locked into place like this when the station started to decompress. This is the only one we have encountered that worked like it should. I'm having trouble forcing it. I'll try to swing my body around to lever it open. Ginger and Scooter help me on three—ready? One … two … three!" Thing2 established a rhythm with his body as he slowly counted. When he reached three, Ginger and Scooter pushed with him hard. The metal of the door buckled further and tore, relieving the tension of the bar and sending the three of them crashing into the door in a heap and collapsing on Thing1, who was still holding the cart.

Red was monitoring the party on the radio from Charlie. The clatter and cries on the channel reminded Red of the confusion during the blowout near Bravo. He paused a moment to compose himself, then asked in measured tones, "What happened? Is everyone okay?" and waited for a response.

The cries of surprise and groans from the tumult turned to laughter as the party sorted themselves from the pile.

"We broke the door!" exclaimed Thing2.

"And crashed into the wall in a pile when the door gave way," laughed Ginger.

"I'm okay," said Scooter.

"Me too," said Thing1. "All of us are in better shape than the door."

The right airtight door still appeared to be fastened at the ceiling, but there was now a tear that paralleled the ceiling where the breaker bar had successfully pried a ribbon of the door away in a strip ten centimeters below the frame.

"Maybe I could pry the door down from where it is fastened now to free it," offered Thing2.

Moments later, the team looked with satisfaction on the mangled door that no longer blocked their passage. Thing2 had pried at it from the top and bottom, and the stubborn door had finally surrendered.

What lay beyond was unlike anything they had seen elsewhere in the station. The walls were blackened by soot. The chemistry lab was at 1:30 on the outside of the ring, but its door lay in the hallway against the inner corridor wall, more mangled that the airtight door they had just vanquished. Two bodies lay in the hallway, apparently burned. The floor was littered with several red cylinders the size of watermelons that had short lengths of hose sticking out of one end. Everything was covered with black soot, with a layer of red dust on the floor radiating from the open doorway.

The chemistry lab itself was chaos, with piles of black debris with a brownish-red patina that more resembled heaps of freshly turned dirt than in other rooms they had visited. Dented and mangled husks of what may have once been equipment were strewn about, some against the wall, others scattered around the floor. Dirty brown light seeped through the windows, filtered through the dust storm still clogging the atmosphere.

"The windows are gone!" Scooter observed with surprise.

The others looked on in amazement as they realized she was right. Their headlamps did not generate a reflection from the glass that wasn't there. The beams just illuminated the dust suspended in the atmosphere outside the station. They could see the dim outline of the East air lock out the windows to their right, receding into the gloom.

"Let's head back," suggested Ginger glumly. "We should conserve the air canisters."

"There might be a few more in the North air lock," suggested Scooter. "We should check while we are here."

"We can get the ones from the East air lock too," added Thing1. "And check the wiring for that big cart in the East air lock. It might have canisters and we can charge it now that we have more power."

Red relayed the suggestions to Cisco and the other Martians, who agreed that a little more exploration to fetch additional canisters was a good idea.

The team continued toward the North air lock on the outer ring. The corridor walls and ceiling were black with soot. The floor was covered with Martian dust. The remains of the twin airtight doors that they would have expected when they got to the twelve o'clock spoke had been ripped from their hinges and lay deformed and broken amid the red dust on the floor in the receiving area.

The receiving area just south of the North air lock was large enough to allow vehicles to drive in from the air lock. The large double air lock doors were swung open in an arc about two meters, blocked by bodies from opening further. The air lock appeared undamaged. The airtight doors to the corridor beyond, designed to protect the outer ring approach to the *Numa,* were off their hinges and lay broken. The airtight doors that should have protected the twelve o'clock spoke to the south were broken and dangling on their hinges. The North air lock itself, a twin to the East air lock but without a vehicle presently inside, appeared intact. There were no signs of soot inside the large air lock. The large outer air lock door was closed and appeared to be intact.

The North air lock was the primary for the station. Inside they found dozens of air canisters and exo-suits. They consulted with Red and the others and decided to leave thirteen canisters here for now and return with the rest, the logic being that in case of emergency anyone could make it from Charlie to the North air lock with only the air contained in an exo-suit. Thirteen canisters meant one for each of them.

They retraced their steps clockwise around the outer ring, gathering more canisters from the East air lock and the large vehicle inside it.

When they returned, they had thirty-eight additional air canisters and Thing1 had identified which circuits ran to the East air lock. He and Ginger made a quick trip to the Utility Access and connected power to the East air lock. They also checked in on the reactor, which seemed to be operating smoothly without their intervention.

The next broadcast to Earth explained what they had seen in the chemistry lab.

In the next broadcast from Earth, Scott seemed somber. "I guess that explains how the station decompressed so quickly. From what you describe, the fire in the chem lab was probably followed by an explosion that blew out the windows and compromised some of the pressure doors. You should probably conserve your remaining air until the rescue mission arrives. Repairing the pressure vessel will be more extensive than you can likely manage without help and additional materials."

The Martians agreed to limit their excursions to rehabilitating Bravo and periodically checking on the reactor and communications systems. Then they settled in for the wait—just seven hundred eighty days to go.